PRAISE FOR THE BILLY LEVINE MYSTERY SERIES

"*Death of a Dancing Queen* is a fast-paced thrill ride of suspense with lots of twists. The characters are sympathetic and believable, and Billie – the PI – is suffused with a fun, dry wit. An absolute must read!"
— *Karen Katchur bestselling author of* River Bodies *and* The Northampton County *series*

"Nothing stops badass Jersey girl Billie Levine from confronting mobsters, meth heads, and crooked cops to catch a killer. Not even her family. Perfect for fans of Liza Lutz's Spellman Files, *Death of a Dancing Queen* is a page-turning PI mystery with depth and heart."
— *Kate Moretti, NYT bestselling author of* Girls of Brackenhill

"Twisty and witty, *Death of a Dancing Queen* delivers a Jersey Fresh private eye whose family troubles leave her little time to dig for clues. Fans of Veronica Mars will cheer fledgling PI Billie Levine as she fights mobsters and neo-Nazis to solve two murders separated by decades but linked by a fabulous diamond. Billie has moxie and grit to spare. I can't wait to dive into Billie's next case."
— *Delia C. Pitts, author of* Murder Take Two *and* Murder My Past

"Kimberly G. Giarratano's start to a new series is crackling with realism, and she's created a savvy, tenacious, and street-smart investigator to root for! PI Belinda "Billie" Levine, holds the weight of the world on her shoulders with her mom's Alzheimer's diagnosis and working to carr~ ~tired grandfather's legacy. She's ~' heart – easier said than done ho ~ung college student/true crime ~ her ex's family business – a strip club. With whip-smart prose, and a plot that will keep you guessing, you won't set the book down until the very shocking and satisfying end!"

– Mary Keliikoa, author of Hidden Pieces, *and the award-nominated* PI Kelly Pruett Mystery *series.*

"Whisking readers from a deli in North Jersey to a club run by the Jewish mob to a true crime podcast session at the local college, *Death of a Dancing Queen* is the best kind of PI novel: gutsy and multifaceted, with a palpable sense of place. This atmospheric mystery will have you craving a black and white cookie and a whole new Billie Levine investigation. A knockout."

– Tessa Wegert, author of Death in the Family

"A spunky take on hard-boiled detective drama."

– Library Journal

"*Death of a Dancing Queen* is a noir lover's dream! If Kinsey Millhone moved to Jersey in 2023, you'd have Billie Levine. The private investigator is quick witted, relatable, and dogged in her attempt to discover what happened to a missing podcaster who pissed off the wrong people – all while dealing with having to parent her parent and avoiding no-good ex whose back in town. I can't wait for Billie's next dance."

– Kellye Garrett, Agatha, Anthony, and Lefty Award-winning author of Like a Sister *and* Missing White Woman

"An exciting mystery novel that connects the past and present of organized crime, all while showcasing the challenges of caring for a struggling family member."

– Foreword Reviews

"Like Henning Mankell by way of Veronica Mars, Billie Levine is exactly the type of PI I love: a badass woman who's as tough as she is smart, full of heart and a willingness to play fast and

loose with the rules to solve her cases. Giarratano finds sharp humanity in characters as varied as skinheads, strippers, true crime podcasters, and mobsters. A thoroughly modern, socially conscious new private investigator for the twenty-first century, I can't wait to see Billie again!"
     – *Halley Sutton, author of* The Lady Upstairs

"Razor-tongued and whip-smart, Kimberly G. Giarratano's PI captivates in the second installment of the Billie Levine series. In *Devil in Profile*, Billie gets tangled in a case pulled straight from the zeitgeist. The plot is a matryoshka of love, betrayal, and murder that Billie peels open, her need for answers at odds with her loyalty to those she loves, proving that this series has serious staying power. I would follow Billie Levine anywhere."
     – *Katrina Monroe, author* Graveyard of Lost Children

"Giarratano does a masterful job of introducing us to Billie's quirky family and then leads us on a roller coaster ride of twists and turns worthy of a Jersey Shore boardwalk ride... Count me amongst Billie Levine's biggest fans. This is a must read!"
     – *Robyn Gigl, critically acclaimed author of* Survivor's Guilt

"What a joy to keep readerly company with Billie Levine, the newly-minted (and somewhat reluctant) private detective who takes her bow in *Death of a Dancing Queen*."
     – *New York Times Book Review*

"An appealing and resourceful protagonist with realistic personal problems complements an intricate plot filled with valid suspects and motives. Readers will want to see more of Billie."
     – *Publishers Weekly*

"Giarratano has created a new favorite heroine. Billie Levine is smart, cool, and above all, human. All I want is a 12-book box set following all of Billie's sleuthing adventures, is that too much to ask for? I couldn't get enough of this slick, sharp thriller."

– Jesse Q. Sutanto, bestselling author of Dial A for Aunties

"Giarratano capably keeps a plethora of balls in the air in the suspect-drenched, tangled plot, but the real draw here is Billie, her family, and the sundry, offbeat characters in their orbit-all fully fleshed and filled with infectious spirit."

– Booklist

"Billie displays some true grit and some impressive detective chops along the way; so tell those corner boys to stop making all that noise-there's a new Jersey Girl in town."

– Deadly Pleasures Mystery Magazine

Kimberly G. Giarratano

MAKE A KILLING

A BILLIE LEVINE MYSTERY

DATURA

DATURA BOOKS
An imprint of Watkins Media Ltd

Unit 11, Shepperton House
89 Shepperton Road
London N1 3DF
UK

daturabooks.com
Hell hath no fury…

A Datura Books paperback original, 2025

Copyright © Kimberly G. Giarratano 2025

Cover by Sarah O'Flaherty
Edited by Desola Cooker, April Northall and Andrew Hook
Set in Meridien

All rights reserved. Kimberly G. Giarratano asserts the moral right to be identified as the author of this work. A catalogue record for this book is available from the British Library.

This novel is entirely a work of fiction. Names, characters, places, and incidents are the products of the author's imagination or are used fictitiously. Any resemblance to actual events, locales, organizations or persons, living or dead, is entirely coincidental.

Sales of this book without a front cover may be unauthorized. If this book is coverless, it may have been reported to the publisher as "unsold and destroyed" and neither the author nor the publisher may have received payment for it.

Datua Books and the Datura Books icon are registered trademarks of Watkins Media Ltd.

ISBN 978 1 91552 343 3
Ebook ISBN 978 1 91552 344 0

Printed and bound in the United Kingdom by CPI Group (UK) Ltd, Croydon CR0 4YY

The manufacturer's authorised representative in the EU for product safety is eucomply OÜ – Pärnu mnt 139b-14, 11317 Tallinn, Estonia, hello@eucompliancepartner.com; www.eucompliancepartner.com

9 8 7 6 5 4 3 2 1

To the librarians who have supported me and Billie.
We appreciate you so much.

CHAPTER ONE

Alan Tran hadn't meant to go after the guy – after all he couldn't give two shits about anyone's YouTube subscribers or video views, which he had to assume were at play here – but he recognized a dangerous situation when it zoomed past him. A teenager on a mountain bike with a GoPro anchored to his helmet was attempting to pedal up Dyckman Hill from the picnic area near the Englewood Boat Basin. A maneuver so dumb it was considered verboten by cyclists and law alike. Literally illegal. The road, having been ambushed by a hurricane years ago, was steep with upturned bricks, downed trees, and debris. Even hiking, a pedestrian couldn't guarantee they wouldn't turn an ankle or fall through sink holes.

So Alan tried to prevent impending injuries like one would smash a spotted lanternfly. Abruptly. Only like the damn bug, the kid was too fast. And Alan's cries of "stop!" went completely ignored.

He's fast now. Wait until he attempts that hill. Although the boy must've been sixteen and Alan was definitely on the other side of thirty, and getting farther away with every cigarette he smoked during a particularly stressful deadline.

The Kentwell investigation was getting to him. It didn't help that he had squashed his embezzlement story (speaking of lanternflies) and that he had gotten into a particularly bad blowup with his best friend Jeremy.

Not for the first time Alan wondered if journalism had been the wisest career path to traverse. Perhaps he should've taken up immigration law like his mother had wanted or worked in his uncle's Vietnamese restaurant in Edison, also like his mother had wanted. Instead, he clamored after corrupt CEOs, shady recruiters, and disgruntled employees whose threats made Al-Qaeda look wimpy. Which was why he was outdoors on an oddly glorious February afternoon in nothing but his cycling jacket and sweatpants. The temperatures had been so mild over the past few days, that ice which had been glued to the road surfaces only a week before, had suddenly given up, leaving behind salty asphalt.

He needed this bike ride. He needed a lot of things. What he didn't need was a teenager being an asshat for views.

So Alan sighed, tore his eyes away from the water, and jumped on his Cannondale. Maybe he could catch the kid.

To say the approach up Dyckman Hill was troublesome was an understatement. The incline wasn't the problem as much as the rocky terrain, made worse by the old storm damage. The road was flanked by a massive stone ledge to his right and a short wall to his left. He felt caged in, but he supposed that was the point, so no one went over.

Labored by the climb, the kid had slowed down, as evidenced by the fact that Alan was able to glimpse his back. At least the boy had the smarts to wear neon yellow.

Alan spied a side mirror on the boy's handlebars. He waved one hand above his head, and yelled, "Kid! Stop!" He really wanted to holler, "You fucking moron! You'll go viral for dying." But realized that such inefficiency of language wouldn't be helpful.

The sun was beginning to set. For all the good climate change did to brighten this February day, it was still winter and the sun was eager to disappear.

Alan found himself slowing to a near crawl, the wheels turning like cranks. Enough with the Camels, he thought. I'm quitting tomorrow.

His bike wheels wobbled under the uneven road. What was he doing?

Sure, Alan was trying to stop the kid from potential doom but, in doing so, was also breaking the law. No more.

He began his descent, this time dismounting so he could walk his bike back down. Just as he halted at the bottom of the hill where it connected to River Road, a black luxury vehicle approached him from behind, likely coming from the marina to the north. Wary of him, he supposed, the car slowed, nearly sidling up to the handlebars. Alan expected the driver to roll down the window and ask for directions, but really – who asked for directions in this day and age?

Hm.

The car then stopped and idled.

Waiting for what?

An uneasiness settled upon his shoulders, so Alan swung a leg over the seat. He hopped back on and pedaled down River Road, picking up speed at such an alarming rate the once warm air now stung his face like hornets. He heard the car, taunting him, the refusal to go around indicative of its purpose.

Alan worried about pedaling faster along a road littered with bits of gravel that had been inadvertently smuggled via truck tires and snowplows. One tiny rock could cause him to crash; it was that simple.

He just needed to get to the Ross Dock Picnic Area, where there might be families enjoying the playground. Or nab the attention of a jogger or a person on a leisurely stroll. Anything to spook the driver behind him.

For a second he thought he felt heat and imagined, like a child, that he was being chased by a dragon – fire breath inches from his butt. He craned his head as far back as he could and spied the car's bumper biting at his tire.

He whipped his head back and pedaled faster. He could jump the tiny raised shoulder, stop his bike, maybe even leap from that rock wall. How far could the fall be?

But even as he was thinking it, he knew it wasn't an option. He just had to make it to the picnic area which, he realized, was now emerging as a stretch of emptiness. But he was nearly there.

The car began to ease up. He could feel the air around him dissipate as if it no longer needed to smother him in protection.

He was coasting until the front tire hit something in the road and lurched. Alan flew over the handlebars, must've been fifteen feet in the air, but he wasn't always great with numbers, hence why he never became an accountant, also like his mother had wanted.

Alan wasn't sure what was meant for him on the other side just that the kid with his GoPro was all but forgotten; his only thought now was of Jeremy Yang and how Alan would never get to tell him the truth.

CHAPTER TWO

Billie Levine knocked on the hotel's service entrance door in a rhythmic pattern, her knuckles tapping out the opening bars to Taylor Swift's "Anti-Hero." At least, that was what she hoped it sounded like.

A Latino kid in gray coveralls opened the door and gave her a judgmental once-over. "Weak rendition," said Diego, while gesturing for Billie to come inside. "And lackluster. You have no rhythm."

"Blame the idiot who suggested it. What's wrong with knock-knock?" Billie followed him down a basement hallway, thick with humidity from the laundry facilities. Sheets and towels churned within tumblers while women folded swaths of graying materials on metal tables. As Billie passed them, sweat bloomed at the base of her neck.

Diego cast her a look, his dark curly hair flopping over one eye. He was nineteen years old and from Dover, New Jersey, the son of Colombian immigrants who had been deported when Diego was a preteen. Now he lived with a cousin who owned a bakery on Blackwell Street.

In addition to selling buñuelos, he worked maintenance at this bougie hotel, decorated like a Swiss chalet so guests could pretend they were in the Alps rather than Sussex County.

"What's the plan this time?" he asked as he led her into a narrow room with rows of lockers. While he spun the dial, his eyes darted to her. "You just gonna go right up to the guy's face with your camera? Ask him to say cheese? Tell him you've caught him red-handed?"

He opened the metal door, reached inside, and tossed her a housekeeping uniform.

"Very funny," she shot back as she caught the fabric one-handed.

"Dude almost took you out last time," he reminded her.

"Almost, but not quite."

"Because I showed up."

"Because you showed up," she agreed. Then added, "Thus a friendship was born."

This got her a laugh. "How many of these cheating spouses cases you running?" Diego asked.

"Enough so I can pay you." Billie dropped her bag onto a wooden bench and shrugged off her jacket. As usual, March was in the midst of an identity crisis, the temperatures fluctuating between arctic cold and Orlando humid. There might've been an hour last week where the air had been perfectly seasonally temperate, but Billie had probably been napping. She tried to do that now. Good for the anxiety, her therapist had said.

We all need a break.

Billie had met Diego a few weeks ago when, as he pointed out, he had saved her ass from an ornery gentleman who didn't like that Billie had snapped incriminating photos of him shoving his tongue into his girlfriend's mouth. Particularly since he was already married and supposed to be in Buffalo for a work trip.

Close call as it had been, Billie earned a few grand for that case and a referral for the one she was working now. As long as there were cheating spouses, Billie's coffers would be full.

And, sure, the dude had been pissed, but his bloated red face was nothing she couldn't handle. Even if Diego hadn't shown up. As long as there were no dead bodies, neo-Nazis or guns, Billie could manage the occasional greasy, middle-aged dude having a midlife crisis in the worst way possible.

And now she was finally earning enough money toward impending roof repairs.

Also the work distracted her from Aaron. Since he had left, Billie could focus on her caseload and her family. Exactly as she should have been doing all along. No distractions. Except for Jeremy Yang whose demise she had been mentally drafting since the smug jerk started poaching her clients a few months back.

Well, she showed him.

The thing about angry cis women peering into the ravine of their shitty marriages was that they weren't all that excited to hire men to do their dirty work. Bad for Jeremy, great for Billie.

Besides, she had freaking had it with him. Diego, on the other hand, was a good guy – the little brother she never had. The buñuelos were a nice perk too.

Billie fastened the uniform buttons and then fished around her messenger bag for the name badge. She held it up and grinned. A ta-da moment that fell flat.

"I don't get it," said Diego as he pointed to the little lacquered tag she held. "Your plan is to disguise yourself as... Maria? Real stereotypical, by the way. You think all Latina women are named Maria? You think all Latina women work in housekeeping? Thought you were more progressive than that."

Billie sighed, then frowned as she examined the pin. "Sorry. I didn't even consider–"

Diego laughed. "I'm just messing with you."

Billie rolled her eyes and examined the badge in the light. "Listen up, my protégé. This name tag has a hidden camera in the letter A. Spy-shit 101."

Diego squinted and then said, "Oh yeahhhh."

"You removed all the towels in the room, right?"

"Had..." he paused, frowned, then said, "Maria Lopez do it this morning."

"Great, so when I go upstairs and deliver them it won't be weird, and I can then record a video of Mr Cheater and his girlfriend. He's none the wiser. Then I get paid; you get paid. And more importantly, no one gets hurt." She smiled while attaching the name tag to her uniform. "Great plan, huh?"

Diego shrugged. "Except you don't look like a Maria."

She blinked at him. "Now who's stereotyping?"

A dark-haired woman popped her head into the locker room with a stack of white towels. Diego jerked his chin toward Billie, and the woman handed them off.

"Showtime," he said. "Room 212."

"Wish me luck."

"I wish you not to be bodily harmed."

"Same thing," she replied.

As Billie rode the elevator to the second floor, she visualized Jeremy Yang trying to pull a stunt like this and immediately chuckled. He lacked imagination. Most men did when it came to this line of work.

Even Gramps couldn't break out of his old gumshoe habits. He'd been taking on small cases lately, investigating petty retail thefts, running background checks, and he did it all by making phone calls. "It works, Billie," he'd told her. "I don't need fancy gizmos to do the job." Then tapping his forehead, he added, "I have smarts."

As if Billie didn't. She had smarts; she had creativity.

The elevator doors opened and Billie's steps were muffled by the soft hotel carpeting. She knocked on Room 212.

"Who is it?" came a deep voice from the other side.

"Housekeeping," she said. Then for good measure: "Towels. We forgot to leave a fresh set in the room."

There was a grunt on the other end, and the door opened to reveal a broad-shouldered guy in his late forties with graying hair and a gruff beard. Just like the photo his wife had sent Billie via text. His name was Mike (weren't they all called Mike at his age?), was a father of three, and worked in telecommunications. He also coached a softball team, which kept him busy – so busy he was able to let his assistant run practices while he banged a sidepiece in his Chevy Tahoe.

Ah, marriage. Between the cases she was running, not to mention the long-ago dissolution of her own parents' union, Billie was reveling in her singlehood.

Mike was wearing nothing but swim trunks. He reached for the towels, but Billie hadn't caught a glimpse of the girlfriend yet so she dodged away from his open arms and slipped into the room.

Billie was nothing if not ballsy. "I'll put them right here on the chair," she said while turning around in a slow circle.

With the camera pinned to her chest, she stuck out her boobs in an effort to ensure she was recording what she could see, which was not much: a king-sized bed, a black duffel bag, a pair of men's New Balance on the floor. Shit. Where was the girlfriend?

Then she heard the shower running and mentally cursed herself. If the woman brought all her items into the bathroom, there was no evidence to record.

"You can go now," said Mike, oozing impatience. So was Billie but for different reasons.

The water stopped running.

"Do you need anything else?" she said, stalling for time. She walked to the phone on the nightstand, picked up the receiver. "If you'd like room service, dial–"

Mike grabbed her by the elbow and pushed her toward the door. "Leave or I'll have you fired."

Billie held up her hands in mock surrender. "Just trying to be helpful."

A voice called from the bathroom. "Mike! I need a towel!"

Before Mike could stop her, Billie grabbed one from the pile on the chair and opened the door slightly, sticking her hand in. A burst of humidity smacked her in the face.

"Thanks," said the woman.

"Out! Now!" Mike cried.

The girlfriend, a blonde with dark roots who was a hair shy of thirty, had just tucked the towel end into her chest when she emerged and balked at the sight of Billie. "Oh!"

"Housekeeper was just leaving," he said.

"I am," Billie said, feeling confident she got just what she needed.

Then the woman squinted and asked, "Do I know you?"

Realization dawned.

Billie shook her head and tapped the name tag. "Maria."

"I've seen you before," she said before her eyes widened. "You were visiting Carrie–" She immediately stopped talking, just as Billie turned to Mike and said, "You're screwing the next-door neighbor?"

And that was the moment Mike lunged for Billie.

CHAPTER THREE

"So then what happened?" Vela leaned forward in her chair, her long dark hair skimming white knuckles that gripped the armrests. One would think Billie was telling a spooky story around a campfire. "You can't stop there."

Billie shrugged. "I dodged out of his way, fled the scene, and ran." Said aloud, the entire incident sounded lame, but Vela only sat back and exhaled.

"Insane." She held up a finger as if making a point. "Only time I will use that adjective." She blinked twice. "Hope the money is worth the aggravation."

"Not gonna lie, it could be better."

Billie was sitting in Vela's office in the psych department of Kentwell College. It was a cozy space with a pine desk, a beat-up chair from Goodwill (most likely), several bookcases, and a floral loveseat, which Billie was sitting on cross-legged, no shoes of course (she wasn't an animal) – her Doc Martens set on the floor next to an almost empty cup of matcha.

She'd been seeing Vela for three months, trying to get a handle on her anxiety disorder. Vela was earning her doctorate in clinical psychology and, as part of clinical hours, saw patients on a sliding scale. In Billie's case, the payments slid all the way down to the carpet.

Vela's counsel helped. So did the meds which Dr Kulkarni had been prescribing since Billie had a freaking panic attack in the middle of a busy intersection in North Jersey. Granted, she had nearly been killed by a maniac. Her reaction was appropriate, if not triggering.

Between the drugs and the talk therapy, Billie's anxiety had been slowly abating, and yet–

"Looks like you're ruminating on something," said Vela.

Billie's gaze naturally pinballed around the room. Every visit she tried to spy Vela's personal touches. There was a framed diploma of an undergraduate degree from Montclair, and a few photos: Vela and her parents on a trip to India; Vela and her sister at a Diwali celebration in Parsippany; and, oddly enough, Vela and Jeremy at Jenn Herman's wedding just last December. That one was new.

"You want to tell me?" said Vela. "Or should I just guess?"

Billie's eyes instinctively returned to the framed photo of Vela and Jeremy, a look Vela caught. She twisted in her chair to follow Billie's line of sight and turned around again with an expression that bordered on confusion, then understanding. Billie hated how easily she could be read. Just stick her on a shelf at the library.

"Are you holding back because of my friendship with Jeremy?" Vela asked.

By way of answering, Billie began picking at the loose threads on the hem of her jeans.

"Let's talk about this," said Vela.

God, let's not.

"Our sessions are entirely, and I want to be clear, one hundred percent entirely confidential. I never discuss my patients with anyone outside of clinical write-ups for my advisor, in which case names are never revealed."

"I know," said Billie. "I wasn't trying to imply that you'd tell Jeremy about my business or anything. But isn't it weird listening to me bad-mouth him all the time? With good reason, I might add. Last week, he undercut his fee and stole a case out from under my grandpa." She leaned over and repeated, "My grandpa. No one does that and lives to tell."

Vela tapped the pen against her bottom lip. She was very beautiful in a way that made Billie self-conscious. Vela wore light neutral knits, flowy and pristine, while Billie couldn't be certain that her T-shirt had been laundered in the past two weeks.

"I admit that this dynamic poses some challenges," said Vela. She set the pen aside on a side table and squared her shoulders. "Perhaps for the sake of your therapy, you should meet with my colleague instead."

"Is it a man?"

"Yes," said Vela. "Eric. Nice guy."

Billie shook her head.

"Gay, if that helps."

That didn't matter to Billie.

Vela sat back and retrieved the pen. "Let's unpack this."

Billie said, "Aaron."

Vela nodded. After three months, Billie could drop a one-word crumb that Vela would trace back to its origin. How could she meet with some dude named Eric now? "You feel abandoned, naturally."

"The weird thing is," said Billie, "I'm over the abandonment issue. He had to leave, no question. A mobster's son was never going to have a normal life in Bergen County. Sure, he could've moved to South Jersey," she shuddered, "or Connecticut or somewhere within driving distance, but he didn't, and I'm OK."

Then again, Billie wasn't sure where the hell Aaron was – he had made a point of not telling her. "It's better if you don't know," he'd said. "Besides, I'm not exactly sure where I'm going anyway. Could be Prague, could be Lisbon."

He wasn't trying to rub salt in the wound, but at the time, it had sure felt like it. Billie had always wanted to travel, but with her mother's early-onset Alzheimer's disease, and her burgeoning private investigation business – not thriving but not tanking either – the farthest Billie had ventured was the Poconos, and only because she had been kidnapped.

"It's understandable to feel abandoned," Vela continued. "First your father left, then your boyfriend. You're having justifiable emotions. It's fair to be angry."

Fair, sure, but lately Billie felt like a gun, misfiring and wounding people who didn't deserve her wrath. Just the other day she'd snapped at David, who had just moved around the corner with his boyfriend Matty, for driving too fast past their house. "It's like you're taunting me," she'd told him. "Speeding away to your new home."

To his credit, he didn't call her nuts, but he did dump her running shoes into her arms and suggested she not come back until she worked off whatever anxiety was coursing through her. "To quote mom during the summer months when we were kids," he'd said, "'Go outside and don't come in until I call you.'"

She ran eight miles that day, doing loops in Overpeck Park.

And then there was Jeremy Yang – stealing potential clients and flaunting his business all over Kentwell College. He was a teaching assistant, but he was no more entitled to exploit campus for his business than Billie was; she was still paying off student loans.

Billie opened her mouth to try and succinctly articulate her jumbled thoughts, but Vela spotted the clock. "Time's up, I'm afraid. We'll bring this back around next session, OK?"

Billie unfurled her short legs, shoved her feet into unlaced Doc Martens, and picked the coffee cup off the floor. She put on her coat while digging around the pockets for crumbled bills which she happily handed over.

As Vela opened the door to welcome her next appointment, Billie spotted Jeremy Yang, stapling fliers to a hallway bulletin board. His back was turned, but she knew it was him by his tall, lean build and that stupid Nike backpack he carried everywhere.

She felt her blood simmer beneath her skin, on the edge of a rolling boil.

"Billie," warned Vela.

As Jeremy faced her, Billie found she had no control of herself, particularly when she lobbed her nearly empty coffee cup at him.

"Hey!" cried Jeremy as it smacked him in the shoulder.

Billie grinned.

There. She felt better. And it had cost her nothing.

CHAPTER FOUR

Jeremy wiped green droplets off his shoulder and gestured to her with the stapler. "You're a child. You know that?"

"You're the child," Billie grumbled, as she bent down to retrieve the paper cup which she dropped into the trash can.

Jeremy scrunched his nose. "Was that a matcha latte?"

"Yeah."

"Gross. Now I'm going to smell like grass all day." He tugged off old fliers and tossed them into the blue recycling bin.

"Don't get hysterical. Besides, matcha odor is the least of your problems. You stole clients from my grandfather. He's gonna retaliate. Gramps holds grudges."

"Family trait."

She wound the strap of her messenger bag over her shoulder and gave him a pointed look. "Your funeral."

He turned to her, his mouth opening and closing as if he wanted to say something but was lacking the language. He'd been weird lately. His competing investigative business had been a betrayal, for sure, but his comebacks to Billie's ire were steeped less in adversary and more in dejection. Like he couldn't be bothered to fight back. Billie found that painfully frustrating.

She grabbed one of the fliers and crumbled it in her fist. He had called her a child and now she felt like one – a toddler trying to incite a reaction. Even negative attention was attention.

There was an exhale of exhaustion before he said, "They're not for my business."

Bille frowned, then unfurled the mangled paper and read the text: *Come to the screening of the Student Documentary Series. Refreshments will be served.* Holding up the paper, she said, "What's this about?"

"Films by the criminal justice majors," said Jeremy with all the enthusiasm of a man forced to sit through hours of amateur footage. Apathy made sense if it was coming from Billie – after all, the last thing she would want to do would be to watch true crime documentaries by smug armchair detectives – but this was Jeremy's pet project. So why the disinterest?

Maybe the stress of juggling his professions – teaching assistant and investigative hack – was getting to him. He did look tired. And slightly malnourished.

She rummaged through her bag for a protein bar she bought from the lobby vending machine. "You want this?" She shoved it in his face.

"They taste like clay." He pushed her hand away.

Billie shrugged, then read the list of student presenters. "Tasha Nichols, huh? Bet she'll be showcasing the Jasmine Flores case." Then, because she needed some response, she added, "You know I worked that?"

He finally turned to her, but rather than offer an eye roll and snark, he whispered, "Beaumont."

Billie whipped around just as a tall, elegant blonde woman rounded the corner. Billie recognized her as the college president. She was appointed last year after an exhaustive search, or so the board of trustees had claimed. There'd been some chatter that the trustees had just put on a show, appearing like they were actually doing the legwork of scouring the country for the best and brightest in leadership, when really they were planning on handing her the reins the whole time. She'd been a dean at a liberal arts school in the Midwest, and before that a professor of business in Texas, maybe even New Mexico. And before that, a CEO or something of a successful shoe company. The woman's CV was long.

Dr Beaumont reminded Billie of a news host: polished, pretty, pretentious, and sporting a slightly southern accent that was manufactured in an elite boarding school. There was a performance in how she addressed faculty, an *I'm every woman* insincerity that needled Billie.

When Beaumont headed straight for Billie and Jeremy, Billie adjusted her posture, imagining the woman would brandish a yard stick and inspect her spine.

Instead Dr Beaumont smiled a row of gleaming white teeth. "Jeremy, how nice to see you." She approached the bulletin board and tapped a manicured nail to the paper. "The documentary series is my favorite event." She gestured to the stack of fliers in Jeremy's hand, the charm on her bracelet swayed with the motion. "May I?"

For a second Jeremy's tongue must've grown three sizes too big for his mouth. Billie elbowed him. "Yes-yes. Of course." He handed her a flier.

Felicia Beaumont turned to Billie and grinned. "Are you a colleague of Professor Yang? I like to think I know all the faculty members at Kentwell, having met everyone at the luncheon last year. Are you adjunct?"

"No," Billie replied, somewhat aggressively. Then she clarified, "I graduated a few years ago. I'm here for a counseling session." She wasn't sure what possessed her to add that tidbit of information. Billie certainly didn't believe in the stigma of mental illness, but she also didn't believe in airing her business to anyone who asked.

"Well, we value our alumni," said Dr Beaumont as she tuned to glance at Vela's door. "As well as our wonderful counseling program." Then to Jeremy, she said, "Come by my office tomorrow. We still need to talk about the funding for your research trip."

Jeremy nodded mutely.

Felicia smiled awkwardly, probably in response to Jeremy's entire vibe. When she was out of earshot, Billie turned to him and said, "What's your deal? You were awkward as hell."

"I wasn't and stop paying such close attention to me."

"I'm not," she said, somewhat affronted.

As Billie and Jeremy watched Dr Beaumont's retreating figure, Billie said, "One thing is for sure, that woman is a liar."

Jeremy glanced at Billie. "Why would you say that?"

"The Student Documentary Series is literally no one's favorite yearly event."

Jeremy nodded wordlessly. For the hundredth time, Billie wondered what had burrowed into his asshole and died.

CHAPTER FIVE

Billie sat at the kitchen table with her new-fangled gizmo (her grandfather's words) attached to her laptop and uploaded the video footage she had taken at the hotel. Despite the end of the camera capturing her blurry and cowardly sprint from the hotel room to the parking lot, she would not make any edits. The client deserved to see everything in its mortifying glory (both of Billie and the soon-to-be ex-husband).

Unfortunately, that was the moment her grandfather popped his scruffy face inside the kitchen and caught a glimpse of fuzzy walls and Billie's labored breathing.

He pointed a finger at her. "Are you being chased there?"

Somehow the footage replayed from the beginning, and Billie swiped at the keyboard, struggling to pause the video. Only when she did, it landed on the still frame of a red-faced man in nothing but swim trunks as his furry arms reached toward her with hands trying to squeeze her trachea.

"I'm clearly fine," she said, while splaying her fingers across the screen, hoping to hide the scene from him. Obviously too late, but she granted herself points for trying.

Gramps wasn't having it. "You take too many risks, even with these cheating spousal cases." He marched over to the coffee pot and grabbed the carafe with such force one would think he was pissed off at Mr Coffee and not Ms Billie.

"If we're to be coworkers," said Billie, "you need to trust my methods."

Gramps poured himself a cup, scoffing the whole time. "Your methods are farkakte. You want to catch two-timing losers, nail them the old-fashioned way – sit in your car with a telephoto lens."

"Stake-outs are passive," she said, as she attached the video in an email to send off to her client and her client's lawyer. Two birds, one paycheck. "This was faster. I got the job done."

A minute later, her phone dinged with an alert. She held it up to him with a grin. "Look at that. I already got paid." No more checks for this agency. Billie had a very young and cheap lawyer draw up new client contracts and the first thing she asked for was electronic payments.

Of course, money in, money out. Her Hyundai needed a new timing belt, an oil change, and tire rotation. The Visa bill was begging to be fed. There was also a bucket by the back door containing stagnant water from the last rainfall.

The Levines were in dire need of a new roof. "Fifteen grand, the thieves want," Gramps had said the minute the contractor was out of earshot. "I've half a mind to replace it myself."

"You fall off the roof and you'll have *no* mind, and likely no body," Billie responded.

So now she had to come up with fifteen Gs. Or get another quote.

Billie heard the front door open and checked her Swatch. Shari wasn't due home from the Safe Horizons day program for another hour. Today her group was making floral arrangements. "Perfect for those with dementia," the director had said in the weekly newsletter, "because they can't get it wrong. Artistic expression is always right."

Billie heard David's whistling and relaxed. He appeared in the kitchen wearing mauve scrubs, his work ID pinned to the pocket. He dropped a sleek black canvas backpack onto an empty kitchen chair. A silver V gleamed back at her.

Billie stared at the bag in disbelief. "Is that a new VHG?"

David ruffled his dirty blonde hair then glanced down at the bag. "Yeah."

"Those cost $500, easy."

"Matty bought it for me," he said slowly, before growing defensive. "For my birthday."

Gramps harrumphed as he sipped his coffee and leaned against the countertop. "So glad I cut you boys a deal on rent so you can splurge on a knapsack."

David glared at Billie, and she shrugged.

"This isn't freaking Prada," he said.

"No," said Billie, pointing to it with the tip of a pen. "It's VHG. Those bags are iconic, not to mention indestructible. Mom had one in the eighties." Then to herself, "I wonder if it's still around."

David turned to Gramps who was eying the bag from his perch by the kitchen sink. "My high school Jansport fell apart so Matty replaced it as a gift. You'd think he robbed a bank, the way you two talk."

Gramps lifted a fuzzy brow. "Did he?"

"No!" said David.

"Wouldn't put it past him," Gramps grumbled.

"Easy," warned Billie as she hefted the new bag off the chair. She began opening pockets, checking out the zippers and the canvas construction. "This feels different from what I remember."

David snatched it back. "Stop groping my stuff. You're just jealous you don't have one."

That hit low, but he was right. VHG was a legend in travel gear. Their Instagram feed featured their products in locations all over the world from the Camino del Santiago in Spain to the markets of Istanbul to the beaches of Ecuador. Billie often felt like, if she at least carried the bag, she'd be ready to travel if the opportunity ever came.

To own a VHG was aspirational if slightly impractical. She wasn't off to a beach in Greece or Italy.

Suddenly, she wondered where Aaron was – had he returned to Haifa or was he shacking up with a new woman in Rio? Johannesburg? Melbourne?

David huffed, disturbing Billie's ruminations. "If you're done judging my birthday gift, can you pay attention to the reason I'm here?"

Gramps set aside his coffee mug and straightened his shoulders, mock battle-ready stance.

"Very funny," said David. "But I'm being serious. A coworker of mine needs a PI."

Billie shifted in her chair so she was facing David directly. He had her attention. Business was always serious.

"Her brother died in a cycling accident," he said. "Police think he swerved to avoid a pothole and went over the handlebars, but his sister is sure he was targeted."

Gramps furrowed his brow. "Targeted how?"

David said, "She believes someone had been following him for a while and purposefully ran him off the road."

"And the Bergen County Detectives Bureau?" asked Billie.

Shrugging, David said, "They say...nothing. So she asked me to talk to you both."

Gramps glanced at Billie. "What do you say, kiddo?"

Billie rose from the chair and stretched. "Let's set up an appointment."

David exhaled with relief. "Great." Then he removed his cell phone from his back pocket and tapped the screen. "Gonna send Billie her number. She's off tomorrow, so maybe you can meet with her then?"

Billie nodded. Gramps nodded.

"Look at us," said Billie as she playfully elbowed Gramps in the stomach. "Teamwork making the dream work."

"Yeah, yeah," said Gramps. "Except this team isn't going to be chased by a scumbag cheater in his underwear."

"Hey now," said Billie. "It was a bathing suit, and we haven't even met this client yet. Who's telling what can happen?"

Gramps rolled his eyes.

CHAPTER SIX

Gramps had suggested Nagel's Deli for the client meeting and Billie agreed.

"Business write-off," she said as they slid into the booth, the hem of her corduroy skirt snagging on the beat-up red vinyl cushion.

As Billie settled in, sticking and unsticking her Doc Martens from the floor, she took a notebook and pen from her messenger bag.

Bernice came by with the coffee carafe, strawberry blonde hair in a French twist, her lipstick freshly applied, and filled up the white mugs. She didn't offer them menus. You don't patronize an establishment like Nagel's for decades and expect to be treated like strangers.

Gramps grinned at Bernice.

Billie sat back, ready to watch a showman perform. "Hey, doll," he said with a wink.

"Hey, yourself," she replied. "What's new?"

"Client meeting," said Gramps.

Billie waited for a flirty comeback but Bernice said, "Hate to be the bearer of bad news but not sure you'll be able to do that much longer. Didn't ya hear? The place is for sale." She jutted her chin toward the front window where a *For Sale* sign was taped crookedly to the glass.

Gramps's shoulders collapsed. "What happened? Marv wants out?"

"Retiring to Boca," said Bernice.

"Jewish cliché," muttered Billie.

Bernice shrugged.

"What about you?" Gramps asked Bernice. "You retiring?"

"Nah, I'll stick around. Someone's gotta train the kids." She took out her notepad. "What'll it be?"

"Bowl of matzoh ball soup and a knish." He smacked a Sweet'N Low packet against his palm and ripped it open, tapping its contents into the mug, while glancing at Billie.

"It's nine in the morning," she whispered. Then to Bernice, she said, "Hamantasch."

"Apricot or raspberry?"

"Chocolate?" Billie asked.

"I'll see," said Bernice in a singsong voice as she strutted away.

"Who eats soup at nine in the morning?" Billie asked.

"I do." Gramps took a sip of coffee. "Can't believe they're selling up."

"We need a proper office," said Billie.

Gramps then jerked his chin at the door. "Our client has arrived."

Billie turned around to see David enter with a young Asian woman wearing a navy pea coat dusted in light drizzle. She had a blunt cut bob and a determined expression. They walked past the dessert cases and a stack of high chairs before sliding into the booth. David sat next to Billie and made the introductions.

"June, this is my sister Billie, and my grandfather, uh, also Billy," he said, suddenly frowning.

If June was confused, she hid it well. Shrugging out of her coat, she said, "Thanks for meeting me."

Billie waited until Bernice filled two more mugs before saying, "I'm sorry for your loss."

June paused in the middle of pouring the cream as if Billie's simple act of condolence reinstalled her grief.

"Thank you." June picked up the spoon, then set it down. Caffeine could wait.

Perhaps June had tricked herself into thinking she was simply headed to the deli for breakfast. A meal with friends. Not about to unload a traumatizing event for two strangers.

"Alan, my brother, was killed last month," she began. "He'd been cycling on River Road, near the Englewood Boat Basin. You know it?"

Billie shook her head, but Gramps nodded. He knew every inch of Bergen County. In vivid detail, he could describe every dive bar, alley, drug den, and chop shop. If it was shady, Gramps had hid in its shadows at various times in his career.

June continued, "The Bergen County Detectives Bureau looked into everything, kept calling it an accident, thinking he avoided a pothole, skidded on rocks and flew off the bike, but Alan was a careful rider."

"The Bergen boys..." Gramps started, and Billie noted how he was taking his time, making sure that what he was about to say sounded sensitive, not jumping to cop conclusions. "Did they tell you why they think Alan's death was accidental and not intentional?"

"Lack of evidence?" June said with a shrug. "They weren't super transparent. The thing is that Alan never cycled that road. Too hard. He wasn't in the best shape. So he always stopped at the river basin. I checked with the local bicycle club and they said you're not even allowed to ride up Dyckman Hill – too dangerous – but based on how he was found, they think he might've tried. So someone forced him that way, maybe. But there weren't any witnesses, no tire marks. Nothing other than his body, found mangled by some joggers." June's voice broke, and Billie wondered how she had managed to keep it together until now.

Billie opened her notebook to a clean page. June took sight of that and smiled. There was an exhalation, her breath wobbling with relief or sadness or both. Being listened to, having one's fears and concerns taken seriously, that was a big part of what Levine Investigations did. What Billie strived to do.

"Alan was a journalist," said June. "He'd gotten into all sorts of altercations with unsavory people while he was reporting. And I don't mean criminals." She gave that more thought. "No, I do mean criminals, just not in the way you might think."

Gramps's soup arrived, but to his credit, he left the bowl to the side. His arms folded, he gave June his undivided attention and said, "Rich ones? Connected?"

June nodded. "And they're scarier with the threats. At least, that was what Alan always said because they could bury you with lawyers and suffocate you with paperwork. You'd never come out."

Billie clicked her pen. "Do you know what story he was investigating? Something that might make him a target?"

Again, June gave that consideration. "Alan's area of expertise, his beat, you might say, was corporate culture and dynamics. He often wrote about unions, sexual harassment, productivity, toxicity, that sorta thing. He was pursuing a few things, but there was one issue he was exploring that is personal. You see, our cousin was – is – being harassed at school."

"Which school?" Billie interjected.

"Kentwell. She had just begun her sophomore year last September. Everything was going great until she decided to pledge a sorority. Long story short, she had been hospitalized because of an asthma attack, an attack she almost didn't survive because none of the girls were willing to call 9-1-1."

"What sorority?" Gramps asked.

"Oh, God." June glanced at the ceiling as if the Greek letters were displayed on Nagel's dropped ceiling. "Zeta Omega Alpha?"

"Zeta Omega Omega," Billie supplied.

June beamed. "That's it. Such a dumb name." This was said with an eye roll and a sip of coffee.

Camaraderie always sounded great until a bratty junior insisted that a pledge drive to Philly for a cheesesteak at two in the morning. Billie was many things, but she was no one's bitch.

"Now Celeste is being trolled by one of the girls," continued June. "She feels unsafe, but the school isn't doing anything to protect her. They claim Celeste is harassing the girl when it's the other way around."

"What do you mean by trolled?" Gramps asked.

"The girl in charge of the pledges leaves Celeste weird *gifts*."

"What kind of gifts?" Billie asked.

"Um…" June scrolled through her phone. "Looking for my notes from my last convo with Celeste. I didn't want to misconstrue this stuff cause it's so unbelievable…" She swiped across the screen. "OK, so one was a cashmere sweater two sizes too small. Another was a bra in a D-cup, also not Celeste's size. And this was super weird… porterhouse steaks."

Gramps frowned.

"Celeste is a vegan." Then, "it gets worse. Celeste is pretty sure the girl peed in her closet."

David mumbled, "Gross."

"Got a name for this girl?" Billie asked.

June checked her notes again. "Brianne Druffner. Double F, one N." She put away her phone. "Celeste was promised by Greek Life that they took these matters seriously, but if 'seriously' means ignoring everything, then that's how they took it."

"And Alan was looking into this?" Billie asked.

"He said he was. He investigated issues like this all the time in corporate America. Harassment that went unpunished, HR only covering their own asses. The victims finally resigning rather than deal with the system. That sorta stuff."

"And you think his death might be linked to this incident at Kentwell?" Billie asked.

June shrugged. "Like I said, Alan made it his business to tussle with powerful people."

Powerful, sure, but Brianne Druffner was just a sorority chick purchasing steaks for a vegan as a way to be a petty bitch. Did she pose a danger?

Billie didn't think she wore her feelings like a scarf, but she must've looked skeptical because June said, "I'm not saying this girl ran Alan off the road. But I'm not saying she didn't. All I know is Alan was looking into Celeste's harassment, and now he's dead. I just want to make sure that if he was targeted, there will be justice. And that I, as his sister, did everything in my power to uncover the truth."

Billie nodded.

Gramps asked, "Did Alan leave notes or files about the harassment?"

June sighed. "Alan's system was erratic. I haven't had the bandwidth to deal with any of it."

David cut in, "Would you be willing to share Alan's notes with Billie and my grandfather?"

June nodded. "If you take this case, I'll give you whatever you want or need. I have a key to Alan's apartment. His rent is paid up until the end of the month. You can go through there, look around. I warn you: someone broke into the place a few weeks back, but a neighbor spooked them and they took off. I installed video security in the meantime."

"And the police were made aware of that?" Gramps asked, stunned.

June nodded. "Yup. Said it could be a coincidence."

Too many coincidences are not a coincidence, thought Billie.

Billie rifled through her own bag and took out the new and improved retainer agreement. June accepted the document and pursed her lips. Billie assumed she might want to take it home, give herself time to consider it, but she simply reached for the pen and said, "Where do I sign?" Then a smile and a "Oh, you take Venmo. Excellent."

Billie said, "Text me Alan's address and anything else you think might be relevant. Oh, and your cousin's phone number. I'd like to talk to her if you think she would be cool with it."

"Celeste is heartbroken. Thinks his death is all her fault," said June. "She's still apprehensive about everything, but if you meet with her in person, she might open up."

"We'll get to the bottom of this," said Billie.

June got up to leave and clasped David's hand, a gesture of gratitude. "I can't thank you all enough. When David had mentioned that his family operated a PI firm, it was such a relief. Especially, since another investigator wouldn't take the case."

That got Billie's attention. "Who?"

"Jeremy Yang," said June dismissively. "He's a family friend so I went to him first, but that was a mistake."

June smiled thinly while Gramps said, "We'll be in touch."

CHAPTER SEVEN

That evening, Billie parked in a garage deck in Montclair. She rounded the corner to meet her best friend Nicole Mercier at Cuban Pete's, an atmospheric place on Bloomfield Avenue where the waitstaff wore Cuban shirts and straw fedoras. In the summer they could eat al fresco beneath stringed lights, but March only lent itself to dining indoors where the pastel walls reminded Billie of spring haze.

She arrived to find Nicole handing the waiter a bottle of red wine, a pitcher of sangria mix already on the table.

Billie didn't drink. Not wine for the resveratrol, nor a summer IPA to quench thirst, nor anything that might zap precious brain cells. If she was to avoid her mother's fate, she would need to err on the side of sobriety. Smart, if not lame. Nicole, on the other hand, enjoyed a good merlot; hell, she enjoyed a bad one too.

Billie watched as her friend curled a tendril of her dark hair around a finger while coquettishly pointing to her phone screen where she had just opened the menu. Gramps would've taken one look at the QR code on the table and noped out of there. "Are we too cool for paper now?"

Draping her bag over the side of the chair, Billie sat down, gave the waiter a grin and an efficient, "Seltzer, please."

When he left, Nicole made a face.

"What?" Billie said, a tad defensive.

"He's delicious."

"Is he on the menu?"

"Very funny."

The waiter returned with fizzy water that Billie then added to the nonalcoholic sangria mix, a virgin concoction that tricked her into thinking she could socialize like any other twenty-four year-old. "Why Montclair?"

The city wasn't far from Teaneck, only there were plenty of other establishments to frequent without having to get on the Garden State Parkway.

Nicole scrunched up the sleeves of her blue blazer, which she wore over a cream-colored silk blouse. She sported heavier makeup than usual, including a touch of highlighter on her dark cheeks, and her hair was in an updo.

"Did you have a job interview today?" Billie asked.

"Good detective," replied Nicole.

Billie waved a hand over the half-empty pitcher. "Did it not go well?"

Nicole shrugged. "It didn't go poorly. I interviewed for a position in campus housing."

"Sorta what you do now."

She nodded.

"You should be a shoo-in."

Again, Nicole shrugged with apathy.

"Are they offering more money?"

She shook her head.

Billie frowned. "A lateral move?"

Sitting back in her chair, Nicole raised the wine glass to her lips.

"Is something going on at work?" said Billie, feeling less like a good detective and more like a shitty friend. She should've been paying closer attention to whatever stress Nicole had been dealing with. The flirting with the waiter... "Is it Calvin?"

"A little. I mean, I feel like he might be getting ready to break up with me."

Billie sighed. "Why do you think that?"

Nicole downed the rest of her sangria. "He's been pushing off dates, making excuses to not come over. Maybe he's cheating on me."

"You want me to tail him?" said Billie. "Because I can do that, happily. Well, not happily. But you get–"

Nicole cut in, "No. I just think it might be time for new scenery. Ever since Dr Beaumont arrived, things at Kentwell have been uncomfortable. Over the last year, she's installed some people in various departments and they can be…" Nicole shifted in her chair, as if her skin was itchy. "Difficult."

"A good boss makes all the difference," said Billie. "That's why I can't fire Gramps."

Nicole laughed, but then her face grew dark. "Remember Ernie?"

"Your favorite person on campus. Head chef at the faculty restaurant."

"Yes. He left."

"But he'd been there since the eighties."

"I know! Something happened, and one minute he was there, next gone. I called him at home, but his wife said that he was prepping for a fishing trip."

"Retirement?"

"And not tell us? So we could throw him a party?"

"He's shy," offered Billie.

"He's not," said Nicole. "But also Stewart – you know, from high school…he worked in the cubicle next to mine and left abruptly last fall. I thought he had gotten a better job, but I ran into him last week and he's working for his dad's roofing company. It's just all so weird."

The waiter returned and Nicole and Billie ordered grilled chicken sandwiches with sides of plantain chips.

Nicole said, "My boss, Deidre, was set to take over the entire department, but then during the hiring process the group they assembled selected this nobody from nowhere person and Deidre is now answering to her. Deidre is also looking for a job elsewhere." Nicole eyed Billie for a second. Then said, "I'm surprised Jeremy hasn't mentioned anything to you about all this."

"Jeremy? Why would he tell me anything?"

"I thought you guys were friends or something, being in the same business."

Billie scoffed. "He's not a friend, more like a client burglar."

"Well, I vented to him about this, so I thought that he would've shared it with you too."

"You spoke to Jeremy Yang about your work problems?" Billie caught the accusation in her tone, her betrayal so evident, she inwardly cringed. Not for the hundredth time did she wonder what genetic trait she inherited that caused her to make other people's problems about herself.

"He's not a dick," said Nicole.

"I didn't say he was." Out loud.

There was a lag in conversation, and then their food arrived. Nicole tapped her fork against her plate, a nervous tic, and asked, "So, what's new with you? How's your job?"

Billie popped a plantain chip in her mouth and spoke around it. "I'm working cheating spouse surveillance. A real moneymaker. I'm paying off bills left and right. There's enough wronged women to last me until retirement."

Nicole raised a brow. "Yeah?"

"Gramps and I also signed a new case this morning. A journalist who had a cycling accident. Sister thinks he was targeted. Police say no foul play."

Without missing a beat, Nicole said, "Alan Tran."

"You know him?" Billie asked, surprised.

Nicole brought the wine glass to her lips and gulped. "He'd been on campus investigating his cousin's issues with another student."

Billie treaded carefully. After all, Nicole worked for the college. "The family claims that nothing was done to help her."

"They're right," said Nicole, deflating. "I took Celeste's complaints, ran them up the chain – including to Greek Life – and then…poof. Nothing. It doesn't help when the college wants concrete evidence. You turn in a signed confession, and they'll want to know if it was written under duress. You show video, and they'll say the footage isn't clear enough."

"Is that what happened?" Billie asked.

"Sorta. Meanwhile, Brianne Druffner gets off scot-free. Something weird is going on."

Billie leaned over and said, "I don't want to put you in the middle of this. I don't want to interfere with your job."

Nicole shot her a disbelieving look.

"Anymore," Billie added quickly. "I don't want to put you in the middle of my cases anymore."

Nicole tossed back the last of the sangria. "If I'm lucky, I'll be out there soon anyway."

They ate in silence after that.

As they left the restaurant and parted ways, Billie walked down Bloomfield toward the parking deck. Her phone rang while she stood at the pay machine, trying to shove wrinkly dollar bills into the slot.

"Levine Investigations," she said, with her cell phone tucked between her ear and shoulder.

"Ms Levine," said a woman's voice. Young and bubbly.

Billie was immediately suspicious. "Who's this?"

"Rebecca Jimenez," said the woman. "I am Katherine Von Holm's assistant. I'm calling to set up a meeting."

"With Katherine Von Holm?" Billie asked, disbelieving.

"Yes. With Ms Von Holm."

"The Ms Von Holm of Von Holm Gear? That one? The CEO?"

"Yes. With her."

Billie wondered if she was being played. "Did Jeremy put you up to this?"

"Excuse me?" said the woman.

"Who is this really?" said Billie.

"Rebecca Jimenez," she said, now sounding more defensive. "I *work* for Katherine Von Holm."

The machine spat out the parking ticket and Billie headed toward her Hyundai on the third level. Billie heard Rebecca whisper, "She doesn't believe I'm calling on your behalf."

A second later another voice got on the line. This one huskier, more self-assured. "This is Katherine Von Holm, calling for Belinda Levine. I'd like to meet you tomorrow afternoon."

"For what? And how do I know it's really you?"

"While I love a healthy dose of skepticism, especially in someone I'm looking to hire, I suppose you'll just have to come to the office tomorrow and hear me out." There was a bout of silence before the phone must've been handed back to Rebecca.

"Fifth Avenue Flagship store," she said. "This is a highly confidential matter, so please let me know if you can clear your schedule tomorrow."

"Text me the time," said Billie, resigned. "I'll be there."

"Excellent." Rebecca disconnected the call and a second later, Billie's cell buzzed with specifics.

What a weird turn of events.

CHAPTER EIGHT

The next morning June Tran met Billie and Gramps outside Alan's apartment. She was dangling a set of keys. "Like I said, the lease is good until the end of the month. Asshole landlord wouldn't let Alan out of his agreement, even though, you know, he died and everything. He's keeping his security deposit if you can believe it."

"Sorry about that," said Billie at the same time Gramps said, "Greedy sharks."

June shrugged, trying to play off her indifference, but her hand shook as she unlocked the front door. They entered the apartment, which was bright but dusty from disuse. Old cooking odors permeated the space.

June darted to a window and undid the latch, hefting up the sash. "I should've deodorized the garbage disposal." She bolted into the small kitchen and flipped a switch that emitted a grinding noise to set Billie's teeth on edge. "Sorry," June called to everyone.

"Where's his office?" Billie asked.

"Second door on the left," said June, who was busying herself with a garbage bag she found beneath the kitchen sink.

Billie glanced at Gramps who nodded wordlessly. Together they entered a second bedroom, darkened from drawn blinds. Billie flicked on the light switch, but a ceiling fan whirled overhead instead.

She shivered and tilted her chin toward the desk in the corner, an Ikea-style Formica setup covered in piles of papers, folders, books, and AP guides. "I'll take the desk; you take the closet," said Billie.

Gramps grunted but went over to the side and pulled open the doors. He pushed aside hangers and lifted dress loafers and Converse from their respective homes. He glanced up at the shelves and hoisted down a box.

Billie rummaged around the desk, lifting books and checking spines, discarding them onto the bed. One pile was made up of employee manuals from all sorts of companies. Another was manila file folders with various people's names written on scraps of papers and Post-its. Sources?

"You know what I don't see?" Billie said to her grandfather.

"A laptop?" he said.

"A laptop," she said. Then, "You think the Bergen County Detectives Bureau took it? Didn't give it back?"

Wagging bushy eyebrows, Gramps replied, "You can ask that detective boyfriend of yours."

Billie exhaled in annoyance. "Esteban Morales is not and has never been my boyfriend."

"Of course not, because he's not a hooligan. God forbid you date a decent, law-abiding man."

"We could call Malley," said Billie.

"He's on a cruise. Left outta Bayonne this week."

"Forgot about that." She slipped her cell phone from her pocket and dialed.

"Levine," Morales answered with an exasperated sigh.

"You don't sound like you're happy to hear from me."

"What do you want?"

"I was hired to look into the death of Alan Tran. The BCDB boys investigated, ruled it an accident, so would they have kept his laptop?"

"Date of death?"

"Thirteenth of February."

"Give me a minute, and I'll call you back."

"OK," she said, staring at her phone in surprise. Was Detective Morales going to help without giving her a hard time? Was there an eclipse?

"He's going to call me back," she told Gramps. "Find anything?"

"This entire box is a pile of manuals and company handbooks."

"Alan did a lot of investigative reporting on corporate malfeasance."

Gramps flipped open a thick packet of stapled papers and said, "This company requires all workers to sign out the sheets of paper they need before photocopying. 'Those who fail to follow protocol will have to have a meeting with HR.' Behoove me to swear, but are you fucking kidding me?"

"Office work isn't for everyone," said Billie.

Gramps said, "HR should stand for Hellish Representatives."

"Very funny," said Billie as she flipped through folders on the desk. "These are employee records from various places. This one is from a woman who worked for a nursing home. She was there twenty years. According to Alan's notes, she was fired when she filed a complaint against a manager who was stealing meds."

Gramps scoffed. "I rest my case." He abandoned his box of manuals and picked up a file from the bed. "This guy worked for an IT firm who promised him a raise after six months, and then said his performance evaluation deemed a demotion. It was changed after the fact." He made a disgusted noise. "Corporate scum."

"Alan dug a lot into corporate crimes. Maybe his death isn't Kentwell-related. Any one of these places could've sent someone after him," she said.

"Makes it sound like a hit job."

"I wouldn't put it past them, would you?"

Gramps said, "Let's focus on what we know. We know he was digging into hazing and harassment on campus. Let's see if there were any interactions between him and this Druffner girl."

"There's a calendar on his desk," Billie said. "I love it when people are analog." She traced her finger along the dates. "He had an appointment with...well, I'll be damned. Tasha Nichols."

"Who's that?"

"President of Sleuth Squad, the armchair detectives at Kentwell. They worked the Jasmine Flores stuff."

"A trip down memory lane," said Gramps without a hint of a smile.

Billie sighed. "Wish I could send you to talk to her. She's not my biggest fan."

"In this business you lose friends and gain informants." Gramps held up another manila envelope and said, "Looky here."

Billie grabbed the folder from Gramps's outstretched fingers. "Let me see that." Jeremy Yang's name was written across the tab. His headshot slipped out and fell to the bedspread like a feather.

Then Billie heard arguing.

"You didn't want the case," came June's voice.

"I still don't," said Jeremy. "Just forgot something I loaned him."

"You can't go in there."

Billie knew what he had come for and was struggling to hide the file under her sweater when he appeared and made a beeline for it, swiping it from her hand.

"Hey!" she cried. "That doesn't belong to you."

Jeremy held it up and said, "Has my name and photo in it, so I'd argue it does."

Gramps hefted out a large sigh and said, "I'll be out there while you kids duke this out."

"We're not fighting," said Billie as Gramps left the room.

Jeremy confronted her. "What are you doing here?"

"Working the case. The case you didn't want."

"Because there's nothing here."

"Says you."

"Stupid sorority bullshit. Celeste is fine." He stepped toward her and leaned down. "I'd like my file."

Billie held it out his reach. "Why?"

"It's my information and I don't want it getting into the wrong hands."

"My hands?"

"Exactly."

Such a hubbub for his photo and some scribblings on half a sheet of paper. Billie caught the words *Spain* and *funding*, but nothing else.

Jeremy leaned in closer. She inhaled his cologne, so familiar she could sniff it out of a lineup at the Macy's counter.

She said, "Alan was clearly investigating shady shit at Kentwell. Why don't you want to help his sister? What are you hiding?"

He grabbed the file folder from her hands. "Alan's biggest problem was that he couldn't leave things alone."

"That was true," said June.

Her sudden appearance startled them both.

Jeremy softened his stance. "June, I–"

"But he didn't deserve to die," her voice harder now. "You should go, Jeremy."

He turned the file in his hands. Again, there was that hesitation Billie had come to expect, like he wanted to explain himself but couldn't find the words. He finally gave up and left.

A moment later, Billie's cell rang. Thinking it was Jeremy, she said, "You regret acting like a big baby?"

Instead, Morales replied, "Seriously, Levine?"

"Sorry. I thought you were someone else."

"Obviously. Anyway, BCDB has no record of a laptop being found in Alan's apartment."

"Interesting," she said.

Morales cleared his throat. "Why do I worry this new case of yours is going to become a pain in my ass?"

"Morales," she began, but then gave up. "With my history, your cause for concern is warranted."

CHAPTER NINE

Later that afternoon Billie headed into Manhattan. She had refused to drive; the efficiency of her own wheels wasn't worth the stress of navigating Midtown traffic, so she had to succumb to the least best thing – a NJ Transit bus. A forty-five minute ride that would take her from Cedar Lane to Ridgefield Park to Union City before dumping her at Port Authority.

Despite the drabness of the March afternoon and a startling confrontation with a rat, Billie felt buoyed by the fifteen-minute walk from the bus terminal to VHG's store on Fifth Avenue. The only downside to being outdoors was the city's aroma, a perfume of weed and urine, that wafted over her as she made her way toward Rockefeller Center. A regrettable decision as she hated elbowing through tourists.

Despite not living in the city, Billie never considered herself an outsider. Teaneck was Manhattan adjacent; she was practically a New Yorker in so many ways. The only thing keeping her out was middle class poverty. Besides, the city could wear on Billie after a while, and its energy oftentimes was no match for her wallet.

As Billie headed up Fifth Avenue, Saks in her rearview, she caught sight of VHG's flagship location within spitting distance (she would have to test that theory later) of Trump Tower.

VHG had retail spots all over the country, including a space in Greenpoint that sold refurbished goods at a favorable discount, but their flagship location was a golden beacon for the world's one percent. Visiting from Dubai and your suitcase wheel broke? You go to VHG on Fifth Avenue. Need a high-end swimsuit for your paddleboarding trip to Lake Placid? You go to VHG. Want a chic photograph on the gondola to Whiteface Mountain? You pick up a $200 hoodie at VHG.

Which made this summons so peculiar. What did Katherine Von Holm, the company's CEO, not to mention the great-granddaughter of its founder, know about Billie Levine?

Despite repeated questions, Rebecca Jimenez, the assistant who had texted Billie the meeting details – *two o'clock sharp! Come dressed to impress!* – had been succinct yet vague.

As Billie caught sight of the copper portico below gilded letters that read VHG she supposed the woman underneath, a curvy silhouette with wavy, dark hair was Rebecca.

Billie understood that VHG was no Patagonia. She didn't expect to see company employees in fleece vests, climbing pants, and Birkenstocks. But she supposed she wasn't ready to confront the jealousy surging inside her when she spotted Rebecca in a vintage VHG Globetrotter Shirt Dress in sapphire blue. The garment once retailed for $300 in the early aughts and had been "guaranteed to never wrinkle, even on a hot day in Santorini." Billie should know the price point; she had tried buying one on eBay last year, only to get outbid at the last minute.

Add in the chunky necklace and delicate bracelets, and Rebecca seemed like she was attending an upscale wedding, not walking out to greet Billie, who suddenly felt schlubby in her thrifted slacks and polyester blouse.

A hand reached out to greet her. Billie noticed a black tattoo near the thumb. "Ms Levine?"

"Yes," said Billie, peeling her gaze from Rebecca's hand to her impatient countenance.

"I'm Rebecca, Katherine Von Holm's assistant. I texted you."

"I know," said Billie, whose own expression quickly manifested into awe when she peeked around Rebecca's glossy hair at the store displays. A very talented window dresser had created scenes: mannequins dressed in VHG's signature button-down shirts and shorts, carrying black backpacks, stylish moss green bucket hats perched on their heads. And behind them, Paris in miniature.

Billie walked right up to the display and pressed her forehead against the glass. "Is that the Eiffel Tower made of," she squinted, "denim?"

Rebecca joined her. She wore a lovely perfume, so incongruous with the smell of pizza and subway heat that had meandered over. "It is," said Rebecca brightly. "We offer a recycling program. Turn in old, outdated, or damaged clothing and we'll give you a $50 voucher for something new."

Billie nearly scoffed. Fifty bucks wouldn't even get her the bucket hat. In moss green!

"Katherine's big on eco initiatives. We're starting a new campaign to highlight the work we do with global partners to cut down on carbon emissions and keep textiles out of landfills." To the uninitiated, Rebecca might have sounded like she was reciting company literature, but Billie caught the sincerity and excitement in her voice. VHG had been known for proactive environmental work for decades.

Rebecca grinned and said, "Mention the display windows. Katherine will appreciate the compliment. She works so hard on the green programs. We all do."

Billie's brow ridged. "Thanks, Rebecca, but I don't need to suck up to anyone."

"I didn't mean it like that," said Rebecca, her voice edging on concern. "Katherine works really diligently on her climate initiatives, and it's nice to be noticed for your hard work."

"Sure," said Billie, still skeptical.

"You obviously love the brand," said Rebecca. "You're not being dishonest if you tell her you appreciate the company and its environmental outreach."

Billie supposed the girl had a point. Still, she was hard-pressed to take conversation starters when she didn't even know why she was here. Katherine had said she wanted a meeting, but to discuss what?

As they entered the store, Billie made sure to wipe away the drool that must've been forming beneath her lips. Rebecca was correct – Billie loved the brand. She owned two VHG travel dresses, thrifted, so they were stained from someone else's journeys. Not hers.

The world wasn't her oyster, more like a melted granola bar forgotten about at the bottom of her backpack.

"Oh, God," she cooed, wondering how in hell she could get a hold of herself. "Is that the Mt Rainier pant in coral?"

Rebecca didn't even glance at the rack. "Spring color. Limited run. That was Katherine's idea. Every March we put out new colors so buyers will want to incorporate them into their wardrobe. Last year the special collection included lilac. Such a hit."

Billie liked lilac.

Rebecca pressed her electronic keycard to a panel beside the elevator, and the doors opened like Aladdin's cave. They went up ten floors – Billie counted – until they emerged into a bustling office.

Rebecca headed straight, giving a nod and a smile to a gorgeous receptionist, who was adjusting a sign that read "peanut-free zone" on the lobby desk, while Billie trailed like a lost child.

"That's our newest hire," said Rebecca. "I did the interviews this year."

"Not HR?" Billie asked.

"Oh, well, I sat in. It was important to Katherine that we selected someone who represented the company well. She's the first person you see when you come through the doors."

A pretty face.

"Dinner Tuesday?" Rebecca said to the girl who responded with a wordless thumbs-up, but not much enthusiasm.

As they passed through the office, several people, all young and inexplicably chic, glanced at them before averting their gaze. Billie wasn't well known enough to draw anyone's attention. Although she supposed that wasn't true. She was here, of course. Katherine Von Holm had heard of her.

In the back, toward a bank of windows, Rebecca stopped in front of a gleaming wood door and knocked.

"Come in," said a woman's voice. Same voice that had jumped on yesterday's call.

Rebecca opened the door, walked inside, and made a flicking motion on the tablet as if ticking off a to-do item. Her bracelet swaying with the movement, she began to say Billie's name. Katherine stopped her with an abrupt hand. As she rounded her large desk, she removed a pair of reading glasses and held out her arms in welcome. "No need for formal introductions. Billie Levine, it's so nice to meet you. In person." Katherine gestured down the length of her body. "As you can see, I am real, and I called you."

Billie found herself smiling. She felt as if she were being greeted by a warm auntie. A warm, Waspy auntie.

Katherine Von Holm was a slim, golden-haired knockout wearing a cobalt merino wrap dress. She noticed Billie staring. "From the classics collection," she said with a wink. "You can wash it in the sink in your hotel in Rome. Or, at least, that's how we market it."

Billie had done her research the previous night, so she knew that Katherine was in her fifties, married to Heath Vickery (a man who made a small fortune in tech), and was not only the company's CEO but its largest shareholder.

She was insanely rich and beautiful and visionary. Vogue called her, "the Karl Lagerfeld of company management." Billie had no idea what that meant, but it sounded like something rich people would find impressive.

Katherine grabbed Billie's hands, as if they had plans to gossip over champagne, and together they sat in cream-colored upholstered chairs.

If only all potential clients greeted Billie like this. Most of her meetings lately had started with: "Catch the bastard."

Was that who Katherine was? A potential client?

Katherine glanced at Rebecca and said, "Two sparkling waters and," she snapped her fingers as if jogging her memory, "that fruit platter sent over this morning."

"Of course," said Rebecca as she nodded and headed outside. Billie heard a rush of office noise, voices and phones ringing, and then silence.

"There," said Katherine appraisingly. "You look younger than I anticipated."

"Oh, uh…"

Katherine laughed. "It's a compliment. Don't look so frightened. Lindsey said you were green, but very competent."

"Lindsey…Delvecchio?"

Katherine grinned. "The one."

Billie had busted Lindsey's cheating husband using a similar strategy to her most recent case. Except Lindsey's ex had been getting his rocks off at the Borgata in Atlantic City. How did Katherine know Lindsey?

"We were boarding school chums," said Katherine. "She was very ashamed after everything that happened with Tony. But she said you were the epitome of professionalism and," she leaned in and Billie inhaled her perfume, the same one Rebecca wore, "discretion." Billie was just about to open her mouth when Rebecca returned with a tray of Perrier and fruit wedges in bright colors that were definitely not in season in North Jersey. Or the entire East Coast. A card had been signed by the current Brazilian president.

Katherine sat back and smiled thinly at the spread while her assistant removed a few papers from a file she swiped from the desk.

"Before we begin and I explain why I've invited you here today," said Katherine, "I must ask that you sign these papers."

That caught Billie off guard. Typically, she was the one who had clients sign things – contracts – so she could get paid. In fact, those same contracts were sitting in a folder in her messenger bag because she never knew when she might stumble upon a case.

"It's an NDA," said Rebecca, hovering above the table.

"Bex, dear, why don't you get that bag you put together?" said Katherine.

"Absolutely," said Rebecca brightly before leaving the room again.

"Don't mind her. She's a wonderful assistant, if a bit enthusiastic. Anyway, yes, it's a nondisclosure agreement, and it's 100% about protecting myself."

Billie picked up the documents, her eyes blurring over the tiny print. Jesus, did she need reading glasses?

"I run a very successful company," said Katherine. "There are competitors who would love to know my trade secrets, as well as personal ones, to take me down. Male CEOs, vultures, buzzing above me, clamoring for my failures so they can feast on my carcass. Women are often the targets of male jealousy."

And yet the insinuation was that Billie, a woman herself, was a potential rat – capable of spilling secrets for her advancement. Unless she signed that document.

She set down the papers, ill at ease. She had never been presumed to be so devious before, at least, not for something she hadn't done yet.

"Ms Von Holm, I can assure you that I'm not a kiss-and-tell type. My business relies on my discretion. Without it, I have no living."

"And I can assure you, Billie, that your assurances mean nothing in a billion-dollar industry. Without NDAs, I have no living."

Billie hadn't heard Rebecca return until a giant shopping bag with the VHG logo was set down on the table next to the untouched fruit platter.

Katherine hefted the bag to Billie. "A gift for you, as a thank you for your time, regardless of what you decide to do today."

Billie was hesitant to accept, but Katherine was insistent, thrusting the bag toward her. "Seriously, it's not going to bite."

Billie said nothing as she examined the contents: a VHG backpack in dusty rose, the Mt Rainier coral pants she had cooed over earlier, some shirts, and a new Globetrotter dress in... "Navy seemed your color," Rebecca said. "Because you're cool toned."

Am I?

"I can't take this," said Billie, desperately wanting to take it. "This must cost a thousand dollars."

"$2,575 to be exact," said Katherine. "But it's a drop in the bucket for what I can pay you."

Billie swallowed a lump. Drops in buckets reminded her of the roof replacement the Levines so desperately needed.

"It costs nothing to hear what I have to say," Katherine said. "If you don't like the terms, you don't have to take my case. The gift is still yours. The NDA protects me." She waved her hands at the bag and then her office. "And my legacy, everything my family built."

Was Billie being bought before she was being hired? Perhaps.

"How much is this NDA worth?" Billie asked.

Katherine said, "How about a thirty-thousand dollar retaining fee? With another thirty thousand as a bonus when the work is completed."

"Sixty thousand dollars," said Billie, nearly stupefied.

"Sixty thousand dollars." Katherine smirked, knowing she had her.

Sixty grand was a lot of money, even though Billie suspected that sum amounted to a day's legal fees in the corporate world. And yet this would be the biggest case of her career. She could afford to hire someone full-time. She could get a proper office that wasn't the corner booth at Nagel's. She could refuse the shitty cases she only took to pay the bills.

She could fix the leaky roof. Times two. She could fix *two* leaky roofs if she wanted.

She could climb out of debt.

"So?" Katherine said. "What harm is there in signing a little document like an NDA?"

CHAPTER TEN

Gramps, aka William Levine, aka the first Billy, aka the "OG" according to his grandkids, sat at the dining room table with a sea of paper before him. He rubbed his hands together like he was about to dig into his mother's brisket.

This was the part of the job that he had missed. Sure, once upon a time he'd loved a stakeout, but that was thirty pounds and several decades ago when his belt was looser and his back didn't hurt simply from bending over. If anyone was going to spend hours crouched in a dirty sedan, sipping bitter coffee and hefting a telephoto lens, it would be his Gen Z granddaughter who jogged – for fun.

Don't get him wrong, the best way to begin a case was to hit the pavement – interview suspects, collect footage, snap photos – but often the trail started with documents. Something he could tackle from his dining room chair. With a cup of coffee. Or with one of those yuppy beers Matthew Goff insisted on bringing, thinking Gramps's affections could be bought with a fancy IPA.

His affections, no, but he couldn't deny the amber bottles smoothed the rough edges and quelled dark thoughts.

He hadn't wanted Billie to get into this business, but he learned long ago that his granddaughter didn't heed advice until she experienced the tough lessons firsthand.

She definitely took after his side of the family.

He trudged into the kitchen, opened the fridge, plucked a bottle from its cardboard container, and went back to the dining room.

Twisting off the cap, he chugged the cold beer, then burped and mentally inventoried the mess before him. Manuals, file folders, Post-it notes, scraps of paper with Alan's scratchy handwriting, even a brochure for a boarding school all meshed together in a slipshod excuse for organization.

Alan's system, June had said.

Poor girl. She was doing her best. Alan had been, too, before all this went down. Before he went down.

Gramps had spoken to his spies at the Bergen County Detectives Bureau – a few retired cops with their ear to the office scuttlebutt – and they all agreed that the leading detective did his job by the book.

Grief was likely clouding June's view of the accident. And yet… Gramps picked up a piece of paper. A diagram had been crudely drawn. Names encircled in black ink, linked together by lines, in a cryptic spiderweb. In the center was a name – Celeste – circled half a dozen times in red.

June had given Gramps and Billie the girl's phone number. She had also warned him that Celeste was skittish about talking to the Levines. She didn't want further trouble from Brianne Druffner or the college.

Gramps dialed the girl's number but she didn't pick up. He left a voicemail that he also expected she wouldn't return.

Kids today. Used their phones for everything but talking.

And that got Gramps to thinking. If the victim was worried about getting in trouble, either the college didn't believe her story or they were covering for someone. Covering their asses most likely.

This all started with hazing. This started with Celeste.

He finished the beer, then sighed. On his way out the door, he glanced longingly at the dining room chair.

This job couldn't be done sitting on his ass, no matter how badly he wanted that to be the case.

CHAPTER ELEVEN

Billie had just finished scribbling her signature when Katherine took a sip of sparkling water. Waiting for Rebecca to leave the office with NDA paperwork in hand, Katherine settled into the couch cushions. If the woman carried the weight of her company on her shoulders, perhaps Billie could relieve her of a small burden. There was a sigh, and then: "Now, we can begin."

Normally this would be the moment Billie would whip out her notebook and pen, poised to scribble down details – names, descriptions, places of importance – but such an action seemed antithetical to the NDA she had just signed, so she held off and listened.

Katherine started, "I'm mortified to even say this aloud but, for starters, I believe my husband is having an affair."

Billie simply nodded. She wasn't surprised by this admission. In the past two months, all sorts of women – beautiful, rich, educated, talented – came to her with the same task. "Tail the bastard." Billie knew that a woman's looks, accomplishments, or wealth could not save her from betrayal.

"Normally, I suppose," said Katherine, "I would just divorce him and call it a day. But there is too much on the line."

"You have a prenup, I assume?" said Billie.

Katherine nodded. "You see, Heath came to the marriage with a fortune as well. The prenup is meant to protect both of us. If we're to divorce, we would split joint assets, but I gave in slightly where I shouldn't have. If he leaves, he still gets shares of VHG."

"OK," said Billie.

"Unless I can prove infidelity." She gestured her hands wildly as if pantomiming a car crash. "That nullifies everything. He walks away with nothing. Maybe if I'm feeling generous, he'll get a gift bag similar to the one at your feet." That was followed by a laugh, even as Katherine rubbed her eyes.

"Do you know who your husband might be seeing?" Billie asked delicately.

"I suspect it's Nina Patchett-Borel, a VP at Tropic Reef."

"Tropic Reef?" said Billie. "Why is that name familiar?"

Katherine's voice pitched. "Instagram? They went viral for their under-the-seat airline bags."

"Right," said Billie nodding.

"They were a fairly successful start-up with a young, fresh eye for Gen Z design and minimalism. And we recently bought them."

"Like a merger?" Billie asked.

"A merger implies we are blending our companies. No, we bought them outright as well as their product lines. We've retained some of their staffing, including their founder and CEO, the VP, social media team, but not everyone. And we don't intend to keep all the original employees. Anyway, it's a sensitive time. And then throw in my cheating husband, who thinks because he married into a legacy business he can select women like he selects ripstop nylon fabric, and...well, his affair could impact the corporation. Heath isn't just my husband; he's an integral part of VHG."

"So this vice president..." Billie began.

"Nina Patchett-Borel," said Katherine, followed by a noise of disgust. "Heath oversaw the whole acquisition. He spent a lot of time at the Tropic Reef offices in Hoboken and continues to do so, getting them acclimated to VHG's policies and procedures. I can only guess why he loves being there so much."

"Typically I tail clients' spouses so I can catch them in the act," said Billie. "I feel like you have something else in mind, though."

Katherine wagged a finger at her. "Smart girl. Ideally, I'd like to install you at the Tropic Reef offices as a plant. You'll work with a team, including Heath and his assistant Webber Brandt. I'm going to make you Heath's intern."

"Won't he get suspicious?" asked Billie.

Katherine chuckled softly. "Doubtful." Whatever she thought of her husband, it was not with respect. Billie didn't think it was wise to underestimate anyone, particularly the mark. "As far as anyone is concerned, I'm finding a position for the daughter of a dear friend of mine."

"All right," said Billie. "You said 'for starters.' Is there something else you're concerned about?"

"Oh, you *are* sharp. Yes. I also suspect that Heath is stealing from the company."

"Embezzling?"

"There's an account he thinks I don't know about, but he forgets who signs the checks for our various money managers and, well, the balance is growing. I suspect he is siphoning money from Tropic Reef."

"Do you think that Nina is helping him?"

"Well, I do now," said Katherine with a slight raise of her brows. "However, that won't be part of your directive. Rebecca and I are currently going through financials. If he's stealing, we'll find out. Your job is to catch him with his pants down." Katherine stared at Billie a beat too long. "This is the part where you say you'll take the job."

"Oh, is it?" Billie said sarcastically.

"Mockery is not a good look on a young lady," said Katherine. "And this is a golden opportunity. Quick money, and a lot of it, which I gather you probably need. Lindsey said you are good at this line of work, and I can use someone with your skillset."

When put like that, how could Billie refuse? Sixty grand for catching a cheater? What was there to think about?

Billie stuck her hand out, expecting Katherine to shake on the deal. Instead, she accepted a badge on a lanyard from

Rebecca, who had just entered the office, and handed it off to Billie.

Billie read the name and snorted. "Belinda Lewis."

"If Heath does get suspicious," said Katherine, "I don't want him googling you. This way, you still have your first name."

And a somewhat goyish last name.

Billie twisted in her chair, trying to remember where she left her messenger bag. "I have a contract you'll need to fill out."

Katherine smiled and subtly shook her head. "My contract will trump your contract, I can assure you. Mine likely has much better terms. I had a gaggle of Harvard men put it together. Rebecca will see to your signature, and a copy will be delivered to you via certified mail."

How could Billie argue against a gaggle of men when the lawyer who put together her contract took five tries to pass the New Jersey bar exam?

Billie barely had a moment to glance at the tiny print when Rebecca handed her a pen.

As if for good measure, Katherine leaned over and pointed to the dollar amounts. "Thirty grand now, thirty when the job is done."

Billie nearly choked on her tongue when glancing at the number. Even if this entire thing went belly up, Billie stood to make a killing, and that, as always, would solve a lot of problems for her.

For a split second, she wondered if she should call Gramps before agreeing to take a case, a case that would cause her to essentially be "undercover."

"I can assure you it's very favorable," said Katherine.

Billie bit her lip, thought of all that money, and scribbled her name. The minute she slid the paperwork across the shiny table, Katherine's eyes gleamed like Ursula the Sea Witch in *The Little Mermaid*.

Rebecca collected the contract and said brightly, "I'll take this to legal."

"No, Bex, call a courier. Send it to Johnson."

"Of course. I should've suggested that," said Rebecca.

To Billie, Katherine said, "My business manager will cut you a check. Might be a small delay, though, since she's in Aruba. You don't mind, do you? She'll pop it in the mail."

"Uh, no," said Billie, minding very much. But before she could ask for more information, the office door opened. A man entered in an exquisitely tailored suit and yellow tie. Italian fabric, if Billie had to guess, but it was just a guess based on some of the duds she'd seen Neil Goff wear. "Never let the clothes wear the man," he'd told her once, like that life advice would come in handy one day.

This man had shoulder-length, ashy blonde hair on a lithe frame, muscles developed from running and cycling rather than the squat rack.

Katherine's face paled. "Heath, honey. I'm in the middle of an interview."

"*Vogue*? *New York Times*?"

"*Job* interview."

If Heath noticed his wife's distress, he didn't show it, or Billie suspected, didn't care. "Seems rather beneath you, doesn't it?" He then shot a look at Billie and brightened. "However, I can't see why you'd hide this lovely candidate."

Katherine recovered quickly. "This is Evelyn's daughter."

Heath furrowed his brow. "Who's Evelyn? College roommate? Sorority sister?"

"Boarding school chum," she replied.

"Zurich?"

"McLean," she said.

"McLean, huh? Feisty girls."

Katherine added, "Belinda is a senior at NYU and is looking to get some work experience."

"Another one? Like the Reilly girl." Heath grinned and leaned into Billie, his arm outstretched, and grabbed her hand, giving it a light squeeze that felt oddly intimate. "I wonder if, like Kat here, your mom got kicked out of two boarding schools."

"That never happened," Katherine said, exasperated. "Anyway, Belinda will be on your team at Tropic Reef. To help with the redundancies and the product launch. There's so much to do, I figured another set of hands would help everyone."

"Excellent," said Heath, his tone a hair's width from outright predation. Billie shrank back.

"Did you need anything, darling?" asked Katherine. "I have another meeting," she glanced at her Rolex, "in twenty minutes with the Women in Leadership committee."

"No," he said. "I just wanted to let you know that I made a hiring decision of my own. No biggie, but I'm telling you so Kyle Olsen doesn't kick him out when he arrives tomorrow."

Katherine excused herself, skirted around the table, and gently took her husband's elbow. As she lead him toward the door, Billie heard her say, "For the marketing team? The recruiter said she was shuffling positions around so we could eliminate the search. None of the candidates had enough experience to warrant the salary requests."

Heath laughed. "No. I hired an intern to help with bookkeeping."

Katherine hissed, "Do you really think that's a good idea?"

"He came recommended," said Heath, his voice tight. Then, lighter and louder, as if for Billie's benefit, he said, "He can fetch coffee and make phone calls. I'm doing this as a favor."

Katherine frowned.

"My dad's old professor friend? He's semi-retired now, but he knows of a bright kid who could use some real-life work experience. Just like Evelyn's girl."

Billie inwardly flinched at the word *girl*. She sensed Heath was using Billie to make a point.

"I see," said Katherine. "I really wished you ran that past the recruiters first."

"Why?" Heath grinned at Billie. "You didn't. Not that I mind."

Katherine sighed. "It's different for me."

Heath leaned into Katherine and hissed, "Oh, yes, I *know*."

"I'm giving women a leg up in this world."

"You do like your legs up," he shot back, all with a grin, as if masking misogyny with a smile made the pill easier to swallow. Not for Billie. Her throat constricted. She grabbed the water bottle off the table, unscrewed the cap, and chugged.

Katherine sighed. "Who did you bring on board?"

"Oh," he said. "You'll be pleased." He whispered, "It's a diversity hire. Asian kid. Student from Kentwell. Jeremy Something."

Billie froze.

CHAPTER TWELVE

Yang!

It had to be.

There was little time to register this information. Heath placed his hands on Billie's shoulders. "Come. Let's get you initiated."

Billie glanced at Katherine for help, but she just exhaled and said, "He wants you to meet his assistant, Webber." Then to Rebecca, she whispered, "Go with her."

"Don't need a babysitter," Heath shot back.

"But you do," Katherine said low enough for only Billie to hear. Which, Billie presumed, was the point.

Grabbing her belongings, Billie followed Heath into the main office, past several cubicles and copiers and into a smaller room. Behind her she heard Rebecca's hurried heels clacking against the concrete floors.

Heath marched straight toward a desk where a handsome guy in a black suit jumped to his feet. He had light brown hair, sharp cheekbones and defined shoulders. In another life he might've modeled. "Mr Vickery, the intern will report to Tropic Reef tomorrow at nine sharp as you requested."

Intern, my ass. Billie was right not to underestimate the mark when he clearly had an agenda of his own. She should tell Katherine; she would have to tell Katherine.

"Webber, this is Evelyn's girl–"

"Belinda," Rebecca cut in, nearly breathless. "Lewis."

Billie wasn't sure what to be offended by more, that Heath referred to her as *Evelyn's girl* or that Rebecca felt the

68

need to interrupt because Billie might not remember the cover story.

Both of them were quite ridiculous. These corporate cogs had no idea how real professionals worked.

Heath pursed his lips, clearly irked by Rebecca's intrusion. "Belinda will be joining us on the redundancies task force."

"Really?" said Webber. "I wasn't aware we were getting a new teammate, especially since you're bringing in that kid from Kentwell."

"I made the decision last minute," said Heath.

"Actually," said Rebecca, "Katherine made the decision."

Webber pressed his lips together, no doubt swallowing a laugh.

"Scurry off, Bex," said Heath, shooing her away. "Go back to the teet."

Billie inwardly cringed. Heath made her uncomfortable, and she'd scuffled with gangsters.

Rebecca hesitated. After all, Katherine did say Rebecca should accompany Billie but, as the CEO's spouse, Heath likely outranked her. Which he proved when he shooed Rebecca away. "Go, Bex. This is outside your pay grade."

So she about-faced. For a moment, Billie was sorry to see her leave. She seemed like the only adult in the room. A little eager, maybe, and a bit obsequious, but happy to help.

"Webber, explain to Belinda what she'll be doing on the project," said Heath, before leaning into him and whispering, "Kat's pets never last long, but I hope she'll be the exception."

Webber nodded, but he had the decency to look awkward about it.

Billie wondered which page in the company handbook specifically prohibited violence in the workplace, and if she'd be the first to stress-test that policy. Glancing at Rebecca's parting look, maybe not.

As Heath went into his office and closed the door, Webber pointed to the chair next to his desk. "I don't have a lot of time. Did you get any onboarding from HR today?" Then as if answering his own question, he shook his head. "Not likely as you're an intern. No W-2s, no paycheck."

"Interns don't get paid?" she said incredulously as she picked up a framed print with an illustration of a giant peanut encased in a red circle and slash.

He raised a dark eyebrow. "Did you expect to?"

Billie glanced around the cubicle farm. Phones rang in the distance. Well-dressed workers buzzed around like bees. VHG owned this Manhattan building. They made billions. Yeah, she expected that they would pay their interns.

But Belinda Lewis could only respond with a sheepish dismissal. "No biggie; my mom gives me an allowance."

"I bet." Webber smirked, unearned. His suit was designer, expertly tailored, and likely worth more than the bluebook value on Billie's Hyundai. But then he said, "I worked two jobs my senior year of college."

Real Billie related. Belinda from NYU could only offer condescension. "That must've been really hard." She hated herself at that moment. "So this other intern..."

"Yeah?"

Play it smart, Billie. "I heard Heath say his name is Jeremy Something."

"Uh huh."

"What's his deal?"

"His deal," said Webber, "is that he needs college credit, same as you."

"Right." She patted a rhythm on Webber's desk. "Right-o." She looked around and spotted another peanut sign, this one hanging from the ceiling. "So you have the peanut allergy, huh?"

His chin tilted down, yet he cast her a brief look. "Don't even think about bringing a PB&J past reception."

"Noted."

Webber asked for Billie's cell phone number, which she provided, and then set a mental reminder to change her outgoing voicemail to "Belinda."

He said, "Although you're interning for VHG, you'll be reporting straight to Tropic Reef in Hoboken. There, you'll work on Heath's team for the expansion and benefits task force."

"What does that entail?" she asked.

"Mostly interviewing employees."

"Interviewing them for what?"

"Heath wants a list of positions he can cut, so you'll be inquiring about everyone's workloads and responsibilities. That sorta stuff."

"So the exact opposite of expansion and benefits?"

Webber didn't find that amusing.

She continued, "You want me to ask people about their jobs so Heath can potentially fire them?" She thought she sounded cynical, but Webber took her question as confirmation that she understood the objective.

"Yep. You'll be taking this off my plate, so do a decent job."

She held back an eye roll.

He logged into his desktop, typed furiously at the keyboard, and said, "I'll get you an iPad so you don't have to handwrite notes."

Billie preferred a pen and notebook to a tablet, but NYU Belinda Lewis likely carried her laptop to lectures so she could watch *The Office*.

Gramps's voice interrupted her thoughts: *you want marks to open up? You get them talking about themselves.*

"How long have you worked here?" she said.

"Three years."

"You enjoy the job?"

"It's a challenging position that provides ample opportunity for growth."

Canned answer that meant nothing.

He turned it around on her. "What are you majoring in?"

"Business," she replied automatically.

He smiled in the manner of a high school principal when the class derelict complimented his tie. "Guess you're in the right place. You'll learn a lot here."

"And you? What was your major?"

Webber scrunched his brow.

Trust worked both ways. "Dude, it's just a question."

"Art," he said.

"Art, huh?" Billie wanted to rest her elbow on his desk and whisper into his ear, "You hear about the Karl Sauer case? I worked that." NYU Belinda said, "How did a degree from..."

"Liberal arts school in Vermont," he supplied with a grin.

Billie chipped at that ice. "How'd you go from art degree to admin at VHG?"

"I tried modeling."

Aha! "Tough business?"

"Cutthroat."

"Like Corporate America?" Billie joked.

Webber didn't laugh.

"So how did you end up here?" she continued.

"I was a barista in Hoboken and met Katherine at a coffee shop. She said her company hired new talent all the time, and to give her a call." He halted abruptly as if the memory was a doorstop. He interlaced his fingers and gave Billie a perfunctory nod. "I'll text you the Tropic Reef address. We'll see you tomorrow."

Billie recognized a dismissal. At this rate, she'd been dismissed more than she'd been welcomed. Webber didn't like to talk about himself, or maybe he was just so infrequently asked he didn't have much practice playing the conversation game. Either way, Billie was ready to go home and try on her new clothes. That was a job perk she hadn't planned on.

As she rose from the chair, she gestured to the photo of a cabin that appeared like it had been torn from a magazine. "Dream home?"

Webber frowned as if he had no idea what she was referring to, before glancing at the clipping with recognition. "One day."

One day she'll visit Europe. One day she'll see pyramids. One day, one day, one day.

Billie suspected people like her and Webber could build a fortress made of *dreams* and *one days*.

Rebecca then reappeared and escorted her to the elevator. "You have your badge for tomorrow, right?" she asked.

Billie dug it out of the gift bag and hoisted it aloft as proof of life.

"Great," said Rebecca, pleased. "I may not see you. I typically don't go to Tropic Reef unless Katherine sends me."

The elevator dinged upon its arrival. The doors opened. Rebecca glanced inside the VHG shopping bag and said, "You're so lucky you can fit into those coral pants."

As Billie entered the downstairs lobby, she peeked inside the bag and ran her fingers over the fabric. Not for the first time, she thought the price for this stuff was just too damn high.

CHAPTER THIRTEEN

Gramps entered the student accounts office, a little weary, clearly confused, holding a paper brochure he swiped from the information desk in the Kentwell student center. He approached the first person he saw, a woman no older than Billie, sitting at a desk and typing frantically at a keyboard.

The woman glanced up. The placard on the desk said KELLY, but Kelly she was not. The photo in Alan's file showed her with darker hair, likely taken before highlights, but the face was the same, perhaps a little slimmer. This was Marissa Gulla. Alan's notes weren't much; presumably everything he had gotten from her was locked away on his computer. Levine Investigations was just going to have to reverse engineer this case.

Gramps tapped a finger to the brochure and said to Marissa, "Can you help me? I'm looking for my granddaughter."

Marissa glanced up. She plastered on a phony smile, the kind Gramps had been given many a times by young people who thought him a forgetful old kook. He might've been old, but forgetful? Only after a few too many at the Clam Bar, and he hadn't been there since his best friend Ken had died. Gramps leaned into the role, though. "I think she's in one of these dorms here, but," a laugh, "I forget which one."

Marissa again smiled demurely, stopped her feverish typing, and leaned over to get a better view of the brochure. "Do you know what year she's in?"

Billie had coached him on this. "Sophomore."

"Wagner House, then, or Schmidt. Maybe Muller, if she's in honors housing."

What was with the German names?

June told Gramps where he could find Celeste, should he choose to interview her, but he couldn't pass up ambushing Marissa Gulla, head of Greek Life, whose file in Alan's hodgepodge system read: *Marissa Gulla – Ohio State, 23, sorority – Zeta Omega Omega.*

And that was it.

She pointed a manicured nail into the hallway as if signaling an exit was all the help required. A bracelet slid down her wrist, swaying with her impatience. But Gramps had a plan for this. He scratched his scruffy chin. "Wagner sounds about right." He twisted the map a few times. "Which direction should I head in?"

Marissa sighed, got up from her chair, and walked into the hallway. Gramps followed. She gestured to the exit sign. "Elevator's on your right. Take it down to the lobby, and out the front door. First sidewalk you come to will take you straight to the sophomore dorms."

Gramps sputtered a laugh. "Could you show me?"

Inside she must've been raging. Good.

Marissa nodded, resigned, and led Gramps to the elevator. She got inside, vigorously tapped the button for the lobby.

Gramps found he was enjoying this. Like that time he got a suspect to practically march himself to the precinct.

He said, "My granddaughter is majoring in biology. What's your major?"

"Not a student," said Marissa. "I work here."

"Oh, you look so young."

"I'm head of Greek Life." It was said confidently, so Gramps replied, "Such a big job for a young woman."

If Billie had heard him just then he would've gotten a detailed lecture about sexism and something called microaggressions. Luckily, he was here and she was not. And this was a mark. Possible suspect.

They exited the lobby and Marissa escorted Gramps outside. A drizzle began and he winced slightly, thinking of the roof repair. Over ten grand easy. He had some money socked away, but that would wipe him out. Billie wasn't the only Levine worrying about bills and home maintenance. The financial burden wasn't just sitting on her shoulders.

Once the brick building for Wagner came into view, Marissa said, "You'll have to use the call button. Do you know your granddaughter's room number?"

He hadn't even replied when she mumbled, "No, of course you don't."

Marissa smoothed down the frizz along her part, then whipped out a white keycard. She hustled up the steps at a quicker clip than Gramps could ever manage, pressed her the card to the reader and the door opened automatically.

Gramps held up his cell phone and waved it side to side. "My daughter texted me her room number. Thank you so much."

If Marissa Gulla had been paying attention, she would've seen that the screen was a text exchange between Gramps and the delivery driver who had dropped off matzoh ball soup when Gramps was too lazy to drive in the rain. But she wasn't paying attention.

Gramps went inside the dormitory with the confidence of a man who knew where he was going. When he glanced outside, Marissa was still on the stairs, her face twisted into doubt.

He continued down the hall.

CHAPTER FOURTEEN

Celeste Tran came to the door after only one knock. She glanced at Gramps's scruff and loose trench coat and said, "Who let a flasher into the building?"

Gramps frowned, then presented her with his PI license. Unlike his granddaughter, he actually had one. "I'm William Levine. I'm working Alan's case on behalf of his sister, June. I'd like to ask you some questions."

He'd made the assumption that the Asian girl standing in front of him was Celeste Tran, mainly because she was Asian. He pictured Billie lecturing him on faulty assumptions, stereotypes and, again, something called microaggressions.

Her eyes widened. She was wearing a coat, her backpack already on one shoulder. "I'm headed to class."

"Great," said Gramps. "I'll walk with you, and we can talk."

But Celeste blew past him, her dark hair practically airborne. Dammit. Gramps's mind was sharp but his body was slow. Too slow to run after a twenty year-old kid.

"Not so fast," he hissed, limping after her once a stitch bloomed in his torso.

Celeste whirled on him, checked the hallway for eavesdroppers, and lowered her voice. "I told June I didn't want to do this."

"Alan died," Gramps said, harsh on purpose.

"From an accident," she whispered.

"Maybe," he said with a slight shrug. "Maybe not."

That stopped her. She checked her phone screen and huffed, exasperated with the clock or Gramps – who could tell? She gestured wordlessly, and a moment elapsed before Gramps realized that he should follow.

Hands in his trench coat, he trudged alongside Celeste as they headed outside, the rain picking up now. That's what the trench coat was for. His old bones could only handle so much moisture.

"June said that you'd been doing some pledge thing when you had an asthma attack."

"We were outside in our bra and underwear in late November when I suddenly couldn't breathe." Celeste cast him a side glance, as if she shouldn't have mentioned *bra* in front of him. He was old, not a toddler. "Dumb, but just a test, you know? See if we really wanted to belong, but my lungs...anyway, I needed an ambulance, but Brianne Druffner ordered the girls to stay where they were, said anyone who broke away would be out – done. One girl defied her, though, and called 9-1-1. I was in the hospital for a few days. I came back for final exams, and that's when Brianne started coming after me."

"Harassment." Gramps sidled past students who gave him a weird look. He supposed it was odd for an octogenarian to be on campus dressed like Columbo. Not one of these kids would even get that reference.

Celeste moved off the path and onto a patch of grass in front of a red brick building. A sign out front boasted another German name. Who established this school? The Weimar Republic?

She suddenly pulled out her inhaler, shook it some, then put in her mouth and pressed down. "Brianne is unhinged. If she sees me talking to you...the abuse was just dying down. I'm pretty sure she broke into my dorm room and took a piss in my closet. She's like the bogeyman. You say her name and everyone scurries."

"And the school did nothing?"

To that Celeste shrugged. "No proof. My word against hers, and every time I went to Residence Life with a complaint, they told me *I* was harassing Brianne, so I stopped." She deflated.

"What does Marissa Gulla have to do with this?" Gramps asked.

"She's head of Greek Life. She should've reported Zeta Omega after the hazing incident; or, at least, she should've investigated Brianne's actions, or lack thereof. I mean, I could've died." Celeste shivered. Gramps noticed she was only wearing a hoodie, no coat. None of these young people dressed for the weather. "But Marissa did nothing, and Brianne is a menace. Word is she got kicked out of her last college."

"Really?" said Gramps. "You know why?"

Celeste shook her head. "I don't even know the name of the school she went to. She's real secretive about that stuff."

He ran a hand over his chin. A lead. He decided to put Celeste out of her misery and bid goodbye, but before he could, a blonde girl emerged from the shadows. She reminded him of Billie a bit, if Billie looked like she'd done time in East Jersey State Prison. Her fleece pullover had the college's emblem embroidered on it, and underneath read, "Ambassador."

The girl stood expectantly, as if Gramps or Celeste owed her an explanation for existing.

"Brianne," Celeste said glumly.

Brianne jerked her chin toward Gramps, then waved her hand around. "Who's this?"

"Her grandfather," Gramps cut in. "I'm visiting."

Celeste's breath hitched, and Gramps worried she'd have an asthma attack.

"She's Vietnamese," Brianne pointed out.

Gramps pretended to be offended. "And how do you know I'm not? That's a microaggression, young lady." He said to Celeste, "Say hello to your mother for me." And then he headed down the pavement toward the parking deck.

CHAPTER FIFTEEN

That evening there would be no cute knock to the tune of "Anti-Hero," just Billie's fist pummeling away at Jeremy's apartment door for several minutes until she heard the deadbolt unlock.

Jeremy appeared, a towel strung about his waist, water dripping from his dark hair. She had suspected he built his physique from some kind of cardio, but now surmised he lifted weights in the Kentwell gym. She briefly pictured dropping a barbell on his toe and shook off that thought.

How would Vela want you to respond?

Definitely not by showing up at Jeremy's place, her temper so charged she could light up the Empire State Building.

"For Christ's sake, I was in the shower," he said as she pushed right past him.

"Trying to cleanse your sins?"

"Please come in," he addressed the empty space she'd just vacated, then shut the door behind her. When he turned, she was standing squarely in his living room.

"I regret not moving the minute you found out where I lived," he said.

"Anywhere you'd go, I'd find you." She sounded sultry when she had meant to be threatening.

He sighed and held up a finger, the other hand grabbing onto the white towel for dear life. Billie was so disgusted by his deceitfulness that she derived no pleasure from the thought of seeing his bare ass. If anything, she wanted to smack it enough to hurt so he knew she meant business. Oh God, was she into kink? No.

Focus, Levine.

"Give me a second," he said. "I need to be dressed to deal with you." He walked backwards into his bedroom, as if retreating from a rabid animal.

Billie paced around the coffee table, picked up a game controller then tossed it onto the couch. Her eyes darted to the corner where they landed on a pair of retro Air Jordans still in the box. She grabbed them and cradled them like a demon baby. When Jeremy appeared, this time in gray sweatpants and a white T-shirt, she hefted them in the air and screeched, "Jordans! Jordans!"

Jeremy yanked them from her grasp. "What the hell is wrong with you?"

She charged him. "You. You're working for Heath Vickery?! Don't deny it. Jeremy Something from Kentwell. Hope the money is worth your double cross."

"My double cross?" Then he sputtered, "How-how do you know this? I haven't even started billing hours."

"Because I took a–" She stopped. That damn NDA. "Because I do."

"Because you took a job at Tropic Reef?"

She pressed her lips together and blinked.

Narrowing his gaze, he continued, "You're working a hell of lot of cheating spouse cases lately. Scorned wealthy women turning to Billie Levine to right their marital wrongs. Were you hired by Katherine Von Holm?"

She blinked several times before blurting, "Can't say."

"That's an answer. She's notorious for NDAs. They all are." A frown, then, "What does a woman like that want with you?"

Billie asked, "What does Heath Vickery want with you?"

They stared at each other.

"You're not going to tell me?" she asked.

"You're not going to tell me?" he asked.

"I need the money," they both said at the same time.

"For what?" they asked together.

"Roof repairs," said Billie. "And a proper office."

"Funding," he said. "My dissertation is due in a year, and I need to spend a few months in Spain."

She exhaled. So did he.

"What are we going to do?" she said. "We both need this job."

"If we tell Heath or Katherine that we know each other, we'll both be sent home, contracts voided."

"With nothing," she added.

Jeremy nodded.

"So we don't tell them," she said.

"Isn't that morally gray?"

"I thought you were getting a doctorate in criminal justice, not philosophy," she shot back. "Anyway, I'm not working for the enemy. You are."

"You don't know what I'm doing," he said. "Worry about Katherine, 'oh, look at my wrap dress that costs $500,' Von Holm."

"Says the guy who bought $400 Air Jordans."

"I didn't buy them," he said. "They were a gift!"

"From who? You got a sugar mama?"

Jeremy paled.

"Oh my God, you have a sugar mama?" She whispered, "Vela?"

"What? No!"

"Then who?"

"Not telling you."

"I'll find out anyway."

"Billie, you don't need to know everything that is going on with a person. Some things are best left secret."

Nothing was best left secret except surprise parties or dubious paternity.

Jeremy marched toward her. "Every time we're in a room together, I want to strangle you. And since I'm not going to end up like that dude in Idaho, you're going to have to leave."

As Jeremy pointed to the door, her cell phone buzzed with a text from David.

Gramps spoke to Celeste.

That caught Jeremy's eye. He grabbed her phone.

"Hey!"

He stared at the message, a storm churning in his gaze. He looked up at her. "Celeste Tran?"

"Not your fucking business," she said, swiping her phone out of his grasp.

He moved toward her, causing her to back up quickly. She fell onto his couch. He leaned over her, boxing her in. "Why did you take June's case? It was an accident."

She pushed him away and scrambled to her feet. "Because your ass wouldn't. She said you were a friend. Some friend. You didn't want to help her? Her brother died under suspicious circumstances. How are you involved?"

"I'm not!" He growled, "You don't know anything about what Alan was researching."

She grabbed the doorknob and twisted, figuring her parting words were best said with an easy escape. "Well, Jeremy. We both know I'll find out. See you tomorrow!" She darted into the hallway and split.

CHAPTER SIXTEEN

Tropic Reef Corp was located in the first two floors of a small, newly-built Hoboken high-rise on 11th Street and Maxwell, close enough to the waterfront to jump in the Hudson River if Billie's day was going badly enough.

The city was only a square mile but had managed to toss aside various immigrant groups – Irish, Italians, Puerto Ricans – like a woman rummaging through her closet and choosing gentrification like a Chanel suit. Now the only people who could afford to live in the city's unofficial sixth borough were those who made chunky salaries working at places like Tropic Reef. Places that saw them as cogs in a wheel.

Cogs like Webber Brandt, who was practically sprinting into the lobby. He nearly skidded to a halt, his dress shoes squealing against the polished floors. His dark hair was mussed and shiny from sweat.

Billie raised a brow. "Did you get caught in tunnel traffic?"

"No," Webber replied, out of breath. "I live in Hoboken. I just had a weird morning. Slept through the alarm. Left in a hurry." Then his face flushed with panic. "Is Katherine here? Did she say anything?"

Billie shrugged. "Is she supposed to be here? I haven't seen her but, honestly, I'm late myself. Traffic."

That got her an indifferent huff, then an eyebrow raise of his own. "You drove here? From NYU?"

Would a trust-fund kid drive from the city? Doubt they'd take the ferry.

Always the consummate professional, she lied. "Uber."

Webber frowned and said, "I see." There was distinct judgement in his voice, or perhaps it was exhaustion. He seemed like the type of guy who abhorred others' ineptitude. Billie could relate, but she found his admonishment misplaced.

He finally exhaled as he took notice of his suit cuffs and plucked off loose threads. "I'll tell Heath that I was waiting for you, and you were late."

Sure, throw me under the bus on my first day. If she was going down, she'd take Jeremy with her. "The other intern is also missing."

Webber nodded as if working this bit of information through the narrative he was drafting. Then he twisted a silver watch on his wrist. His tall frame cast a long shadow on the polished floors. He was handsome. Billie couldn't understand the modeling industry if they tossed out a looker like Webber.

As if by demon's conjuring Jeremy Yang appeared, slightly breathless and wearing a slim-fitting navy suit. Billie cast him a warning glare and watched as he hurried past the security guard and awkwardly yelled, "I'm with them!"

Webber opened his mouth but Billie cut him off. She thrust out her hand, essentially stopping Jeremy's momentum, and said, "I'm Belinda *Lewis*. Nice to meet you."

Jeremy nodded, glanced down at her outstretched fingers, and shook. His hand was sweaty. "I'm Jeremy *Chen*." His grip was firm, almost too firm. "Nice to meet you, *Belinda*." Billie yanked back her arm and wiped off the dampness.

"Great," said Webber, holding out Jeremy's ID tag. "Now that you're acquainted, let's quickly get inside and down to work. Mr Vickery is particularly looking to speak with you, Mr Chen."

I'll bet.

"And remember, you were late and I was not."

Webber led the way like a mother duck. Jeremy leaned into Billie and hissed, "Do not blow this for me."

"Believe me," she whispered, "if I wanted to blow anything it would not be you."

Webber turned around. Billie grinned. Jeremy smiled. Webber faced front as his loafers treaded along the shiny floors. He stopped in front of a glass door with pink vinyl letters that read *Tropic Reef* and then, lower in a severe black font, *A Division of VHG*. He pressed his ID card to an electric scanner. A mechanism clicked and the door unlocked. As Webber ushered them through, he said, "Tomorrow, you can do this yourself."

"Like big kids and everything," said Billie without thinking, but it indulged Webber to laugh.

They entered a small lobby where a pert receptionist, who could pass for a high school cheerleader, sat behind a round counter. She was flanked on either side by large ficus plants. A *peanut-free zone* sign was taped crookedly to the desk facade.

Billie would be making egg salad sandwiches for the foreseeable future.

Webber greeted the receptionist with a nod of his chin. The girl stood, blushed, then handed him a folded brochure. "From the new place on Washington and Tenth. Katherine said to order whatever you want."

Webber nodded wordlessly and shoved the paper inside his suit pocket. Billie peeked at the interior label. Armani. Jeremy noticed as well.

They continued past reception into a wide open area. Like VHG, this space was bright and sun-filled. Billie smelled coffee brewing and heard the whooping of a photocopier. Phones rang. To her left sat conference rooms, each with a large whiteboard. And, straight ahead, rows and rows of cubicles, desks, and office chairs on clear, plastic mats clustered in a group like walruses on a cliffside. Most chairs had a butt in them.

"Nice dress," said Jeremy as he scanned Billie's figure. It was a compliment in name only. "Looks *expensive*."

"From the new Tropic Reef spring collection," Webber replied. "Wrinkle-free fabric made from recycled plastic bottles. A gift from Katherine."

"What a nice perk for an *intern*," said Jeremy, which caused Webber to frown. Jeremy was practically drawing an arrow to Billie's temple and declaring, "Be suspicious."

Billie asked, "Where's my desk?"

Webber pointed to a group of darkened computers in a corner by a water cooler. "You can set your belongings over there. Just pick any drawer you want for your bag."

"Is there a key?" she asked.

"A key?"

"Is it secure? Does it lock?"

"No," Webber replied. "This isn't Costco. You don't get a locker." Then more frankly, "No one is going to take your stuff."

"Fair enough." Billie was adjusting the strap on her bag when Heath Vickery appeared from the shadows. He had flushed cheeks and sheen to his skin. He was wearing a gray suit jacket with a plain white T-shirt underneath. He grinned with outstretched arms. "My interns." Then he glanced at his Rolex, frowned, and stared at Webber. "Why so tardy?"

"They were late, sir," said Webber. "Tunnel traffic."

"You should cycle here, then, like I do."

"From Teaneck?" Jeremy said.

Heath clamped a hand onto Jeremy's shoulder. "I have a special project for you, young man. Why don't you come into my makeshift office and we'll get started?" He turned to Billie next. "Hopefully I'll get to snag you for lunch."

As a guest or the meal?

Billie was so preoccupied watching Jeremy and Heath disappear from view, she startled as an object skirted past her vision. An iPad.

"Let's get you earning that college credit," said Webber as he tapped the screen awake.

Billie's eyes darted all over the office searching for Nina Patchett-Borel. She wasn't here to be an intern; she was here to catch a cheat. Unfortunately, the only ones aware of the con were Katherine and Rebecca and they weren't around.

Billie inwardly sighed. "Can't wait."

She was a professional investigator. She'd stared down the barrels of guns on multiple occasions. She could ask a bunch of worker bees questions. This wasn't going to be hard.

CHAPTER SEVENTEEN

Billie held the stylus and stood across from a forty something year-old woman wearing pink hair, several nose piercings, and a tailored black blazer. She looked like she'd been dipped into neon paint and tossed inside an Ann Taylor.

"So, Sylvie, how long have you been working for Tropic Reef?"

"Five years. I was one of the first marketing hires when the company got established." The woman's chin tilted upward in a defiant *fuck you*, except Billie was the wrong target for such ire.

Billie checked off a box. She wasn't sure why she was being asked to do this: if it was a missive from Katherine to give Billie the aura of legitimacy, or if Heath really needed this information for company staffing reshuffles, especially since much of the data she'd collected could be found in the employee files. And yet she continued.

"Would you say your job responsibilities take longer or shorter to perform than your current schedule allows?"

She frowned. What a tricky question. If Sylvie was to answer yes then it might appear that she didn't know how to work efficiently. If she said no, then it would seem as if she didn't have enough to do and, therefore, expendable.

This conflict was no doubt playing on Sylvie's face as her brow scrunched and eyes narrowed in thought.

After a moment, she said, "I would say 'just right.'"

Well done.

But the victory was short-lived. Sylvie threw a pen down on her desk and huffed, "I knew this acquisition would fuck us all over. Kyle insisted that we would all keep our jobs. He promised."

Kyle Olsen, the venerable president and founder of Tropic Reef who had initially started the company in his garage, selling used travel gear from corporate closeouts and bankruptcies. He originally called the business TrekTrendz until a well-meaning girlfriend said the moniker sounded like a Chinese drop-shipper selling dupes on Amazon. He changed the trademark immediately after, then dumped the girlfriend.

He was in his mid-thirties, physically fit, and sported a perpetual smile. His profile in *Outdoor Magazine* called him a "captain of travel." He was a younger, gentler version of Heath Vickery.

But did the world need two?

Kyle's outline appeared against the cubicle wall.

Sylvie rose from her chair and addressed the shadow. "Kyle, she's questioning my ability to do my job."

Billie was doing no such thing. She wanted to pat her chest Tarzan-style and grunt, "messenger."

"Stop stressing, Sylvie," said Kyle, whose jeans and sports coat made it seem like he was headed to a wine tasting rather than a business meeting. Maybe that was the plan. He sold Tropic Reef so he could blow the windfall on a vineyard. "This is information collecting." He took off his jacket, and Billie noted sweat stains in his armpits. Men could always perspire in an air-conditioned office.

But Sylvie didn't seem relieved. "Remember, I put off my vacation for three years while the company was up and running. I missed out on my sister's timeshare." She aggressively tapped a finger on the desk. "Write that down. Three years. No vacation."

Somewhere a French person was cursing out America.

Kyle laid a heavy hand on Sylvie's shoulder as if he was a parent trying to quell a toddler's tantrum. Billie noticed that these men did that a lot. Like women needed to be anchored by them; the action so infuriating, Billie imagined grabbing his hand and tossing him over her shoulder in some kind of ninja-style fight scene.

She wondered if Detective Malley could instruct her on how to do that, or book her a session with the police academy trainers.

"I protect my best workers," said Kyle, wiping at his nose with the edge of his knuckle. "You know that."

He waited until Sylvie nodded, which she did, a placating performance meant only for Kyle. When he left, Sylvie exhaled and said, "I better start redoing my resume." Then, as if remembering Billie was still there, she said, "What's the next bullshit question you have to ask?"

Billie looked down at the tablet screen and said, "Would you be willing to take a pay cut to keep your current position?"

"Are you fucking kidding me?"

A head popped over the cubicle wall. A bearded man with blue eyes. "Start sending out those resumes."

"Not helping, James," said Sylvie.

Billie tapped the screen. "James Compton?"

The face slid down, melting behind the cubicle wall until he disappeared altogether.

"No," he said weakly.

"Can I ask you some questions?"

"James isn't here right now."

Billie sighed. She had better luck getting information out of crooks.

CHAPTER EIGHTEEN

There wasn't a lot Billie appreciated about her life, but she'd take her broke ass and dysfunction over stuffy office culture any day.

Especially when Heath called out to his employees like they were a herd of sheep.

"Sylvie! Toby!" he bellowed. He pointed at a desktop computer in a cubicle with a view of the Hudson River.

Billie hugged her tablet to her chest and glanced outside longingly. The trees were beginning to bud; soon the entire East Coast would glow green. One wouldn't anticipate that shivering inside the Tropic Reef office building with the air conditioning cranked down to tundra.

Webber followed her gaze and sighed. No matter how old they got, Billie imagined they all wished to be kids allowed out for recess.

Heath's hand coasted the waist of a beautiful woman in a black suit and pumps. Billie caught a glimpse of her profile. Young, early thirties. Leggy. Mediterranean coloring. Pale skin where a wedding ring would sit. Recently separated? Nina Patchett-Borel, vice president of operations. Billie recognized her from last night's Google session. She had stayed up way too late building dossiers on the big players at Tropic Reef, and chatting with Nicole about the nearly three grand in freebies she had been given. *That* was not part of the NDA.

Heath and Nina's heads were bent toward each other. Laughter permeated their conversation. The air felt thick with sleaze.

"How's the interviews going?" Webber asked her.

"Um, a bit touchy," Billie replied, not taking her eyes off the pair. Katherine's intuition was right. Heath and Nina screamed office affair.

Webber patted around his suit jacket and swore.

"Something wrong?"

"New suit," he said. "With the alarm fiasco this morning, I forgot something in another jacket." He shrugged. "No big deal. So things are tense?"

"Everyone's just a little worried about losing their jobs," Billie offered Webber as Jeremy sidled up beside her.

He asked, "How's your day going?"

The question was posed innocently enough, but Billie suspected his interest for what it was: fishing. She would not be bait. "Fine. And yours?"

"Also fine."

Webber gave her a weird look before pressing a finger to his lips. Heath and Nina stood in front of them, a pair of high-powered executives, appearing as if they were about to address a group of children. As Billie glanced around, she supposed they kind of were since most were batting under thirty. Except for Sylvie.

Kyle dropped into a desk chair with a huff and ran a hand through his hair. He appeared to Billie like he was late to a spin class and this whole 'owning a company' was an infringement on his day. Sweat glistened across his temple.

Heath grumbled, "Now that everyone is here, I wanna show you something Nina found." He wiggled the mouse and brought the screen to life.

A girl appeared. Pretty. Familiar. YouTube famous.

"Guys," she said. "I got the new TR backpack in chartreuse and look at all these compartments." She shoved the bag in front of the camera. "I'm going to show you how I pack it." Fast forward later, the bag was stuffed. "It's light too. I don't know how they do it. I know it's expensive, but you can't beat this zipper construction. It's so much better than my old VHG bag, and it comes in all these cool colors. If you want my opinion, VHG is on its way out"

Heath paused the video. "This account has over a million subscribers."

Kyle swiveled in his chair and said, "I've been saying this for months now. There's a reason TR bags are so coveted. They come in fun, young tones. People don't want black anymore. They want neon and pastel and camo."

Heath grimaced. "Katherine's fine with some TR lines in those hues, but VHG classic bags need to remain classic."

"Yeah, but you guys stopped our production on the Florence backpack in cerulean, celeriac, and cherry."

"They weren't selling, Kyle. We told you that. We've put them on sale. And we hate doing sales. Besides, this is not a production meeting. We need the Tropic Reef social media team to start building brand awareness around the new line."

"Send the reviewer free goods," said Kyle.

"No," said Heath.

Toby, who occupied the cubicle closest to the bathroom, rolled her eyes and leaned into Sylvie. She whispered, "Last time I did a social media campaign presentation, the team in New York stole my concept and ran with it. Heath came back telling me I needed to do more if I wanted to keep my place."

"Thieves," whispered Sylvie.

Toby, the tattooed Irish pixie, had been an international hire for the social media team. Her job for Tropic Reef had been to expand the brand into international regions.

Just last year, Kyle had sent her and two others on an Ireland walking tour using only their signature all-in-one Globetrotter Go Backpack. The campaign had been such a raging success that Tropic Reef sold out of the bag and unscrupulous eBay sellers were asking three times for it, and getting it.

Toby's creative ad campaign was the entire reason they got on VHG's radar, and now Billie was asking if her job could be done by fucking AI, or James in sales and, if so, could she kindly gather her belongings and say goodbye to her coworkers? *We'll give you a great reference, but it's back to Dublin with you.*

If Billie was being honest, Dublin sounded a lot nicer than being stuck inside a stuffy Hoboken building on a sunny afternoon.

Heath said, "We need to flood out the critical review. Legal's working on taking that video down anyway. Girl has a grudge."

The group was dismissed, and Billie wandered over to the water cooler.

"They're going to close the TR office," said Sylvie as she strode toward Billie. "I know it. And I'm not commuting into the city. I was told during COVID that I would be able to work from home."

Toby laughed. "Load of shit."

"I swear, sometimes, I want to strangle Kyle and ask him what he was thinking selling Tropic Reef to the highest bidder."

"Money, Syl. Sports betting isn't going to pay itself."

"He promised me there wouldn't be this hustle culture. How many times did he say, 'no hustle culture.'"

"A thousand."

"Right. And now we've been taken over by a bunch of Gen X workhorses."

"You're Gen X, Syl."

"Not like them," she said, clearly insulted. "I had asked for a week off in June and HR came back and asked me if I could do five days instead of seven because we have a big product launch set for mid-June. I was like, 'the new backpack line isn't really a big launch. We do it every summer.' Then I heard Katherine say if we don't care about the company, we can find other jobs. Like, for real? She wasn't in the office last month because she went to three global women's summits in Europe!

"I can't do it much longer, Toby," Sylvie continued. "I've been trying to find some work-from-home gigs, but it's all bait and switch. The job listing said 'virtual,' only when I got to the interview, they said that I'd need to come in three days a week. They don't care because there's just another poor schmuck lined up behind me and another one behind them. We can't all be Rebecca Jimenezes – eager for the crumbs cast at our feet."

And Billie thought private eye work was tough.

She looked at her watch. Nearly noon.

Webber found her a few minutes later. She was staring outside at passing joggers. "This isn't the tough part," he said. "Summer is."

"Is that when you leave for vacation?"

"I try," he said, softly. Then, "Oh, Heath wants you to join him for lunch."

"Really?"

"Yeah." He adjusted his cuffs, checked the time, and exhaled. "Don't take long, all right? He can keep you out all day."

"How am I supposed to handle that? Do I just ditch him after an hour?"

"Make excuses. Katherine will lose her shit if she thinks for a second…"

"What?"

"Nothing. Heath's just extra."

In this case, *extra* was likely a euphemism for *philanderer*.

Billie sighed, then excused herself to find Heath's office. The receptionist had dropped a smoothie on his desk. As she left, her ass managed to snag Heath's gaze.

"Belinda!" Heath smiled, all cheeks. "You fancy Italian?"

Normally she fancied anything she didn't pay for, but a meal with Heath would cost her something. Nothing was free.

Heath didn't wait for her to respond before grabbing his phone and jacket. "Let's go. There's a bottle of Sassicaia that I'm itching to try."

"Mr Vickery," said Jeremy, entering the office with his eyes cast down on a file folder. "I may have figured out–" He spotted Billie and stopped talking. "Oh."

Heath glanced at his phone and grumbled, "Change of plans, Belinda. Sassicaia tomorrow."

"Sure."

He flew past her, smoothie in one hand, his suit jacket in another. Billie and Jeremy both watched him leave alongside Nina Patchett-Borel.

Billie smirked. This was almost too easy.

As she motioned to grab her coat so she could follow, Jeremy pulled her back. "Where are you going? Your lunch plans got cancelled."

She shook him off. "Just out; I'm hungry."

"You brought an egg salad sandwich for lunch."

Billie needed to leave now if she was going to stay on Heath's tail, but Jeremy must've sensed that because he refused to let her go. Billie caught Webber's gaze. "Back away, *Chen*. Webber's getting suspicious."

"The fact that he isn't already is suspicious."

Billie smiled at Webber and deflated slightly. His face was better than her anti-anxiety meds.

"You're attracted to him," said Jeremy.

"What can I say? He's a good-looking man," she replied. "And what does that have to do with anything?" Because while she admired Webber's looks, she wasn't that done in by them. Men complicated things.

"Clouds your judgement," said Jeremy.

No shit.

Billie turned back to him. "Says the man working for Heath Vickery, whose eyes haven't met a woman's ass he didn't like."

Jeremy sighed.

Billie started for her bag, not likely to catch up to Heath now.

"Where are you going?" asked Jeremy.

"To eat my sandwich in the broom closet. Is that all right with you?"

CHAPTER NINETEEN

Billie hid in the supply closet, her tablet charging via the nearest socket while she sat on an upturned bucket and talked to Nicole.

"Jeremy is at my undercover gig. The bastard blindsided me. He's working on behalf of...this guy, under the pretense of being an intern."

"Stealing your thunder?"

"Not like that," said Billie. She huffed, "Or maybe like that."

"Did you ask him why he's there?"

"Of course. He wouldn't say."

"Did you tell him about your case?"

"I didn't because I signed an NDA, which is why I'm being so vague with you."

Nicole's voice hitched. "Did you learn nothing from those Fox News blondies?"

"It's different. I'm helping scorned women."

"Uh huh. And what's your grandfather think of this?"

"He wasn't pleased that I took this case without checking with him first – until I mentioned the fee. Then he quickly changed his tune." Really he said, *That check better be in the mail.*

But a woman like Katherine Von Holm, a CEO for God's sake, wasn't going to stiff Billie. "Forget me," she said to Nicole. "How was your job interview in Union?"

"Good, I think."

"You think? Did it pass the vibe check?"

"Oh, there was a vibe. Just not sure it was a good one. Something feels off."

"Like what?"

"I went in and the guy, Dr Fredericks, seemed so pleased to see me. Said my resume was impressive. We were chatting about campus life and then he got a text or something. He glanced at his phone, and immediately everything changed. He was curt and said he'd have to cut the interview short."

"OK, well that may not have anything to do with you. Maybe his wife called to tell him she was having an affair with their pool cleaner."

"Who's using their pool in March? Also, the man is gay."

"Well, I stand corrected."

"You need to take on some new cases."

"Can't, the money's too good. Like really good. But seriously, perhaps, it has nothing to do with you. He's a dean, so maybe some academics dissed his article. I saw Jeremy toss a textbook into a Kentwell fountain because a review journal rejected his research on Spain's cardboard recycling thefts, claiming it was 'inconsequential to the study of criminology.'"

Nicole took a beat. "When did that happen?"

"I don't know," said Billie. "Few weeks ago."

"I thought you two avoid each other because he's a client burglar."

"I ran into him when I was at a counseling session. Totally random."

"Right." There was a tone of disbelief in her voice. "Well, I have another interview in twenty minutes. I'm in a parking lot at FDU."

The door opened, and Webber stuck his head inside. "I thought I'd find you in here," he said. "Sadly, lunch is over."

Billie glanced at her Swatch. "Oh, crap. Didn't know the time." She said into the phone, "Gotta go, love you, and good luck."

Nicole muttered, "Go forth and detect."

Billie ended the call and brushed dust off her dress. She unplugged the tablet and followed Webber into the hallway as he turned back and whispered, "Far be it from me to overstep, but maybe business might not be your major, seeing as how you were eating your lunch in a closet. Gotta talk to people in this field."

Billie shrugged. "I don't know anyone here. I feel a little weird." It was the truth.

"Sorry your lunch *date* with Heath didn't work out."

"Me too," she said, not bothering to disguise the sarcasm. "Man's not subtle."

"He's not." Webber leaned in conspiratorially. "Keep your guard up."

Billie wanted to ask for specifics, but Webber seemed preoccupied. "In here."

She couldn't overcome the sleaziness that came with being undercover. Her stints pretending to be a housekeeper at a fancy hotel to catch a cheating spouse were brief. By the time she could consider how she felt in her skin, the con had ended. The jig was up.

But, here, parading as some wealthy NYU student made her itchy, the costume being so ill-fitting. And the only person who might see things her way was Jeremy Yang, and she definitely didn't want to talk to him right now. Although she supposed she would have to at some point.

Webber led her into the conference room, only now the table was littered with several boxes and a takeout container. "Employee records for the past ten years," he explained, pointing with his fork.

"Tropic Reef's?" Billie asked.

"VHG. Heath had them sent over for some reason."

"You don't know?"

Webber shrugged. "I suppose this is what the intern is doing; Heath's working on something." The last part was said cryptically.

Billie surmised then that Webber didn't know the con. Maybe to Webber Jeremy Chen was just a diversity hire and not a private eye.

Webber sat down and unwrapped a waxed parcel.

"You didn't eat?" she said.

He shook his head. "Katherine has me doing product inventory with one of the designers. She wants to see what Tropic Reef had in the works before the takeover."

"Anything good?"

"A bag with rollerblade wheels," he said. "In recycled vinyl." Then, for emphasis: "Neon."

"I like neon."

"Katherine loathes it. Neon, she has said many times, does not look classy."

"If you don't mind my saying, there seems to be a real conflict between what Katherine wants and what consumers do."

"You like that navy dress?" asked Webber, gesturing to her clothes.

"Yes, but I also like neon."

Webber unwrapped his sandwich.

Billie sniffed the air. "What's that?"

"Vegan tofu burrito."

"I had egg salad."

"How pedestrian."

"That's a nice way of saying cheap."

He glanced at her. "Figured you'd order a fancy Cobb salad."

NYU Belinda would have, but Billie saw all those peanut-free signs yesterday and erred on the side of mayo.

While Webber began nibbling on his burrito, Billie began removing files from the boxes, overcome by a desperate need to snoop. She opened one folder, caught a name, and a red stamped word: RESIGNED.

She saw another labeled: RESIGNED.

In fact, the entire box was full of employees who had left the company. It was a thick box.

102 MAKE A KILLING

She heard Webber slurp from his straw. Then he coughed, likely recoiling from the carbonation. He stopped, coughed again.

She heard him wheeze and say, "Oh no."

Billie turned around just as Webber abruptly stood up and pushed the chair behind him. His hands first went to his throat. Then he wheezed as he tried to pat down his suit jacket pocket. His skin grew blue. He gasped, and Billie spied his tongue, swelling to twice its size.

"Shit!" Billie darted over and frantically opened his jacket, sticking her hands into the internal pockets, trying to feel for an EpiPen. Nothing.

"Not there," he wheezed. "Desk."

His breath was becoming more labored and shallow. She turned to run from the room, but he grabbed her wrist. "Don't go."

Billie realized with a sickening feeling that Webber thought he might die alone. She screamed, "Help!" And then fumbling for her cell phone, she dialed 911.

"Jeremy!" she cried again.

He came flying into the room and said, "Are you insane?" Took one look at Webber and said, "What's happening?"

"Anaphylactic shock. Check his desk. EpiPen. Now!"

She heard Jeremy cry, "Which one is Webber's desk?" just as Webber collapsed to the floor.

CHAPTER TWENTY

Fuzzy, black caterpillars. The kind that turn into spongy moths. His eyebrows are the babies and that mustache, well, that's the dad.

Billie found herself staring at the officer's facial hair, imagining the thick bands as sentient beings, ready to jump ship the moment a razor came within inches of his skin.

It was the only way to keep her from falling apart in front of everyone.

"There was no EpiPen in his suit jacket?" the detective asked, the hair above his lip twitching as he spoke.

"No," she said. "I checked his pockets. He was wearing a new suit, I think."

"Was that the only one he carried?"

Billie felt her body on the verge of a shrug. After all, how much information could she provide on a guy she only met yesterday? "There supposedly was one in his desk, but Jeremy couldn't find it."

"I see," he said.

Webber had been taken away by ambulance to the nearest hospital, in this case, Hoboken University Medical Center.

"Is he...is he OK?" she asked. "Detective..."

"Abadi," he replied. "Mo Abadi."

The problem with a freak accident happening in Hudson County meant that her Bergen County Detectives Bureau connections were no good here. Maybe Morales could inquire on her behalf; likelier he would not.

The detective didn't answer Billie's question, which rankled her more than she wanted to admit. Instead he thanked her before moving on to other parts of the office. Billie caught sight of Katherine, who had apparently jumped in a hired car the minute the ambulance had been summoned.

Tossing off gloves, Katherine had entered the Tropic Reef offices alone, expecting fanfare, only to be met with the red-rimmed eyes of the higher-ups. Nina. Heath. But no Kyle Olsen. He had dipped out for lunch and failed to return. Nina had been calling his cell for the past half hour.

Rebecca had come through the doors next, her coat billowing behind her like a cape, and her phone held out in front. "Got your text. What happened?"

"Oh dear," said Katherine. "An accident with Webber. I was at my meeting…"

Now Rebecca was stopping at each cubicle, pollinating the office in niceties and tissues. "I'm sure he'll be OK." She knew everyone's names as she set down cups of water. "I have Motrin if you need it, Toby. I know how you get headaches when you're stressed."

Meanwhile Katherine spoke hurriedly to the detective. She was wearing a white wool coat, patterned scarf, and bright red lipstick. She had been in a meeting when Heath had phoned her. Billie had overheard one side of the conversation.

You must come now. It's Webber.

…

He was taken away by ambulance. Allergic reaction.

…

Fuck, Kat! Get here now! This is a crisis you need to handle. Get your PR people looped in.

Jeremy sidled up beside Billie, and she jumped.

"Sorry," he said, and he actually sounded sincere.

She wasn't in the mood for him right now, which he must've realized. "I didn't mean to bother you; I just wanted to know the name of the detective."

"Mo Abadi."

Jeremy considered that for a moment. "I have some contacts with Hoboken PD. I can ask around."

"We need to see how Webber is doing."

"Billie–"

"Find out if he's in the ER, or ICU. I'm sure he was admitted."

"Billie–"

"God, I think his parents live in Vermont. Will take them forever to get here."

"*Belinda,*" his voice grew firm.

"What?"

He jerked his chin toward Abadi who was carrying an evidence bag. Inside was Webber's lunch.

"Oh no," she said, falling into the nearest chair. "Do you think he's–"

"We don't know anything, yet. He could be in the ICU." Jeremy, to his credit, was being kind. Billie hated that.

The detective answered a call Billie was not close enough to overhear. He then walked straight to Heath and whispered in his ear.

"This isn't good," she said.

"For once I agree with you," said Jeremy.

Billie, either by intuition or something far more primordial, watched Heath closely.

He raised his hands, trying to quiet the mournful murmuring of a corporate office where its worker drones were barely used to living.

"I'm so sorry to report, but–" Heath's voice faltered, and Billie found herself suspicious of every wobble. What was sincere and what was performative?

"Webber has passed away."

No one said anything, except for Jeremy who whispered "fuck" under his breath.

"I think," said Heath, "it would be understandable if we ended the day early. HR will be made available in both our companies to help you through this time."

Billie waited until the office drones buzzed once more before she grumbled, "what a cold address."

But Jeremy had bigger thoughts on his mind, such as, "You should tell Katherine you're off this case."

"What?!" That caught her a few stares.

Jeremy tugged on her sleeve and ushered her into the copier room. "If Webber was targeted then Katherine is a suspect."

"One, how do you figure and two, are you nuts?"

"There's some things you don't know about Katherine," said Jeremy.

Billie crossed her arms over her chest. When Jeremy said nothing, she unfurled her arms and gestured in a wild motion. "Are you going to tell me or not?"

Jeremy shook his head. "Are you going to tell me why you're working for Katherine?"

"I signed an NDA, so I couldn't tell you if I wanted to," she said. "I assume you've done the same."

Jeremy nodded. "Then I guess we're at a standstill. If we tell each other, we defy the NDAs."

"I'm not backing off this case," she said. "I didn't know Webber, but he was a nice guy. A guy I could have been friends with."

His nostrils flared as he stepped back. "I'll prove to you that Katherine isn't who you think she is. While I'm at it, I'll find out what really happened to Webber."

"Pfft," she said. "And I'll prove to you that Heath is not who you think he is. And if anyone is going to avenge Webber, it'll be me because I'm the superior investigator here." Billie held her hand out for a shake. "May the best private eye win."

Jeremy hesitated for a second and then grabbed her hand. It felt warm and soft.

Billie was disgusted with herself.

CHAPTER TWENTY-ONE

"So what story was Alan investigating for you?" Gramps said into the phone. He was talking to Mary Tanaka, Alan's editor at *The Atlantic.*

"A fraud story," she replied.

"At Kentwell?"

"No," she said. "At least, I don't believe so. Months ago, he said he was given some shady financial statements, recordings about a charity that seemed to be embezzling donations. He said if it turned out to be true then it would be a huge deal. He even referred to the piece as Pulitzer-worthy. But then his cousin Celeste had that hazing incident and Kentwell became his focus. He blew through the deadline."

"Did you confront him?"

"I did, yes. I told him that he had promised me an award-winning exposé." She laughed, but her laughter quickly diminished. "He said he was onto something bigger, but he couldn't give me details yet."

"Bigger?"

"Yes, that's what he said."

"He said he stumbled upon a bigger story than the fraud one?"

"Yes," said Mary, and this time, he caught her tone. She was growing frustrated with Gramps's questioning, but he wanted to be certain of information. "In your opinion would the hazing incident be a bigger story than the fraud one?"

Mary hesitated. "I'm not sure because frankly I hadn't seen much evidence of either. I had pressed him for more details on the fraud story and that was when he admitted that he had fallen behind on the investigation. I warned him about being scooped by another outlet, but he assured me that likely wouldn't happen as the person who sent him the materials was unlikely to trust another journalist. I then told him that he had an obligation to see this through, and he said he would tackle it the moment he was done with Kentwell. I didn't think there was anything there other than his cousin getting treated pretty terribly by the college." She stopped for a moment, and Gramps thought he might've heard her crying.

"And then what happened?" Gramps asked kindly.

"He told me I was wrong. We hung up after that, but I did send him an email later in which I laid out my expectations. If I were to publish the story, I wanted details. I wanted the hook. No more ambiguities."

"I take it he never got back to you."

"No, he died within the week." Mary sighed, a shaky exhalation.

"Thanks for your time, Ms Tanaka," he said.

He didn't hear a reply, just a growing silence. She had disconnected the call. He wrote in clear block letters so, if he ever kicked the bucket, Billie could decipher his work: ALAN THOUGHT THE KENTWELL ANGLE WAS BIGGER THAN THE FRAUD STORY.

Gramps now wondered if the story was actually bigger or was Alan just more personally invested? Was he looking to punish those who did nothing to help his cousin?

Both, Gramps supposed, could be true.

He was considering this while he searched the table, notes and documents organized in an array. He stopped once he found a list of names with letters written beside each entry. Again with the initials. For once, why couldn't Alan have just written out the words? He needed an Enigma machine to decipher the man's notes.

James Compton

Stewart DeVries KC

Calvin Anderson KC

Brendan Taylor

Paul Cohen

Mitchell Lott

Sighing, Gramps began searching for email addresses.

CHAPTER TWENTY-TWO

As Billie toed off ballet flats and tossed her messenger bag into the foyer closet, Gramps appeared with a dishtowel slung over his shoulder. "There's my working girl. How was your day?" His eyebrows shot up at her slumped posture, the exhaustion of work and death pressing on her spine. "That good, huh?" He gestured to follow him into the kitchen. "Tell your old man about it over dinner."

"Did you actually cook?" she asked with clear surprise.

"I did," he said proudly. "Baked ziti. Come eat while your mom is napping."

Billie sighed, her exhalation a razor's edge from a complete mental breakdown. She'd need help processing all this; she'd need Vela.

Billie collapsed into the chair and rested her cheek against the kitchen table while Gramps donned oven gloves and hefted a giant CorningWare out of the heat and onto the counter. She grumbled, "A guy died at work today."

"Jesus Christ," said Gramps, shucking off the oven mitts in such a huff that one would think she had killed Webber.

"I'm *not* responsible," she said, lifting her head up. She rubbed at her eyes.

"Cause of death?"

"Anaphylactic shock. Allergic to nuts."

"Airborne?"

"In his food maybe?"

"Cops came?"

"Yes."

Gramps rummaged through a draw for a large serving spoon, which he then used to punctuate his words. "Is it foul play?"

Billie frowned. "Not sure yet."

He groaned.

"Saw an officer bag the guy's lunch. The victim's name was Webber Brandt. He was Heath Vickery's assistant."

Gramps stabbed the ziti with a spoon that stood straight up as if was cemented in place by shredded cheese. "You're not to go back there."

"You know I have to," she said. "The amount of money I'm being paid will fix the roof issues and a whole lot more. Besides, there isn't proof that he was targeted; it could've been a freak accident."

"We can only hope," said Gramps.

"And honestly, this death isn't the worst part of this job."

"It is for the dead guy."

"You got me there. Jeremy Yang is also working a case. He's posing as an intern for Heath Vickery."

Gramps scooped such a large portion onto the plate that his hand dropped from the weight. He set it in front of Billie with a fork and napkin. "You want seltzer?"

She nodded and stared as steam coiled from the pasta. Did she have an appetite? She stabbed a noodle, popped it in her mouth.

"This is nice." She couldn't remember the last time Gramps had cooked. He must've learned since David had moved out. She supposed she would have to learn too. Maybe she would check out a French cookbook from the library; travel via her stomach. Have some culinary adventures. Who was she kidding? Visiting Paris via boeuf bourguignon was as pathetic as only seeing the Eiffel Tower on a screensaver.

She then thought about Webber's parents and the news they had received today. She dropped the fork and pushed away her plate.

"If you're not hungry, follow me into the dining room," said Gramps.

Billie reluctantly rose from the table and trudged after her grandfather. The dining room table, which was only used for holiday dinners, was covered with manuals and documents from Alan Tran's apartment.

A bucket in the corner sat half full with rainwater. Billie's eyes shot to the ceiling where brown veins stained the paint. The roof really needed to be addressed. And it would be. Once the check came.

She said, "We need a proper office."

"One day, but, for now, the dining room will have to suffice. I was going through and found a bunch of notes on various Kentwell people of interest."

"People Alan was talking to for his story," said Billie.

He held up one file in particular. "I think we should start here."

Billie placed her hands on the table and leaned forward, squinting at the names. She said, "Shit."

"What?" said Gramps.

Billie faced the paper toward him so he could read the name. She said, "Calvin Anderson. Nicole's boyfriend."

"I can see that being a headache. Anyway, I emailed each of them asking about their connection to Alan. I'll report back once they reply."

"If they reply." Billie rubbed the ridge between her brows. "I'm going to have to tell Nicole. Right? That's the correct way to go about this?"

"As a friend, probably, but as an investigator I caution against. Not until we find out what this is all about. You could get Calvin in trouble or, worse, she might sideline your work."

"That's what you think is worse?"

Gramps shrugged.

Billie squeezed her eyes shut. Outside, she heard the gentle patter of rain. Only a matter of minutes before the bucket saw some action.

"Let's circle back to that," she said. "I'm thinking we should first check in with Alan's editor at *The Atlantic*. Make sure we have our ducks in a row."

"Way ahead of ya," he told her. "I called her earlier." He unpeeled a yellow Post-it note off a file folder and held it up for Billie's inspection. "Mary Tanaka."

"Get anything useful?"

"She said Alan was hyperfixated on the story at Kentwell. But that wasn't the issue."

"You're burying the lede."

"Mary said he was supposed to be working on a fraud story but blew through a deadline."

"Because of this harassment with Celeste?"

"That was her understanding. But she said that Alan claimed the Kentwell story was 'bigger' than the fraud one." He made air quotes.

"Bigger, huh? Objectively so?"

Gramps shrugged.

Billie said, "I have to think that whatever Alan was working on might've gotten him killed."

"Possibly. I'm not ready to draw conclusions."

"Anything else?"

Gramps leaned back in his chair. "I spoke to Celeste."

"On the phone?"

"Of course not. I ambushed her on campus. Anyway, she said that Brianne got kicked out of another college before she transferred to Kentwell." He tapped on his phone. "I looked up her social media, but it's all blocked. I have to friend her first." A long sigh. "This'll take time. Especially with you working for corporate America."

"It's for a case," she said. "A case with a big payday for our roof."

He sighed again.

She said, "I have a kid, Diego, that helps me out sometimes. I can offer him some hours, help take the load off."

"A stranger?"

"He's nineteen and lives in Dover. Eager."

"Broke you mean?"

"Who isn't? He's also cute and college aged. Students might be more willing to talk to him than you. No offense."

Gramps waved away that bruise to his ego.

Billie yawned, her arms stretched above her head. She wanted to get out of this dress. It might not wrinkle but it wasn't as comfortable as threadbare sweatpants and a ten-year-old camp T-shirt. "Tomorrow I'm hitting the pavement. I want to check in on the takeout place that served Webber his last meal."

Gramps nodded before picking up a can of seltzer from the table. He toasted the air. "To working stiffs." Upon the realization of his accidental cleverness, he smiled and said, "Working stiffs? Get it?"

"Tasteless." As she trudged upstairs, she texted Diego.

Fancy meeting a girl?

CHAPTER TWENTY-THREE

Later that night Billie embarked on a little research. She typed Heath Vickery's name into Google and scanned the CVS-receipt-length fluff pieces on what a great businessman he was.

GQ did a profile on him, calling him the first gentleman of *green goods*. According to the article, Heath was the mastermind behind some of VHG's most daring product launches – luggage made from patches of dead stock nylon – if daring was synonymous with ugly. "It's important we don't add to fast fashion waste," he said.

He was also erroneously associated with being a CEO, as evidenced by the headlines in various publications.

America's Cycling CEO travels to conventions by bike

Cycling CEO does it again and builds a better bag

The Cycling CEO infiltrates the Tour de France, will cycle through Europe to raise environmental awareness

Other articles had to do with charity events, mostly bike races Heath had sponsored to raise money for environmental causes. There actually seemed to be quite a lot of them. He rode for Sierra Club, Greenpeace, California Redwood, and even raised money for a Kentwell College eco club that had planned an awareness trip to the Amazon rainforest.

But his charity, Vickery's Victors, fundraised for low-income kids to attend outdoor excursions. According to the *New York Times*, the Victors had raised over ten million dollars to send thousands of kids to a series of outdoor adventure camps around the United States and Canada. "I'm hoping if enough people get into nature, they'll want to protect it more."

Fair enough, but for some reason Billie struggled to buy this whole green activist vibe he was building around himself. Maybe because Heath leered at her like she was a meal, or because he treated Webber like property and Rebecca like a bothersome gnat. Or perhaps because Heath looked like a billboard for expensive designer suits, leather loafers, and sports cars which, as far as Billie understood, were not eco-friendly.

Heath seemed lauded in the press as a quiet eco-warrior, but Katherine was the face of the company. And yet reporters painted him as the man behind the curtain, pulling the strings and creating the successes simply because he was a *he*.

Oddly, Heath's Wikipedia page was almost a dearth of information, his early years a few measly sentences. Born in Ohio, went to college in Swarthmore, created a small company that was bought out, which gave him enough money to invest in start-ups. He met Katherine in graduate school. They had both been earning MBAs.

But most of the information lacked detail until he met her.

Even the articles didn't pop up until he was made vice president at VHG.

The Tropic Reef acquisition was also Heath's brainchild. "If VHG wants to extend its legacy, it needs to reach new generations," he'd said in a *Time Out New York* column.

But not all his endeavors had survived. Heath's European cycling tour company had bled money. Poor reviews and low enrollment forced them to shut down. "You can't take a bunch of out-of-shape Americans on a cycling tour and expect them to have fun when their asses get sore," Billie muttered to herself.

Heath had publicly said, "I only put in my body what nature creates. That's how you live a long life."

Billie wanted to gag on the sanctimony.

So Heath spent his days puttering around the VHG offices, and what? – hitting on interns while everyone worked?

No wonder Katherine thought he might be cheating on her. Besides his leery demeanor, he had the DNA of a man who couldn't sit still. Billie could understand why Katherine didn't want to divorce him and watch as he got half of what she had built.

Billie was exhausted seeing men receive credit for standing upright in a woman's wake.

Heath Vickery may not have had much of a Wikipedia page but the man left a trail. If Heath was cheating on Katherine, and Billie suspected he was, then it was only a matter of days before she caught him.

In some ways, Billie admired Katherine. Like Billie, Katherine had inherited a legacy business. Of course unlike Billie, Katherine had turned her inheritance into a global powerhouse. Billie could only credit herself with bringing Levine Investigations into a mobile-payment era. So sorta the same.

But as Billie had learned, even the most accomplished, wealthy women still picked the worst fucking partners.

Her phone rang, and Billie glimpsed the screen. Speaking of... "What do you want?" she asked Jeremy.

"What are you doing?" he said.

Billie pulled her phone away from her ear and frowned. His voice sounded sultry, inviting even, as if he was asking her, *what are you wearing?* "Nothing," she said dryly. "What are you doing?"

"Oh, not much." A long exhale. "Just checking out Webber's social media accounts."

Billie tucked her cell between her ear and shoulder and frantically pummeled her keyboard. "Why? What's on there? Where are you? Instagram?"

"God, you type so loud. I can practically hear the desperation."

"Fuck you. I'm purposeful, that's all. Ah. Found it." She inhaled a breath. "Those are his modeling pics?"

"Calm down, Levine. It's all phony."

"Phony hot, though."

The first image to appear was Webber in jeans and nothing else. His hair tousled with product. His abdominal muscles were glistening with sweat, and shiny like chrome.

They were both quiet for a moment until Billie said, "God, what a tragedy."

"Because he was hot?" Jeremy asked.

"Because he was a person. A person we knew. A person we duped."

"We didn't dupe him. We just weren't upfront with our identities. Totally different."

"I guess...you sure he didn't know your real name?" she asked.

"No," Jeremy said. "Heath didn't trust him."

"Interesting."

"Don't read into that," he said. "So you think his death was an accident?"

It was a question she had been asking herself for hours. "Only one way to find out," she said.

"We find out."

"Yeah," she said. Then, "But I'm going to find out first."

She could practically hear his eyes roll. "Your competitive streak is annoying," he said.

"I'm a woman so I'm annoying. Is that it? Because when men are competitive, they're just good at business?"

"Jesus. I shouldn't have called."

"Why did you?"

"Asking myself that very question right now." The line went silent. It took Billie a moment to realize he had hung up.

Fine by her. She had shit to do. Like look up Webber Brandt's Hoboken address.

CHAPTER TWENTY-FOUR

Billie kept the takeout menu in front of her as she walked from her metered parking spot to the aptly-described "hole-in-the-wall vegan joint even your dad would love." Presumptive. She doubted Gramps would be so open-minded as to consume a chicken bacon Caesar salad wrap that contained neither real chicken nor bacon. Hell, he wouldn't even eat the salad.

Before leaving Tropic Reef offices yesterday, Billie had approached the young receptionist and fanned out the restaurant takeout menus from Webber's desk. "Which one did Webber order from today?"

As the receptionist scanned the print, eyes red, a tissue pressed under her nose, her gaze stopped at the last one. She blubbered, "This place."

Billie thanked her, folded the menu and left.

Now as she approached the cafe's navy blue awning, she wondered how she should play this. Go around back and see if she could bribe a kitchen worker for information? Ask for the boss and pretend she was from the city health department? Impersonating a police officer was definitely out, and while she knew she could run circles around the boys in blue, faking a badge would get her ass tossed in a cell. And it didn't matter if Esteban Morales used to see her naked, there was no way he would bail her out.

So she decided to do the sensible thing and order Webber's last meal. Luckily it was circled on the menu.

She went inside and stood in line. A man with a dark beard barked orders in Arabic as he signaled to customers. When it was Billie's turn, she said, "I'd like the tofu wrap."

"Fries?"

"Uh, sure." Then she added, "Only if they're not cooked in peanut oil."

"They're not," he replied without glancing up. "One tofu wrap!" he called to the men in back.

And because she was feeling dramatic, "Maybe I should change my order because I can't have peanuts. I'm really allergic to peanuts."

"No peanuts in the tofu wrap," he said.

"Are you sure because I'm severely allergic. Like I'll need to be hospitalized."

That got her a look she didn't like.

He glared at her while scribbling the order on a notepad, shaking his head the whole time. "No peanuts."

"Not even oil? Cause I'm seriously, like, seriously allergic to them."

The guy straightened, tossed the pen on the counter, and again shook his head as if mentally saying, *how many times do I have to tell you?* "We don't use peanut oil and we don't include peanuts in this dish."

"Are you sure–"

"Listen, lady, I'm sure because I own the restaurant, and I have a peanut allergy."

"Oh."

"Yeah, so you can be assured that I wouldn't serve you anything with peanuts."

"I'm so appreciative of that," she said, subdued.

He seemed pacified until he muttered, "First Hoboken Police, now you."

She leaned so far over the counter, she almost tumbled over, then caught herself. "Did you say Hoboken Police Department?"

The guy shook his head. "No."

"You did."

"I didn't." He stared at her in challenge. "You want the wrap or not?"

Billie nodded several times. She was hungry. "Yeah. Yeah. Sounds good."

"Can I get a name for the order?"

"Billie," she said.

She stepped off to the side while he catered to the customer behind her, a bald gentleman in a sweater vest.

Eventually, a paper bag was waved in her periphery. The man was holding up her lunch which she grabbed with a sheepish thanks. As she headed toward the door, the balding man said, "You don't have to worry. I have a peanut allergy, and I've never had an issue."

"Really?"

"Coming here three times a week since it opened. That's a lot of times to toss a dart, you know?"

"And never hit a bullseye?"

"Never even hit the board. Take care, young lady." He moved toward the counter when his order was up, and Billie went outside.

She opened the takeout bag as she crossed Washington Street and inhaled the aroma. She couldn't smell peanuts, but that meant nothing. She wasn't a bomb-sniffing German shepherd.

Rather than move her car and fight for another spot downtown, Billie unwrapped her lunch and began the pleasant walk of heading toward Webber's apartment. She could eat and devise a plan on how to break in at the same time.

CHAPTER TWENTY-FIVE

Webber lived on the third floor of a five-floor walk-up on Willow Avenue and 1st Street. At first glance the building appeared quaint with bay windows that ran down the center of the facade and a small entrance. A black iron fence hemmed in a weedy garden. There was no doorman, which simplified the situation.

Watching the entrance from the corner, Billie waited until a man exited with his eyes on a cell phone, oblivious. She held out her own house keys and dangled them as if she was just about to open the door herself.

The resident smiled and propped open the door for her.

You could be letting in a serial killer.

Billie walked through the small vestibule, past the mailboxes, and up three flights of stained carpet and scratched beige walls.

She found Webber's place immediately outside the stairwell door and went to work getting out her lock-pick kit. Within moments she had to pretend to tie her shoe when someone left the neighboring apartment. As the footfalls retreated she jumped up, finished the job and was inside.

As suspected, the entire studio was no bigger than Billie's cramped attic bedroom. There was a kitchen off to the side, so narrow her shoulders could almost touch both walls. Then presumably a bathroom on the other side of that. The ceilings were high, which helped to offset the apartment's small footprint.

Webber's decorating style signified thrift. His loveseat was threadbare. The dresser was sturdy with several coats of paint. A birthday card sat atop the worn wood. Billie read the inscription: *Hope this will tide you over for a while. –Mom*

Likely cash had been inside at one point.

Billie then glimpsed a copy of the rental lease taped to the fridge. She tugged the paper loose and flipped through the pages. Webber had been paying a whopping two grand a month for this unit.

Granted the location was stellar. A short walk to the PATH train and Webber could be in the West Village within ten minutes. As far as commuting went, Hoboken wasn't a bad place to live: a Jersey address, Manhattan vibes, and limited interaction with rats. But was the locale worth two Gs? A real estate agent would argue going rate, but going where? To the poor house?

With exasperation, Billie tossed the papers onto the small kitchen countertop before opening cabinets.

Webber had certainly kept a tidy home. Dust at a minimum. A few dishes stacked beside the sink, but they were ceramic, not paper, so that counted for something. A French press, toaster oven and small air fryer cluttered the only available workspace.

She then opened the fridge and found a six-pack of beer, condiments, and cheese stamped for a quick sale. Generic cereal boxes sat on top of the fridge next to cans of tomato soup.

The living/sleeping area was minimal but masculine, and she wasn't sure if this was a style choice or by default.

Two closets flanked the narrow hallway to the bathroom. Billie opened one door only for it to fall off the track. Inside were several suits, all high-end and tailored.

She was rummaging through a jacket pocket when she heard a sneeze. And not hers.

She stumbled back, and hastily unzipped her bag, grasping for her Taser, when the shower curtain flicked open. Jeremy climbed from the bathtub with his hands held high.

"You scared me." She sucked in a breath. "No wonder I picked the lock so easily. You undid the deadbolt. How?"

He dangled a set of keys from his fingers. "Stole them from Webber's desk before the police had arrived."

"You shit. What are you doing here?"

"Same as you. Looking for clues."

"I hate when you say *clues*, like we're part of the Scooby Doo gang."

"What would you say we're looking for then?"

"Evidence," she put plainly.

Jeremy rolled his eyes.

"And I think I just found some," said Billie. She removed her hand from Webber's suit jacket and held up a square of embossed stationery.

"What is it?" Jeremy reached for the card, but Billie tugged it out of his grasp.

"Not so fast." She stepped back and ran her eyes over the messy handwriting and squinted. "So sloppy. Jason's...no."

Jeremy grabbed the note and said, "Jurgen's Custom Tailoring appreciates your patronage." He raised his dark brows into questioning arcs.

"Custom tailoring isn't cheap," she said.

"Neither are the suits Webber wore."

"Do you think VHG purchased these clothes for him? Like as a dressing allowance?"

"Or Heath did."

"I can't see Heath caring what Webber wore to the office," she said.

"Don't be so naive. Katherine gifted you clothing, didn't she?"

"From the new Tropic Reef line. She hasn't plied me with Diane von Furstenberg wrap dresses."

"Don't know who that is."

"You wouldn't."

Jeremy roamed around the apartment, which really was just a matter of taking ten paces to the left then ten to the right. Buried treasure was located with more wiggle room. He picked up various framed photos and set them back down. Billie opened the nightstand drawer and found the typical fare: condoms, lube, and a printout of a Zillow listing for a cabin in Ontario. The one taped to Webber's desk in Manhattan.

Dreams and one days.

"Do you think Webber was sleeping with someone from work?" she said suddenly.

Jeremy looked at her. "And you think that person poisoned his food?"

Billie blinked several times.

Jeremy said, "I went to the takeout place after work yesterday."

"I went this morning," she said. "Interviewed the owner."

"Spoke to the kitchen staff," he said while opening up dresser drawers. He rifled through undershirts, boxer briefs, and ties.

"Motive?" Billie asked.

"Lover's quarrel."

"They'd have to work at Tropic Reef, no? To sabotage his lunch?"

He pursed his lips. "Toby? The Tinker Bell lookalike?"

Billie dismissed that idea. "Didn't get the impression she's into men."

Jeremy furrowed his brow as he located a yellow tie with a paisley pattern. "Familiar?"

Billie stared at the fabric until the print swirled in her vision. "I think Heath wore one like that on the day I came in for the interview."

Jeremy examined the fabric. "Hundred percent silk."

"It's possible Heath gifted Webber the tie." Billie glanced over his shoulder. "Are they all silk?"

Jeremy tossed aside several. "Seems so."

Billie had an idea. "Do you think Heath was sleeping with Webber?"

"That's a leap just because they wore the same ties," said Jeremy as he located an envelope and unfolded the paper inside.

"What's that?" Billie asked.

"Student loan statement."

Billie's stomach cramped at the thought. Could she get secondhand anxiety from someone else's debt? "What's he owe?"

"Almost a hundred grand."

She shuddered. "Two thousand in rent and student loans. No paystubs around, but I have to guess he wasn't banking much as an assistant. At least, not enough to cover his expenses."

Jeremy said, "I overheard Rebecca mention that she commutes from Staten Island to save money."

Billie marched back over to the closet and stuffed her hand inside more jacket pockets.

"What are you searching for now?" Jeremy asked.

"I don't know. An ATM receipt. Bank balance. EpiPens. I haven't found any. That's weird."

"I agree."

She inhaled deeply. A light fragrance permeated the wardrobe. She took down a pair of brown leather loafers – Gucci – and stuck her hand inside.

"Why do you assume everyone hides shit in their shoes?" said Jeremy.

"Because they do." His eyes widened as Billie's fingers came free, pinching a keychain and a...

"Is that a thumb drive?" asked Jeremy.

She slid the silver cover away from the USB connector as it dangled from a plastic yellow keychain, shaped like the number one and stamped with a credit union's logo.

Jeremy glanced around the room. "Did you see a laptop anywhere?"

"No."

She examined the flash drive in a beam of sunshine as if the tiny device's secrets would reveal themselves with a smidge of light. "When I get home," she said, "I'll see what's on it."

"Don't you mean *we*? You're not getting dibs on that."

Billie cupped the drive in her palm, tightening her grip like she was protecting a gold doubloon. "Finders keepers."

"Fine," he said. "I'll just come with you to your house."

"Or," she said. "I'll open the drive and report back."

"You'll withhold information."

"How dare you suggest that I would–" She darted for the door. Jeremy immediately charged her in an attempt to grab the drive, but she quickly sidestepped him only to bash her knee into the coffee table. "Fuck."

"That'll bruise," he said, blocking her exit.

She hissed as she rubbed the skin to ease the sting. "Dude, I'm not giving you this." She shoved the keychain into her coat pocket.

"You're ridiculous." Jeremy blocked her path. "Let's just go to the public library and use their computers."

"Love to, but I have an appointment." She pushed up her sleeve and revealed her watch as if she needed a prop as proof.

"Where?"

"Not your business," she said. "I have a private life."

"Fine." Jeremy stepped aside and gestured dramatically. Billie waited a beat, expecting the drop until he moved toward the window, blocking the light. "Go. I'm serious."

Walking backwards, she eyed him the entire time until she was safely in the hallway.

"See you after therapy!" he called after her.

Billie wondered if she had time to locate his car so she could let the air out of his tires.

CHAPTER TWENTY-SIX

"You found a flash drive?"

"We found it actually."

"You and Jeremy."

"Yes."

"Hmmmm."

Billie found herself sitting across from Vela, her socked feet tucked under her butt, her Doc Martens on the floor beside her bag, her breath slightly raspy as she had sprinted to the counseling office from the parking garage.

Billie had mentally balked at mentioning the VHG case to Vela until she remembered that her counseling sessions were confidential, the only traces of Billie's loose lips were scribblings on a notepad. More had been destroyed by less, and yet this was liberation.

Only Vela seemed awfully quiet like she was chewing on Billie's information as if it were tough steak.

Billie cut through the silence with a "what?"

Vela shifted her weight slightly revealing more of the upholstery's floral pattern. To Billie, Vela seemed contemplative as if she was weighing her thoughts on silver scales. What followed then seemed cautious. "Your relationship with Jeremy appears to be changing. The antagonism is subsiding."

Of course Vela wouldn't be saying that if she had seen the two of them fighting over the thumb drive as if it were the only inflated ball at recess. Billie fidgeted with the loose threads on the hem of her jeans as she too contemplated the meaning behind her response. "We have our moments."

"Does it make you uneasy that you might get along with Jeremy?" asked Vela.

"What do you mean?"

"You seem to – not enjoy – but prefer the adversarial relationship."

"*Professional* relationship."

"Right, but adversarial nonetheless. I'm wondering if that is a comfortable baseline for you."

"You think I like fighting with Jeremy?"

"I think you're more comfortable there." Vela reclined slightly, waiting for Billie to jump in. But Billie was tuned inward, thinking about whether Vela's point was true. Was she more comfortable in conflict than peace? Was that not just true for how she dealt with Jeremy as it was for Gramps or David? What about Aaron?

When Billie still hadn't responded, Vela continued, "Changes in the status quo can cause anxiety. You and Jeremy challenge each other by default."

For this she had a response. "We're both working the same game. He's my competition."

"Fair point," Vela mused.

But something had clicked inside Billie's brain. A mechanism had turned, releasing gears. "I don't want Jeremy to suddenly be nice to me. Because then he'll then be looking out for me or trying to protect me, and I've had enough of that from men to last a lifetime. I don't want coddling in this business. I want respect."

Up until that point, Vela had been jotting notes, but that diatribe caused her to put down the pen. "You're a woman in a largely male-driven industry where your gender is seen as a weakness."

"Exactly," said Billie.

"And Jeremy is a representative of that industry. Do you think your anger is misdirected?"

"I think my aim is fine," said Billie. "Jeremy really puts the dick in private dick, you know?"

Vela laughed. She picked up the pen and scribbled notes again. "Fighting with Jeremy puts up walls, and those walls protect you."

They certainly didn't hurt.

"I wonder then," said Vela, "why he does the same?"

"Because I'm a threat to his business," Billie said, but it sounded like she was guessing.

"He has clients and a solid case load," said Vela. "Doesn't he?"

Billie found herself growing bitter. "What are you getting at?"

Vela shrugged. "Not sure." A sigh, then, "So what are you going to do about that flash drive?"

Billie noted the time and began unfurling herself from the couch like a cat. Sliding her feet into the boots, she laced them up and said, "I'm going to see what's on it. Could be something, could be nothing."

"And is Jeremy going to help you?"

Billie stood and stretched. She looped the strap of her messenger bag over her shoulder. "Is Jeremy going to help? Well, I'd like to think he's gotten distracted and has completely forgotten, but we both know that isn't true. In fact," she opened the door to reveal Yang standing directly in front of her, "I bet he's waiting for me right now."

"My office, Levine," he said. Back turned and halfway down the hall, he added, "Bring the thumb drive."

As if she needed the reminder.

Billie exhaled. She'd take rivalry over friendship any day. Billie had enough friends, but a combatant like Jeremy…well, he kept her sharp.

CHAPTER TWENTY-SEVEN

After having just dissected the spongy part of her brain that housed reflections on Jeremy Yang, Billie shifted slightly on her heels as she stood awkwardly in his office. A movement he noticed.

"You wanna pull up a chair?" He eyed her. "Or rock back and forth like a lookout during a 1940s bank heist?"

"Weird comparison, but OK." Billie dragged a folding chair over to the desk. With Jeremy centered she had no place to put her knees and kept knocking into him while he set up the laptop. Sunlight grazed the computer screen and Billie was tempted to wipe away dust and fingerprints with the hem of her sleeve. His desk was mostly bare except for a photo of himself and his parents standing in front of a monument, most likely in China, but she couldn't be sure, and didn't feel like asking about that right now. Not while he was waiting for her to plug in the flash drive.

Jeremy exhaled and she smelled mint. He said, "You wanna place bets on whether we'll find photos, video footage, or..."

"Porn?"

"No. Why would you go there?"

He clicked on the drive and opened up a file with several blue folders. "Not porn," he said. "Well, maybe. This one says *Dirty*."

"Click on that."

"If it is porn, we're both going to be very uncomfortable," he said before hovering the cursor over the file and clicking twice.

132   MAKE A KILLING

A document opened that was most definitely not porn, to their relief. Billie squinted. "What is that? A spreadsheet?"

"I swear you need glasses," said Jeremy.

"I wear glasses," she said. "Contacts, actually."

"Time for bifocals." Pointing to the screen, he said, "They're camps." He read from the list. "Camp Moss. Camp Mohawk. Camp Sunny Days. Camp Setting Sun. Camp Sunshine. Jeez. What's with the sun theme? There's addresses, too, and a director name, and a phone number." He ran a hand through his dark hair, upsetting the coifed style.

"And these numbers next to them," she said. "Dollar amounts."

"Heath's charity," they said together.

Billie turned to him. The office door rattled, and she worried they'd be interrupted by one of Jeremy's students. But the passing bump was just that. Passing.

She said, "Vickery's Victors raises money to send kids to camp. Do you suppose these are the financial contributions? Scholarship money?"

"These lists go back a few years," he said.

Billie set her phone on the desk and opened Google.

"What are you thinking?" he asked.

"Read me off one of the camps."

"Camp Mohawk. Honesdale, Pennsylvania."

She entered the terms into the search engine. A listing popped up. "Verified."

"Check another listing," said Jeremy.

Billie typed Camp Sunny Days and a California address into Google. "Yup."

"So these check out," he said.

"All we did was corroborate that they exist," Billie pointed out. She tilted the laptop toward her and opened another file. This one labeled, "Transactions."

"Electronic payment receipts," said Jeremy.

"Into a bank account with a long number," added Billie.

"Offshore."

"Oh, that's not shady at all." Then, more quietly, "Katherine told me she thinks Heath's embezzling from the company."

"Is that why she hired you?" he asked.

"Not quite." She'd revealed more than she should have hoping Jeremy would reply in kind. Instead he said nothing.

She gently elbowed him. "Why aren't you more excited? This is your domain. Criminal financial shit. I figured you'd be gleeful. You can write it up for one of those weird peer-reviewed journals you're so desperate to get into? *Journal of Modern Criminals and Psychos.*"

"We don't know this is criminal," he said, before tapping on another document. "And it's just *Journal of Criminology.*"

"Whatever." She crossed her arms, nearly sulking. "Open up another file."

There was a huff and a double click. They both leaned forward. A video played.

The film was grainy, slightly gray and fuzzy as if recorded outside on an overcast day. A Black woman stood center-frame, her hair covered in a silk kerchief. Behind her was a brick building, but the camera only caught angles of the litter-strewn street behind her. Her face was serious and determined. Her anger, as she began to speak, palpable. "They did one of those charity races, right through here. Closed off the streets and everything. Caused my neighbor Mr Mitchell to walk with his cane down several blocks before catching a cab. Anyway, I looked up the charity – Vickery's Victors. Saw they raise money to send kids to camp. Well, what do you know? I have an eleven year-old who wants to be a park ranger one day. So I apply to send him." Her posture grew stiff as she punctuated her words. "Four weeks, he'd be away. A dream for him. Sent in the application and everything, including references for an eleven year-old, if you can believe that. We met the deadline. But we never heard back. You can be sure I keep getting emails from the charity asking for money though."

A voice from the other side of the camera lens – female – said, "So what did you do?"

"I called one of the camps listed on the charity website. Camp Lenape up in Rockland County. I asked to speak to the director. I thought maybe I'd just plead our case straight to them instead of waiting on some supposed charity to help us out. They dismissed me right off. Said they didn't accept scholarship campers. She said it real nasty like." Her voice changed, grew haughty as she mimicked the director, "'We don't take city kids.' Oof, if I didn't recognize the racism in that statement."

The video ended.

Billie said, "Heath's charity sounds like a scam."

"It sounds..." Jeremy began, "questionable."

"Stop being so deferential to Heath Vickery of all people. Heath Dickery is more like it." Billie rose from the chair, needing to pace. Katherine suspected Heath of embezzling from VHG, but what if he was embezzling from a charity? A kids' charity? That was even worse.

Maybe Billie didn't need to catch Heath cheating on his wife; she just needed to catch him cheating on the company.

Jeremy remained seated. He once said he did his best thinking stationary. "Katherine's no saint," he began. "And we don't know if this video is indicative of anything illegal. For all we know, Heath sends kids to camp, but there wasn't enough funds to send that one eleven year-old."

"I'm not an idiot," she said.

"About what?"

"I know your bogus internship with Heath has something to do with former employees. I saw the files the day when Webber..." she trailed away.

"You don't know anything."

"Your niche is international crime, and suddenly you're hired by Heath Vickery to go undercover as an intern. He's digging up dirt on his wife. And using former employees for what? Testimonies?"

"That would be no different than you sniffing around Heath for adultery."

She gave him a look.

He said, "I'm not an idiot either."

"What's Heath paying you?" Billie said. "And, like, did he mail you the payment?"

He made a face. "I'm not telling you that. What's Katherine paying you?"

"No comment." Billie leaned over the desk and swiveled the laptop around. She began typing furiously.

"What are you doing?" Jeremy asked.

"Copying the files to your hard drive." She pulled out the thumb drive and slipped it inside her pocket. "I need more time to figure this out and I can't stay here all day."

"Why?" Jeremy smirked. "Got a date?"

When she didn't respond, his face morphed into a frown. "*Do* you have a date?"

"Roofer coming to give me an estimate," she said.

He deflated some as if that answer alleviated the pressure from his shoulders. What would fix the stick in his ass? "Why can't your grandfather take care of it?" he said.

"He has plans." A half-omission.

To Jeremy's credit, he didn't press for more information. Perhaps because poking one's nose into William Levine's business never ended well. Jeremy was irritating but not suicidal.

"What are you doing for the rest of the day?" she asked nonchalantly.

Shrugging, Jeremy grabbed his Nike backpack. "Dinner." He checked his watch. "Then grading. I'm still a teacher."

She wrapped the strap of her messenger bag across her head and shoulder. "I don't know how you're balancing your fake-ass internship with your real-life class schedule."

"Honestly, not well. I'll be in the library for the rest of the day."

"Well, have fun." Billie headed out of his office and into the stairwell. As she scuttled down the stairs, she texted Diego.

Got a surveillance gig for you.

Diego typed back a thumbs-up emoji.

CHAPTER TWENTY-EIGHT

Billie watched her grandfather descend the stairs in a trench coat and fedora. Hands stuffed inside his pocket, Gramps looked like Columbo and Dick Tracy had morphed into an old Jewish superhero. He paused in the middle of the living room, blocking Billie's and her mother's view of the television.

Shari said it first, "You look like Humph...Humph... that guy from the movie with the piano."

Gramps beamed. "Humphrey Bogart?"

Billie grinned too. "If you're meeting any femme fatales in red lipstick promising you a payday to retrieve valuable loot, say no. It's a set-up."

Gramps dropped his smile and said, "You should take your own advice." He pointed a thick finger at her. "For your information, I'm headed to Kentwell."

"You'll meet Diego, right? You can't pass for a student."

"Yes, I'll meet Diego," he said, mocking Billie's voice. "Although I don't see why we need to take on strays."

"Be nice. He's a good kid," she said.

"You're a kid." Gramps pursed his lips and examined the living room. Billie's laptop was open, begging to reveal secrets. "What are you doing now?"

"Roofer." She pointed to the ceiling before gesturing to her computer. "Then research."

"Hmph."

"What?"

138   MAKE A KILLING

"It's just funny how I'm hitting the pavement and you're sitting home on your ass."

"I was out all day, not sitting on my ass." The doorbell rang. "And if you'd like to deal with the roofer, be my guest. I think I'm being hosed by these guys the minute they see I'm a woman. During one estimate the guy asked if he could speak to my husband. I nearly committed felony murder."

"Try to keep your cool." Gramps checked his reflection in the mirror above the loveseat. "OK, I'm off. Wish me luck."

"Bye," said Shari, her attention now returned to the news. The kitchen door closed as Gramps headed to his car parked outside the garage.

Billie opened the front door and found a man her age dressed in a flannel shirt. He had short dark hair, stubble, and bright blue eyes. He was handsome the way Webber had been handsome. Sharp jaw line, bright skin, and, in his case, a physique built upon slanted roof lines. He hadn't changed a bit since high school.

A greeting fell from her mouth like a stone. "Stewart."

"Billie?" He lifted the clipboard, read the name, and pursed his lips.

He was obviously expecting her grandfather, just as she had been expecting a paunchy, middle-aged *Sopranos* extra. Color them both surprised. "It's been a while."

Nicole had mentioned Stewart was working for his father's roofing company. Billie should've made the connection, but her preoccupation with cases meant she was a shitty observer of the benign.

Stewart glanced at the clipboard, eyelashes dusting his cheeks. He looked back up at her and smiled, revealing a dimple. A thousand vessels would have sailed into battle for a face like that. Too bad she wasn't interested in boarding a ship.

"I'm going to get the ladder and climb up," he said.

She gestured toward the sky. "Have at it."

He excused himself, and Billie watched his tool belt bob with his gait above an admirably nice ass. Only she felt nothing. Not horny nor intrigued. She shut the door.

Inside, she listened to his steps while she examined the keychain attached to the thumb drive: yellow plastic shaped into a number one, a freebie from an unknown credit union. Not just old but old-fashioned, the kind of thing her mom would've gotten from the bank to use as an extra set of house keys when Billie and David were kids. So did the thumb drive not originate with Webber then? Was he given these files, and if so, why?

She attached the drive to her laptop and settled into the couch.

"Homework?" asked Shari.

"Kinda."

"For class?"

"For a case."

"A case," Shari repeated.

Billie nodded. "A puzzle really."

"I used to like puzzles," said Shari.

"I like them...most days," said Billie.

Katherine had stationed Billie under Heath's nose so she could catch him in the act. Right now all Billie had caught was paperwork: spreadsheets and PDFs.

"Ma, did you ever go to sleepaway camp?" Billie said without thinking.

She did that sometimes; asked questions that her mom likely couldn't answer. But to her surprise, Shari said, "No. Too expensive."

"Overnight camps cost a lot," Billie mused. "Jay from around the block, he went to a sleepaway camp in Pennsylvania. Gone for weeks." He'd been Billie and David's only playmate so his absence had been keenly felt at the time.

"That's because his parents were getting a divorce," Shari said.

"Hadn't known that," said Billie.

"His mom had that boyfriend. I don't remember his name."

"Oh yeah, Mike. He was an asshole to Jay."

"I remember him yelling a lot," Shari said.

Billie smiled as she clicked on an audio file. This one labeled *Judith Wilcox*. "Sorry," she told her mother. "I just gotta listen to this for a second."

A woman's voice said, "Vickery's Victors said they were going to send us fifty grand to support several campers from urban areas. With that amount, we offered scholarships to ten kids from an elementary school in the Bronx. But the charity only sent a check for five thousand dollars. When I complained to Vickery's Victors, I was told that the original amount had been a clerical error, and that they needed the funds for other area camps. So we had to cancel the stays of nine campers that we had promised spots to. I was gutted for those kids. I complained to the state but no one ever returned my call."

"What does that mean?" asked Shari.

"Kids were promised a free sleepaway camp but the money was taken away, so they couldn't go."

"Sad," said Shari. "You can't give someone something and then take it away."

"No, you can't."

And there's the smoking gun, thought Billie. "They promised to send the camp fifty grand, but they only sent five." She clicked around the spreadsheet, the one she and Jeremy had reviewed early. She scrolled through the list of camps and spotted Camp Salutations. Sure enough the number next to it was $50,000.

Careless error or deliberate cover-up? Nonprofits filed with the IRS like everyone else. So did camps. But how would the IRS know if they lied? Without an audit, Vickery's Victors could fudge the numbers. They could claim to donate fifty grand but only send five. What was done with that $45,000 difference? Had it gone to another camp? Or was the money transferred somewhere else? Like an offshore bank account?

Either way, this should've been enough for the IRS to investigate Heath Vickery and his charity.

Which then begged the question: what was Webber doing with these files? If Heath had found out, Webber would lose his job. Why kill the golden goose?

Unless it wasn't too golden to begin with.

Billie itched to call Jeremy, but he had a copy of the flash drive and had no doubt combed through the files. He would naturally come to the same conclusion, and if he hadn't, well...she wasn't going to fill in the gaps. After all, they were on opposite teams.

Katherine needed to know about this.

Billie googled Judith Wilcox and Camp Salutations and was gifted with an email address. She drafted a quick note asking Judith to call her. Seeing as it was March and a weekend she might not respond right away, but Billie could wait.

She was bouncing on her heels with excitement until Stewart climbed down the ladder, knocked on the front door, and handed her an estimate. She glanced at the number, a barely perceptible improvement over the previous one. "Thirteen grand, huh?"

To his credit, he shrugged apologetically. "You need to replace the whole thing. No patch jobs," he said. She followed him outside and watched as he collapsed the ladder.

The sun was drifting away, and Billie found herself squinting at the burst of dying light. For a minute, she forgot all about buckets of water and weeping ceilings.

"Hey, Stew," she began, "Nicole said you left Kentwell College."

"Yeah." He didn't look at her.

"Can I ask why?"

As he slid the ladder into the van, he said, "Job wasn't working out."

"In what way?" she asked cautiously.

He shifted his work belt around his waist and dropped the clipboard into the passenger's seat through the open window. This, Billie recognized, was a stall tactic. He didn't want to respond.

Finally, he said, "Roofing is a hell of a lot less problematic than academia. The people there were…let's just say that I feel more sure of myself on roofs." He went around to the driver's side and hopped in.

Billie folded the estimate and slipped it into her back pocket. She approached the open window. "Stew, my grandfather and I are working a case on campus. What's really going on over there?"

He scoffed. "The women are insane."

"Insane, how?"

"Power hungry."

Billie deflated some. She didn't want to get in a complex conversation about gender dynamics, particularly when it came to the unfair characterizations of women in leadership. He must've read that on her face because he said, "This is why I didn't want to talk about it." Then, a sigh. "I'm probably not explaining it right. Talk to Calvin. He can shed more light on things than I can." And, with that, he started the truck and was gone.

CHAPTER TWENTY-NINE

Gramps met Diego in the visitor parking lot of Kentwell College. The sky was gray like smoke, but the forecast promised only clouds. Gramps had his doubts.

Billie had said to look for a Latino kid, not much younger than her, but this was a college campus in North Jersey and that description could've fit any of the half-dozen students who passed him within minutes of his arrival. Gramps decided the boy would more likely find him. And he did.

"Mr Levine?" he said, his hand outstretched.

He was scrawny, scrappy even, with a floppy mess of dark hair, and an earnest expression. He reminded Gramps of David around that age.

Gramps shook the boy's hand, then said, "Bill is fine."

Diego seemed hesitant to accept that moniker but he nodded just the same. They walked from the visitor lot to a building in front of a sparse flower bed.

"So what's the game plan?" Diego asked, his hands shoved in his pockets.

Gramps leaned in a bit so he could lower his voice, lest eager freshmen catch his words. "Not sure how much Billie filled you in, but Brianne Druffner is a student ambassador. I looked that up on the college website. Apparently, she gives tours of the college campus to prospective students."

That got an eyebrow raise out of him. "Really? The girl who's trolling another student is giving tours?"

"Yes." They stopped next to a garbage can. On the other

144   MAKE A KILLING

side of the brick building would be the green lawn where they were to gather in ten minutes. Gramps would not be going past this point.

"You're gonna have to go alone," he said. "That Brianne girl has already seen my face. She'll know we're not together. That you're not my grandson."

Diego narrowed his brow. "OK."

"She's blonde, thick and, frankly, a little mean looking. You can't miss her. I need background information, particularly the college she went to before this. Pretend you're a transfer student."

"Ah," said the kid, pulling at the collar of his jacket. "You want me to use my Latino charm." He was being cocky, but he was right.

"Whatever works," said Gramps. "I'm going to get a cup of coffee and sit in the student center. Find me when you're done."

Diego gave a playful salute.

Billie trusted the kid so Gramps would too. He said to him, "Play it as straight as you can. Use your real first name if asked. You're a kid from Dover, no need to make up a new hometown or anything. You're interested in attending the school."

Diego nodded, seemingly pleased with this piece of advice. Gramps could only imagine what shenanigans he and Billie got up to. Cover stories and spyware. Running from angry men.

Gramps leaned in and whispered, "Brianne is deceptive."

"Right, a total puta. I get it." Diego nodded, having accepted his assignment, and headed down the sidewalk toward the tour group meeting place.

Gramps itched to go with him. Instead he walked off in the opposite direction, a cup of coffee calling his name.

Gramps was fishing off a wooden dock, somewhere in the Poconos. Ken Greenberg, his best friend, stood next to him, casting a line over shimmering water. Ken turned to him and said, "I got invited to a party."

"What?" Gramps asked.

"I'm in," he said again.

A shove to his shoulder, and Gramps fell off the dock and into the lake.

He woke up before he hit the water.

Diego stood over him, a hand on his shoulder. Gramps shifted around, disoriented slightly by the unfamiliar surroundings. He had fallen asleep in a club chair near the cafe. The empty coffee cup sat by his feet.

He straightened up, checked his watch, and glared at the kid. "What took you so long?"

Diego pulled up a chair, sat down, and leaned over. "Billie asked me to follow some professor while I was on campus."

Jeremy Yang. The lack of trust that fueled their relationship...

Diego tapped Gramps's knee, as if he was a dog that needed redirection, and then held up his cell phone. "I friended her on Instagram."

Gramps immediately sat up as Diego flicked the screen, revealing Brianne's profile. "That's it? Did you get anything else? Get her to talk? Open up?"

"What do you mean, 'that's it?' I flirted with her and she gave me her Instagram. This is progress."

"I'm not sure how useful pictures of Brianne's dinner are going to be."

"That's not all Instagram is for," said Diego. "There's a photo that I think you'll want to see."

Diego dragged his finger over the phone, and then turned it around so Gramps could view it. "Well, I stand corrected."

Diego grinned, and for a moment Gramps felt a spot in his chest, hardened from years of stakeouts and perp chases, soften for this kid. Rubbing at his eyes, Gramps asked Diego, "You got somewhere else to be?"

Diego shook his head. Billie mentioned that he had family in Dover but his parents had been sent back to Colombia. Gramps stood up, his bones creaking so loudly, he flushed. He might look old, but did he need to sound old too?

"You want dinner?"

"I could eat," said Diego.

Of course he could. He was nineteen and scrawny.

As they walked to the car, Diego said, "You're not going to believe it but she also invited me to a party."

"You should've led with that," said Gramps. They stopped in front of his car, keys out, but something made Gramps hesitate. "Don't go alone, and don't let down your guard."

Diego nodded in that perfunctory way that Gramps couldn't decide was respect or mockery.

Kids today, Gramps thought to himself as he unlocked the doors.

CHAPTER THIRTY

Billie was taking a lasagna out of the oven when her grandfather returned home with Diego in tow. She shucked off the oven mitts and turned to them. "How'd it go?"

Gramps shrugged as Diego said, "Great. Your abuelo gave me good advice."

Billie raised her eyebrows, impressed. She knew her grandfather was a highly skilled detective, but it had been awhile since anyone had complimented him, probably because he was often calling someone a yenta or putz or schmuck.

She grabbed plates from the cupboard and set them on the table.

"Did you make this?" Gramps asked her.

"Stouffer's."

Diego plopped down. "I'm starving."

"*Abuelo* wouldn't stop for McDonald's on the way home? Welcome to my childhood," Billie joked before placing the lasagna on a trivet in the center of the table.

"Why would I waste money?" said Gramps. "Where's your mother?"

"She ate earlier and fell asleep. The new meds make her tired."

Gramps nodded, then grabbed a beer from the fridge.

"Can I get one?" asked Diego.

"When you're legally allowed to," Gramps shot back.

"Anyway," said Billie, "don't keep me in suspense. What happened?" She joined him at the table and scooped a portion of lasagna onto her plate.

Gramps pulled out a chair and sat. "He signed up for a college tour."

"I pretended to be a transfer student, interested in engineering," said Diego in between bites.

"Are you interested in engineering?" asked Billie.

"Not even a little, but it was fun to pretend. Anyway, you'll never guess who was the tour guide?"

"Brianne Druffner," she finished. "Celeste's troll."

Diego frowned. She had ruined his big reveal. "So I went on the tour, and after, I chatted with her."

"And she talked?"

"Sorta."

Billie turned to Gramps and said, "How did you manage it? Threaten? Bribe? Intimidate? All three?"

"Very funny," said Gramps before a belch. "I wasn't there."

"Oh no?"

"I had to lie low," he said, sheepish.

Billie wanted more of that story, but Diego was too eager to spill, so she said nothing.

"I had a cover story," Diego added.

Billie turned to her grandfather. "You told me to back off cover stories."

Gramps dismissed that with a wave of his hand. "No elaborate scheme like you cook up. A simple plan, made successful because Diego over here is a natural. He blends in."

Billie glanced at Diego. "You flirted."

"*Latino charm*," he emphasized before wiping his face with a napkin. "I asked her if there were any good parties and she invited me to one tonight. And she friended me on Instagram."

"Can't believe we're paying you for that," said Gramps before he tilted back the bottle of beer and took a swig.

"This job is better than my bakery gig and my hotel gig combined," Diego said, but Billie's brain was churning.

"This is good. We can ask the other Zeta Omegas about Brianne, but be subtle. Alan was digging into this so there must be something there. I want to find out where she was the night Alan died."

"Brianne's a wacko," said Diego. "She has crazy girl energy."

"Wacko is a relative term," said Billie, tapping her fork against the edge of her plate. "I'll go with you to this party."

"Really?" said Diego.

"I can pass for college aged," she replied, offended. "Perhaps there's a history of hazing that the sorority and college were intentionally ignoring. We can also find out where she went to school previously."

"Way ahead of ya," said Gramps, nodding to Diego. "Show her."

Diego slipped his hand into his jacket pocket. He took out his cell phone, swiped across the screen and opened the Instagram app. He slid the phone across the table. Gramps and Billie peered over it.

Diego pointed at the screen. "She curates her account. Very few photos. But this one is from her freshman year. Look what she's wearing in the pic."

"A Washington and Franklin sweatshirt," said Billie.

"I did some googling and she was a part of Greek Life there. But nearly the entire school is," said Diego.

"OK, so Brianne likely went there, but are we sure she was expelled, though?" said Billie. "Hate to be the doubter."

Gramps dipped into the dining room, then returned a moment later with a piece of paper. Billie spied Alan's scratchy handwriting.

"Alan wrote *Jeff Pearson-WF* next to Brianne's name," said Gramps, "and a weird decimal number. My guess is he works at Washington and Franklin, so I'll call Monday," said Gramps.

Billie nodded, satisfied. They were balancing two cases. Successfully, she might add.

"Oh," said Diego. "I also followed your homeboy."

Gramps pointed at her with the tip of the beer bottle. "You have him shadowing your boyfriend."

150 MAKE A KILLING

"He's not my boyfriend," she replied defensively. "He's our competition and if I've learned anything working in a corporate office, it's understanding how the other side plays."

"You're full of crap," said Gramps. "You're just trying to figure out what he's doing for that Vickery fellow."

"That too, although I have my suspicions."

Diego swiped through his cell phone until he got to the notes app, which he opened. "Okay, after Abuelo went to the student center for coffee, I followed your dude. He gabbed with some students for twenty minutes, then he went to his office – or what I assume was his office because his name is written on a piece of paper near the door, and shut himself inside. He was in there for ten minutes before he left and headed toward the student center. There he got a slice of pizza, and a matcha latte. Weird combo."

Billie groaned.

"Yeah." Diego made a face. "Gross."

"Dude, he made you. That was a test, and we failed." Billie huffed. "He knew you were following him."

Diego frowned. "I had a feeling he was onto me. Damn. I should've realized it when he walked across campus to that building by the fountain."

"The glass building?"

"Yeah. Why?" asked Diego and Gramps in stereo.

"A lot of pre-law classes. Did you see who he was talking to?"

"Do you one better. I snapped a photo," said Diego as he tilted the screen toward her.

Billie stared at the picture. She recognized the professor. Grizzled with a goatee. "He's a lawyer."

"What flavor?" asked Gramps

"Labor law."

Gramps ran a paw over his scruff. "Could be connected to his VHG stint."

Billie sighed. "Possibly."

Except Jeremy was getting his doctorate in criminal justice and it was certainly reasonable for him to meet with lawyers for research. But Jeremy's niche was international syndicates. Labor and employment law were not in his wheelhouse. One could argue, thought Billie, that it had been in Alan's.

"Earlier you said you had more work for me," said Diego.

Billie awoke from her daze. "I do." She slid over a piece of paper with an address in Mendham. "I'm investigating this woman."

"Who's she?"

"Nina Patchett-Borel. A VP at Tropic Reef."

"Anything else I should know?"

Yes, but then Billie would be defying her NDA. "Just report where she goes and who she talks to. Take photos."

Diego nodded. "Sure thing, boss."

Gramps then said, "I think it goes without saying, but don't get made." He clamped Diego on the shoulder. "After you digest, I'm going to give you some tips on how to properly shadow a mark."

Diego grinned. "This is so much better than working at the hotel."

CHAPTER THIRTY-ONE

Billie couldn't remember the last college party she had attended. Maybe because she had rarely been to any. Shari's Alzheimer's disease had started during Billie's sophomore year. By the time Billie was legally allowed to imbibe – not that she ever did – she was back home juggling her thesis seminar with her mother's care.

So when she stepped onto the porch of the Zeta Omega house with Diego she nearly balked at a cover charge. "Twenty bucks for the red solo cup."

Billie wasn't going to drink, not from a keg, and certainly not here where some frat boy could spike her drink. But to refuse would evoke suspicion. She slipped the girl a Jackson and handed Diego, too excited to hide his underage glee, the cup. "Easy," she warned him as they entered the foyer, welcomed by techno music. The beat pummeled her skull like nails in a two-by-four.

He yelled into her ear, "I'm a pro now."

Billie leaned into him and said, "Find Brianne."

"On it, Chief!" He disappeared into the crowd, swallowed up by a sea of tank tops and T-shirts. She wondered what the odds were that she'd find him later puking in the shrubbery. Pretty high.

She was only a few years out of school and yet it might as well have been eons. The girls all looked so young.

She followed one, a brunette wearing a Zeta Omega printed tee, to a hazy room off the kitchen where the music had been reduced to a soft din.

Several guys sporting their own Greek letters sat on couches, vaping, drinking, and scrolling through their phones.

Billie scooped an abandoned solo cup off a lone speaker and carried it around like a prop, the beer long disappeared down someone's throat. She took a seat next to the unlit fireplace and pretended to drink.

A girl leaned across the coffee table and drunkenly tapped Billie's knee several times. "Hey, you. You."

"Yes?" said Billie.

"You go here?"

"Yeah," Billie lied.

"I don't know you."

"I'm a senior."

"Me too."

"It's a big campus," said Billie.

"Who invited you?" said the girl.

"Brianne," Billie said. Everyone was drunk. Who was coherent enough to verify her story?

"Pffft. No way. Brianne doesn't invite girls like you."

Never underestimate a mark, Levine.

Billie deflected. "Why's that?"

"Competition," said the girl, sloshing beer. She uneasily got to her feet and pawed her wet shirt. More beer spilled. "Shit." Billie jumped out of the way as the girl rounded the coffee table and all the liquid hit the floor.

What was Billie doing here? She should've just stayed home, snuggled under bedcovers, and trusted Diego enough to glean information from a suspect without training wheels.

Billie wandered around a bit until she eventually found herself in a wood-paneled dining room with framed photos on the walls. Pledge classes. Billie looked for the most recent and noticed that Celeste's headshot was noticeably absent. Honestly Celeste hadn't lost out on anything but drunken parties. Billie didn't see the appeal.

Her eyes scanned the walls reading names that flowed with the times: Ashleys to Amandas to Jessicas, Patricias then Barbs and Susans.

"Jesus Christ," came a girl's voice, startling Billie.

A figure emerged from the shadows. Black skin, curly hair in a messy bun, dressed in a long coat with fur trim. The stench of weed trailed after her.

"Billie Levine," said Tasha Nichols. "What are you doing at a Zeta Omega party?"

Billie faced her. "I could ask you the same thing."

Tasha was the president of Sleuth Squad, a mostly-female, but inclusive, group of armchair detectives who gathered on the second floor of the Kentwell Student Center, an area so inconsequential the college had probably forgotten all about it. And yet Tasha ruled the room like a queen.

Billie said, "Didn't think an overachiever like you came to these kinds of soirees. You seem more at home in a pretentious brownstone sipping bourbon than at the college equivalent of a middle-school hangout."

Tasha sighed heavily as if Billie's characterization was a misfired dart and not a bulls-eye.

Tasha might've reigned with strength, but Billie's bullshit detection typically sawed through that unearned authority. "Anxious?"

"Got a lot going on," said Tasha, hoisting her red solo cup in the air. "Just blowing off steam. I'm busy."

"Oh, I bet." Billie began ticking off Tasha's jobs on her fingers. "President of Sleuth Squad. Managing editor of the Kentwell Chronicle. Resident Advisor. Am I missing anything? I assume you're not on the board of the Safety Brigade anymore. I would think the officers don't like members who lie about their fight with a murder victim."

Tasha sneered. "You're really keeping up to date with my life, aren't you?"

Billie said, "I'm not too current, apparently, since I can't imagine why you're here. And yet the serendipity of this meeting is truly," Billie kissed her fingers. "My luck never runs like this. I'll be straight. You had an appointment with Alan Tran weeks before he died. For once I think your Sleuth Squad gig is the wrong tree, so was he barking up your newspaper job or...nope. He wanted to talk to you about your RA gig, and I think I have an inkling as to why."

"Celeste," said Tasha.

"Ding, ding, ding."

Tasha came closer. "I feel really shitty about everything that happened."

"I bet you do."

"I hate your cynicism. You know that?"

"You wound me," said Billie with a hand to her chest.

"I do feel bad. I didn't get into a criminology major to see more people become victims of crime. I really tried to help Celeste, but...I got sidelined."

"So you were the RA on Celeste's floor?"

"Still am," said Tasha with all the enthusiasm of a soldier who missed the last chopper out.

"I imagine holding onto that precious RA position is why you," Billie rounded the table, "got *sidelined*."

Tasha shot back, "The RA job pays for my housing. I literally can't afford to lose it."

"So paint a picture for me. Celeste is the victim of a sorority hazing incident. How do you come into play?"

Billie heard the sound of a door opening and closing. Tasha froze. Then, coming closer, she said, "I know you're not going to believe this, but I actually did the right thing."

"Explain," said Billie.

"The girl who's harassing Celeste?"

"Brianne Druffner?"

"Shhh." Tasha motioned for Billie to lower her voice. "I told Celeste to report her to Campus Police. I caught her – Brianne – going into Celeste's room with a package and coming out empty-handed. I recorded the whole scene on my phone, so I thought we had the proof."

"And then what?"

"Escalation."

"To Campus Housing?"

"And Greek Life."

"Then the review board?"

"But there was no review board."

"What do you mean?"

Tasha shook her head. "There was *no* review board and no involvement from anyone outside the college."

"The video?"

A door again opened and closed.

"Tasha?"

She stood directly in front of Billie, their faces separated by inches. "I showed Campus Police the video; I also showed it to Nicole Mercier in student housing, but both agreed that it wasn't obvious what," Tasha swiveled her head, but the room remained empty aside from them two, "Brianne was actually doing. She only got cited for entering a student's room without permission."

"You spoke with Nicole?"

"Yeah, and she said there wasn't enough evidence. If I've learned anything, it's that it's really hard to prove harassment. It's your word against theirs."

"You mean Celeste's words."

Tasha whispered, "I got a visit from a woman in administration who said that my RA position was not guaranteed, although she didn't say it so succinctly. She had said that there were many students who would love to be an RA, and that perhaps my job would be better filled by a student without my many commitments."

Billie hated to ask this, but she had to. "Was it Nicole who told you this?"

To Billie's relief, Tasha shook her head. "No. A white woman, Marissa Gulla, who said some heinous shit about me being a diversity placement, and now I think I understand how some people commit murder."

Marissa Gulla was mentioned in Alan's files. Gramps had met her when he went to talk to Celeste. Marissa worked in Greek Life, not Campus Housing. Why would she threaten Tasha's resident advisor position?

"Alan died in a cycling accident," Tasha went on.

"Yeah," said Billie.

"But you think there's more to it than that. Right?"

Billie wondered how much of her hand to reveal to Tasha who presided over a club that ran on the fumes of unsolved murders. Finally, she replied, "Why are you at this party? You're clearly scared of Brianne for some reason."

Tasha chugged the last of her beer, which, at this point, must've been warm and flat. "As I said, I'm just blowing off steam."

"Uh huh."

"You're not going to tell Marissa Gulla I spoke to you, are you? I'll definitely lose my RA position."

Billie said, "I have many principles, and one of them is that I don't fuck around with people's livelihoods."

"Sure." But Tasha didn't seem convinced. Billie wasn't insulted. Most of the time, she didn't even trust herself.

Billie crushed her red solo cup and left it on the table. She'd had enough; it was time to find Diego. She was shimmying around Tasha, when a sound caused her to turn. "You got something else you want to add?" Billie asked.

Tasha sighed. "You're not the first person to ask me any of this, you know?" Her voice sounded louder now, more assured as if what she had to say could be said without the fear of rats in the walls listening in.

"Oh, really?"

"Professor Yang had questions like this for me too."

"Of course he did," said Billie, turning toward the door.

"You leaving?"

"Yeah, as soon as I find Diego."

"You came with a guy?"

"A coworker. A trainee actually."

"Cute?" Tasha asked, which seemed like a weird question. Billie wasn't certain of Tasha's sexuality but she had thought it had skewed toward XX chromosomes.

Billie huffed, impatient. "Why?"

"You better find him," said Tasha. "You know the first rule of college parties: don't lose sight of your drink, or your man."

"Shit," said Billie.

CHAPTER THIRTY-TWO

Billie squeezed through narrow hallways. Party goers, like mice, curled up in tight spaces. She'd step then apologize for jostling an elbow, sloshing a drink. Nasty looks pinged off her like hail.

She made her way through the living room, pushing past a drunk girl crying on the sofa. Another sorority sister was comforting her but was also drunk; tears mixed with beer.

Billie remembered that the house had once been grand, likely belonging to a nineteenth century state senator, or something like that. Now the floors were sticky with beer, the walls perfumed with weed. The marble mantle was chipped and neglected. Like everything, grandiosity had to be maintained.

Billie called Diego's name but he didn't respond. Likely he couldn't hear her above the mashup of music and conversation. An old Bon Jovi song suddenly came on and the entire house was screaming the lyrics.

New Jersey being New Jersey.

She pushed her way toward the kitchen where the noise sank into a dull hum. Tasha appeared then and pointed toward the window. "Is that your boy passed out on the lawn?" Then, she grumbled, "And look who's out there with him."

Billie leaned over the counter and peered outside. A blonde girl encased in shadows was leaning over Diego and tugging on his arm. If she wasn't careful she'd pull his shoulder from the socket.

Billie darted for the backdoor and bolted outside, down cement steps and into a bare yard.

Diego lay prone on the grass, his sweatshirt pushed up slightly revealing dark hair above the waistband of his pants. His boxer shorts peeked out from a loose belt, the buckle undone. What the hell?

Billie charged Brianne who took several steps backwards. "What are you doing?"

"Nothing," said Brianne, and Billie took pleasure from her cowering.

Billie then fell to Diego's side. Dampness seeped into her knees. She lightly tapped Diego's cheek.

"He drank too much," said Brianne. "I was trying to get him up. Can't have dudes laying on the grass. The neighbors might see, call the police."

"The neighbors are Phi Epsilon," said Billie, not buying the excuse. She struggled to get him upright. He groaned as she wrapped her hands under his armpits. "Come on, Diego. Let's get out of here." She grunted and he finally seemed to register her presence. "I'm tired."

She hadn't left him alone all that long. How did he get wasted so fast?

Billie whirled on Brianne. "You did this!"

"Did what?" Brianne held up her hands like a gun was pointed at her. "I didn't bring him here. You did."

Billie took out her phone, held it like dynamite. "One call and this is over."

"Please. The police don't give a shit."

"The Bergen County detectives might," said Billie, a threat with no backing.

"Don't do anything stupid," said Brianne. "I can make your life hell."

"I don't go here!" she snapped back. Then, for good measure, "Your threats are meaningless. Maybe you should go back to Washington and Franklin. Oh, right, you can't."

Billie wasn't sure what possessed her to show her hand like that, but Brianne's widening eyes and quivering lip told her she was on the right track. Billie hissed, "Where were you February 13th?"

Brianne blanched. She stepped back, looked at the kitchen door, then turned around. Her expression morphed from surprise to resolve. Billie didn't like that. Brianne took off.

Billie went back to Diego and gently tugged on his hand. She then felt a tap on her shoulder. Tasha said, "I'll help you get him to the car."

Billie nodded, thankful. Together, they each draped one of Diego's arms over their shoulders and hoisted him to his feet. Diego likely weighed almost as much as Billie, a fact he would deny. Right now, his light weight worked in their favor.

As the girls hobbled through the fence gate, Brianne called out to Tasha. "Nichols, you weren't invited!"

"Blowing off steam, huh?" said Billie. "More like inviting trouble."

"Says the girl who brought a kid to a college party notorious for lacing drinks."

Billie jerked her chin down the street to where she parked the Hyundai under lamplight. Together they half-carried, half-dragged Diego to the backseat of the car, holding him awkwardly while Billie fumbled for her keys and opened the door. He practically fell inside.

"What were you really doing there?" Billie asked, shivering. Spring was en route but winter was loathe to give up her grasp.

"Film project," said Tasha, pushing off the car. She aimed her body away from the Zeta Omega house. Now that Brianne had clocked her she wouldn't be welcomed back.

Billie wanted to ask follow-up questions but her responsibility was to Diego, who was likely going to puke in her car if she didn't quickly get him home.

"We're not done," Billie called to Tasha's back as the girl walked into evening darkness. Tasha waggled her fingers but didn't turn around.

Billie considered driving Diego to his cousin's place in Dover, but after staring at the Zeta Omega house until her vision blurred she was struck by a thought – vengeance.

CHAPTER THIRTY-THREE

Billie's gas tank was so dangerously close to empty she wondered if she had driven to her brother's house on fumes of rage. By the time she deposited Diego onto David's sofa she was vibrating so violently that Matty whispered that his Glock was in the safe and all she had to do was give him an address. A joke, presumably, but she didn't nix the idea.

"You gonna tell us what happened?" David asked while the three of them gathered in the kitchen. It was well after midnight, at least according to the digital clock on the microwave.

"I fucked up," she said as she leaned over the counter, her fist pounding the old Formica. She straightened, waiting for the inevitable pats of sympathy, but David was too familiar with Billie's patterns to assume she'd been the victim of her own misfortune.

"I took him to a party and I think he was roofied," she said.

"Oh shit," said Matty, his eyebrows raised in surprise.

She turned her attention to David. "I need him to pee in a cup."

"Bring him to a hospital," said David. "They'll run tests."

She shook her head. "I took a nineteen year-old to a college party, bought him a red solo cup, and let him loose. I don't have a PI license yet, David, but I definitely won't if I bring him to the ER and explain what happened."

"So that's what you're worried about? Yourself?"

"Not everything is black and white. Matty, help me out."

But he was already inching toward the living room. "I'm going to check on the child," he said.

Fucking coward.

"Please, just get me one of those urine cups," said Billie. "I'll turn it over to Morales and he'll get it examined, OK?" He didn't seem convinced, so she added, "Please, David. You have your medical shit here, don't you?"

David sighed, then wordlessly left the room. Billie knew he would help her, but his silence was worse than if he had just refused.

She watched as her brother roused Diego from the couch and positioned him upright. Flicking on a light, David encouraged Diego to get up and use the bathroom. Meanwhile Diego muttered something about *beer* and *a girl* and *college was whack*.

Handing him a plastic container, David said, "Please tell me you can aim into this. I don't want to help you."

Diego nodded like a bobble head and unsteadily got to his feet. Matty flicked on the bathroom light and pointed to the open door.

Diego grunted but made his way there.

When Diego had finished, he handed the cup to Matty who shook his head. "Give it to your girl there."

Holding a paper towel, Billie accepted the urine sample.

David said, "He can stay here tonight. He should text his parents or roommate."

"He lives with a cousin." Billie rubbed the tension above her eyes. "He's got a complicated home life."

"Made more complicated by working for you," said David.

"Not fair," she said.

"Pff. It's not me you have to worry about. Wait until Gramps–"

Billie charged David, forcing him to back into the wall. "Do not tell him."

"You think you're going to keep this a secret?"

"He knows he went to the party but I don't want him knowing about the rest of it. OK?"

David scoffed.

"Not until I talk to Morales."

David exhaled, but gave no more opposition. That was the best Billie was going to get out of him for now.

She checked on Diego, pushing aside his sweaty dark hair. Leaning down, she said, "I'll be back tomorrow morning."

"He's going to have a wicked headache," said David.

"I'll bring coffee," she said.

David cleared his throat.

"And bagels."

Now Matty chimed in, "And lox."

"See you tomorrow." Billie exited into a cool night, the quiet unnerving as if underlining her colossal mistake. Diego was roofied. Had he been a target? Or the recipient of a tainted beer meant for an unsuspecting sorority sister?

Billie glanced at the urine cup, willing a revelation.

One thing was for sure: Morales would not be happy to see her.

CHAPTER THIRTY-FOUR

Billie stood outside Esteban Morales's home, a two-family house that he shared with his sister and her kids. She had texted him prior to showing up but still had to pound on his door to get him to wake.

Something he was decidedly not thrilled about.

"The hell," he said groggily, rubbing his eye sockets like he was a little boy. He held the door open for her to come in, but she remained firmly outside holding a plastic bag with Nagel's insignia across the front.

Morales accepted the bag, noted the weight, and frowned. He glanced inside. Then hissed, "What *is* this?"

She explained what she wanted from him.

"Should've gone to a hospital," he said, parroting David.

"Can't for a myriad of reasons."

"Do you really think I can just send this to a lab without a case attached to it?" he asked.

She shrugged. "You'll find a way or excuse or whatever. Cops have gotten away with much worse than running toxicology reports on random urine."

"It's against protocol." He eyed the plastic bag but didn't relinquish his hold. Rather, his eyes flitted back and forth, a wheel turning, cranking slowly but deliberately.

The detective was known around his precinct as a boy scout, a rule follower, but even rule-followers got inflicted by cases of raging curiosity.

He wrapped the plastic handle tighter around his hand,

and then pointed at her, the bag swinging underneath.

"Fine," he said. There was no question Morales was doing her a favor, but he was also potentially getting something out of it: catching a criminal.

While she had him here, she asked, "Do you have any contacts in Hudson County?"

Morales closed his eyes and yawned. "What do you want?"

"A guy died at my undercover job," she said.

"Suspicious?"

"We think so."

"We?"

"Jeremy Yang and I."

He frowned.

"Don't be like that," she said.

"You want my help so you and your boyfriend can get a collar?"

"He's not my boyfriend. Why do you do that? I can't work with someone of the opposite gender without you assuming I'm sleeping with him. Very sexist."

He sighed, then rubbed the tension from the bridge of his nose. "You're right. I shouldn't have made that assumption." Another sigh, but Billie would chuck that up to exhaustion and not exasperation. "I'll ask around. Text me the details."

Billie nodded, and that was enough for Morales to shut the door in her face.

CHAPTER THIRTY-FIVE

Later that same morning Billie yawned loudly into a cup of coffee.

"You all right there?" Nicole asked.

They were sitting in Nagel's. Billie had a mug of dark roast that was brewed too bitterly and a hamantasch. With her hand around the handle, she said, "Late night."

By way of response, Nicole arched her brow.

Billie was mentally strategizing on how best to broach the subject of Calvin's name having been written on a sheet of paper in Alan Tran's handwriting without coming across as accusatory – a skill Billie hadn't aced in a long time.

She tried something else. "You'll never believe who gave me an estimate on the roof repair?"

Nicole said nothing.

"Stewart."

"Really? Did you ask him about why he left Kentwell?"

"He mentioned power-hungry women," said Billie with a shrug. "If I hadn't spoken to you about how things are on campus, I would've assumed Stew was another man who couldn't handle working under a lady. But you said it's toxic over there."

"It is..." Nicole trailed.

"He suggested I speak to Calvin," Billie broached.

"Stew did?"

She nodded. "What department does he work in again?"

"He had started out in Student Accounts, but he got

promoted recently. Now he's working under the bursar. I had thought he'd feel better about work, but ever since he took that job he's been a different guy."

"Who oversees his department?" Billie asked.

"I forget her name, but she's new."

"A Beaumont hire?"

"Yeah." Nicole twitched her nose, reminding Billie of a mouse considering its options. "You think his demeanor change could be attributed to work? He's under a lot of pressure."

Shrugging, Billie took another sip of coffee, before making a face.

Nicole then said, "Let's talk about something else. Something that would have us pass the Bechdel test."

"How'd the interview go at FDU?" Billie asked cautiously.

"Great," said Nicole, straightening her shoulders, the confidence oozing back into her posture. "I feel really confident about this one, but I also said that about the last one and the dean never called me for a second meeting."

"It's possible they just have a lot of candidates. Takes time to make calls."

Nicole sat back as if she was considering that to be the case. "The dean did mention that. Then, after telling me I had an impressive CV, he said, 'Seeing a lot of candidates from Kentwell. Do you know what that's about?' And how was I to respond? If I mentioned that the departments are being shook up by a new president it might sound bitter."

"What did you say?"

"I changed the subject. I discussed my ideas for efficiency, mentioned a systems upgrade I heard about in one of the trade magazines. The dean sounded impressed."

"Then he was impressed." Billie sipped again, winced, and reached for a sugar packet. "Don't doubt yourself."

"Hard not to when you get ghosted by department heads." Nicole crumbled up a napkin. "Speaking of, how's stuff going with Jeremy and VHG?"

"Lousy. A guy died."

Nicole choked and sputtered. Reaching for another napkin, she dabbed her lips. "What is with you and people dying?"

Billie shrugged. "Occupational hazard."

"Funny business?" Nicole asked.

"Still figuring that out."

"With Jeremy's help?"

"Guess so," Billie said, which caused Nicole to smirk.

"What?"

When Nicole's bemused expression didn't appear to abate, Billie emphasized, "We're *not* friends."

"No, because you want to bang each other."

"Hey!" A woman in another booth glanced over at Billie's outburst, so she lowered her voice, "It's not like that. Also I thought we were adhering to the Bechdel test."

"This is more fun. I swear you and Jeremy act like the *Hating Game* meets Philip Marlowe."

"Clever," said Billie. "But, seriously, Jeremy's difficult. I already dated a difficult guy. I'd like my next boyfriend to be easy."

"Girl, the easy guys get snatched up first."

"Once we're both off our VHG cases, we can go back to ignoring each other."

"Well, he heads to Spain this summer. He'll be out of your hair for a while."

"As long as he gets the funding," Billie pointed out.

"Oh, he has the funding. I know because one of my friends is setting up his housing in Seville."

If Billie had still been drinking the coffee, she would've spit it out. "He secured the funding from the college?"

"Oh yeah," said Nicole. "Three months in Spain, paid for by Kentwell College. Generous weekly stipend too."

Billie grabbed a napkin off the table and crumbled it in her fist. If only it had been Jeremy's face. "Son of a bitch."

CHAPTER THIRTY-SIX

Later that afternoon, Billie was brewing a pot of tea when her phone rang. She caught the number but was still surprised by the voice – gravelly and worn – on the other end.

"Belinda?"

"Katherine?"

"Rebecca and I will be joining you at Tropic Reef from now on. Given everything...with Webber's death, it's important we're there, keeping the company together and focused..." Billie heard an audible swallow. "And I'll help Kyle and crew with the summer product launch. Can't fuck that up. Heath's useless, of course. Doesn't know what to do with himself and has taken to pestering me with new ideas..." Another swallow, then a discreet belch. "Get this. He wants to start a fitness camp for the elderly." She laughed, then hiccupped, and Billie imagined Katherine slugging from a mossy green wine bottle unearthed from some ancient French cellar.

Poor people got drunk off Natty Ice and no-name vodka better used for disinfectant than martinis. Rich people mostly got drunk off their money.

And yet Katherine sounded loose. Somber. Maudlin.

So this probably wasn't the time to bring up the flash drive and Heath's charity irregularities. If Katherine wanted to get rid of her husband, other than murdering him, catching him hanging a coworker was still her best bet. Assuming the prenup didn't have an embezzling-from-kids clause. *We'll talk about it tomorrow. When she's sober.*

Billie had been considering all this when Katherine cleared her throat, obviously waiting for a response. Billie said, "Heath must be very upset about Webber. You all must be."

This was a test, of course. For guys like Heath, one assistant was as good as any when you were a billionaire.

"Oh, yes," said Katherine. "We're all heartbroken."

"I assume the funeral is in Vermont?" Billie asked.

A sigh. "Rebecca has the details. Family only."

"Right."

Another exhalation, this one sounding like a huff. "I just can't deal with all his half-assed schemes, and I can't have him distracted. Luckily he doesn't find Rebecca attractive." At its core, this conversation was nothing more than a wife calling to complain about her husband. "Webber's parents are coming to VHG offices tomorrow."

"To get his belongings?"

Katherine cackled, and now Billie was certain she was shit-faced. "They're coming for a payout."

"Oh."

"It's fine. Least we can do. Webber ran Heath's life. Saved me so much aggravation. And Webber's folks, well, they weren't around much. Kept their distance."

"That's sad to hear," said Billie, thinking of her own absent father. Gramps, on the other hand, was so far in Billie's life that they practically shared a brain.

"Webber said he preferred it that way. His career kept him busy."

This gave Billie pause. If Webber had been so integral to Heath's day-to-day, then wouldn't he have known about any affairs? Why hire Billie when Katherine could've asked Webber all about Heath's dirtiest deeds?

"My lawyers will draw up a nice agreement," Katherine grumbled. "Not our fault the stupid restaurant poisoned him."

You could tell her, Levine. The restaurant is not at fault. Tomorrow.

Katherine went on, "I'd sue them, but VHG is sponsoring scholarships for two of their female waitstaff to attend Stevens in the fall."

At a loss for words, and not even sure if they were needed, Billie said, "How kind."

"Make no mistake, it's not kindness, Belinda. It's done out of necessity. Women need to support other women because men will stand on our necks every chance they get."

Billie thought of Jeremy; how easy she could blow his cover right now over the phone. *Jeremy Yang's a spy!* Maybe not in such a dramatic fashion. Of course, to do so would ruin her too. Jeremy would tell Heath that she wasn't Belinda from NYU but rather Billie from Teaneck, and they'd both be out of a paycheck. Stewart was cute, but Billie suspected she'd have to marry him to get the roof replacement for free. And maybe not even then.

"VHG won't be the same without Webber," Billie said, because that seemed like the right thing to add.

Katherine laughed, a sound so out of context Billie wondered if she had missed an entire part of the conversation.

By the time Billie said, "See you tomorrow," she was met with silence. Katherine had disconnected the call.

CHAPTER THIRTY-SEVEN

That night her phone buzzed with a text message: *come outside*.

Jeremy Yang stood on the sidewalk, hands in his jacket pockets, the streetlight bathing him in a glow of lemon light. He was wearing Nike sweats and old Air Jordans, creased and dingy at the toes. He looked polished but tired. Like he always did.

Billie greeted him in her hoodie and fleece pajama bottoms. She realized she looked ridiculously sloppy, but Jeremy was not the kind of guy she wanted to impress. At least not via her appearance. That wasn't how she saw him, despite what Nicole insinuated.

And not how he saw her, apparently, as evidenced by his look of disgust when he said, "Jesus, you're not wearing a bra?"

Billie looked down at her chest and crossed her arms. "What do you want?"

"I caught your little brother's tail," he said.

"So I gathered. How was that matcha latte, by the way?"

"Expensive and shitty, but worth it because you figured it out."

"You shouldn't have celebrated your win quite so early. What were you doing talking to Bob Whitlock?"

Jeremy shook his head ever so slightly as if to say, "not sure what you mean."

"Diego caught you. Whitlock teaches labor law, doesn't he?"

Jeremy began to turn around. "Keep your kids off my lawn, Levine."

"What are you so scared to tell me?" she called after him.

He turned around. "Not everything is your business."

"You've been stealing my clients for weeks and then you turn down your best friend's sister, essentially thrusting the case into my lap. Why?"

"Alan's death has nothing to do with Kentwell."

"How do you know?"

"I just do."

"That's not a reason. You can't *because I say so* and think I'll walk away. Unless you caused Alan's accident," she held up a hand, "which I know you didn't. How are you so sure that this Kentwell story isn't a factor?"

Jeremy closed his eyes and exhaled. For a second, Billie thought he might have an emotional breakdown, and she would be at a loss as to how to handle it. Crying she could handle, Jeremy crying she could not. To her relief, he just shook his head and began to walk away.

"You lied about why you took the Vickery case," she said.

He turned around. "What are you talking about?"

"Nicole said your Spain trip got funded with a very generous weekly stipend. The college is paying for everything."

Jeremy paled. "That's not...that didn't...I'm not accepting that money."

"Why not?"

"Have you ever made a deal but realized the terms were not on your side? The consequences too great?"

Deals with the devil.

"I suppose."

"Well, that's what taking the money would mean."

"Does any of this have to do with why you were sniffing around Tasha Nichols?"

"I take offense to that phrasing," he said. "I wasn't sniffing."

"No. You were investigating...on a case you begged off. Why?"

He took a step toward her, and then halted. There it was – that look on his face. A secret bubbled beneath his skin.

Billie felt herself grow enraged. "My little brother, as you described him, may have gotten roofied last night at a Zeta Omega party, so I ask you, does Alan's reporting have anything to do with that?"

He stared at her a beat too long, but his silence was response enough.

"Dammit, Jeremy, you didn't take June's case, but you seem to be working a side investigation. What the fuck is going on?"

But he refused to answer, choosing instead to walk away along the sidewalk and toward his Corolla parked across the street.

Billie called after him, "I'm going to tell Katherine about the flash drive!"

He paused, keys in midair, and turned around. "Why? So we both get fired?"

"I won't get fired. And she deserves to know."

He threw his head back and laughed. "You think she'll reward you once she finds out? You're wrong." He pointed at her with the key fob. "You'll see."

Billie watched him click the button on the remote. The lights flashed and the car beeped.

He got inside and within seconds was gone.

CHAPTER THIRTY-EIGHT

Monday morning, when Billie entered the Tropic Reef offices, Rebecca was there to greet her, holding up a brown shopping bag with gold VHG letters emblazoned on the front. Billie caught the tattoo – possibly a Greek letter although it appeared smudged out by makeup – on her hand. Katherine must not like tattoos. She probably found them trashy. And Rebecca struck Billie as the kind of girl that believed whatever Katherine believed.

Dropping her belongings at her desk, Billie eyed the bag. "What's that?"

"The Florence dress in black," said Rebecca, the package swaying in her fingertips.

"And?"

"Katherine wants you to put this on…today."

Billie glanced down at her ensemble. She was wearing one of the vintage VHG dresses she had bought on eBay – an emerald green number from the discontinued Alcazar line – and platform Oxfords. She envisioned herself in this dress outside the Alhambra. Wouldn't that be something?

Rebecca leaned in close and whispered, "She thinks this new dress is more appropriate, all things considering, and I have to agree."

Of course, she has to agree.

Billie asked, "When you say appropriate, do you mean for mourning? Because I own black. But I didn't think Webber was being buried in the office building." The moment that left her mouth, she winced. "Sorry. Uncouth."

That elicited a shrug from Rebecca.

"I never asked how you're doing," said Billie.

"I didn't know him real well," she said.

"You seem to know everybody, and you worked together for years."

"He didn't really talk to me. Saw him in a bar once; he didn't even say hello. He never came to the company hangouts. He begged off McBride's when Sylvie's band was playing. He didn't chip in for a holiday gift for the custodial staff. And he only stayed twenty minutes during the last company picnic."

"So you don't know if he had a girlfriend...or boyfriend?" asked Billie.

Rebecca shook her head. "I wouldn't know if he had a sister or a dog. He wasn't a sharer."

He didn't have a dog; that Billie knew for certain.

Billie then took the bag and went to the ladies' room. If Katherine wanted Billie to wear the goods, she would wear the goods. As she put the dress over her head, loose threads snagged on her hoop earrings.

"You want me to zip you up?" came Rebecca's voice.

Billie hadn't realized the girl had followed her inside, and yet as Billie twisted awkwardly in the bathroom stall, she found she needed her help. "Actually, yeah." She undid the door latch and stepped out.

Rebecca seemed pleased. "Black looks good on you."

Billie looked down at the grim fabric. She turned around as Rebecca zipped up the dress. Her hands rested on Billie's shoulders for a brief second. "Chic."

Billie glanced in the mirror at the low neckline and cinched waist, a flattering fit, if a little immodest for workwear. Definitely not suitable for a meeting with Webber's grieving parents, not that she expected to attend. So why bother mandating Billie's wardrobe? Was it because Katherine didn't think Billie was accurately portraying Belinda from NYU or because Katherine just liked playing dress-up with her employees?

"The brand is really important to Katherine, isn't it?" Billie asked while she rummaged in her messenger bag for makeup.

Rebecca watched Billie apply lipstick in the mirror. "It's her company, her whole life."

"No, I mean Tropic Reef."

"It has to be a success," said Rebecca. "They spent a lot of money on it. Plus, Heath was the one who convinced the board it was worth the gamble."

Billie blotted her lips with a tissue while Rebecca faced the mirror and said, "The only new dress I can wear is the Lake Como design because it has stretch."

"It seems the company would do well to expand their sizes."

"Katherine says that VHG is an aesthetic and a lifestyle. Tropic Reef is meant to be the more inclusive brand. That's why they acquired it."

"I thought they acquired the company because Tropic Reef was squeezing them out of the marketplace."

"Do not say *that* to Katherine. She didn't want Tropic Reef but, because Heath had made such a great pitch to the board, she was outvoted. She said we just have to make the best of it. Take Heath's impulsive acquisition and turn it into something amazing. If anyone can do that, it's Katherine." Rebecca opened the bathroom door and waited as Billie shoved her own clothing into the brown shopping bag.

When Billie entered the large office space, she stopped short at Heath, who was scurrying around desks like a chipmunk. He cornered Sylvie first; the poor girl was sipping coffee from a mug that said *Fuck Mondays*.

Heath rested a butt cheek on the tip of her desk, essentially covering whatever paperwork she had been reviewing. "What do you think about a camp for the elderly?"

Sinking low in her desk chair, Sylvie muttered a "sounds great," but her voice lacked enthusiasm. No doubt she was used to his manic energy, but still she recoiled.

Katherine, however, had bigger demands of Sylvie. "Send

Rebecca a zip drive of all the short marketing videos you've created for the Tropic Reef Euro line. I need the spreadsheet, too, of their engagement levels."

Sylvie nodded. "Sure thing."

Katherine endorsed Billie's appearance. "Add five inches to your height, and I'd hire you for a shoot."

Billie set her bag down on an empty chair. She appreciated the clothes, but she'd value them more if they didn't come with expectations.

A breeze brought the smell of cologne. Trailing behind was Kyle Olsen, dressed in a button-down shirt and no tie. His dress shoes gleamed like they had been shined by a Dickensian street urchin. He tweaked his nose, then clapped his hands in rapid succession and said, "Tropic Reef, are you ready to talk product launch?"

His infectious energy stopped at his cufflinks.

"Kyle, dear," said Katherine softly.

"What?" He glanced around at Heath's glower, Rebecca's wide eyes, and the cast of Tropic Reef employees who were still shell-shocked that a man died in the conference room only two days ago.

"Sorry." Kyle pinched his chin between thumb and forefinger and paused for several seconds as if genuinely weighing Katherine's admonishment. He said, "If anyone needs time or counseling, please don't hesitate to come by my office."

Billie caught Heath smirk in response. Kyle caught it too. "Prick," Kyle muttered. Heath replied, "Douchebag."

Where the hell was Jeremy?

Heath gestured toward Billie. "Belinda, dear, follow me to my office. I'd like an update. And by the way, you look exquisite in that dress."

Billie swiped the iPad off the desk and brought it with her, a ready-made shield if she needed one.

Heath dropped into his chair with a huff. There was something about him that reminded Billie of a young boy whose energy often outmatched the pace of the adults around him. Heath spun in his chair before picking up a large tumbler and sucking down its contents via straw. He caught Billie watching him and said, "Smoothie? You want? I can have Bex make you one."

"No," said Billie. Then, "Did you need something specific, Mr Vickery?"

"Call me Heath, please." He winked then and said, "And should I call you, Billie?"

Her stomach dropped. "Uh…"

"I heard Jeremy call you by that on Friday. Edgier."

Billie glimpsed Jeremy's shoulder just out of frame. If he blew her cover, she was going to kill him, and then Webber wouldn't be the only murder in this building.

"Are you two dating?" Heath asked suddenly before sipping from the straw.

"Excuse me?"

"You and my intern. I mean, it wouldn't be the first time interns got a little freaky here, you know? But you can do so much better than him."

Outside Heath's office, an object fell to the floor, followed by "shit" in Jeremy's strained voice.

"No, Mr Vickery. I don't really know him." And then, because a lie only worked when it contained mostly truth, she whispered conspiratorially, "I find him very irritating."

Heath picked up his cell phone, glanced at the screen, then set it back down again. Sighing, he shook the tumbler and set that back down as well. "I understand you didn't know Webber, not really. He was a wonderful guy. A great assistant. He could cycle a century and not break a sweat. Well, that's not exactly true, but he held his own. He volunteered his time with Vickery's Victors. Did you know that–"

Could that explain how Webber came in possession of the thumb drive?

"–I'll need a new assistant." Heath glanced at her. "You'd be perfect."

Billie hugged the iPad tighter. Having a direct line to Heath would certainly hasten this case, but it would be like jumping onto the roof of a train in order to make the 2:45 arrival to Penn Station.

Luckily, the office door opened and Jeremy entered. He stared at Billie, and cleared his throat. Whatever he wanted to say wasn't something he wanted her to hear.

"Jeremy," said Heath. "We should catch up on that *project.*"

Subtlety had skated past Heath's notice.

Rebecca appeared behind him then, calling over Jeremy's shoulder, "Mr Vickery."

Heath nodded, but there was a bit of mirth in his expression. Three young people all vying for his attention and approval. To a man like Heath, it was cocaine. Not that he would snort cocaine.

"Nothing in this temple that doesn't come from nature," he'd once said in a magazine profile.

Kyle, on the other hand…

Rebecca said, "The Brandts rescheduled for four o'clock."

Heath groaned. "I'm meeting my trainer then. Bex, call Klaus and see if he can fit me in at six. And another smoothie. This time no banana."

"Absolutely," said Rebecca.

Outside, Kyle set down his coffee mug and said, "I can fill in for you at four."

"Wouldn't you like that," muttered Heath.

"Actually, Katherine probably prefers I attend in your stead," said Kyle with a grin. "You're a little too hyper during the staff meetings."

Heath purred, "I don't think a coke fiend should be talking to me about excitability."

Kyle's smile melted like candle wax.

Then, with more exuberance, Heath said, "Besides, you hardly knew Webber, so I expect you'll easily move on with the day. Make those summer launch plans." He cast Kyle a glance and added, "You gotta cold? Your nose is running."

Kyle wiped moisture from his nostril, before turning around and striding away.

Billie felt like at any moment Heath and Kyle would take out their dicks while calling for Rebecca to fetch the measuring tape.

CHAPTER THIRTY-NINE

Gramps dialed Jeff Pearson at Washington and Franklin University. The phone rang a few times and Gramps figured he'd have to leave a message until a breathless voice got on the line.

"Jeff Pearson, Student Affairs."

"Yes, hello, Mr Pearson, I'm Bill Levine, a private investigator."

A laugh. "Doug, is this you?"

Guy thinks this is some kind of prank.

"I can assure you, Mr Pearson, I'm not Doug." Quiet. A moment for the putz to register that this was a serious call because Gramps was a serious man. "Do you have a moment to speak?"

"Seriously, Doug, who do you think you're fooling? Are you trying to get me back for the pool incident last July? Oh God, that was an accident. I swear I didn't put the dog up to that."

OK, so the putz wasn't registering the situational gravitas. "Again," Gramps coughed, hoping that if he cleared his throat, he wouldn't pass for Doug, who sounded like a real winner, "I am Bill Levine, a private investigator."

"Bill Levine, a private investigator," Jeff mocked Gramps's voice.

"For Christ's sakes!" Gramps barked as he pinched the bridge of his nose. He inhaled deeply, let out a breath and said calmly, "You still there, Jeff?"

There was an audible swallow, and a meek reply. "Yes. So not Doug?"

"No," said Gramps. "Not Doug."

Jeff's voice lowered an octave. "So sorry about that. My buddy is a jokester, and he calls sometimes and – you don't need to hear this. Did you say you're a private investigator?"

"Yes. I'd like to ask about a former student at your college, Brianne Druffner. She transferred last year to Kentwell College."

Gramps knew silence had no mass, but this one weighed heavily.

"I can't give out any information on a student, former or otherwise," said Jeff. "As per college guidelines."

"Guidelines shmidelines," said Gramps. "I just want to talk."

"You're asking for information on a student, and I can't provide that because of federal reasons. I'm not allowed to just give out records," Jeff said, followed by a huff of indignation.

"I don't need documents, although that would be nice. I want to chat."

"About Brianne Druffner?"

"Yes," said Gramps.

Jeff said nothing. How telling that when Gramps had first said *Brianne Druffner*, Jeff didn't need a moment to jot down the spelling or ask Gramps to repeat himself. There were thousands of students at Washington and Franklin University, but the moment Gramps said *Brianne*, Jeff knew who he meant. Whatever she had been expelled for, it must've been pretty bad. Jeff likely wanted to talk, federal regulations be damned.

Gramps loved long shots.

"Forget Brianne," said Gramps. "What about a nonstudent you spoke to?"

"Who?" said Jeff suspiciously.

"Alan Tran?"

"I'm sorry, I don't know – Wait, did you say Alan Tran?"

Bingo. "Yes," said Gramps. "My investigation is in relation to his death."

"He died?"

"He did," said Gramps.

Another audible swallow. "Was Brianne involved?"

"Do you think she could've been?"

"I shouldn't have said that."

"But you did," said Gramps.

"Listen, I can't give out *any* information about a student." Another heavy silence. "How did he die?"

"Cycling accident. Maybe."

"Jesus."

"I can tell you that Jesus wasn't involved."

"This isn't funny," said Jeff. "Alan was a good man."

Feeling somewhat chastened, Gramps asked, "Did you know him well?"

"Not really, but I know he was on the right side of things."

"How so?"

"Are you recording this conversation?" Jeff said.

"No," said Gramps.

"If you are, you have to tell me."

"I'm not," said Gramps. And also New Jersey was a one-party consent state, but he was going to keep that nugget to himself. Gramps heard the sound of a door closing, then muffled noises.

Jeff whispered, "If you tell anyone I told you this, I will deny it."

Gramps said nothing, which must've sounded like acquiescence.

"And I'm only telling you this because of Alan." Jeff didn't speak again right away, but Gramps knew he was on the line. Heavy breathing, followed by a phone rustling as if Jeff was squirreling himself away somewhere, maybe under his desk. "Brianne Druffner was…asked to leave…because she was accused of drugging male students. No definitive proof was found so local law enforcement wasn't involved."

How lucky for Brianne.

"Drugging? Drugging how?" asked Gramps.

"GHB," Jeff said. "Roofies. A student went to the hospital, got tests. There was a review board and a hearing. I wasn't involved. And no one could prove she was responsible, but she was..."

"Asked to leave," Gramps filled in.

"No criminal charges were filed. It was all done in-house." He said this so rapidly, Gramps worried he'd miss a detail. He scribbled down the information on his notepad. "I'm not sure how Alan got my name, but he had called me – God, many weeks ago – and asked me questions. I didn't talk to him then. Not on the phone, at least. He took a train down to see me. I can't believe I'm telling you this now, but when you said he died...I don't know...that means something. Anyway, that's all I'm willing to tell you."

"Well, thank you, Mr Pearson. You've been helpful."

"If anyone asks, I haven't been helpful. Not at all." Then he hung up.

CHAPTER FORTY

"So, would you say your job responsibilities overlap with anyone else's in the office?" Billie read from her script on the iPad. She was addressing Toby.

"Are you fucking kidding me, Belinda?" Toby said, but in her accent it sounded far more charming. "Is Kyle seriously going to send me packing?"

"It's not Kyle," said Sylvie from the other side of the cubicle wall. "It's Heath. *She* works for him."

Technically, Billie worked for Katherine. "I'm just an intern." *Good one, Billie. That'll smooth things over.*

"You're more to him than that," said Sylvie.

"What does that mean?" Billie asked, stunned. She certainly could guess what it implied.

Sylvie swung an arm over the cubicle wall and clucked her tongue. "You're pretty and blonde and just Heath's type."

"I'm not sleeping with Heath," Billie sputtered.

"Well, no. Not yet, but something tells me you will," said Sylvie.

"I won't!" Billie hit back.

"I don't know," Sylvie singsonged. "He's been looking ravenous lately, and his favorite food are blondies."

"Except for me," said Toby.

"That's cause you bat for the other team and, luckily for you, Heath knows it."

"OK," said Billie. "I think we're getting off course."

But Toby and Sylvie carried on their salacious conversation as if Billie wasn't even there.

Sylvie whispered, "Seems only fair since poor Heath has had to watch from the sidelines while Katherine banged Webber."

Billie reeled back. *What*?

Toby hissed, "Sylvie!"

Sylvie shrugged, then slid behind the wall like an enemy sniper who had hit her target and was moving on.

Billie turned to Toby, who she trusted more than Sylvie for some reason, and asked, "Is that true?"

Toby pinched her shoulders in that affable way people did when they weren't exactly sure.

Billie said, "Hm." If Webber had been sleeping with Katherine, there was an additional motive right there. For Heath, getting rid of Webber was a viable solution to a problem that he himself had created.

But for Katherine to have been sleeping with Webber, well that really crossed the line.

"I can see the gears churning inside your head," said Toby.

"Is she finally realizing that precious Katherine Von Holm isn't the feminist icon she portrays herself as?" Sylvie said.

"I don't...I don't think of Katherine as a feminist icon," said Billie, chastened.

"Sure you don't."

"You and Rebecca fawn over her like she is God's gift to corporate women everywhere."

Billie had done no such thing. She'd been an intern all of two days. And maybe she got some new clothes out of the deal, and maybe they were worth a deposit on a new car, but she didn't think she carried herself like an obsessed fangirl. Only Sylvie didn't view Billie that way. She saw Belinda, an NYU intern, daughter of Katherine's boarding school chum. To Sylvie, all wealthy people got dumped into the same bucket, which she proved when she added, "Rich people just don't care about regular folk," and then gave Billie a pointed look.

"Rebecca should get that memo," Toby added.

"The poor girl just loves working here," said Sylvie. "Someone should."

"I hear what you're saying," said Billie, "but that doesn't mean Katherine was sleeping with her assistant." Because if she was, then she was a massive hypocrite and Billie was the stooge.

"She's beautiful and powerful," said Toby.

"So?" Billie said.

"Maybe Webber felt like he couldn't say no."

The women might've had a point. Billie felt her cell phone buzz in her pocket. She glanced at the screen and frowned.

"Bad news?" said Toby

Brianne got kicked out of Washington and Franklin for drugging guys, Gramps had texted.

"Unsettling," Billie mumbled, before putting the phone away. She had waltzed Diego right into the lion's den. Was that why Tasha Nichols had been at the Zeta Omega party? She was keeping tabs on Brianne? Trying to catch her in the act? To get her expelled from Kentwell? That certainly seemed plausible. Tasha proclaimed herself a victim's advocate. She hadn't become president of Sleuth Squad and the Safety Brigade to sit on the sidelines.

Sylvie smirked then, a wicked look that jostled Billie into the moment. "Hey, girl, if you give me a glowing review on that iPad of yours, I'll tell you something else."

"What?" Billie said.

Sylvie raised her brows, an expectant gesture.

"What power do you think I have here?" Billie said. "Tell me what you want to tell me, or don't."

Sylvie huffed. "Fine." She leaned in and whispered, "Heath can't get it up."

Toby hissed, "Sylvie!"

"I'm sorry, what?" said Billie.

Sylvie clarified, "Heath's impotent." She wagged her thumb at Toby. "We heard him and Katherine arguing once about his sex drive." She shuddered, then made a disgusted face. "Because he won't take medications for it."

"How long has this been going on?" Billie asked, her mind suddenly quiet from confusion.

Sylvie shrugged. "A few months, at least."

"And Katherine knows this?" Billie said again, her voice nearly disappearing into the office workspace, floating away as if being sucked into the air vents.

"Of course," said Sylvie. "Why wouldn't she? Although…"

Billie looked at her hopeful. "Although, what?"

Shrugging, Sylvie spun in her chair, before sizing Billie up. "He seems different lately."

"Really?"

"Ever since you arrived, he seems more…" She stared Billie down, "Jaunty. Like he has a spring in his…" She let the implication hover in the air like a stench, "…dick."

CHAPTER FORTY-ONE

Eager to get out of the building, Billie took her lunch outside and called Diego. He answered by retching.

"I've got a headache and I've puked three times."

"Still?"

"I think it's all out now."

She set the brown bag at her feet, abandoning the egg salad sandwich Gramps had packed her, appetite lost to anxiety and confusion. "Are you hydrating? Tell me you're hydrating."

"Your brother bought me Gatorade. I've puked that up too. Maybe I'm allergic to date-rape drugs."

Billie dug her fingers into her eyes. She had hoped the fresh air and sunshine would alleviate the strain of florescent lighting and lying bosses but, so far, no dice. "I'm so sorry," she told him.

"It's not your fault," he said wearily.

"I should've been more careful," she said. *Never underestimate a mark.*

"I'm grown up enough to look after myself." There was a belch. Then, "How's Corporate America treating you?"

"Like I'm the other woman."

"Huh?"

"Nothing. It's fine. Everything's fine."

Clouds gathered and Billie smelled rain. She imagined streaming water and overflowing buckets. *Stop. The roof will get fixed soon.*

Billie heard snoring on the other side of the line. Diego had fallen asleep.

She disconnected the call, slid her phone into her pocket, and scooped her lunch bag off the ground, her appetite stolen away by guilt and impending flood waters and a check still in the mail. She had a half hour to eat, but found she'd rather roam the waterfront and glance out at the Hudson River than consume a soggy sandwich in abject misery. Although she supposed the misery wasn't going anywhere and she'd just be hungry.

She needed the money. But so far this case had been nothing but bogus office work disguised as a lie. If Heath was impotent, then what the hell was she doing here? Why pay her sixty grand for a lie?

She needed to speak to Katherine. Billie was being used and she didn't like it. She turned toward the office building.

And that's when she saw Nina Patchett-Borel, wearing a checkered coat and black pumps, carrying a briefcase. Not the most damning scene, but it was the way she scurried across the street, furtive, glancing around as if expecting shadows. Billie ducked her chin, pretended to be scrolling through her phone, and tailed her. Nina rounded a corner and passed pedestrians, a deli, and a real estate office before disappearing underneath the red awning of a swanky restaurant.

Billie followed, then grabbed a seat at the bar, which gave her clear sight lines. The joint was fancy but understated, with cream-colored linens, floral wallpaper, framed art and curved doorways. Aaron had offered to take her here once for a birthday but she had opted for low-key Mexican food instead. Billie was more at home near a bowl of chips and salsa than she was around lit candles and polished silverware.

She ordered a club soda with pomegranate juice that cost more than a plate of loaded nachos and kept her eye on Nina as she settled into a four-top near the back. She was presented with a wine menu, which she quickly waved away.

Nina then eyed the front door as if anticipating her companion to arrive.

Billie averted her gaze and took interest in the cocktail napkin while the hostess led a couple, mid-fifties maybe, toward the back and sat them at Nina's table.

Billie pretended to be scrolling through her phone while she snagged a few photos.

The woman was ashy blonde, dressed in a maxi skirt and turtleneck sweater, totally at odds with Nina's designer dress. The gentleman was equally out of place. He had white hair, pale skin tinged pink by the cold. He wore a wrinkly dress shirt and corduroy slacks. But what struck Billie most was their countenance: white skin underlined by red-rimmed eyes and downcast gazes.

A waiter came by and presented a bottle of red wine. Nina again motioned to send it away, until the woman nodded, almost vehemently, and Nina acquiesced. The waiter poured a tablespoon into the glass, expecting Nina to swirl it, smell the bouquet, but she gestured to the wine glasses. Smiling but clearly uncomfortable, the server filled their glasses.

The woman gulped down her wine and went back for more.

"Another club soda?" The bartender asked.

Billie nodded. Then she had a realization. *Webber. Could these be his parents?*

If that's the case, why wasn't Katherine here? Or Heath? Why hadn't they been invited to this meeting? And why was Nina the one conducting it?

A hand tapped the bartop. Billie followed the slender fingers to the chunky timepiece on his wrist all the way up his sports coat.

"What are you doing here?" she hissed.

Jeremy ordered a beer, and said, "I followed you. Those are Webber's parents."

"I gathered that," she said.

"They're supposed to be at Tropic Reef around four," said Jeremy.

"And yet here they are with Nina."

"Why do you suppose that is?" They watched as Nina patted Mrs Brandt's hand. It wasn't the patronizing gesture she expected, the *there-there* for a grieving mother. Billie sensed genuine sympathy.

Nina removed an envelope from her leather bag and handed it to Webber's father. The man peaked inside and shook his head.

"Is she buying them off?" Billie whispered to Jeremy.

"I didn't see money, did you?"

"A check doesn't take up much space." She stared at Jeremy and sipped her soda. "This is shady as fuck. Do you think Heath sent her? And is he keeping Katherine out of the loop on purpose?"

Webber's parents rose from the table. Mrs Brandt faltered.

Nina, too, rose, and reached for Mr Brandt's hand. To Billie's surprise, he clasped it sincerely before draping an arm around his wife and turning to leave.

"Shit!" hissed Billie. The space was too small for them to hide. Both she and Jeremy pretended to drop a napkin on the floor, their heads bent for an oddly long amount of time while the Brandts, and then Nina, exited the restaurant.

Billie glimpsed the door closing. She slapped a few bills on the bar and exited. Jeremy was on her heels.

Billie whipped her head up and down Washington Street. "You shadow the Brandts, and I'll go after Nina."

Nina was several yards ahead. A light drizzle began, so Billie dug around for her vintage fedora.

Nina stood out in the crowd. Beautiful women in well-tailored suit dresses often did. Money, like cream, had a tendency to float to the top.

Billie stopped short. Jeremy jostled her. She smacked his sleeve with the back of her hand, then said, "You're on the Brandt tail."

"They got into an Uber," he explained.

A man, short and slim, greeted Nina from the opposite side. He wore an Italian suit jacket, dress shirt and no tie.

"Kyle," they said together.

Nina paused and Kyle reared back slightly. Billie sensed the tension from this side of the street.

She got her phone ready, wondering if this evidence was worth collecting when Jeremy put a hand on her arm to stop her. "Watch," he whispered.

Kyle had tugged Nina's coat sleeve, pulling them out of the way of busy pedestrians, and toward the corner of the intersection, tucking themselves against a building's brick exterior.

Billie glanced at Jeremy and together they sprinted toward the couple, making sure to camouflage themselves among the crowd.

"What did you do?" Kyle said angrily.

"Nothing," Nina bit back. "Nothing that will get back to us."

But Kyle wasn't buying that. He said, "We're both doomed now. You've signed our death warrant."

"Don't be so dramatic," said Nina, shrugging off Kyle's grasp. "Heath sanctioned this."

Kyle gave her a dark look – angry and violent – that Billie had seen from the men she caught with their pants down. The only thing stopping Kyle from lashing out was the street full of witnesses. He stared at her, nostrils flaring, for an uncomfortable beat before finally giving up and heading downtown.

Nina exhaled, her shoulders dropping. She pressed a hand to her chest, then crossed Washington and walked toward Maxwell Place.

"What do you suppose that was about?" Billie asked when she could be certain they were in the clear.

"No idea," said Jeremy.

"They're conspiring." Billie turned back uptown, toward the office, her thirty minutes gone. Katherine would notice if she was late.

Jeremy gripped her arm and tugged her back.

"Heath isn't having an affair," Billie said.

"What?" asked Jeremy.

"You were right; I was hired to tail Heath. Katherine suspected he was cheating on her, but he can't."

Civilians walked past them, some grazing Billie's coat as they stood in the middle of the sidewalk.

"He's impotent," she said.

"Why are you telling me this?" Jeremy said.

Billie stepped back, nearly into the street. The only thing stopping her was a trash can. "I'm being used, and I don't know why."

Jeremy ran his hands through slightly damp hair. "Billie, it's obvious." He faced the street, then her. "You're bait."

CHAPTER FORTY-TWO

"I'm telling you these young people don't want to work anymore. Have you heard about *lazy girl jobs*? No?! I saw it on TikTok, and get a load of this bullshit. These women who I'm trying to empower just want the nine-to-five, and that's it. The recruiter was livid, said she had a candidate walk out when it was understood that the money she was requesting would come after six months and a performance review. Another candidate asked about overtime. Honey, if you want overtime, become a plumber. You want to get to the gilded egg, you gotta climb the beanstalk. Oh, and now my VHG department heads are angry because suddenly several of our people are insisting on leaving at six. Where's the drive? The ambition? I worked my ass off for this company, all I'm asking for in return is loyalty. How are women supposed to end the wage gap if we're not rising to our potential to compete with men? I know you know. You deal with this too. CEOs, presidents, all the same." Sigh. "The board wants another sit-down regarding the new factories in Guangdong, but I'm going to propose we move our manufacturing to Bangalore. Vietnam is on the table too. The Tropic Reef summer line is going to be streamlined. We're running focus groups for our new ads, and we're thinking of bringing back a few items from our discontinued VHG lines from the nineties. I know, the nineties are hot again." A laugh. "I feel so old."

Finally, Katherine cast Billie a glance. "I gotta go, dear. Yes, I'll have her call you later. Smooches."

She put down her cell phone.

"Sorry about that. Old friend of mine."

"School chum?" Billie asked, recalling Katherine's words.

Katherine brightened. "Yes, as a matter of fact." There was a languid sigh. "I think when a girl leaves her parents she truly finds herself. For you it was probably college, but for me, it was boarding school. Without adults, I really learned who I was. I think we all did. All the girls. Because there were no boys at this school. No distractions, you see. We could focus on our needs." She smiled, almost to herself, as if Billie wasn't even there. "Oh, the mischief we got into." Then Katherine added, "Anyway, my friend and I are both women overseeing the many. She's the only one I commiserate with." She gave that consideration. "Oh, and you. You're a small business owner."

"I have one employee, two if you count my grandpa," said Billie uneasily. "And technically he's my supervisor."

That earned Billie a laugh. "How quaint."

Quaint, right. What the fuck was Katherine's angle? Had she been hired for some kind of experiment? Was she, as Jeremy suggested, being dangled in front of Heath like an earthworm?

Sylvie kept saying she was Heath's type. Did Katherine seriously hire her, hoping her impotent husband would want to bang her? And succeed? And for the low, low cost of $60,000?

Billie had worked her ass off not to climb some imaginary feminist staircase to the top but to pay bills, take care of her family, and create a company that could sustain her over the years. She, like Katherine, was building a legacy. Unlike Katherine, Billie didn't want to build that legacy on the corpses of young people. She remembered Diego and thought she might be sick.

Do I tell her about the thumb drive?

"Don't tell her about the thumb drive," Jeremy had implored. "Katherine can't be trusted."

Billie caught Sylvie slinking around outside the office door. *Sure, just like Webber wasn't sleeping with Katherine.*

Billie was a soldier, flailing in the dark, unsure of the target. No evidence Heath was cheating. No evidence he was impotent, or that Katherine had been sleeping with Webber. Everything was office rumor and paranoia.

Then there was the issue of the Brandts meeting with Nina. Nina arguing with Kyle. Both of them scared of Heath?

Billie had one job: find evidence of Heath's affair. A nonexistent affair.

She was being played.

Katherine laid her hands on the shiny lacquered desk and looked hopeful. "Any updates?"

Standing here in this sanitized office, Billie felt dirty.

Katherine wanted to divest herself of Heath so badly, she was willing to tempt him with his type: Billie.

Tell her about the flash drive.

Tell her something.

She blurted, "Is the check in the mail–"

But she was interrupted by Kyle's shoulder brushing past her. He gave Billie no consideration. He just barked to Katherine, "We need to talk."

Katherine pursed her lips before wordlessly dismissing Billie with a wave of her hand. She backed out.

Billie was barely outside the office before the door closed in her face, inches from her nose.

She was slow to turn around. In her deliberate hesitation, she could see Kyle's countenance through the glass window, the way he leaned over the desk, whispering in Katherine's hair even though walls and concrete separated their secrets from the workers' ears.

Whatever happened on the street with Nina was obviously being discussed. And, by the scowl on Katherine's face, her employees' work-life balance wasn't the biggest problem she was facing right then.

CHAPTER FORTY-THREE

Later that afternoon Billie was watching the interactions between Heath and Rebecca the way one might observe a moon orbiting a planet. Or an asteroid about to hit Earth.

In this case, Heath went about his business and Rebecca circled him, peppering him with questions and reminders. Blending concoctions in the break room for him to suck down.

Did you use a full two scoops of protein powder, Bex? Are you sure? Doesn't taste like there's two full scoops of powder in here. I can't make gains without protein.

Billie wanted to scream, "Then fucking make it yourself!" Heath could put anyone off smoothies.

Heath was the kind of guy who wheeled his bicycle into the office, all decked out in cycling gear: skintight biking shorts that showed off his junk, cycling jacket, helmet. Screaming, "Come on, people. It's a beautiful day. Get out there." Meanwhile his employees were stuck in the office, toiling away, while he took a two-hour lunch because who in their right mind would question the boss?

A man with money and time didn't seem to recognize the privilege bestowed upon him. And he didn't extend that generosity to anyone else.

When Rebecca removed a salad from a bag under her desk, Heath walked by and muttered, "An 800-calorie salad is still 800 calories," before retreating into his office.

Rebecca acted like she hadn't heard him but the droop in her mouth, followed by a phony smile, told Billie she had. Also

Heath wasn't a low talker by nature. So Billie asked Rebecca if she would mind company. The girl was incredibly friendly to everyone in the office but the goodwill didn't appear to be returned. Billie saw Toby roll her eyes on more than one occasion when Rebecca had suggested everyone meet for a drink in Webber's honor.

But Billie's kindness was appreciated as Rebecca pointed to the neighboring chair.

"That salad looks delicious," said Billie.

Rebecca pushed the container toward her. "You want half? It's a lot."

Billie shook her head. "I'm not eating your lunch. It's a salad, not Thanksgiving dinner."

Rebecca rubbed the skin along her wrist, smudging more of the makeup she used to hide the tattoo, before stabbing a fork into the center and coming away with spinach, egg, and what looked to be dried cranberries. "Well, you're pretty thin so I guess 800 calories wouldn't matter," she replied.

Billie said, "Don't listen to Heath."

"He's right, though," Rebecca replied. "I lost over fifty pounds in college and I'm not about to gain it back."

"Wow. Um…good for you?"

"My sisters and I did it together."

"You have sisters?" Billie asked.

"Oh, no," said Rebecca with realization. "I'm an only child. I meant my sorority sisters. One was our coach. She would wake us up at six o'clock every morning. We did this army-style bootcamp. It was so fun."

"It was?"

"All us girls working toward one goal. I don't think I would've been able to lose that weight alone."

For some reason, this peaked Billie's interest. "Which sorority?"

"Lambda Theta Beta," said Rebecca.

"Ah, that explains the tattoo," said Billie, pointing to her own hand as if in demonstration. "A Lambda."

202 MAKE A KILLING

Rebecca quickly covered that part of her skin. "My concealer never lasts."

"Not sure why you cover it up," said Billie.

"Katherine doesn't approve. She says tattoos are trashy."

Called it.

Rebecca stabbed her fork further into the salad, scooping up a tomato. Before taking a bite, she asked, "What about you? Were you into Greek Life?"

Billie shook her head. "Never really had an interest. I'm always reminded of that Groucho Marx quote about not joining any club that would have me as a member."

"I've heard that," Rebecca said with a slight chuckle. "There were a few sororities that wouldn't have me. Lambda Theta was different, though. They welcomed me and became my best friends. None of the other houses would have us, so we sorta had ourselves."

"I have a bestie like that," said Billie. "We met in college. I love her. She's my sister."

Rebecca grinned. "Bet it's hard to hang out now, though?"

"A little," said Billie unconvincingly. "I mean, it was, but we're making an effort to have dinner a few times a month. I call her a lot. I bug her a lot." *I do background checks on her boyfriends. A lot. She passes me insider information. A lot.*

"Really?" said Rebecca. "I haven't talked to any of my college friends in a long time. It's mostly Instagram chats now and then."

"That's normal, from what I hear."

"A stupid part of me thought that being in Greek Life would mean having a built-in friendship forever, but it hasn't worked out like that. When I was struggling to get a job, my Lambda connections didn't help. Maybe because we weren't popular on campus."

"Thought popularity went away with high school," said Billie.

To that, Rebecca fully laughed.

"In adulthood, no one gives a shit about popularity," said Billie.

"Except, they do." Rebecca waved her fork around. "Take the office, for example. Kyle is constantly struggling for Katherine's attention. Nina wants to be in charge of all Tropic Reef's decisions. And Heath..."

Billie eyed the closed office door. She leaned in and whispered, "Heath wants everyone to like him."

Rebecca's mouth quirked into a small indulgent smile. "Pathetic, right?"

"Very," said Billie.

Rebecca said, "I followed him once to the gym."

"Really?"

Nodding, Rebecca glanced at Heath's closed door. "Thought maybe I could save Katherine the expense of hiring outsiders, no offense."

"None taken. And?"

"I watched him attend a spin class. I sneaked into the locker room, but he was just changing." She sat back, her cheeks flushed. Billie bet Rebecca had never admitted that to anyone before. It was sneaky, devious, and something Billie would do. She admired the chutzpah.

"Heath was overweight in his younger years. That's why he's so health-conscious now. He makes such a point about only putting natural products into his body, but really, how natural is protein powder? Although I sorta get him in that regard," Rebecca offered. She took several bites, chewed, then said, "I was saving up to do his cycling tour in Ireland before he shut down his company. I just wanted to prove to him that I could do it."

"There are other tours," Billie pointed out.

"Yeah, but it lacks the pettiness."

Billie laughed. "I'd love to travel abroad, but I can't. Not with work and my mom."

"What's wrong with your mom?"

"She's got dementia," said Billie, not wanting to elaborate. "I help take care of her."

Rebecca nodded. "My mom had cancer, but she's in remission."

"That's great," said Billie.

Rebecca nodded again. "Yeah." But it sounded like Rebecca wasn't sure. "My mom's not that nice. After I graduated college I struggled for two years to get a job. There were so many applicants and the companies wanted experience. Impossible to get experience when you won't get hired. But my mom blamed me. Said I must be acting weird in interviews or it was because I didn't know how to dress properly. I mean, she wasn't wrong. During the VHG interview, I broke down in tears."

"Really?"

Rebecca nodded. "The HR person looked like they wanted to jump out the window, but then Katherine showed up. She talked to me for thirty minutes which, if you know Katherine, is a large chunk of her time. She hired me on the spot."

"That's some story," said Billie.

"The whole reason I'm here for Heath, and not Katherine, is because she trusts me." This was said with a source of pride. Billie found it interesting that Rebecca didn't see the obvious. That to Katherine, Rebecca wasn't trusted because of her competence. She was trusted because Heath valued thin, beautiful young women, and Rebecca posed no threat to Katherine's marriage.

Billie was going on a fishing expedition. If Heath was impotent, would Rebecca know?

"Katherine is an incredible woman," Billie ventured. Then, "No man should take her for granted."

Rebecca nodded like she was in church. "Totally agree. She's the reason I'm here. If she hadn't given me this job, who knows what would've happened to me."

Billie made a questioning face.

"I could be waitressing in a diner," Rebecca explained.

Billie rocked a bit back and forth as if ruminating on something. "Sounds to me like Katherine could have any person she wants. Makes me wonder why she settled for Heath."

"He's charming when he wants to be," said Rebecca. She glanced at the closed door, making sure that what she about to say couldn't be overheard. "But he's sneaky. For example, I know he's having his intern look at employee records for the past ten years."

"Any reason why?"

She whispered, "He needs to make his charity appear legit, so he's using old records to build a staff. He even rented a dump in Jersey City so he'd have an address."

Billie glimpsed Jeremy's figure in the reflection of the door window. Did Jeremy know this? Or was he being played too?

Rebecca had opened her mouth to add something else, but that's when Heath opened the door and hollered her name.

"I shouldn't have said that," whispered Rebecca, her eyes alit with panic. "Promise you won't say, or do, anything. I don't want this to blow back on Katherine. She's not to blame. My stupid mouth…"

"I won't say anything," said Billie, but because Rebecca looked a feather's touch away from a complete mental breakdown, she added, "Promise."

Rebecca exhaled. She pushed away her salad and tossed the plastic fork in the garbage. Then she got up to deal with Heath.

CHAPTER FORTY-FOUR

Gramps had knocked several times before the old lady answered the door. She was elderly – even by his standards – pushing ninety maybe.

She stood hunched like a candy cane, dressed in all pink, and leaned against a walker. "Can I help you?" she said, her voice phlegmy and rough.

Gramps pointed to his left and said, "I'm an investigator working on behalf of Alan Tran."

"Who?"

He raised his voice. "Alan Tran."

"Who?"

"Your neighbor!"

She frowned, narrowed her brow, and finally waved him inside her place, trudging away like a snail.

Gramps hesitated. The apartment smelled like cat litter and stale cigarette smoke, but he'd been in worse places. He sighed, followed her inside, and shut the door behind him.

"Can I make you instant coffee?" she said.

"No, thank you," he replied, glancing around. These garden apartments were built in the seventies and typically had thick walls, not like these new-fangled quick builds with paper-thin sheetrock. The old lady seemed deaf anyway.

Could she have heard anything? Seen anything?

June had said the neighbor had scared an intruder. Gramps was only wasting his time if this turned out to be a nothingburger.

"Ah, Mrs…"

"Millie is fine." She positioned her walker next to a worn sofa, then fell backwards.

Gramps took that as his cue to sit opposite her in a recliner. He shifted slightly to remove a notepad and pen from his interior coat pocket. "Again, I'm investigating the death of Alan Tran."

She reached up to her ear and adjusted her hearing aid. "Nice boy," she said.

"His sister said you scared off someone trying to break into his apartment."

Millie dismissed that with a flick of her wrist, as if every day she confronted burglars. "It was just some kid."

A kid to Millie could be a forty year-old man with a beard. Better try again. "Do you remember what he looked like?"

"Sure. Tall. Young. Handsome."

"How tall?" Gramps said. "My height?"

"With all due respect, you're not tall."

Everyone's a critic.

"I'd say above six feet."

Gramps jotted that down.

"And how young would you say?"

To that, Millie made a face. It wasn't her fault; that skillset became harder as one aged. The amount of times Gramps had asked the young woman working the Nagel's counter why she wasn't in school at 10am, and she would always reply: "Mr Levine, I'm twenty-five years old." It was a game he liked to play with himself: how senile can I appear to a young person?

"He looked older than my grandson, but younger than Alan, I suppose."

"How old is your grandson?"

"Twenty-one," she said.

Fair observation. He wrote that down.

"You say he's handsome. That's quite subjective. Can you describe his face? Jawline? Skin? Race?"

"White man, definitely. Clear skin. Lean. A looker."

208　　　　　　　　　MAKE A KILLING

Gramps glanced at her. "A looker?"

"My grandson is a pudge ball with acne. It's hard for him to date." She shrugged. "This man would have no problem." Suddenly, she gripped the walker and hoisted herself up.

"Funny you should ask about that man," she said, inching herself toward the kitchen counter where a stack of mail, magazines, and supermarket circulars sat heaped in piles. She plucked an item from a ceramic bowl, turned around and held it up. "I found this outside on the ground. I think the burglar dropped it when I scared him."

Gramps also rose from the couch, his joints protesting as he did. He squinted, then accepted the item. "Where'd you find it specifically?"

"Outside the sliding glass doors of Alan's patio. I was smoking a cigarette and spotted it in the grass. I should have mentioned it to June but it seemed silly at the time, and she was already so upset. I had forgotten until you reminded me."

Gramps twirled the EpiPen. "Is it possible that this belonged to Alan?"

Millie shook her head. "No. I've never seen him carry one, and I've lived next door to him for five years. I also cooked for him a few times, and he never mentioned any food allergies."

Gramps nodded. "Mind if I keep this?"

Millie made a face. The Jewish expression for *what do I care?*

He thanked her and said he would see himself out. As he turned toward the door, Millie said, "It's possible, I suppose, that the thing belonged to the woman."

Gramps turned around. "The woman?"

"Not long ago I saw a woman prowling outside Alan's door."

"Can you describe her?"

Millie shook her head. "Sorry, no. She took off the minute I went to the door. I just saw black clothing."

"How do you know it was a woman?" Gramps asked.

"She sneezed, and it sounded very feminine."

Gramps held up the EpiPen and bade his goodbye.

CHAPTER FORTY-FIVE

Billie waited until Jeremy had been ordered to meet the FedEx guy – "Fabric samples," Heath had called out – before sneaking onto Jeremy's computer. She had just enough time to slide into the desk chair, wiggle the mouse, and wake up the desktop.

Jeremy was here to make a buck. Same as Billie. But would he do something corrupt for a paycheck?

No.

But would he *pretend* to do something deceitful for money?

Yes, she decided.

A spreadsheet – the aura of legitimacy – greeted her. Her shoes hit a box underneath the desk, so she pulled it out and shuffled through the files. She selected one folder, read the name, and searched the mini database Jeremy was building. Billie glanced from the file to the spreadsheet boxes, noted the red stamped DISMISSAL on each form. The information matched, but these people were being entered in the database as current employees. Was Rebecca right? Were Heath and Jeremy building a fake staff from old employee records? Rebecca was terrified at this admission, worried for Katherine and the company, so there must be truth to it.

A voice growled, "Belinda."

She startled and closed the tab.

Opening up a fresh one earned her a scoff and a, "are you fucking kidding me right now?"

Jeremy.

"You're at my desk."

Voices rang out above the din of office work. Toby and Sylvie sat huddled together, their fingers pointing at the computer monitor like two FBI agents trying to decipher fuzzy security footage. Billie heard Toby say, "This launch is going to fucking kill me." And Sylvie responding with, "If we're employed long enough." Then, "You're stressing me out, Syl."

Sylvie wasn't the only one agonizing over her job. Billie was counting on her fee to repair her roof. Money that hindered on Heath Vickery having an affair with anyone that wasn't Billie. And so she had to resort to Plan B. Bust Heath for murder. Webber's murder. Katherine might pay a pretty penny for that outcome.

The motive was right there. Heath had been stealing from his own charity, and Webber found out.

But did Heath know that?

Jeremy raised his brows, waiting for Billie's response.

"I don't owe you an explanation as to what I'm doing," she said, before adding, "At your desk."

"Certainly not," said Katherine who had swapped out reading glasses for chic, black frames. She bore the heir of a wealthy British aristocrat, minus the accent.

She addressed Jeremy. "Mr Chen, my husband hasn't really informed me about the specifics of your role on his team. What are your responsibilities for the summer launch?"

Jeremy squared his shoulders, but under Katherine's gaze, he faltered. "Uh, well, I'm ordering supplies for the launch party...and organizing vendors in this spreadsheet." On instinct, Billie pushed the box of files under the desk.

"Very well," said Katherine, but her tone suggested anything but pleasure. "And now you can help Sylvie and Toby with the tripod."

Jeremy nodded, a gesture so subdued and weak, Billie tried to implant the image in her brain to conjure during Jeremy's future cocksure moments.

As he shuffled off, Katherine put one hand on the desk and leaned over. She said, "Never let a man insist on knowing your business."

Since Billie literally built her career on secrecy, she didn't argue.

Then Katherine whispered, "I have it on good authority that Heath is having dinner at Sushi Lounge. He's being cagey as usual on the details, so I need you to follow him."

Billie nodded outwardly, but inwardly she wondered if Katherine was being purposefully obtuse. She also wondered if the prenup contract covered emotional affairs or just the physical ones. Because even if Heath was getting his rocks off with someone, and the office gossip was wrong, why would he flaunt that in town? Why wouldn't he slink off to a hotel room? Then she wondered how one-sided was that prenup?

Because if Katherine had been sleeping with Webber, and Heath could prove it, couldn't he sue for divorce and still get his shares?

Katherine patted Billie's shoulder. She then pressed her cheek to Billie's and said, "We can only count on each other." Walking away, her voice rang out, "James, let's see if those hours well spent were actually well spent, shall we? I want to see the reports for last quarter."

Billie got up from the chair and scurried to the bathroom, the one place Jeremy wouldn't look for her.

CHAPTER FORTY-SIX

Billie inadvertently followed Sylvie and Toby into the ladies' room, a move that Sylvie misconstrued almost immediately.

"Not really into women," she told Billie. "I mean, I could be tempted, but not by you."

"Christ," said Toby, her accent somehow amplified with that one word. "Leave the poor girl alone."

"I'm just here to wash my hands," said Billie, heading toward the sink. "Messy lunch."

"Yeah, I could smell that egg salad from my desk." Sylvie examined a pimple in the mirror, while Toby stared at the reflection and rearranged her bangs. Neither woman was in any hurry to return to their desks. The restroom, Billie realized, was a refuge since the higher-ups had their own private facilities. A place to talk and not be overheard. The door was fairly thick. The walls, maybe, even thicker.

But just to be sure Billie turned on the faucet and said, "So do you really think Katherine and Webber were screwing each other?"

Toby cackled, more likely surprised at Billie's audacity than the question itself.

But Sylvie paused, her eyes lingering on Billie. "I probably shouldn't have said that earlier, especially to Heath's lackey."

"I'm not his lackey," she said, pumping the soap.

"You're definitely his type," Sylvie grumbled. "I'm not surprised Katherine has you working so close to him. She wants to see if your presence will stir something in him."

"Gross, Syl," said Toby. Then she added, "Sylvie also thinks Katherine is banging Kyle."

"I know that for a fact," said Sylvie. "I caught them once. Webber, though, was just a hunch. And maybe a weak one. Look at Katherine. Webber died days ago, and does she look upset? She's done nothing but hassle me about social media content for the better part of the day."

People grieved differently; inward sorrow didn't always manifest outwardly.

Stop cutting her slack.

Billie turned off the faucet, her hands dripping into the sink basin, unable to move a muscle. She had to temper her response here. Nothing would quell this discussion more like an unnatural interest. If she seemed too eager, she had no doubt that Sylvie would move off.

"Katherine had been sleeping with Kyle *and* Webber?" Billie asked.

Sylvie suddenly hunched over as she meticulously checked under each stall. Popping back up, she said, "I don't know if it was at the same time, or anything. I mean, it could've been."

Toby tilted her head back and forth, a wordless gesture Billie interpreted as agreement.

Billie grabbed a paper towel while she digested that nugget. Coworkers gossiped, and these women thrived on it. But gossip wasn't gospel.

"Do you think Heath knew?" Billie asked.

"Couldn't say," said Toby as she checked her smartwatch and sighed. "Although he hates Kyle."

"Please," said Sylvie. "Heath would be threatened by a greyhound if that dog was leaner and faster than him. Man is insecure as a chubby eighth-grade girl."

"Made ya wonder why he had Webber Brandt working for him," said Toby, taking the words out of Billie's brain.

"Such a hottie." Sylvie fanned her face just as Toby crossed herself. "May he rest in peace."

"I barely knew him," Billie added, "but he seemed like a nice guy."

"He was, actually," said Toby. "He'd only been working in the Tropic Reef offices a few months, since the beginning of the acquisition. But he seemed to care about our products. He was interested in the new clothing line. You could tell he wanted to leave VHG; he was just biding his time."

"Until what?" Billie asked.

Toby shrugged. "Not sure. He didn't say much, but I once caught him looking at real estate listings for cabins in the Canadian wilderness. I said, 'If you want cheap homes in the middle of nowhere, there are towns in Italy that will pay people to move there.' It was something I saw on Reddit once. Anyway, it was the most we had ever spoken." Toby grew quiet, only stirring when Sylvie grabbed Toby's hand and squeezed.

Billie said, "Rebecca mentioned that Webber didn't socialize much with coworkers."

"Not sure how he would've had the time," said Sylvie. "He was constantly at Heath's beck and call, working until ten, sometimes eleven o'clock at night. No overtime pay, mind you. And while I appreciated Rebecca coming out to hear my band, I'm totally OK with a strong delineation between work life and personal life. I don't want to attend company picnics. At the end of the day, I just wanna go home."

"Speaking of work," said Toby as she checked her phone screen. "I have a Zoom call with the social media team in Manhattan, and the last time I popped on a minute after the hour, someone messaged me *time is money* via the chat."

As Sylvie reached for the door handle, she turned to Billie and said, "You seem like a nice girl, different than others that were here, but corporate life sucks. If I were you, and I could start over, I think I'd pick a quiet job, the kind I could do in my living room."

If only they knew Billie's actual profession.

"All I'm saying is accounting seems nice in hindsight."

Billie honestly couldn't agree more.

CHAPTER FORTY-SEVEN

The office had emptied out but Billie couldn't go home until she tailed Heath to Sushi Lounge. Jeremy had left but he smartly took home his shady files or shut them away someplace.

Shut them away. Hm. The supply closet? Worth a shot.

But when Billie opened the door, she found Rebecca lining up cartons of pens.

"Didn't expect to see you here still," said Billie.

"I leave when Katherine leaves," said Rebecca.

"That can be pretty late," Billie pointed out.

Shrugging, Rebecca stood back and admired her work. The office products did look neat and orderly. "I don't mind. I'll head to the gym after this. Someone in accounting said there's a killer kickboxing class. Might try that. Then I'll go home."

After what Rebecca had said about her mother, Billie imagined the girl spent as little time in Staten Island as possible. Like most sane people.

"Your accent isn't very strong," Billie remarked.

Rebecca blinked several times as if Billie had picked up on something she thought she had hidden away. "Katherine said my diction was doing me a disservice. No one would take me seriously."

"The way you sound?"

She hid her hand. "And maybe the tattoo. She wasn't wrong; I wasn't being hired."

Billie didn't exactly sport a subtle Jersey accent either, but she felt her pronunciation only added to her charm. Screw the haters.

She checked her watch. "I gotta go."

"What did you come in the closet for?"

Commit to the bit. "Pens." Billie plucked a few off the shelf and wagged them about. Then she left and rounded the corner to grab her bag.

Raised voices came from Katherine's office. Billie glanced around, noting empty chairs and desks. Bags missing, their owners gone. Standing outside, she crouched down, pretending to tie the laces on her Oxfords.

"Told you an actual intern would be best, but you had to hire a private eye!" barked Katherine.

Billie's eyes went wide.

"What are you talking about?" said Heath lightly.

"That Asian guy is a private investigator," Katherine hissed. "I had Rebecca do some digging. I knew something was off about him. And not just a PI, but a professor at Kentwell, too."

Heath laughed maniacally, but there must've been something off in his tone because Katherine then said, "I'm not joking."

Heath blanched. "Nina said–"

"Nina?!"

Nina?

"She's the one who found him," said Heath. "She assured me that he would help my project."

"And you believed her? You idiot! Always thinking with your dick. She's trying to sabotage us."

"You don't know that," said Heath softly.

"Kyle told me what she's up to. She met with the Brandts."

"I paid them off," he said.

"You did what?"

"Figured it was the best way to put this mess behind us," said Heath. "If the Brandts had come to the office, everything would be on record. Now it's quietly dealt with. But I should've figured Kyle would rat me out. I want him out of the brownstone."

"Heath–"

"It's *our* place," he said. "He's a drug addict and a gambler. God knows what he's doing there. Can't he afford his own home? I want him gone. If you don't take care of it, I will."

"He's made some bad investments," she replied.

"Not my problem."

"What about Nina?" said Katherine. "We have no idea what she said to the Brandts. What she insinuated. And, you idiot, payment is admission."

"I'll take care of Nina," said Heath. "She won't be a problem."

Billie tried to unveil the tone in that response. Was he making a threat? Or simply suggesting an agreement?

She could never tell with him.

A voice said, "I thought you were leaving."

Billie glanced up from her pretend shoe-tying to see Rebecca standing above her.

Heath said, "I gotta run. I have that dinner meeting, I told you about. Investor."

"Uh huh," said Katherine.

As Billie rose from her crouch, she spied Heath kiss Katherine's cheek. "Don't be like that. My ideas are golden. With the right direction, who knows where I can take us?"

Billie darted out of the way just as Heath opened the door. He noted Billie and Rebecca standing together, sized them up, and said, "You ladies like to band together." He shrugged on his sports coat and headed toward the lobby.

CHAPTER FORTY-EIGHT

Billie waited outside the Sushi Lounge for an hour, but Heath never showed. Since Heath couldn't get it up, perhaps he was fucking her this way.

Hoboken's streets glistened with rainwater and motor oil as she headed down 1st. She was parked nearby, having managed to snag a spot that didn't require a residential permit, but bypassed her car and moved toward Webber's apartment building. Glancing up at his third-floor window, she saw the light on and shadows skating across the blinds.

The building door had been propped open to accommodate a man carrying out boxes. Billie recognized him as Webber's father, Mr Brandt. Which likely meant that Mrs Brandt was upstairs.

Billie slipped inside and climbed the three flights of steps. Webber's door was ajar, his mother sobbing inside.

Billie hated herself for what she was about to do. She gently knocked on the molding.

Mrs Brandt turned, her eyes so red and swollen Billie wasn't sure how she could see.

"I live down the hall," said Billie and, not for the first time, she considered the marvel of all the lies that lived inside her. "I'm sorry about Webber."

Mrs Brandt brought a tissue to the tip of her nose and took a seat on the edge of Webber's tiny loveseat. "I'm still in shock."

"I didn't know him too well, but he was always such a nice guy." Then for good measure, "Always offered to take in my mail or feed my fish if I was away."

"That sounds like him."

Of all the awful things, lying to a dead man's parents ranked among the worst. Even her kind fibs wouldn't absolve the deceit. But it was for a purpose, she reminded herself.

"He told me about his modeling days," Billie continued. "I have to admit I had always hoped he'd ask me out." Shame, disguised as a blush, crept hotly across her cheeks. "Was he seeing anyone?"

Mrs Brandt attempted a smile beneath her sorrow. "I'm sure he would've been so happy with a girl like you, but work was his life for so long."

"He wore the hell out of a suit," Billie attempted, and to her relief Mrs Brandt smiled.

"He received a generous clothing allowance."

"Few companies do that," Billie offered.

"I know," she said. "He really valued his position at VHG, or at least, we thought..." She stopped, and Billie was aware that Mrs Brandt caught herself just in time. Hiding a revelation that she'd been paid to keep secret?

That was when Mr Brandt returned, sans boxes this time, ready to haul out the last dredges of Webber's life before movers likely came for the rest. Either that or they would abandon the furniture for the landlord to handle. No one cared about a used loveseat when their kid was dead.

"This is a neighbor," Mrs Brandt told her husband. "She heard about Webber and came to pay–" but there was no finishing that sentence. Mrs Brandt erupted into sobs.

Billie felt sick. "I'm so sorry. I should go." She then remembered the lube and condoms in Webber's nightstand drawer, and wondered if it would be kind to remove them and save them the secondhand embarrassment.

Billie spied a little succulent on the windowsill by Webber's bed. "Could I take the plant?"

Mr Brandt frowned, then nodded, not likely hearing Billie, his arm wrapped protectively around his wife. "You wanna wait in the car?" he whispered to her.

"We'll be back," said Webber's dad. "Just going to…" They went into the hallway.

Billie decided now would be a good time to swipe any offending sex paraphernalia from the nightstand. She opened the drawer, grabbed the lube and remaining condoms and shoved them in her jacket pocket. She went to shut the drawer, stopping only when a bit of metal glinted in the lamplight.

She peeked again and nudged various objects – tissues, bookmarks, an old Kindle – out of the way.

A bracelet lay coiled. Solid gold. A delicate chain with a charm of a crescent moon. Feminine. Familiar, only Billie couldn't place the memory. She pocketed it and left.

CHAPTER FORTY-NINE

At home, Billie ran a photo of the bracelet though a reverse image search, a frustrating exercise that amounted to nothing. Bracelets with crescent moons might as well have been infinity tattoos. Ubiquitous and unimaginative.

She then found herself scrolling through social media.

She had been watching so many videos on VHG products, her algorithm was a mess of expensive travel gear reviews, their subsequent Amazon dupes, and those who wanted to shit on Tropic Reef for selling out to VHG.

What did make the rounds was disgruntled travelers holding up their VHG backpacks, bitching about shoddy workmanship: loose seams, thin fabric, and weak zippers. "This thing broke on me in Milan," said one girl.

Another influencer stitched her video with a Tropic Reef bag. "Look at the quality difference. See how TR's bag has a thicker polyester lining. This thing is waterproof. I'm so glad I got one of these bags before they were bought out by VHG."

Billie also noticed that VHG was not capitalizing on the youth market. How could they? Young people didn't have money. People Billie's age needed the dupes and travel hacks. If they were buying quality, they were thrifting it via brick-and-mortar shops and eBay. Billie was wondering when there would be that great backlash to consumerism but she hadn't seen it yet. People liked owning shit, particularly shit many other people couldn't afford.

Billie had seen everyone's Europe trip videos last summer, watched them with agonizing envy, but also sorrow. She had always wanted to travel to Italy, but she didn't want to be one more annoying tourist trying to elbow her way to the Trevi Fountain. Billie didn't want to see landmarks just to snap a photo for the *'gram*. She wanted to experience life in another place – rent an apartment for several weeks, find the best markets, pick up useful phrases at the bakeries.

She wanted to live inside an Elena Ferrante novel, apparently, but without the drama.

To do that required money, or at least, a fervent imagination, because for Billie to plunk herself down in a quaint Italian village or Spanish town on her savings was a fantasy.

Not for the first time, she was jealous of Jeremy. He had that opportunity. He was headed to Spain on the college's dime. Hell, they were paying him to go – to study in Seville for months!

But he wouldn't take the money. Was it pride turning him into a total dick?

To her great shame, she imagined joining him. Crashing on his couch while he complained about her presence. She would return the favor by bringing him palmeras and Spanish tortilla. Maybe they'd go to a soccer match together. Maybe she'd try Rioja from the actual region of Rioja. That would be worth her self-imposed sobriety.

Maybes and one days.

Billie went back to social media. There was a subreddit devoted to traveling light and so she decided to search "VHG" and read what popped up.

VHG Madeira bag: worth it?

I'd save my money if I were you. Mine lasted only through four trips. Broke in Bermuda. Had to buy a Samsonite from the hotel boutique. Never again.

My mom's old bag lasted for twenty years before I got it. Unfortunately, the strap broke and they wouldn't honor the lifetime warranty. Just as well since I heard their new stuff sucks.

I love the new design, but I noticed they jacked up the price $100 and shrunk it by an inch.

VHG won't honor warranty

My Edinburgh Rolling Duffel crapped out on me after two trips, and they won't honor the warranty. The zipper ripped off the lining. Customer service said it was due to carelessness from the luggage carousel. But I used it as a carry-on!

See if a local luggage place will repair it.

I did, but the guy said they can't fix it. Told me to just use duct tape. For a $700 piece!

I feel like they care more about fast fashion than their luggage now.

Fast is right. Their clothing lining got panned on the Reilly McReady's account. Although, all those videos got taken down for some reason.

Billie paused. Reilly McReady.

She clicked on the hyperlink and went straight to Reilly's YouTube page. Her name rang no bells but her face set off an alarm. She recalled seeing her on the computer monitor at Heath's little staff meeting.

Billie grabbed a shovel and dug. Reilly was an NYU graduate who majored in business and marketing. She loved to travel and many of her videos showed her in exotic locales. The girl had money and so traveled. Then she got products to review for free.

Billie scrolled all the way to the bottom and reached one video where Reilly was twirling about in a blue wrap dress.

Billie pressed play. "This was my mom's. A vintage VHG Globetrotter from 1995. Look at that fabric and the stitching. If you can find these on eBay, get one! Check your moms' closets, ladies."

Billie combed through her memory. What had Heath said in the VHG offices in Manhattan? When Katherine had told Heath that Belinda was a student from NYU…

Like the Reilly girl?

Just as Billie began drafting an email, Gramps yelled from downstairs, "Found something I think you should see!"

CHAPTER FIFTY

Billie went into the dining room where she found Gramps sitting, glasses on the tip of his nose, going through Alan's files.

"You called," said Billie.

"Wanted to bring you up to speed." He tilted his chin toward the stack making itself comfortable by the potted spider plant. He then pointed to a pile of manila folders. "Those are Kentwell employees who have recently left the college."

"By choice?" she asked, sitting down and thumbing through the various files.

"Fifty-fifty. I've been making calls."

"Does anyone pick up?"

He shook his head and sighed. "I miss the days before Caller ID. I've been emailing as well."

"Any replies?"

Gramps read off his bulleted list. "One woman said she found a better opportunity elsewhere. Another said toxic work environment. Another said she got her dream job across the country. And another said she left to travel."

"OK," said Billie. "They all seem like legitimate reasons."

"Yes," said Gramps. "All the women said fairly innocuous things."

"All the women?"

"The men haven't emailed me back."

Stretching, she rose from the chair. "Well, if there isn't anything else, I'm going to shower. Got an early day tom–"

"I also went to Alan's apartment today. I spoke to the neighbor," he said. "The one who flagged the break-in."

"Did they give a description?"

"Male, over six feet, slim build."

"Catch his face?"

"Handsome." Gramps touched his own bulbous nose as if to demonstrate. "Looker."

"You or the burglar?"

"The burglar," Gramps replied, unamused.

"Wait, did you say a *looker*?"

"Yeah, handsome. According to the neighbor. An older woman, bordering on elderly, so take that lightly. She called me 'young man' at one point."

"Are you questioning her eyesight?"

"No," said Gramps. "Just providing context. Anyway, that's not all I found out." He turned slightly in the chair and reached down into a box. Groaning, he raised himself back up with a closed fist. He unfurled his fingers to reveal an–

"EpiPen," cooed Billie.

Gramps nodded, pleased.

She plucked it from his open palm. "Where'd you find this?"

"I didn't. The old lady found it outside Alan's patio door," he said, gesturing toward the floor. "So then I called June and asked her if Alan had any allergies?"

"And what did she say?"

"Seasonal, like the rest of us. But nothing that would require epinephrine."

"Webber," said Billie, her voice trailing.

"Your dead office worker?"

She nodded. "Could this be an actual coincidence?"

"You know what I think of that," he said with disgust.

"Why would Webber have tried to break into Alan's apartment?" she mused.

"Not sure. And it's not like you can ask."

Billie's brain churned, the gears clicking, the clock keeping time.

"Could Webber have taken Alan's laptop?" Gramps asked.

"We didn't find one in Webber's apartment," she replied.

"You broke into his apartment?"

"Jeremy did it first," said Billie quickly. "I just followed. But then I went back."

Gramps held his hands up which was Billie's cue to stop confessing. He couldn't deny what he didn't know.

"And I found this," she finished, holding up the bracelet she discovered in Webber's nightstand. "It's dainty, and I never saw Webber wearing jewelry. I think it belongs to whoever he was sleeping with."

Katherine?

"Did you do that reverse photo thing?" he asked.

She had. "Nada."

Gramps gave that thought. "You might have to start working these cases like they're related."

"You think Alan's death and Webber's death are connected?"

Gramps shrugged, which was response enough. Billie then scattered documents to her grandfather's dismay. She was looking for a name.

"I have a system here!"

Billie asked, "What did Alan's editor at *The Atlantic* say? Didn't she say he blew through a deadline on a fraud story?"

Gramps stretched across the table, and seeing his notebook, he rummaged through, flipping past pages of black ink. His eyes skimmed notes, then he nodded once. "Yes. She said he was investigating a charity that was embezzling donations."

"That's the connection!" Billie said. "I bet that Alan was initially investigating Vickery's Victors. Specifically Heath pilfering the donations and fudging IRS documentation. So why would Webber want to get into Alan's apartment? Protecting Heath doesn't feel likely."

"There's something else," Gramps said. "The old lady mentioned another potential break-in."

Billie frowned in confusion.

"A woman tried to get into Alan's apartment but, again, she scared her off."

"A woman?" Billie said.

Gramps pointed a pen at her. "These cases are related and we need to compare notes." He patted the chair next to him. "Buckle up, kiddo."

CHAPTER FIFTY-ONE

When Billie headed back upstairs, her cell phone rang.

"Hello."

"Is this Billie Levine?"

"Speaking."

"This is Judith Wilcox. You emailed me about Vickery's Victors," she said. "Is it too late?"

Billie paused on the landing, realized who was on the line, then scrambled to her bedroom for a pen.

"Yes!" Billie said, a little too exuberantly. "I mean, no, it's not too late."

"Honestly, I'm surprised you got my name. I was told my interview would be confidential," said Judith. "The camp I work at won't be pleased to know I'm talking to journalists."

"I'm not a journalist," said Billie, "if that helps. And to be upfront, the reporter looking into this has died."

"Oh dear. And she was so young too."

"I'm sorry – *she*?"

"Oh, yes, I assume you mean the woman who approached me."

"It wasn't a man?"

"No. It was a woman. Pretty, thirties."

"Name?"

"Oh, uh, I don't remember her surname off the top of my head because it was hyphenated…"

"Hyphenated?" Billie took a beat, then said, "Nina Patchett-Borel?"

"Yes," said Judith, with relief. "She called me, asked about the charity funds, and I was upfront, mainly because I was just so angry, but she seemed to already have the information. I was just confirming numbers."

"I see."

"I had reported Vickery's Victors to the state, but they're a New Jersey charity and the camp is in New York. I was told that I needed to contact Trenton, only for the man there to say I should call Albany. It was incredibly frustrating. So I spoke to a lawyer friend. He works at Kentwell, so–"

"Kentwell?"

"Yes, the college in North Jersey somewhere."

Billie took a gamble. "Bob Whitlock? He's a Kentwell professor and labor lawyer." And a confidant of Jeremy's, but she didn't say that aloud.

"Yes!" she responded with obvious surprise. "He and I go way back. Anyway, he said he would look into the charity as he heard rumors."

"When was this?"

"Oh, many weeks ago."

"OK." Billie's brain swirled with information. She began sketching out a mind map on the paper with Jeremy's name in all capital letters. "Thank you, Ms Wilcox. I appreciate your help."

"Not sure how I helped. You seem to have all the information already."

Billie did have what she needed. She just needed to piece it together.

CHAPTER FIFTY-TWO

The problem with modern-day sleuthing was that no one picked up the goddamn phone anymore. Gramps had gotten the numbers for the men on Alan's list and not one answered when he had called, except for Stewart, and that's because he thought Gramps was calling to schedule the roof repair. So Gramps had responded, "Yes, let's do that. Get us on the schedule." Never mind that he hadn't cleared this with Billie, but she would understand. She'd do anything for a case, even put a deposit down on a much-needed, and super costly, roof job.

Gramps said, "While I have you on the phone, Stew – can I call you Stew? – I was just wondering why you left Kentwell College."

Silence.

"Hello?" Gramps said.

"Yeah, uh, how does this relate to the roof?"

"Well, you see, your name is on a list belonging to Alan Tran. Did you ever talk to Alan Tran?"

"No," said Stew, but Gramps thought the boy was asking a question, not answering one.

"You sure?"

A clearing of the throat and three seconds of weird noises before Stew said, "I mean, he phoned and left a message but I never returned his call. I thought he forgot, or found someone else for his story."

"He died, actually."

"Alan died?"

"You didn't hear?" said Gramps.

"Jesus. No. How?"

"Not entirely sure."

"Accident?" Stew asked, but the way he said it made it seem almost hopeful.

"Again, not sure. Why?"

"No reason, just wondering."

Uh huh. And Gramps only suffered from indigestion.

"Billie said you run a private investigation firm," said Stewart.

"We do," said Gramps.

"I don't want to talk to Billie about this," he said. Then he quickly added, "She's great, but we went to high school together, and I feel weird. I'd prefer she didn't know."

"Fair enough."

There was a longer stretch of silence now, but this was where Gramps lived – in the gaps. When a person was arguing with themselves. He only had to wait to see who won.

Finally, Stew cleared his throat and said, "Could I meet with you?"

CHAPTER FIFTY-THREE

The following morning, Jeremy hadn't taken two steps inside the Tropic Reef lobby before Billie grabbed his elbow and forcibly pirouetted him inside the restroom.

He spun like a top, only stopping when he gripped the edge of the sink.

"The fuck, Billie?" He straightened, then rearranged his ID badge and tie. Billie glanced under the stalls, before kicking open each door for good measure.

She pointed a finger at Jeremy. "I figured out shit."

He didn't look amused but he did gesture sarcastically for her to explain herself, which she would do with aplomb.

"You knew Heath's charity was a sham because Bob Whitlock got a call from Judith Wilcox, who basically said her camp was scammed out of funds."

"You spoke to her?"

"Don't act surprised," said Billie with disgust. "I'm not to be underestimated. Also you had to figure I'd follow up those witness accounts. I can't believe you watched as I sat next to you and copied those files onto your computer when you knew everything already. How could you?"

"I didn't know everything," he said, sounding exhausted. Good. He should be.

"So what was the plan?" she said. "Besides icing me out."

Jeremy sighed. He went to the door that opened into the lobby and locked it, then rattled the handle for added security.

Took all of Billie's willpower not to grab him by the collar and shake the information loose.

Turning to her he said, "Bob Whitlock approached me, wondering if I would like to share credit on an investigative piece. He suspected Vickery's Victors of fraud, but with the IRS and law enforcement so underfunded, he couldn't do anything but report them and wait. He had told Alan to work on the story but Celeste and the Druffner girl were taking up all his mental energy, so, enter me. Then lo and behold Heath Vickery, who has Kentwell connections, is in need of an intern for his charity."

"So Whitlock suggested you go undercover?"

"Not exactly," he said. "I volunteered." He stepped toward Billie. His voice quiet, but earnest. "Look, I'm knowledgeable. I know how to document evidence. We're building a case. But that flash drive? That was treasure. Heath has only given me employee files. I'm to build a staff using those old records."

"Well, Katherine knows you're a private investigator," Billie said. "She told Heath who you really are!"

Jeremy paled.

Billie said nothing, just leaned against the sink and dropped her chin to her chest. "How is Nina connected to all this?"

Jeremy pressed his lips together. "She's the one who contacted Whitlock. She knows him from her prelaw days."

"Why would she do that? Why would she bust Heath for fraud? He's her boss. I thought they were close."

"I believe because Heath is blackmailing her."

"About what?"

He shrugged. "Whitlock wouldn't tell me. I didn't ask."

Some PI. Billie would've asked.

Jeremy checked his watch and moved toward the door, but Billie blocked his way. "Is this what you and Alan were arguing over? He wouldn't work this story and you got stuck getting involved?"

"Yes," said Jeremy, but he almost seemed relieved, and Billie wondered if she had asked the wrong question. He unlocked the door and headed into the lobby. Billie ran after and followed him into the elevator.

She whispered, "What are you going to do? Katherine knows who you are."

"Clean out my desk? Now that I have the flash drive, I might have enough material to expose Heath for good."

The elevator doors opened. But rather than head toward his desk he turned on her, backing her into the corner. He whispered, "Why are you still here, though?"

"What do you mean?"

"It can't just be the money," he said.

"Why not?" she said. "It's a lot of money."

Jeremy softened before shaking his head, like he couldn't believe he had to explain this to her. "Because you're too earnest, and you care too much about justice."

"I think you answered your own question," she said. "I want to know who killed Webber."

Jeremy's eyes flitted around the empty reception area. He leaned in and whispered, "Katherine is dangerous. I'm begging you to leave before you get hurt."

Billie reared back. "Are you protecting me?"

"Yes."

She immediately turned and walked away. He grabbed her elbow and tugged her back, but she snatched her arm out of his grip. "Get this straight, Yang. I don't need a man's protection. Certainly not yours."

This earned her a beleaguered sigh, so she added, "Maybe, Jeremy, you should be more concerned with your own self-preservation because you seemed to be steeped in a huge pile of shit."

Then she walked away.

CHAPTER FIFTY-FOUR

A few hours later, Nina Patchett-Borel approached Billie with a key. "I haven't seen Kyle in two days and he won't answer my phone calls. I have a meeting with China in twenty minutes. Would you be so kind as to go down the block and see if he's there? He has a brownstone on Garden and Tenth. You can walk."

Billie stared at the keychain, wondering if she was being set up.

Nina looked at her expectantly.

"Why do you have his house keys?" Billie asked.

"It's not really *his* house," said Nina. When Billie still didn't look satisfied at that answer, Nina added, "I've had to rouse him when he'd gotten loaded a few too many times, so he gave me an extra set. You happy?"

Not really.

"Do you know Alan Tran?" Billie asked. She was likely blowing her cover, but this would be her last missive. Billie was going to end her contract with Katherine. Not because she was heeding Jeremy's advice – *God no* – but because she needed to move on; she needed to help out Gramps.

Nina's widened expression proved unequivocally that she did know Alan Tran, but rather than admit that, she repeated, "Kyle."

Billie wordlessly took the keys and grabbed her coat.

She left the building just as Jeremy was crumbling up sandwich foil and tossing it into the trash can. He had his Nike backpack stuffed like a suitcase. He seemed in no hurry to get out of Hoboken. "Where you headed?"

"Nina sent me on an errand. Kyle is MIA." Then she had a thought. "You wanna come with me? The dude is likely sleeping off a bender or in the afterglow of an orgy, and I don't want to go there by myself. I might need protection." The last part was delivered in a facetious tone, but if she was to discover Kyle Olsen coked out of his mind, she'd want a witness. Corroboration.

Jeremy made a weird face, then glanced at his watch. "I should get going."

"Forget it," she said. "If he's naked and high, I'll use my Taser." Which was a lie as she had left it in her car.

But that got him up. "I'm coming." He pushed off the brick wall and followed her as they walked along 11th Street, across Hudson and down 10th.

They were silent for several moments, their paces firmly in step, their strides matched. "Please quit," he said.

She wanted to torture him but found their constant battle was leaching energy from her. So she replied, "I will. Later today when Katherine comes back."

"Oh. Good."

Then, angrier, she said, "The entire case is yours. Nail Heath, gain your recognition. Go to Spain."

He stopped short and placed a hand on Billie's shoulder, essentially stopping her from continuing down the sidewalk. "What are you really mad about?"

"Nothing." Billie huffed and headed toward the apartment. "I don't care about your dissertation or European trips or you eating tortilla de española outside La Geralda."

"You know an awful lot about Seville," he said.

"Let's just go wake Kyle up so I get back to the office, get paid, and get out of this very charming, and egregiously expensive, city."

She stomped off in a state, fuming until they got to the stoop of a gorgeous brownstone with red brick and a bay window. Billie whistled. "Jesus."

Jeremy brushed past her and up the stairs. "You gonna gawk all day or unlock the door?"

She stuck the key into the lock and said, "If he's coked out of his mind, you have to deal with it. I can't handle douchey rich dudes and their vices."

"Oh, and I can?"

"You've done a great job so far."

Billie pushed open the door. The first thing she was met with was a smell, like rotting garbage. They walked in. Staircase directly in front, the living room to the right, the kitchen in the back. Every surface and wall had been renovated.

"Looks clean, like no one has been here."

"You think he left? Kyle's known for drugs and gambling. Maybe he got into it with bad people and hightailed it out of Jersey."

Jeremy moved back to the kitchen and dining area, and paced around the giant marble island. He peeked into the backyard.

"Basement?" asked Billie.

Jeremy disappeared downstairs and a second later, re-emerged. "Nothing weird."

"Um, then I guess we should go upstairs."

Billie and Jeremy looked at each other, then glanced up. They climbed the stairs together.

"Smells vinegary, like vomit," he said.

"Let's call," she whispered. "So we don't barge in on him naked, or worse."

"Kyle!" they called together.

No answer.

Billie felt the dread. They opened up a bedroom door. Nothing but a dresser, desk, and club chair. Office, she decided. They opened the master bedroom – untidy but empty. "The bathroom next."

She allowed Jeremy to do the honors. He swung open the door. Billie gasped, then turned her face.

A body lay naked in a bathtub. Pale, waxy, his cheek lobbed against the surface of still water.

"Something worse it is," said Jeremy.

"And not Kyle," added Billie.

"What the hell is Heath Vickery doing here?"

CHAPTER FIFTY-FIVE

Gramps knocked gently on the doorframe of a small office where Nicole Mercier sat behind a desk, frowning at her phone screen. When she looked up and glimpsed him she did not appear any happier, only confused. Appropriate response, since Bill Levine did not make a habit of touring college campuses that his grandchildren were no longer attending. Nicole recovered and smiled. "Mr Levine, what a surprise."

"Call me Bill," he said. He did not suggest she call him Gramps. That moniker sounded too much like *grumps*, which was likely how he acquired it. Also his identity was not solely wrapped in being a grandfather. He'd been a beat cop, police detective, and now private eye. He'd been an ass-kicker and crime solver. His family was a blessing, but they did not define him.

Nicole rose from the desk and pointed to the chair in front. "What are you doing here? Can I get you a water?"

"Sure," he replied.

Nicole scurried around and popped over to the water cooler visible from her office. He heard the glugging noise of liquid being displaced by air. She returned a moment later with a plastic cup that she set on the desk.

Nicole was being kind, but Gramps sensed the tension she carried in her politeness.

"You're probably wondering what I'm doing here," he began.

"I am," she said, as she returned to her office chair.

"I'm working on behalf of Alan Tran's sister."

"I heard that," she replied. "I'm going to assume you need my help since you're in my office."

Nicole was savvy. Gramps wouldn't do her the disservice of insulting her by making that point. Instead he sighed. "I hate to ask."

"You Levines hate to ask, and yet...here we are," she pointed out.

"Listen," he said, before glancing around. He gingerly rose from the chair, and shut the door.

"This serious?" Nicole asked.

Gramps nodded as he returned to the chair. "Like a lapsed mortgage payment."

He finished the cup of water and leaned forward. "How much do you know about students when they come here?"

"Nothing," said Nicole. "I work in campus housing."

Gramps figured as much. "Brianne Druffner got kicked out of her former college for drugging male students."

"I'm sorry, what?" Nicole said.

"Roofies," he elaborated.

"With intent to..."

"My source at Washington and Franklin didn't expand upon that, but yes, I imagine, with intent to assault."

Nicole leaned back in her chair. "Fuck." She slapped a hand over her mouth. "Sorry, Mr Levine."

Gramps waved that off. He wasn't a pearl-clutching society maven from the 1950s. Even his mother swore like a sailor. In Yiddish and English.

"I want to know how she got into Kentwell," he said.

"You mean you want to know *who* got her into Kentwell," said Nicole.

Gramps grinned. "Smart cookie."

"I know how you Levines think." She hesitated for a second. "I can't get into Brianne's records. I can't see her transcript, or..."

Gramps waited and watched Nicole's brown eyes flit back and forth, calculating, considering. "But I know someone who can." She picked up the phone and dialed. "Tammy, it's Nic. Gotta minute?... Great... No, I didn't hear back from Kean. You?... Thank God we're not competing for the same gigs... Girl, I know. Listen, I have a favor to ask, and I need you to keep it quiet too." Nicole smiled. "I'm trying to find information on Brianne Druffner. Specifically, her records from Washington and Franklin... Lunch on me? Excellent. No, no email. Just call." Nicole hung up. "Tammy said she needed five minutes."

Gramps nodded before turning around. He spied a woman through the small window and recognized her as Marissa Gulla. He slouched down, hoping Nicole's frame would block her view.

"Again, you Levines never cease to surprise me." Nicole smiled, but he sensed a tinge of disappointment. Gramps remembered how his friendships always seemed transactional. How he would pump neighbors, cousins, teachers for information. Anything to aid a case. Billie was likely doing the same. Could their selfishness be genetic?

The phone rang and Nicole answered. She uh-huhed a few times, smiled, but then her eyes widened. She said, "Why am I not surprised?" Finally, she set down the receiver. She exhaled long and slow and said, "Brianne Druffner is supposedly a legacy admission."

"Supposedly?"

"There's no record of her parents or grandparents being alumni." Nicole tapped a pen against the desk surface and chewed her bottom lip.

"What aren't you telling me?" Gramps asked.

Nicole dropped the pen. "Dr Beaumont wrote Brianne's letter of recommendation."

"The president of the college encouraged your admissions department to enroll Brianne Druffner?"

Nicole nodded.

"Is it possible that Beaumont wouldn't have known about the allegations from Washington and Franklin?"

Nicole shook her head several times, and Gramps suspected she was more likely trying to convince herself than him. "Her GPA from Washington and Franklin was a 1.9 and that's way below our standards. She went to an elite boarding school, but even that was unremarkable. This explains a lot. Why Greek Life and Campus Housing wouldn't pursue the harassment allegations? She's being protected."

"By Felicia Beaumont," said Gramps.

"Yeah," Nicole whispered. "You know what this means..." She glanced at him with wide, brown eyes.

Gramps sighed and tapped the desk twice. "Proceed with caution." Nicole stared at her cell phone for a second before waking up the screen.

"Something else on your mind, kiddo?" Gramps asked.

Nicole's expression morphed from concern to odd relief. "I think I'm being blacklisted from jobs."

"Because you're Black?" Gramps said cautiously.

"What? No." She considered that. "Maybe. No." Shaking her head, she huffed out a sigh. "Maybe Dr Beaumont is making phone calls to these other colleges, warning them away from me. Persona non grata."

"Why would she do that? I mean, if she has it out for you, wouldn't she want to get rid of you?"

Nicole stared at him as if the answer was obvious and he was an idiot for not seeing it. Perhaps he was.

"As a show of power."

"Huh," said Gramps, rising from the chair. "I can play the game. Show my hand. Where would I find this Felicia Beaumont person?"

CHAPTER FIFTY-SIX

Jeremy handed Billie a cup of warm liquid.

"I can't drink coffee right now," she told him, thinking of Heath Vickery's naked and gray corpse.

"Good, because it's hot chocolate," he said. "I didn't think your nerves could handle a jolt of caffeine."

She smiled appreciatively. They were sitting outside, their butts perched on the bumper of a parked car. Inside Kyle's brownstone, police officers and detectives milled about. Billie caught sight of several techs in white jumpsuits, their pale silhouettes appearing like ghosts in the windows.

The leading detective, Mo Abadi, had been cordial until his inquiry into evidence contamination forced Jeremy and Billie to reveal their roles as private eyes. "We know our way around a crime scene," she had said.

"You work at Tropic Reef."

"We do that too," said Jeremy.

Not technically a lie.

"The VP sent us here to find Kyle Olsen," Billie added.

He tapped his pen against a notebook several times, never taking his eyes off them. His eyebrows were so fuzzy and thick, Billie expected them to morph into monarchs and flutter away.

He exhaled, then told them to hang out in case he had more questions.

"He just wants us to sweat," said Jeremy once the detective was out of earshot.

"Shows him," she said. "We're pros at making other people uncomfortable."

Jeremy laughed softly, reflecting both their uneasiness.

"So Webber's dead and now Heath Vickery," mused Billie. "Kyle's in the wind?"

"Seems so."

"I really thought it would be Kyle in that tub." She blew across the hot liquid. An officer nearby grumbled, "Another rich drug addict."

"What if it's a homicide made to look like an accident?" she said. "Just like Webber."

Jeremy remained quiet. Billie wondered if his thoughts churned like tornadoes too.

"There's something you should know," they said together.

"You go first," they both said.

Jeremy gestured for her to speak. Billie hesitated a second, wondering if she was being set up, and then decided she didn't care. "Webber tried to break into Alan's apartment. Alan's neighbor found an EpiPen on his patio. I suspect – well, Gramps does too – that Webber and Alan's deaths are connected. I considered that Heath was the killer, and maybe he's still good for Webber's murder because Katherine might've been sleeping with Webber. She took advantage of him. She bought him those suits. And Webber knew about Heath's fraud. Also I found this in Webber's apartment." She held out the bracelet.

Jeremy's eyes widened.

"Is this familiar to you?" she asked.

He frowned, his brain working at the memory. "I've seen it before, but I can't place where."

"That makes two of us." Billie gestured with her cocoa, signaling to Jeremy that it was his turn for a revelation. He paused too long and Billie was certain he was pulling a fast one until he said, "So in an effort to fake his charity documents, Heath had me combing through years of employee records. Interns. Temporary hires. Contractors. All given generous severance packages."

"Why?"

"I suspect that Katherine wasn't sleeping with just Webber."

"Kyle," she added. "Probably why Heath was here. Catch her in the act."

"Katherine has a history of predation. All those files cite her as the reason for resignations. HR buried it."

"Jesus." Billie felt her body grow heavy, practically melting into the car bumper. For a savvy private investigator she sure felt stupid.

"So, she's screwing around, and Heath isn't? Or wasn't?" She hadn't expected to be used by a woman. She set aside the cocoa and crossed her arms across her coat. "Now what?"

"Katherine is no better than a man in her position. She uses her power and wealth to intimidate and abuse. Her company makes all this money at the detriment of Asian workers, of debt-saddled college graduates. She doesn't even pay her interns."

"She's clearly a garbage person," said Billie.

"Katherine is good for murder," said Jeremy. "We just have to prove it."

"Three men are dead," said Billie. "If she killed Webber, Alan, and Heath, that makes her a serial killer."

"So?"

"What's her motive for killing Alan?" Billie asked. "He was investigating Heath's charity. If anything, Alan's reporting could've saved her the hassle of using me as a lure. She needed Alan."

"If Alan's article came out, accusing Heath Vickery of stealing charity funds from children, Katherine's brand would've gone down with him. Influencers complaining about faulty stitching would be the least of her problems."

Billie pushed herself off the bumper. Detective Abadi was no longer in sight. Even a few of the beat cops had left. No one would care if they went back to the office, or home. "The Kentwell stuff is tied to this. There's shady shit happening on campus, and too many coincidences."

The minute she mentioned Kentwell, Jeremy started walking toward the Tropic Reef building, not even waiting for Billie to catch up.

"They're not related," he said without looking at her.

But Billie didn't believe him. Jeremy had been acting weird – not just about Alan but about the funding for his Spain trip, and Dr Beaumont – nearly everything Kentwell-related. Something was clearly going on with him, something he didn't want Billie uncovering.

If anything, these cases had taught her not to underestimate a mark.

And Jeremy was definitely her mark.

CHAPTER FIFTY-SEVEN

Dr Beaumont's office was up one flight of stairs and down a corridor, taking up the entirety of the east side of the third floor. In fact, signs pointing Gramps in the right direction referred to this part of this building as the Presidential Wing.

Who does she think she is? Eisenhower?

He stopped in front of the young Asian woman who manned a desk outside double doors, and said, "I'd like to speak with Dr Beaumont for a few minutes."

"Do you have an appointment?" She asked this in a kind manner, but her voice seemed coated in condescension. *Look at this old man trying to get in to see the president of the college. How quaint.*

"I do not," he said, before flipping open his private investigator license.

The girl frowned as she glanced at him. "Are you a police officer?"

The private eye asks the questions. "I'm investigating the death of Alan Tran. Is Dr Beaumont available?"

Suddenly, the girl scrolled through a tablet. Gramps surmised paper calendars went by way of the dodo. She nodded, satisfied with some unseen information, and shook her head. "She's in a meeting right now. I can schedule you for another date."

"When would that be?"

"Next month. Wait, no, the month after next."

Right. These self-important people whose time was more valuable than gold. Bullshit.

Voices emanated from behind the double doors. Gramps waited, not giving the girl an answer, nor wandering away.

"Sir?" said the girl.

He recognized one of the voices. And when the door opened, a familiar face appeared. Young, blonde, hardened, like she could instigate a prison brawl. Eventually she would. He was sure of that.

"Now, don't worry about a thing," Dr Beaumont said to Brianne Druffner. The girl was sporting a Kentwell sweatshirt. Gramps pictured a dresser drawer filled with hoodies from the various institutions she got kicked out of.

Dr Beaumont glanced at Gramps, frowned, then recovered with a pressed smile. She could not place why an old man in a trench coat was standing outside her pristine office. Gramps loved these moments. He was often underestimated; his age caused many to write him off. "Dr Beaumont, got a minute?"

The Asian girl bolted to her feet. "I was just asking him to make an appointment for two months from now."

"Do you have a minute?" he repeated.

Felicia Beaumont held up her hand, a signal for her young secretary to remain quiet. "Who are you?"

"Bill Levine. I'm looking into the death of Alan Tran. I'd just like to ask you some questions."

Shaking her head, Beaumont said, "I don't see how I can help you."

"Answering my questions would be a start."

"Are you a detective?" she said.

"Investigator," he replied.

"I don't speak to civilians posing as police," she said. "You can understand that." She gestured to the girl. "Chloe will see you out."

Then with a smile as taut as wire, she patted Brianne on the shoulder. A get-lost gesture if Gramps had ever seen one.

Standing next to each other, Gramps noted the similarities beyond blonde hair and brass balls. Brianne and Felicia each wore a thin gold bracelet with a charm.

Identical to the one Billie found in the dead boy's apartment.

CHAPTER FIFTY-EIGHT

A round table of women. Not what Arthurian legend suggested, but surely what Katherine had always wanted.

Next morning Billie sat in the conference room, her chair sandwiched between Sylvie and Toby. The rest of the office drones hunkered around with disappointed countenances. After all, one boss-man was dead and the other had disappeared, and yet they were expected to clock in?

Outside was Katherine, a cashmere coat draped across her shoulders. Rebecca stood next to her typing frantically on her phone, and beside them a team of women in sleeveless dresses and visitor tags were barking into cell phone speakers.

They entered the conference room like a cyclone. Files dropped to the table, chairs pulled out only. One would sit down, only to immediately jump up to take a call by the photocopiers.

Billie felt like she was watching a colony of bees make honey; they were industrious and hectic. They had purpose.

Katherine addressed the congregation. "We're in crisis mode," she began. "But we'll muddle through. It's what Heath would've wanted."

Her worker bees began passing out documents, sliding the papers across the shiny table like hockey pucks. Sylvie was the first to ask the obvious. "What's this?"

"Nondisclosure agreements," said one of the women. "News outlets will be calling you. They might offer money–"

"How much?" grumbled Toby.

"You are not to tell them a thing," the woman continued. "Anyone who is caught talking to a reporter about–" She stopped herself, clearly unsure of how to address the elephant in the morgue. Was Heath's death an accident? A murder? "–Mr Vickery," she continued, "will be dismissed. If you are contacted by any major news outlet, you are to refer them to our PR team." Business cards then skidded across the table like skipping stones. Billie scooped one up.

None of this was directed at her. First, she never spoke to reporters and second, she knew she was waiting to be fired. Even though she had been prepared to quit she felt a dismissal was better: she'd still get paid the thirty grand, minus the bonus. She supposed Heath's charity investigation would also collapse; any fraud allegations would be dismissed as speaking ill of the dead.

Heath's demise definitely solved one problem for Katherine, even as it created many larger ones. For starters, the president of Tropic Reef, Kyle Olsen, was completely in the wind.

What was this hive of damage control going to do regarding that?

Billie glanced around as everyone sighed, then scribbled their names to the NDAs. Billie signed hers and turned it in to Rebecca who was gathering the paperwork onto a clipboard. She didn't even glance down to verify the signature. Which was good since Billie wrote 'Veronica Mars' in place of her name.

Everyone filed out the conference room. There had been no talk of grief counseling or time off to process feelings. Katherine, however, flustered by the buzzing of her crisis team, yelled, "We still have a product launch, people!"

Billie flinched.

The murmur of voices died to a low hum.

Katherine repeated, "Von Holm Gear has been around for a century, and it will continue to do so. This changes nothing."

Billie heard Sylvie mumble, "The grieving widow." Her mouth snapped closed the minute Rebecca sidled up to Billie.

"I'm sorry to tell you but Katherine has ended your contract," said Rebecca with a frown. "I really enjoyed getting to know you. I felt like we could've hung out had we had more time. I also hope you learned a lot from Katherine while you were here. She's a true visionary. A real leader. Here's your payment. Katherine said the business manager never got it in the mail – she is sorry about that – so I'm to give it to you in person." She handed Billie an envelope with the check for thirty grand – no bonus, of course – but more than enough to square away her bills. And yet Billie oddly hesitated to accept the money. The cash seemed tainted.

She took it anyway – roof wasn't going to fix itself – and in doing so, accidentally offset the balance of Rebecca's clipboard which was cradling a cell phone.

Billie noticed the wallpaper photo. A headshot of Katherine in a blue dress, hand demurely under her chin. A gold chain with a crescent moon gently grazing her wrist.

Billie swallowed as she handed Rebecca the phone. "What a beautiful picture."

Rebecca made a face, clearly confused by Billie's train of thought. Then glancing down, said, "Oh, that's Katherine's phone. She asked me to answer press calls should they come in. The photo was taken by *Vogue*. She looks amazing, right?"

Billie's mouth quickly went dry. "And the bracelet? Was that a piece *Vogue* lent her…or?"

"No, that's hers," said Rebecca who, hearing her name being called from across the office, jerked her chin.

"I've seen it before," said Billie.

"Yes, all Gunness girls receive one at graduation."

"Gunness?"

"The boarding school," said Rebecca. "To own one is very special. Means you're somebody. That crescent moon is, like, a ticket to success."

"Are you a Gunness girl?"

"No," said Rebecca with a slight laugh. "I wish. Gunness girls do not struggle to find jobs, that's for sure." Again, her name was called. "I gotta go handle whatever that is. Take care." And she left.

Billie stood there stunned as if a bucket of rainwater from the Levine dining room had been spilled over her head. Gunness.

She googled the name while simultaneously walking toward her desk to collect her remaining belongings: change from the vending machine, the parking pass she'd sadly have to return.

Gunness Academy for Girls. A boarding school in McLean, Virginia.

She was so engrossed in her phone, she didn't see Detective Abadi until he brushed past her, accompanied by several uniformed cops. He displayed his badge and said, "We're looking for Nina Patchett..." he checked his notes "...Borel. Anyone see her?"

Several people shook their heads. Only Sylvie spoke up. "She hasn't come in today."

The detective wiggled his mustache before heading toward Katherine and her protective beehive. She took one look at the cavalry and the search warrant and quivered her lip. Billie would've bought the performance if she hadn't just been threatened to keep her mouth shut.

A moment later a police officer popped his head out of Kyle Olsen's office and called for Abadi.

Billie shoved her phone into her pocket and trailed after him. She peeked her head around the open door and watched as the cop pointed to a cabinet with a gloved hand. Billie saw the orange container as Abadi stroked his chin.

Peanut butter powder.

"Do I bag it?" the cop asked.

Abadi nodded and turned around.

Billie zipped out of the sightline.

As she gathered her things and turned in her ID badge at the security desk, she took out her phone and texted Diego. He claimed he was feeling better – two quarts of matzoh ball soup and a few days in David's guest room would cure any ills – and looking for an assignment. She'd been reluctant, but even David had begged her to give him something to do that wasn't binge-watching *Suits* on Netflix, so she sent him an address and a missive: *Keep an eye on her*. He'd know what she meant.

As she was walking to her Hyundai she turned her attention to her payment. Sliding a fingernail underneath the envelope flap, she slid out the check, eager to get to the bank and deposit the quasi-windfall. This was more money than she had ever earned on a case. Thirty grand would give her breathing room. But when she examined the numbers, they were missing a zero. She hadn't been paid thirty grand, but three.

Billie cursed so loudly, her voice echoed throughout the parking deck, scaring an errant pigeon into flight. She crumbled the check in her hand, squeezing the paper like she wanted to squeeze Katherine Von Holm's neck.

That cheap bitch, thought Billie.

The CEO was going down. Billie would do everything in her power to make that so.

CHAPTER FIFTY-NINE

Gramps agreed to meet Stewart outside a job site, where he was promised ten minutes of interview time in exchange for a deposit on the roof repair.

Two grand just to get on the schedule. He could scrounge up the cash, but he'd have to sell Ken's Oldsmobile to pay the balance. He'd ask David how to make an ad on Craigslist. Or Facebook? That should make for a swell afternoon, he thought bitterly. David didn't have much patience when it came to Gramps's computer skills.

Perhaps, though, he wasn't salty about the money but the drive to Clifton to stand outside a duplex as it drizzled. Latin music blared from a speaker while the guys chucked shingles into a dumpster. Bits of Spanish peppered him as he stood there, hands in his trench coat pocket, wondering when the crew broke for lunch.

Gramps was checking the time when Stewart appeared, removed his tool belt, and opened the back doors of his van to retrieve a meatball hero.

His employees scattered toward the pizzeria a block away.

Unwrapping the foil, Stewart leaned against the bumper. "Got the check?" he asked.

Gramps frowned, feeling like this was more of a shakedown than a legitimate business exchange. He removed the folded paper from his coat pocket and set it on the clipboard. "Don't lose it."

"I won't," said Stewart.

"Busy guy," Gramps noted.

"Always work in roofing."

Gramps supposed that was true. Recession-proof, inflation-proof.

"OK," Gramps began, "So let's talk Kentwell and Alan Tran."

Stewart swallowed a lump of meatball. He set down the sandwich and grabbed a bottle of water, slowly twisting off the cap. Gramps thought Stewart was stalling, but perhaps Stew was just collecting his thoughts.

"I was being sexually harassed at my job at Kentwell," Stewart said. He leaned over, checking to see if his remaining crew members were lurking by the truck. They weren't. Gramps would've noticed.

"By who?"

Stewart raised a brow as if saying, "isn't it obvious?" but Gramps wanted confirmation. He didn't want to put words in a witness's mouth. Give people the space to speak their minds, and they will gift you with information.

"Dr Beaumont," Stewart said, picking up the hero. He tore off another bite.

"How did it happen?" Gramps asked.

"Not immediately, or anything like that. She's calculating, knew what she was doing. She invited a bunch of the new hires to a fancy event. An opportunity to network with the deans, supervisors, and higher-ups. It was a nice party. Appetizers and wine. She mingled, came around to everyone, introduced herself, asked us questions. Honestly, we felt so special. I know I did. And then a month later, I got invited to a cocktail party at her house. My boss said the president had zeroed in on candidates she thought had the makings for leadership. So I went. I worked in student accounts, but I really wanted to manage the scholarship program. I was a recipient of it, and I wanted to give back. I told her as much. Said my dad was a laborer, and college gave me an out from that lifestyle."

Gramps nodded along.

Stewart set aside the hero, appetite lost or stolen. He wiped his mouth with a napkin. "She came on to me at the party. It was subtle, but I'm not an idiot. I know when a woman is into me. She touched my arm and, at first, I thought she was being friendly. But she kept plying me with this weird beer. Some local brew. I'm a wine drinker usually but I must've had a few bottles. She cornered me in the kitchen. Whispered in my ear that I should stay when everyone else left. She grabbed my hand and forcefully placed it between her legs. She wasn't wearing underwear." He shivered. "I know, right? Every man's worst nightmare." He uttered this lightly as if trying to convince himself that he had overreacted. Then he sighed while rubbing the tension from his forehead with his fingertips.

"What did you do then?" Gramps asked.

"I told her that I had to leave. I still lived at home, and my mom was anxious about late nights. Which wasn't the right thing to say because then she said if she and I got cozy, she'd make sure I was put in charge of the scholarship program." He looked at Gramps then. "It comes with a raise. Anyway, I freaked the fuck out. I think I stumbled into the dishes on the drying rack. One broke, made a loud crash. That might've saved me, I don't know, because a head popped in. Her assistant, I think, checking to make sure everything was OK."

"Did that end it?" Gramps asked. "Not just for the night, but in general?"

Stew scoffed and shook his head. "First, she started texting me these pornographic images and videos from some unknown number. My mom almost caught one of the messages when I left my phone out on the kitchen counter."

"How did you know Beaumont was the one sending the pornography if she was using an unknown number?" Gramps asked. Likely the woman was using a burner phone but Gramps wanted to be sure.

"She'd follow each message with a line like, 'this is what we'll do together' and some of the most vulgar descriptions that I will not repeat to you. Totally unnerved me. This went on for several weeks."

"Gotcha," said Gramps. "What else happened? How did it escalate?"

"One day I went out to my car in the staff parking lot and found my tires deflated. I had noticed that I was being given extra assignments that kept me in the office until dark. So I was about to call for a tow when a town car approached. Driver said Dr Beaumont had sent him to pick me up."

"She trapped you."

"Yeah," said Stew. "Fucked, right?"

Not Gramps's first choice of words, but yes, fucked.

"I called an Uber and got out of there." Stew shook his head, the memory probably feeling as incomprehensible as it sounded aloud. "I kept getting invited to more cocktail parties, but I refused to go. So Beaumont sent her assistant to my desk, basically saying I was expected to attend the presidential functions as a job responsibility. But still I stayed away. A month then went by, and everything suddenly stopped – the porno texts, the vandalism to my car, all contact – and I thought I was in the clear, like she had moved on. Until suddenly, I'm getting poor performance reviews. Then I wasn't invited to a campus-wide brunch, hosted by the deans. Everyone gets invited to that. My boss said she heard a rumor that I was caught ogling some of the female undergrads. Apparently, Dr Beaumont was telling staff and faculty that I was a sexual abuser in the making. Can you fucking believe she said that?" His voice shook. "I'd had enough, so I quit that day."

Gramps said, "Who knew about the harassment?"

"Alan had figured it out. Somehow. But that's it. I didn't even tell my dad – I was too ashamed. I worried that if I had told him what was going on he would've laughed at me. Said something gross like I was looking a gift horse in the mouth. I mean a beautiful woman wanted to sleep with me, and I turned her down? So I just told him that he was right and academia wasn't for me, and I should take over the business like he always wanted." He shook his head while rewrapping the hero. "I wanted to succeed in my job because I cared, not get a promotion because I pimped myself out. I like Kentwell a lot and I wanted to give back, and she fucking took that from me."

Gramps squeezed Stewart's shoulder and said, "I'm sorry, kiddo, that this happened to you."

Stewart nodded and shifted slightly.

"Is that why you didn't want to talk to Billie about this?" Gramps asked. "Because the perpetrator was also a woman?"

To that, Stewart scoffed. "No. If anyone could understand, it would be Billie. Who knows what crap she has dealt with in her profession? No, the reason I didn't want her knowing is because I'm not the only one she has harassed. Calvin was another victim, and I know Billie is tight with his girlfriend Nicole. Calvin doesn't want Nicole to know what happened. Only reason I knew about Calvin was because the day I walked out, Calvin met me in the parking lot. He said I was brave to leave. He said Beaumont needed to be stopped, but he wasn't sure how. He told me what had happened to him and then begged me not to tell anyone."

Sighing, Gramps thought of Calvin. Poor boy. The secret he'd been carrying, the shame he must be feeling. Gramps sorely doubted Nicole knew what was going on. If she had, she certainly wouldn't have been in her office while Gramps wandered into the presidential wing, trying to catch Dr Beaumont off guard. No. Nicole would've been front and center, ready to throw fists.

Gramps ran his hand over his scruff. He was in desperate need of a shave, but he thought his five-o'clock shadow supplied him with a gruffness he could use to his advantage.

"Do you know where Calvin lives?" Gramps asked Stew.

Stew shook his head. "But I know where you can find him."

CHAPTER SIXTY

Billie pulled up in front of Nina's house in Mendham, a massive colonial that made a mockery of historic charm.

The town was uber wealthy with an odd New England aesthetic. The real estate taxes alone gave Billie heart palpitations.

It was also an hour's commute from Hoboken.

To each her own, but Billie didn't think Tropic Reef was worth that kind of drive, particularly in rush-hour traffic.

Diego shifted beside Billie and said, "There's a guest house in the back." Then for emphasis, "Near the pool."

"Rich people," they said together.

Billie was still understandably salty about being cheated by one of the wealthiest women in America. She had told Gramps earlier that they would have to sue Katherine and VHG, but he had only laughed and said, "That's the whole point. She has a ton of lawyers and you only know a kid who took five tries to pass the bar exam. She's counting on you letting this go because you can't afford the legal fees associated with a litigation."

Billie felt cheap and used. The thirty grand had been a retainer that she had never retained. Gramps had told her to get the money upfront, but Katherine kept putting her off. *Business manager is handling it.* So Billie didn't push it.

Why hadn't she pushed it?

Because she was taken in by a bag of designer clothes and the promise of a lofty payday.

She wouldn't make that mistake again. If Billie was to dismantle Katherine's kingdom, she'd have to first shake down Nina Patchett-Borel.

Unbuckling the seatbelt, Billie told Diego, "Stay here." She sounded like she was directing a child, but an admonishment floated around her head: *he's your responsibility*.

"What are you going to do?" said Diego.

"Knock on the door."

Which Billie did before finding the bell. A jaunty tune played, but there was no sign of Nina. Diego texted her from the car: *I see movement in the upstairs window*.

Billie pressed the button on the door cam and said, "It's Billie, uh, Belinda from the office. I just want to talk." Then: "I know about Vickery's Victors, and I know you're involved. I also know you paid off the Brandts." She motioned like she was going to return to the car, and then Nina's voice said, "Ugh, fine."

Nina was already there, dressed in sweats, holding the door wide open as if Billie was an invited guest.

Billie went inside. She'd been right about the manufactured charm. The foyer had stonework and wide planked floorboards, but the masonry was too pristine and the hardwood too polished.

"This way," said Nina as she headed down a short hallway and into an open space with leather sofas and white painted furniture.

Nina dropped onto the couch, leaving Billie most comfortable in the opposing club chair.

Unscrewing the cap on a bottle of fizzy water, Nina sipped and drew up her knees. "You're not an intern, are you?"

"No," said Billie, fishing for her business card. "Private investigator. I was initially hired by Katherine to tail Heath. She suspected him of philandering."

That elicited a snort out of Nina. "Katherine got one over on you. That man was as limp as a cooked noodle."

"She told me he was sleeping with *you*."

"I'm not his type," said Nina as she brought the bottle to her lips. She gulped the rest of the water before adding, "Too tan. But you, dear girl. You're perfect."

Billie felt a need to assert dominance. "I wasn't just hired by Katherine Van Holm. I have another case on behalf of Alan Tran's sister. You know Alan, don't you?"

Nina briefly closed her eyes as if the information pained her.

"Explain to me how you are connected to Alan?" said Billie.

"Why should I?" said Nina with a dismissive wave of her hand. "You're not police. They were here earlier, so I'll tell you what I told them: I don't know anything."

"I bet they believed you too," said Billie. "You're very pretty and sophisticated and accomplished, but I know things they don't."

Nina blinked at her, challenging. "Like what?"

Billie grinned. "Like how you secretly paid off Webber's parents. Or how you may be covering for Heath's fraud. Or that you have a very improper relationship with Kyle Olsen, which I'm going to guess is not something you want broadcasted to your husband. Where is he, by the way?" She rose from the chair but took no more than two steps before Nina grabbed her wrist and tugged her to sit back down.

"I'm not the bad guy here," said Nina.

"You're shady," said Billie. "In my experience, shady people aren't on the right side of anything."

Nina rolled her eyes. "You wear the sanctimony well. You don't know what the corporate world is like, especially around women like Katherine. You have to go around their backs."

"Is that what you did when you paid off Webber's parents?"

"The Brandts needed money to bury him. Katherine would've tossed them ten grand and referred them to her counsel if they wanted more. Heath said I could give them fifty."

What was a life worth?

Billie said, "I'll ask again: how do you know Alan Tran?"

There was another huff of breath and a gulp of water before Nina finally said, "Long story, but Heath asked me to do an audit of the finances for Vickery's Victors. I had told him that I didn't have the time to help him and that he should get his staff to handle the tax documents. But, as I later learned, there was no staff because the money never reached the summer camps. He'd siphoned ninety percent of the funds and cut checks for meager amounts, insisting the camp directors buy technology from one of his old business associates. I was honestly horrified, and yet he had come to me thinking I would enable this. I told him that he was embezzling from his charity and I would not be a part of such a scheme. He said he just wanted his ducks in a row, but really he wanted the documents to look legit for the IRS because complaints had been made. Charities like Heath's can fly under the radar forever if no one flags them. Although when Judith Wilcox had complained to the state, she got the runaround. Still, Heath got spooked."

"Then Judith spoke to Bob Whitlock," said Billie. "Whitlock was your professor at Kentwell once upon a time, wasn't he?"

Nina first looked impressed, but then she frowned as if in disappointment. "You did your homework."

"Always," said Billie, sick of being underestimated. "What happened after you told Heath *no*?"

"He threatened my marriage. Said if I breathed a word about the discrepancies – that's what he called them – he would tell my husband," she swallowed a lump in her throat, "that I had slept with Kyle."

"So you did sleep with him?" Billie had been bluffing on that part.

"Once," Nina said, holding up a pointer finger. "We were drunk at a conference in San Diego. Only ever happened that one time. I don't even know how Heath had found out, except that people talk. Coworkers aren't family."

Billie's were. "Is that why your husband isn't here? He find out about the affair?"

Nina shook her head. "Not yet. And, hopefully, not ever. He's away on a business trip. Sacramento."

Billie didn't think the secret would stay secret but that wasn't her problem. "So you copied the files onto the thumb drive and handed them to Alan Tran?"

Nina nodded. "I read an article Alan had written in *The Atlantic* about corporate malfeasance. I thought if anyone could handle this it was him. By the time the scandal went to press, Heath would be powerless to do anything other than damage control. Only…"

"Alan's investigation never came to light."

"Alan had said he was working on another story but would look into the mess. I believed him, but then he died, and the story would've died with him," her gaze clouded over, "until Dr Whitlock and Jeremy Yang hatched a plan."

"And you got Jeremy the internship?"

Nina nodded. "Was easy enough. Heath is lazy."

"What do you think Webber's role was in all this?"

She tugged her sleeves over her arms. "You saw the picture of the cabin on his desk?" Billie nodded. "He said he was going to buy it once he had enough money. Now I know what Webber earned and, unless he came into an inheritance, I couldn't see how he'd ever get his hands on that property. And then I caught a text message on his cell phone screen when I'd been setting documents on his desk."

"What did it say?"

"'Put your bid in now.'"

"When was this?" Billie asked.

"A week or two before he died, I think." Nina tugged at a loose thread on her sock.

"So, theoretically, Webber had plans to blackmail Heath – and Katherine – about the charity scheme in order to buy his dream property," Billie said. "So he stole the thumb drive with the documentation from Alan's apartment. Why, though? I have to imagine he would've had this information. As Heath's assistant, he was privy to everything Heath did."

"Heath didn't trust Webber," said Nina with a shake of her head. "Maybe I shouldn't have either because I told him about Alan and the investigation. I had a feeling Webber could help, but he clearly had an agenda of his own."

"Did you know that Webber was sleeping with Katherine?" asked Billie.

"We all thought that was office gossip. Webber never gave any hint..."

"I'm sensing a *but*," said Billie.

"But Webber always looked afraid of Katherine," said Nina. "Like she was a shark, and he was chum in the water." Nina sipped from the nearly empty water bottle again, a lengthy pause, but not long enough to toss off Billie's suspicion.

"You mentioned the cops have been here," said Billie.

"Yes."

"They think Kyle is good for Heath's murder. Webber too?"

Nina swallowed, then looked at Billie. Really looked at her.

That's when Billie heard a noise coming from a room off the kitchen, the sound of weight shifting against a door. Billie stood. "What was that? You alone?"

"Yeah," said Nina. "Damn wind."

"It's a still night," said Billie. "I was just outside." She spied a shadow glide across the kitchen window and saw the distinct silhouette of a man on the run.

Billie darted to the French doors, pulled them open, and gave chase. "Hey!" she cried.

Nina sprinted after her. "It's nothing! Just the neighbor! The kid is a peeper!"

"Call the police!" Billie yelled back as she sprinted farther into the yard, watching the figure race toward the fence. If he got away, there was no capturing him. Billie was moments from leaping toward him – hoping if she could just grab the hem of his shirt, she could catch him – when suddenly another body emerged from the darkness and slammed into the man.

Two figures mashed together and went down. Billie skidded to a stop.

Diego grunted. "That hurt."

Underneath him was Kyle Olsen.

CHAPTER SIXTY-ONE

Kyle sat at the kitchen table with a cloth staunching light bleeding from a small scratch, but he was carrying on as if Diego had stabbed him in an alleyway. Meanwhile, Diego held an ice pack to his shoulder. He too was moaning, but he'd been through a lot in the past few days so Billie was in a more forgiving mood. Besides, he was a kid. Kyle was a privileged douche.

"You're harboring a fugitive," Billie told Nina who had been filling glasses of water, as if hydration was anyone's problem right then.

"Kyle didn't kill anyone."

"I didn't," he whined.

"Then why hide? Why not go to the police?" said Billie.

"I was high," Kyle said, almost exasperated, as if Billie's questions were an inconvenience to his evening. God forbid the man answered for his misdeeds. "I needed to dry out first."

"You were listening to our conversation," said Billie. "You ran like a man in possession of his faculties. So what the hell happened to Heath?"

"I don't know." He huffed. "Honestly, if my neck wasn't on the line, I wouldn't even care; guy was a prick."

"Why was he at your place?"

"Not my place," grumbled Kyle. "Katherine's name is on the deed. I just live there."

"Can't afford your own digs?" Billie asked, remembering Heath and Katherine's argument.

"I'm not great with money," said Kyle. "Invested poorly, blew through some. Seemed easier to just live there since we were…" His eyes, for some reason, darted to Diego who said, "Oh, it's OK. I'm nineteen."

"He's my associate," Billie explained, handing Kyle her business card. "I was hired by Katherine to find evidence of Heath cheating."

Kyle barked out such a surprising laugh, Billie thought he was momentarily choking on his tongue. "You're really Heath's type. Pixie blonde dream girl. Katherine was at her wit's end, wanting him out. You have the perfect face. She hoped he would fall for you."

"Then hire a sex worker, not a private eye."

"Heath would never," said Nina. "He was worried about diseases."

Well, if that wasn't some presumptive bullshit. Particularly since his wife wasn't monogamous.

"There's something you should see." Kyle took out his phone, dragged his thumb across the screen, and pressed play on a recording. "You're lucky I'm showing it to you."

"Thank you so much, Mr Olsen," said Billie sardonically.

At first all Billie could hear was shuffling. Papers moving about. On a desk, perhaps? Were they in the VHG offices? Then Webber's voice: "Katherine, I sorted the documents for the Oahu line. The production team wants to set up a meeting for next Monday."

Katherine: "That's fine."

Billie could hear the clacking of heels. Then a door shut.

Katherine: "Has everyone left?"

Webber: "Yes."

A moment of silence before the sound of objects being thrown to the side. Something landed with a clang.

Katherine: "Those heels were killing me."

More silence.

Then Webber: "I don't think we should do this here."

Katherine: "Why not? You said everyone left."

Webber: "Heath might come back, or Rebecca."

Katherine: "I don't give a fuck about either of them. They both want me, but only you can have me. Doesn't that turn you on?"

Billie cast a quick glance at Kyle, who rose and leaned against the kitchen counter. He exhaled painfully and ran a hand over his ribcage. Big baby.

Webber: "Katherine, please."

His voice sounded desperate, pleading. Billie wanted to reach inside the recording, turn back time and help him escape.

More rustling sounds, like Webber was being stripped of his tie.

Then Webber's voice, stronger: "I'm serious, Katherine. I want to end this. It isn't fair to me."

Katherine: "Fair? I think I'm being more than fair. You're an administrative assistant. You have an art degree from a podunk Vermont college. You work for one of the most successful and wealthiest companies in the world. I provide you with a living, designer suits and shoes. I give myself to you. This arrangement is more than fair to you."

Webber: "I want out. I think it's best I find another job."

"Another job? Webber, dear, I don't want to call every single CEO in Manhattan, but I will. They don't like disloyalty any more than I do. You try and leave for another company in this city or within the entire tri-state area, you'll see how far my reach is. The only job left for you will be in a Vermont Cracker Barrel."

More papers rustling. Then Katherine's voice: "We're done here. You go on home to that shoebox you live in."

Webber: "I'm sorry, Katherine. I'm just tired. Forget I said anything."

Katherine: "Already forgotten. But you'll have to make it up to me."

The recording stopped.

"Holy shit," said Diego.

But Billie had other concerns. "Did Webber send this to you?"

"No," said Kyle, making a face. "That would've been weird. He didn't trust anyone in the office, particularly me."

"So how'd you get it?"

"My cousin."

"Your cousin?" said Billie. "Who the hell is your cousin?"

"A girl who interned for VHG a few years ago."

"I want a name," said Billie.

"Reilly McReady."

"The influencer?"

"Yup."

Billie checked Kyle's phone screen again, then grabbed a pen off the counter and wrote down the number on the top of her hand. "Corporate America has to be the most incestuous place in the world."

"I didn't sleep with my cousin," said Kyle.

Billie cast him a look. "I was being metaphorical." Sighing, she signaled to Diego that it was time to leave. "Hope your lawyer is good."

"Money always pays for a great defense," said Kyle.

"Yeah, but you're broke," said Billie on her way out the door.

CHAPTER SIXTY-TWO

Jeremy was not delighted to see her, but he let her inside his apartment.

Billie had dropped Diego off at his cousin's place in Dover. "I gotta man the bakery counter tomorrow," he had told her, which worked out well. Billie craved buñeulos and Gramps wanted to return to walking around the house in boxer shorts.

"Can't be free around company," he'd told her.

"You shouldn't be so free around me either," she had said.

And now, as she stood in Jeremy's apartment, the adrenaline fueling her dissipated. Jeremy didn't look great. His eyes were dull with exhaustion. His skin, normally so clear, was splotchy.

"Whatever you've come here to say, say," he said.

"There's been some developments," she told him.

"Right. Otherwise why else would you be here?" He went into the kitchen. Billie watched him fill a tea kettle. "You want?"

"Uh, sure," she said.

"So Kyle Olsen is alive and well, and hiding out at Nina Patchett-Borel's home."

The faucet stopped running. "Really?"

"He was drying out," said Billie. "So coked out of his mind he wasn't sure he didn't hurt Heath."

"Did he?"

"Unlikely."

"Lying?"

"Didn't get that impression." She waited for the kettle to stop whistling before she added, "I want to play you something. I must warn you, though, you'll feel debased just listening to it."

Jeremy sighed and snatched her phone. "Christ, Billie, enough with the preamble."

He pressed play and Billie listened again as Katherine threatened Webber. Thirty seconds of torture. When it was over, Jeremy remained quiet. He was pale, almost sickly.

"Are you OK?" she asked.

Jeremy nodded, but still said nothing. He went into the kitchen, and calmly poured the boiling water into two mugs. He dropped in tea bags. His whole demeanor was oddly controlled and placid.

"What's wrong?" she said.

"Nothing," he said.

"Something is."

He shrugged, then dipped the bag into the water, several times, as if on autopilot.

"You're being weird. Don't you find this disturbing?"

"Of course."

"But not that disturbing?"

"Webber made a choice."

"You think he had a choice?"

"Yeah, I do." Jeremy sipped from the mug, winced, then set it back down.

Again, Billie found herself unsettled by his rigid response.

"He could've said no. He could've quit and worked at Cracker Barrel in Vermont."

"She's a monster," Billie said. "You did warn me. What's changed?"

"Nothing," said Jeremy. "She's still horrible, but I don't think Webber is a victim. He willingly slept with her."

"Coercion sounds more accurate."

"Those suits we found in his apartment. Those gifts. He could've returned them. Said no. The first time she came onto him, he could've said no. He didn't."

"Let me ask you this," Billie began, "when a woman is sexually harassed, do you think she has a choice? Do you think she could have just said no and returned to work?"

"That's different."

"How? Katherine used her power and position to control Webber. She knew he was broke. Knew he had loans. She dangled wealth in front of him like a carrot. The only thing he had to give her was sex, a transaction he clearly wanted no part in."

"You don't know how it started out," said Jeremy. "Maybe he wanted her too. Maybe he was excited by the attention. Maybe he had no idea how everything would turn on its head."

Billie stared at him dumbfounded. "Doesn't matter how it started out. Only matters how it ended. With Webber's death. Katherine is a dirty manipulator." Billie shook her head. "I'm getting nowhere with you."

"Why? Because I'm not sympathetic?"

"Yes. That." She made a face, then a decision. "I'm going. I don't know why I do this to myself."

"What?"

"Try to talk to you."

"Just remember," he said. "I didn't invite you over. You came here."

"My mistake. I won't make it again." Billie didn't glance at Jeremy as she grabbed her coat and bag. When she left, she thought she heard Jeremy exhale. Like a weight had been lifted the minute she was no longer near him. As if she was some burden he carried. Or a disease he didn't want to catch.

CHAPTER SIXTY-THREE

The following morning, Billie sat cross-legged on her bed and dialed the number scrawled in pen on her hand, the number Kyle had given her against his better judgement.

A voice answered cautiously, "Hello?"

"Reilly McReady?" said Billie.

"Speaking."

"This is Billie Levine. I sent you an email about Katherine Von Holm." Then, sensing Reilly would disconnect the call, she quickly added, "I want to discuss Webber Brandt and Kyle Olsen."

There was a bout of silence, but Reilly was still on the line. She said, "Be quick."

Billie heard street noise on the other end. Honking horns, motorized scooters, and sirens. Finally the commotion quieted to a distant hum.

And then Billie told her everything: her undercover work at Tropic Reef; witnessing Webber's death; finding Heath's body; Kyle Olsen; and finally the video Reilly had sent her cousin.

"What I don't understand is why Webber texted that to you?" Billie asked.

"We were friends," she said. "I worked at VHG for several weeks, and in that time we grew close. I had told him to stay with me in Milan, but he said he couldn't quit his job. He needed the money. I knew he was miserable at VHG but I didn't realize why until he sent me that video. For safekeeping, he had said. In case anything should happen. But when Webber died, I truly thought it was an accident until I got your email asking about my connection to Katherine Von Holm. That's when I texted Kyle the video. He's, like, a second cousin once removed. I thought I could trust that he would bring it to the police. I'm in Milan; he's in Jersey."

"What is your connection to Katherine?" asked Billie.

"She and my mom had attended the same boarding school."

"Gunness?"

"Gunness Academy for Girls in McLean, Virginia. That's how I got the internship at VHG. I had an *in*."

"You didn't stay in the job."

"Because Katherine is a royal bitch, not to mention a master manipulator. Once I realized she was cheapening the product lines and her company's green initiatives were a bunch of bullshit, I quit and started vlogging. I make more money on YouTube than I ever could in a corporate gig. Plus I can live in Italy."

"The green initiatives are lies?" Billie asked.

"Totally. VHG doesn't use recycled scraps. The company dumps them into landfills. Smoke and mirrors. When an NGO called them out for pollution, Katherine's lawyers sued them into oblivion. She even sent them after me. I received a cease and desist letter for a video where I accused VHG of lying to consumers about the fair trade partnerships they presume to employ. Spoiler alert: they use sweatshops."

"So you quit."

"Technically I was fired by Rebecca, because Katherine is a coward. My suggestion is to just get out while you can. My mom excluded, but that boarding school births nothing but psycho women with their dumb brand of toxic feminism and their stupid bracelets. And their fundraisers. I told my mom that she was *not* to give that school any more money. Of course, what does she do? Attends a dumbass fundraiser at Kentwell and cuts them a check."

"A fundraiser?" Billie asked.

"God, yeah. Like they need more cash. School costs a fortune. The tuition is insane. It's so like rich people to have their hands out, you know?"

Billie did.

"And this fundraiser was at Kentwell?" Billie said.

"Yeah, cause Felicia Beaumont is an alumnus."

That got Billie to thinking. "Do you remember when the fundraiser was?"

"I don't know. My mom was talking about it in February. I think it was near Valentine's Day."

"Huh," said Billie. "And everyone would go?"

"If you mean former students? Then yeah. Katherine, and of course she brought Heath. Felicia. They all were there. My mom saw them. Kept saying how much work Katherine had done. Like I care." A huff. "This is why I live in Italy."

"Thanks, Reilly," said Billie. "I'm glad to know that Webber had you as a friend."

"Yeah," she replied. "I wish I had been a better one, though. I had no idea how bad things were for him. He never said, but I could sense something wasn't right. I saw how Katherine looked at him, like he was a piece of meat. I knew deep down that he was in trouble, but I did nothing. I should've…" A sigh. A sniffle? Billie couldn't tell. "…I should've asked. I should've pushed." At this point, the city noise had died away completely and Billie wondered where Reilly had hidden herself – a cemetery? A church? "You forget sometimes," she said sadly.

"Forget what?" said Billie.

"That not all monsters are men," she said.

CHAPTER SIXTY-FOUR

Gramps pressed the button on the crosswalk. He stood outside Kentwell College's gates, squinting against a gunmetal sky as he stared at a light blue Victorian that housed Alpha Phi Alpha, the school's only Black fraternity. According to Stewart, Calvin was helping the boys repaint the old backyard fence, and that's where he would be this morning.

"Tell him I sent you," Stewart had said, "otherwise he might get skittish."

Gramps wiped donut crumbs from his mouth and dialed Billie as he waited for the light to change. She picked up and said excitedly, "You're not going to believe what I found out." And then proceeded to tell him.

"Felicia, Katherine, and Brianne are all tied together," she said. "They all attended a charity fundraiser for that evil boarding school on February 13th. Someone could've slipped away and mowed down Alan. Might be a conspiracy."

Gramps pressed the button again, getting impatient. Vehicles zipped by. The speed sending tufts of exhaust through his trench coat. "Speaking of, check your email. June sent over security footage from the camera she installed at Alan's apartment. Now that we know the neighbor saw a woman, I want you to be on the lookout."

"You think Brianne could be on that footage?"

"Can't rule her out." Finally, the sign turned green, and he headed across the street. Out of nowhere, a car honked, startling him. He pressed a hand to his chest as he continued to the safety of the other side.

"Where are you?" Billie asked.

"I'll fill you in later. In the meantime, check the footage."

"Yeah, yeah," she said, and then hung up.

Gramps ambled up the front steps. He had one fist poised to knock before he heard rap music blaring from somewhere behind the house. He sighed, then shuffled down and went around back, confronting a wooden gate with an iron latch.

He went through.

The minute he entered the yard, a sea of Black men stared back at him. Buckets at their feet. Their shirts and sweatpants covered in wood stain.

A kid spoke up, "You lost?"

Gramps could see how this looked. He, a white man, dressed like authority, showing up out of nowhere. He realized the folly of his actions in not calling ahead.

"Sorry, fellas," he began. "I'm looking for Calvin."

"You a cop?" the kid said, slowly putting the paintbrush down.

Gramps felt foolish and apologetic. "No. I mean, I was, like thirty years ago." Then quickly, "No one is in trouble. I just want to talk to him. Is he around?"

The boys said nothing. Finally, a voice said, "Mr Levine?"

A head poked out from the screen door. He wore a baseball cap and had a mole on his cheek.

"Calvin," said Gramps.

"You know this old man?" another guy asked. "He said he was police."

"Thirty years ago," Gramps reminded him.

"Guys, it's fine," said Calvin. To Gramps, he said, "I'll meet you out front."

Gramps nodded and turned to go. He said, "Sorry, fellas, I didn't mean to intrude."

The kid from before grabbed a paintbrush. Gramps heard him mumble, "White man shows up outta the blue. Says he used to be a cop. What the hell we supposed to think?"

"Fence looks great," Gramps offered lamely, and then walked through the gate and out the way he came.

Calvin was waiting for him on the front lawn.

"Stewart said we could talk," said Gramps.

Calvin's eyes widened. "What did he tell you?"

"His own story," said Gramps. "And that you might be willing to speak to me about Felicia Beaumont."

Calvin retreated a step. "I can't discuss this. I don't want Billie to know; she'll tell Nicole." Calvin walked toward the yard. Gramps stepped in front of him.

"I wouldn't be here if it wasn't important," Gramps said. "Extremely important."

One of the fraternity brothers reappeared. "Everything OK, Cal?"

Calvin glanced from Gramps to the kid and back to Gramps. Sighing, he hunched his shoulders and said, "Everything is fine, bro. Girl drama."

"With an old man?"

"Yeah," said Calvin impatiently.

"If you say so," said the kid but to his credit, he returned to his buddies.

Gramps said, "I know it may seem weird, but we are professionals. This is our job. Billie will respect your privacy."

Calvin didn't look convinced.

"I'm her supervisor," said Gramps. "I tell her what to do." Not really. Not ever.

Calvin exhaled and, for a second, Gramps thought he might break down. "I'll talk," said Calvin, "but it can't be here."

"Come to my office," said Gramps.

"Nicole said you work out of your dining room."

He rephrased, "Come to my house."

Calvin nodded. "Fine."

Gramps said, "I'm in the book."

Calvin made a confused face.

"You can google my address," Gramps clarified, quickly heading toward the intersection. He did not want Calvin changing his mind. Plus Gramps had parked at an unfed meter because the payment required he download an app. What ever happened to using quarters and dimes?

The crosswalk glowed with approval and Gramps stepped into the street.

At which moment a black sedan rounded the corner and hit him.

CHAPTER SIXTY-FIVE

Billie had been searching *Gunness Academy for Girls alumni* for the better part of an hour when Gramps had called asking if she could check the Levine Investigations email account. Which she did. There was so much spam she could host a luau.

Billie opened and downloaded the attachment June had sent, a file so heavy Billie was surprised her laptop wasn't crying from the weight.

June had included a message: *As requested, the footage from February. There's a lot.*

Billie exhaled, anticipating a slog. The video opened with a tight view of Alan's backdoor patio, more specifically the sliders. She hit fast-forward and stared blearily at her screen while cats, birds, and the elderly neighbor moved in and out of the image. At one point a ball bounced off the glass window, followed by a kid sent to retrieve it.

Finally, on February 20th, a figure skated across the lens, camouflaged by both a moonless night and their black clothing. Their head, of course, covered in a knit hat. Their skin darkened with makeup? A backpack slung over their shoulder. A flashlight shining into shadows.

Alan had died the week before, so whoever this was knew he wouldn't be around to confront them. They also had taken the laptop. So what were they coming back for?

"Killer," Billie whispered to her screen.

The figure shimmied open the sliding glass door and slipped inside. They were gone for ten minutes – Billie noted the time-lapse – before coming back out. The backpack looked no heavier, so what had they taken?

What was so important they had to risk getting caught?

She watched as the thief attempted to lock the door from the outside. Tough to do with a slider as the bolt prevented them from closing it properly. The person struggled, tugging, trying to get the door to lock.

Billie paused the footage, then rewound. She played it again. A second, no, two, then paused.

The thief was holding something inside their gloved hand. An object that glinted in the flashlight beam.

Shiny, like a speck of a gold.

The thief had gone back for her bracelet.

CHAPTER SIXTY-SIX

Gramps saw a blurry man's face hovering over him.

"Mr Levine," said the man.

Another voice: "Is the old guy dead?"

"Conscious."

"Seriously, Cal, if an old white dude dies on our property, we're done for."

"He's not dead, just disoriented. I think."

"You think?!"

Gramps felt cold blades of grass on his cheek. He blinked several times before gingerly propping himself onto his elbows. He glanced at his body. Half of him was on the scraggly patch of lawn that bordered the sidewalk. The other half, his legs, were dangling in the gutter. Cars were now giving him wide berth.

Calvin leaned over and said, "Can you get up? Are you OK? We called an ambulance."

Gramps groaned. "I'm great."

"You know the cops are gonna show up," said the kid from the backyard. "And blame us."

Gramps heard murmuring of confirmation. The fraternity had gathered around him.

"Did he hit his head?" asked the kid, pointing aggressively at Gramps. "He could have a stroke."

There wasn't anything Gramps enjoyed more than a bunch of twenty year-olds arguing over his demise on a public street corner. He tried to stand but found himself woozy. Did he hit his head?

284 MAKE A KILLING

He heard the sirens of emergency vehicles, as recognizable to him as his own face. That's what a decades-long career in law enforcement had given him. Familiarity with crisis.

"Calvin, help me up," he said just as the ambulance pulled over to the curb. A second later, two paramedics jumped out, stretching on latex gloves and carrying medical bags.

One of the Alpha Phi guys hurriedly said, "He got hit by a car. We're helping him."

The other men chimed in.

Gramps began worrying for them. "He's right," he said, his voice strained, phlegmy and a bit garbled. "They're helping." *Helping me remember how fragile I am.*

One of the paramedics sat Gramps on the sidewalk and shone a light into his eyes. He called to his partner and said something about "pupils" and "head trauma."

The police showed up next. Immediately Calvin stiffened. So did his friends.

Luckily Gramps recognized one of the officers. A Black cop from Lodi. Gramps blanked on his name.

"Bill?" the cop said, before gesturing to his partner, a woman. Indian. Hispanic, maybe. Didn't matter. What mattered was that everyone remained calm. Including himself.

"I got sideswiped," Gramps said to the police while his vitals were taken and a stretcher was rolled out.

The fraternity boys all started talking at once.

Hit by a car.

Had nothing to do with it.

Minding our business.

Staining our fence.

Calvin knows him.

Don't throw him under the bus.

Poor choice of words.

"Was he hit by a bus?" asked the Black cop.

"No," said Calvin. "A dark sedan. Fancy. Expensive. An Audi, maybe. Or Volvo."

The cop nodded as he retrieved a notebook from his pocket. His partner said, "Who saw the car that hit Mr Levine?"

Only Calvin's hand raised, but then when he saw Gramps being helped onto the stretcher, he said, "I should go with him. I'm the only one here who knows him."

The female cop nodded, then said, "We'll meet you at Hackensack Medical."

The last thing Gramps saw was the Alpha Phi guys releasing a collective breath as his ass was tucked inside the ambulance, Calvin climbing in after him.

When the doors closed, Gramps said, "Volvo or Audi, huh?"

Calvin frowned. "What?"

"Maybe it's my head, but I'm pretty sure it was a Mercedes that hit me."

Calvin swallowed a lump. "Was it?"

The paramedic took a seat, watching the exchange. "When we get to the ER, we're going to have a nice long conversation."

CHAPTER SIXTY-SEVEN

"What's new since we last spoke?" Vela asked, but it was the way she did so that raised Billie's suspicions. Like she knew the finer details of Billie's life but wanted Billie to be the one to reveal them.

"I'm dealing with conflict," said Billie carefully.

Vela nodded, grabbed a pen, and began jotting down notes. "What kind of conflict?"

Paranoia seeped in. Hedging, she replied, "I had an argument with a friend."

"Nicole?" Vela asked.

"No," said Billie. "The friend's name doesn't matter."

"I see," said Vela, putting down the pen. "Do you think your work causes personal conflicts with friends and loved ones?"

"Yes," Billie replied automatically. "All the time. But in this particular case my conflict is with a colleague."

"You called him a friend."

"I misspoke, and I never said he identified as a male."

"Fair, but I don't think you misspoke. We have talked about this, your inability to trust."

"My profession makes it hard to see the best in humanity," said Billie, a bit defensively. "Every time I think a person might have a modicum of honesty and integrity I'm proven wrong."

"Billie, you know there are good people out there."

Sure. Gramps and Diego. David and even Matty, although

outwardly one would not associate his business dealings with goodness. And yet she shrugged, feeling insolent. Her head bent down, she took interest in the hole in her sock.

Vela said, "Have you ever considered a different profession? The job isn't everything."

Billie jerked up her chin. "The job isn't everything?"

"I take it that's upsetting to you."

"Of course it is. What am I if not a private eye? What else do I do to pay my bills? Be home for my mom?"

"There are other careers," said Vela, gesturing with her pen. "So many work-from-home options."

"Like a corporate gig? Baiting me with a telecommute contract only to switch it out at the last minute? Working for a wealthy prick who's going to nickel and dime me out of overtime to save a few bucks for the bottom line? Or shareholders? No thank you. I do something I'm proud of."

"You just said that your job causes personal conflict. That will heighten anxiety."

"The world makes me anxious!" Billie snapped. "What difference does working in an office make for me? At least as a PI I work for myself."

She then thought of Webber, a prisoner to his debt. Student loans and expensive rent. Coerced into a sexual relationship for dress clothes and professional mobility. Desperate to purchase a cabin in another country so he could live on his terms. Be his own person. Escape his life.

Billie often wanted to escape hers.

She leaned over and grabbed her unlaced boots, tugging them on as Vela protested.

"We need to talk about this, not avoid it."

"I'm done talking," said Billie, stopping only to say, "My job causes problems, but I'm not qualified to do anything else. I'm stuck. Like most people."

"You can change your life," said Vela.

"Not without hurting my family," said Billie as she rose from the couch. She left cash on the table and headed out of the office. Vela sighed loudly behind her.

When she opened the door, Campus Police stood outside with expectant expressions.

"Ms Levine," said one of the cops, a young guy Billie was fairly certain had been in her political science class sophomore year.

"Yeah?"

He stepped toward her. "We're here to escort you off campus."

Vela came up behind her and addressed them. "What's going on?"

"We've been ordered to take Belinda Levine to the front gate."

"Why?" said Vela.

A woman appeared from behind one of the cops. Asian. Young, but in command. "Levine Investigations is overstepping their campus privileges," she said.

"Do you have an order?" Vela asked.

Billie turned to her and raised a brow. Like a court order? What the hell was she talking about?

"Some kind of document that gives you permission to do such a thing," Vela continued.

But Campus Police wasn't having any of that. One of the cops roughly grabbed Billie by the elbow, a move that caused Billie to halt and wrench her arm free. "Get off me!"

The Asian woman said, "Ms Levine is mentally unwell, thus, for campus safety, she will be escorted off the property. With or without cooperation."

Vela darted for the girl, but Billie stopped her, and whispered, "I got this. I'm OK." She put her hand on Vela's shoulder and gently pushed her back inside the office.

Billie grabbed the lackey's wrist. She seemed to enjoy doing Felicia's dirty work. Could she have broken into Alan's apartment? "No bracelet," she hissed.

The girl snatched her arm back. Campus Police then shoved Billie forward. "Move," the cop barked.

She snarled at him.

They drove her to the Hyundai, sirens wailing as if she was a criminal, only to find her car was blocked by another person.

Nicole stood there, arms crossed. "I've been texting you," she said, ignoring the police. "I'll drive."

"What's happening?" Billie asked.

"Your grandfather got hit by a car. He's in the hospital."

CHAPTER SIXTY-EIGHT

Gramps lay on a gurney in the emergency room with curtains drawn around him. He'd had more peace urinating in the Penn Station men's room. He'd been handed a hospital gown, which he politely refused. Instead he took off his shoes and leaned back against rough bedsheets. He'd been seen by several nurses, all young enough to be his granddaughter, and one doctor who uttered few words before ordering a CT scan and then promptly leaving.

Outside Gramps's medical prison, machines beeped. He smelled antiseptic and coffee. He was reminded of his wife's final days in the ICU – a stroke had taken her – and of Ken, his best friend, who had slowly slipped away from a hell of his own making.

Well, that would not be Gramps. He had merely been sideswiped by a car, a Mercedes as he remembered. Recalling the make and model of a car that almost killed him had to count for something. He had his faculties.

So he turned to Calvin, who was sitting in a plastic chair beside the bed, and said, "Your buddies are probably worried about you."

Calvin wiggled his cell phone in the air. "They're actually more concerned about you."

"They asked?"

Calvin nodded and read off the text messages. "How's the white guy doing? Is the white man OK? Dude, please tell me the old dude is alive."

"Well, it's nice to know they care," said Gramps before smacking his lips a few times. "Can you pour me some water?" The pitcher sat on a side table out of Gramps's reach, which seemed like a form of torture for dehydrated patients. Calvin jumped to his feet and poured a cup of ice water, clearly anxious to help in any way. This made Gramps feel cruel for what he was about to ask.

"So, Cal, can I call you, Cal? You wanna talk about what happened with you and Felicia Beaumont?"

Calvin paused, then set down the cup gently. He exhaled, his eyes darting to the partition.

"Thinking of making a run for it?" Gramps asked before taking a sip. The liquid cooled his throat, sharpened his speech. He was a spider plant, hard to kill, that just needed a little watering.

Calvin fell into the chair, leaned over and rested his elbows on his knees. His head dropped.

"You spoke to Stew," Calvin said.

"Were your experiences the same?" Gramps asked. "Did Felicia Beaumont sexually harass you?"

Calvin straightened, his eyes again darting to the space between the curtains. Freedom.

"Listen, Cal, you know I'm not here to judge you. Only to listen. And hopefully to solve the mystery surrounding Alan's death."

"Do you think Felicia Beaumont killed Alan?"

"I'm interested in why you think that," said Gramps. He finished the rest of the water, but held onto the cup, uneasy about losing the only thing saving him from turning into a raisin. "Is she capable of murder?"

Calvin exhaled. "Nicole and Billie are going to be here any minute."

"So talk fast," said Gramps. "I'm not going anywhere."

Calvin nodded, drew himself up. "I got promoted this year," he began. "You want to know how?" He stared at Gramps and blinked several times before adding, "I was drugged."

CHAPTER SIXTY-NINE

Billie got signed into the emergency room and directed to Gramps's bed, but she was already flying down the hall. She only stopped when she heard Matty call. He was poking out from behind a curtain.

She halted and caught her breath, then slipped inside a little claustrophobic space.

Gramps stuck a thumb at Matty and said, "Your brother got a flat tire, so he sent *him*."

Billie went over and kissed the top of her grandfather's head. His hair, thinning and white as bone, stuck up in different directions. Billie wanted to ask if he had been electrocuted rather than hit by a car, if just to make him laugh. "Since you got run over, we're going to ignore your rudeness," she told him.

"I was kidding," said Gramps, even though he wasn't.

Matty began walking backwards. "I'm going to hit up a vending machine. Want anything?"

Billie shook her head, but Gramps said, "A Corona."

"You're not at Club Med," said Billie. "How hard did you hit your head?"

Matty chuckled as he parted the curtain, leaving Billie and her grandfather alone.

Gramps gripped her sleeve. "What kind of car does Felicia Beaumont drive?"

"I don't know," said Billie.

"Can you find out?"

"You think she ran you over?"

"*Tried* to run me over," he said. "I'm fine. They're just being cautious."

"You're an old man. You fall in the shower, it's a medical emergency. You get hit by a car? You're here for a few days."

"Very funny," he shot back. "You think I like how often you remind me that I'm old? I've been doing this job for decades, longer than you've been alive. I've been shot at, stabbed and, one time, I'm not proud of it, left naked in a hotel room, handcuffed to a bed frame."

"I don't even wanna know–"

"The point is, yes, I got sideswiped. But I'm fine. I'm not feeble. I'm capable. I'm just…not young. Enough with the old man jokes."

"Jesus. What hit you in the head? Oh right, the asphalt." Billie fell into the empty visitor chair and exhaled. At some point, the exhaustion in her body had made contact with her brain. She closed her eyes for the briefest of seconds and patted her grandfather's hand. "For Dr Beaumont to try and take you out, she'd need to be following you."

"She could've been," he said.

"I don't know," said Billie. "Doesn't seem likely. She'd have to sit on you for a while. The woman is busy being evil. I'm not sure–"

"I was right near campus," said Gramps, growing defensive. "She could've spotted me and seized an opportunity."

"Maybe," said Billie, relenting. "I can guess why you went to Calvin's fraternity house, but are you going to tell me what actually happened with him? What did he say?"

To that, Gramps shook his head.

Billie shifted in the chair. "You're not going to tell me here? Or at all?"

"He asked me not to, Billie."

She leaned forward and whispered, "We're partners. Colleagues. I need to know what you know."

"Not this time. Or at least not yet. Let him talk to Nicole first. Let him tell you on his terms."

Billie sighed, a noise of exasperation she refused to tamp down.

The curtains opened and David entered, a little out of breath. "Did Dr Simon see you? Or was it Kasper? What nurse is on shift?" He glanced at the whiteboard. "Kaylee? I don't know her."

"You don't work here. Of course you don't know her," Billie said, standing up so her brother could take the seat. "I'm going to the lobby so I can check in with Nicole." She gave her grandfather a look; he gave her a look back. David made a face at both of them.

When Billie went into the waiting room she spied Matty sitting in reception, scrolling through his phone. "Where's Nic?" she asked him.

"Outside," he said, without looking up, "but I don't think you want to–"

Billie headed outdoors but halted at a cement column. She saw Nicole and Calvin standing ten feet away, engaged in an argument. Billie ducked down by a shrub and pretended to tie her shoe.

"You're so secretive," Nicole said. "Ever since the promotion. You won't talk to me."

"There's a lot going on," said Calvin.

"Like what?" Nicole's voice came out pleading. "Tell me. Are you stressed? Is it your new boss?"

"It's nothing," he said. "Only stress, like you said."

"I don't believe you. Tammy thinks–"

"You're talking to Tammy about me? She's a gossip!"

"She's a friend." A beat. "She said you've been having private dinners with Dr Beaumont. Is that true?"

"No," he said, but the response was weak. As if Calvin was out of ammo.

"Are you sleeping with Dr Beaumont?"

Calvin said nothing.

Nicole went off. "That's it, isn't it? She's a raging bitch who has ruined the college, and that's who you chose to have sex with?!"

Again, Calvin said nothing.

Billie rose to her feet, ready to duck inside, when she saw Nicole slap her vintage Coach bag against the hospital's exterior. "You know what? I don't even blame you. It's me. I attract assholes! Personal flaw. Won't make the mistake again." Nicole turned and yelled, "Billie, I know you're listening. I'm taking an Uber home!"

Calvin swallowed a lump and reached for Nicole but she was already several feet ahead, walking with the determination of a high-speed train.

Billie knew that Nicole had the wrong idea so she ran after her, while calling to Calvin, "I'll talk to her!"

But Nic was not having it. "Go away, Billie!"

They were nearly at the parking deck when Billie grabbed her friend's coat hem, essentially forcing them both to a stop, otherwise risk tearing the fabric lining. And if Nicole didn't end their friendship over Billie's eavesdropping, she would certainly excommunicate her if she ruined vintage Chanel.

"Please, Nic, let's discuss this."

"Why?" Nicole snapped. "You want insider info again?"

"You're not being fair," said Billie.

Nicole whipped around. "I'm not?!"

"OK, you are, but let's have a discussion rather than a fight."

Nicole gestured wildly with her handbag. "Maybe I want to fight instead of quietly letting you and everyone else walk all over me."

Oof. Billie deserved that. So much of her relationship with Nicole teetered on Billie's selfish behavior. What kind of friend listened in on her bestie's breakup simply to glean information? Answer: a shitty person. "I'm sorry I was eavesdropping."

"You're sorry because you got caught," said Nicole.

"No, I'm sorry I did it. I was worried, but that's not an excuse."

An ambulance drove past – no sirens, no emergency – but the moment gave Nicole some space. "He's cheating on me," she said, finally.

"I don't think that's what this is," said Billie.

"Then what is it?"

"Dr Beaumont has a history of sexual harassment," said Billie. "It's possible that Calvin is – was – a target, but I don't know for certain. He spoke to Gramps, not me. I think that explains his distance. But, again, I'm not super certain."

"Ha," said Nicole bitterly. "First time Billie Levine doesn't know something."

Billie replied softly, "I don't know a lot of things."

Nicole stared at her for a beat, then blinked rapidly. Tears began sliding down her cheeks. She vigorously wiped them away, leaving a smear of makeup on her skin. "I gotta go home. I'm not about to have a breakdown in a fucking parking garage."

"I'll drive you," said Billie.

"No," said Nicole, holding up the phone. "Uber is here. I want to be alone anyway." She brushed past Billie before retreating a step and grabbing Billie's hand, giving it a tight squeeze.

That would have to be enough for now.

CHAPTER SEVENTY

The next morning Billie awoke to her cell phone ringing, startling her from a sleep so deep she managed to whack her hand against the nightstand and drop her glasses, thus ensuring she would fall out of bed. Somehow, she landed next to her phone.

"Hello. Hello."

"Billie?"

"Oh, Morales." She huffed, then patted around for her glasses, which she located inside her Doc Marten, next to a dirty sock. "What time is it?"

"Seven."

"Early."

"I'm sorry, but did you not show up at my door before dawn with a bag of urine?"

"Not a bag, a cup of urine." She brought her knees to her chest and noted the dust bunnies rolling beneath her bed like tumbleweeds.

Gramps was still in the hospital, to his horror but Billie's relief. She was still pissed at him for freezing her out. Working for – no, *with* – her grandfather had its challenges. For example, he seemed to make up rules that he failed to disclose. Luckily, David had slept over to ensure Billie got a decent rest and that their mother didn't decide to suddenly roast a chicken in the middle of the night.

She'd deal with Gramps later.

Morales said, "I figured this was news you'd want to be woken up for, since you're doing undercover work at VHG."

She hadn't even told him that. Detectives gonna detect. "I *was* undercover. No longer, but go on," she said.

"I'm sure you know but since Hudson County doesn't have its own medical examiner's office, they use Bergen County's."

"Yes. I did know that." She didn't.

"Anyway, the word is Heath Vickery drowned."

"OK." Billie gave that some thought. "Not gonna lie, was hoping for something a little more salacious."

"I'm not done. He died with tadalafil in his system: a vasodilator."

"A vasodilator?"

"Erectile dysfunction med, Billie."

She scrambled to her feet. "No way. Heath was self-proclaimed straight edge. That's why he was impotent – because he wouldn't take anything to fix it."

You're bait, Billie.

"Well, he had it in his system. So either he was a hypocrite who took the drug willingly, or he was–"

"Unknowingly fed the medication," she finished.

Morales said, "There's something else."

"Really?"

"He also had gamma-hydroxybutyrate in his toxicology report."

Billie gasped. "GHB."

"Ding, ding, ding."

Billie began to pace around her room. "This doesn't make sense. The ED meds make it seem like Katherine Von Holm was involved."

"Well," said Morales. "Slipping boner pills into someone's drink isn't the same as slipping GHB."

"But GHB is Brianne Druffner's MO."

"Speaking of, the urine you had me test did come back positive for roofies. Your instincts were right."

"Diego was at that party, so was Brianne. Could she have also drugged Heath?"

"Why?" Morales asked. "I don't see the connection."

"Honestly, me neither. But you'll bring her in for questioning, right?" Billie asked.

"I can bring her in for Diego," said Morales.

"Great–"

"As long as he comes in to give a statement first. Let's do this in the order nature intended."

"I'll call him right now." She was about to hang up when a thought occurred to her. "What if she's gotten wind? What if she destroys evidence?"

"I don't know what to tell you, Billie. This is a tricky case. Without proof...well, you know the struggle."

"Proof," she whispered. "Right."

"Billie," Morales warned, but by the time he had finished his thought, she had dropped the phone in favor of getting dressed and getting her ass to Zeta Omega.

CHAPTER SEVENTY-ONE

Billie knocked on the Zeta Omega door but she might as well have been knocking on the lid of a coffin, the good it did her. No one was home. Spring break had officially begun, and the Zeta Omega girls were likely on a flight out of Newark, heading toward Cancun.

Billie didn't really require their presence anyway. She took out her lock picking kit and set to work. Gramps might shit on her methods but they got the job done.

Billie was in.

She stumbled over the threshold, tripped by a bunched rug. She cursed the sorority girls then shut the door behind her. A dirty coffee cup sat on the table near the television. Curious, she picked it up and sniffed. Still fresh. Either they didn't clean up before they left or someone stayed behind.

Billie stilled her breathing, trying to discern the noises of the living, but heard nothing other than the settling of an old home.

She decided to make quick work and headed upstairs. Brianne had drugged Diego, and maybe Heath, so if Billie wanted evidence she expected to find it among Brianne's possessions. Locating her bedroom was easy, as the sorority sisters labeled their doors with their names in pink wooden letters.

Brianne's space, like much of the sorority house, was dirty. Carpet that had never seen a vacuum. Dust that had seeped into the furniture now merged with the varnish. The bed hadn't been made; clothes were flung about, sweatshirts lobbed into corners.

Billie rummaged around the top drawer of the nightstand, cradling a stupid hope that she would stumble upon a bottle that said Date Rape Drug in bubbly letters.

Billie then opened dresser drawers, fumbling over numerous pairs of underwear. She went to the closet and found upturned shoe boxes. Sandals. Heels. She stuck her hand into boots – nothing.

There seemed to be an awful lot of summer clothes left behind for a girl who had jetted off to Riviera Maya–

"What are you doing in my room?"

Billie whirled around. Brianne stood in the open doorframe with crossed arms. She was wearing a Kentwell hoodie in the college's signature colors. Brianne had hopped from one school to another, eager to assimilate. Becoming an ambassador, joining Greek Life. She was a parasitic woman; her only goal was a complete and utter corruption of the host.

As a response, Billie flopped onto Brianne's bed. The springs bounced beneath her ass. *Unsettle her.*

"I know you drugged Diego," said Billie. "And B-T-dubs, so does the Bergen County Detectives Bureau."

"What are you talking about?" said Brianne. "If anyone is getting in trouble with the stupid cops it's you, for breaking into our house." But she spoke with false bravado. A sheen had erupted along her hairline. Stress sweat? Billie hoped so.

Billie languished on the comforter, reveling in her boots touching the ruffles of the bedspread. "Call the cops. I dare you. And while they're speaking to me, I'll let them know that you were kicked out of your previous college for drugging frat boys. Washington and Franklin didn't nail you for sexual assault but the Bergen boys will."

Brianne swallowed a lump. When she spoke, her voice came out gravelly, raw. "What do you want?"

Billie sat up. Play ball. "I want to know your connection to Heath Vickery."

Brianne paled. "Heath Vickery? Nothing."

"Did you slip him GHB?"

"No."

"You're tight with Dr Beaumont," Billie said. "And she and Katherine Van Holm are besties. After all, you're Gunness alumni and you girls stick together. Isn't that right? Isn't that why you're a Kentwell junior now? Because Felicia got you enrolled as a legacy admission."

"So?" Brianne's voice hitched.

Billie got to her feet and, as she did, Brianne took a step back. "I did some digging. You got kicked out of your Connecticut high school too. Felicia got you into Gunness."

"She's my godmother."

"Almost like a fairy godmother. She really creates miracles for you. You've fucked up a lot, and she keeps bailing you out. I couldn't think why, unless she doesn't see what you're doing as wrong."

Brianne charged forward, but stopped at the sight of Billie's Taser. She paused and cracked her neck. "I don't do anything men don't do. And I'm not doing anything they don't want me to do."

"It's sexual assault," said Billie, disgusted. "They can't consent when they're drugged."

Brianne hissed, "It's not assault when they're into it."

"Consent means–" Billie began.

Brianne cut her off. "You don't see them flirt with me at parties. Offer to buy me a beer, or pay the cover charge at the Phi Sig house. Stick their tongue down my throat in a dark corner before they pull me into the bathroom and unzip their pants for a blowjob. And you know what? I give them that blowjob. Willingly. I consent. And then they slip out the door, move on to the next girl. Their mistake is thinking that they can take and not give. That they can hold out." Then she whispered, "I want what they promised, and if they won't give it to me, then I'll take it." She huffed, the sound nearly a laugh. "And they say women are teases."

Billie shuddered as she held out her Taser and maneuvered around Brianne, backing her way toward the door. Brianne was sick, and Billie felt gross having listened to the girl's horrifying defense. "I've met a lot of sociopaths in my line of work, but you really win the award for Best Nut Job. Congratulations. There were a ton of great nominees." Billie then turned and ran.

She was halfway down the steps when she felt a shift change in the air. A shadow coasted over her, like an albatross in flight, and then a body slammed into her back. She and Brianne rolled down the remaining stairs. The Taser had long left her grasp. Billie's cheek slammed against the hardwood. She shifted onto her back and blinked painfully at the ceiling. "Fuck." Brianne then straddled her stomach and squeezed Billie's neck. "Bitch! You're not going to pin this shit on me."

Bucking her hips proved useless as Brianne had twenty pounds on her side. Billie wasn't able to catch her breath from the fall.

She twisted abruptly, forcing Brianne off-kilter. Brianne loosened her grip, giving Billie a chance to turn on her stomach. Which was a bad move as Brianne settled on her back and started pummeling her head.

The blows landed hard as knuckles slammed into the base of her skull. Billie tried to protect herself with her hands but then Brianne grabbed a finger and started pulling.

Billie screamed.

The front door flew open, and suddenly the pain stopped. Billie heard the hiss of a spray and a woman's voice yell, "Stay down!"

Tasha Nichols to the rescue.

Brianne was coughing, likely choking on air. Billie caught a whiff. Pepper spray. The hairs inside her nostrils burned as if someone had started a forest fire inside her nasal passages. Brianne must've been feeling the same way because she was screaming and hacking. Billie army-crawled out the front door and kept going until she was safely under the protection of a boxwood bush.

Brianne flung herself onto the grass. Snot ran down her chin.

Tasha stood over both of them, looking scared but also really proud of herself. She helped Billie to her feet.

"Thank you," said Billie.

"You're welcome," said Tasha, tugging off the face mask she was wearing for protection.

Brianne vomited into the grass. Her cell phone, miraculously unscathed, was in her grip, her thumb dancing over the screen. "I called Campus Police. They're gonna arrest both of you and kick you out of school, Nichols."

Billie grabbed onto the fur lining of Tasha's coat. "We should go."

"Brianne, you bitch!" cried Tasha, as Billie was tugging her along without much resistance. "Bitch!"

When they were firmly a quarter mile from the campus boundary, Billie fell against a small tree.

"Girl has Campus Police in her pocket," said Tasha. "And apparently on speed dial."

"Because Felicia has them in *her* pocket," said Billie, regaining her strength. "But she'll get her comeuppance. Detective Morales is going to bring her in once Diego gives a statement."

Tasha scoffed. "*If* he gives a statement."

"He will."

"Felicia Beaumont has hurt a lot of men in her life, but she's still around. I'll tell you this though: her days are numbered."

"Be careful with how you talk. That sounds like a threat," said Billie.

"A promise." Tasha looked hardened. Brianne brought out a ferocity that Tasha's other pet projects never did.

"How did you know I'd be there?" Billie asked.

"I didn't," said Tasha. "I'd been staking out the house since the rest of the girls left for Cancun. Figured that if Brianne was going to strike she'd do so when there were no witnesses, and I could catch her drugging some poor guy and record it all. I just happened to have my eye on the place when you showed up."

"You're such a yenta," said Billie, "and I'm so grateful."

"Speaking of yentas, why were you there?" asked Tasha.

Exhaling, Billie started walking in the direction where she had left her car. "I wanted to ask her about Heath Vickery."

"The charity dude?" Tasha said.

"Sure, the charity dude. Anyway, he died. Was killed. Not sure if you saw it in the news. But he had GHB in his system. I thought maybe she killed Alan, and then I don't know…I'm not sure I've forged the connection yet."

"Well, I can tell you that she didn't kill Alan," said Tasha.

Billie halted abruptly. "How do you know?"

"Alan died on February 13th, right? There was a fundraising event on campus for a boarding school. A scholarship thing. Anyway, she was there. So was I."

"Gunness Academy for Girls?"

"Yes," said Tasha.

"Alan was run off the road. Is it possible she left the event? Dyckman Hill isn't that far. She could've followed him there."

Tasha shook her head. "I had eyes on her."

"The whole time? Are you sure?"

"I'm positive. I've been suspicious of Brianne Druffner since she set foot on campus. I watched her; I watched her like she stole money from me. She didn't leave that event."

"Well then," said Billie. "Do you know who did leave?"

"Felicia Beaumont stepped out for a bit," said Tasha. "But so did Katherine Von Holm. I remember because their names were called to give a toast and they were missing. They held off on the champagne for thirty minutes."

As they were in distance of her car, Tasha grabbed Billie's arm and squeezed.

"What?" said Billie.

Tasha pointed. They inched closer. Someone had spray painted *TRAITOR* on her back windshield.

"Motherfucker," said Billie with a groan. "Does glass insurance cover vandalism caused by a psychotic bitch? Also, traitor to what? What does that even mean?" She stomped around the vehicle, assessing damage. "Am I traitor to Kentwell?"

"Brianne couldn't have done this," said Tasha. "How would she know you were here? You surprised her at the house, right?"

"Yeah." Billie threw her hands up in the air. "God! Well, if not Brianne, then who did this?"

Tasha just shrugged. "You have enemies I don't know about?" Billie said nothing so Tasha answered her own question. "Of course, you do."

CHAPTER SEVENTY-TWO

Billie drove her *TRAITOR*-mobile to pick up Nicole outside her condo.

Billie had been trying to remove the spray paint with an ice scraper when Nicole had called asking for a ride.

"I'm kinda busy with a bunch of murders," said Billie.

"It's Ernie," said Nicole, curt. "He asked me to return some stuff he left on campus. I wanna know why he was fired, and I want you to come along. For moral support. You owe me this."

Since Billie owed her friend way more than a ride, this favor no longer seemed inconvenient. "I'll be right there," said Billie.

Ernie and his wife lived in a first-floor rental in Little Ferry. A starter apartment for most, in this case a finisher. The unit was nestled in a courtyard with weeds creeping between cement blocks. Dead potted plants slowly began their rebloom. Gutters ended in puddles of rainwater.

Nicole, carrying the box of Ernie's things, nearly tripped over a red stone walkway that had been pushed up haphazardly from unseen tree roots.

"Guess they downsized," she said with a frown.

Ernie had agreed to welcome them, seeing as they were bringing him his chef knives, but with a caveat: they come after his wife left to volunteer at Hackensack Medical.

The wife could entertain Gramps, thought Billie.

Nicole readily agreed, although Billie had to wonder what Ernie didn't want his wife to overhear. After a half-century of marriage, Billie would've thought nothing was sacred. Then again, what would she ever know of a relationship lasting longer than six months?

Ernie welcomed them inside, but not before pointing to the shoe rack and asking them to remove their footwear. "Wife hates the dirt."

Neither Billie nor Nicole minded, even if it took Billie an awkward minute to untie her boots.

The girls were led into a small dining room with a plate of cookies on the table. Billie smelled coffee brewing. "How do you take it?" he asked.

"Sugar and milk," said Nicole at the same time Billie said, "None for me." After Nicole shot her a look, Billie hissed, "I had some this morning."

"I have hot water for tea," said Ernie from the kitchen.

"Yes, please," Billie replied.

Ernie was a tall, Black man with cropped salt-and-pepper hair, and sloping broad shoulders. He was likely a defensive tackle in his youth. His hospitality seemed second nature, which made sense seeing as how he had been a trained cook for his whole life.

Billie felt like precious company and she could see how this man had been a beloved Kentwell fixture. Only fixtures lasted. Not chewed up and spat out by the same people who claimed to value loyalty.

Billie reached for her notepad but was stopped by Nicole's subtle shake of her head. *If we want honesty and openness this can't look like a transaction. Can't look like business.*

Nicole cleared her throat. "Ernie, you've really been missed."

"Have I?" Ernie fussed with the creamer and sugar. He got up from the table to retrieve napkins.

"Of course," said Nicole, shifting awkwardly in her seat. "The faculty are complaining. The new chef doesn't have your creativity."

"I'm sure he's a fine replacement."

Nicole slouched, the fight leaking out of her like helium. She straightened as Ernie returned to the table and pushed the plate of cookies toward them.

"Can't thank you enough for bringing my knives," he said.

"Not a problem," Nicole said. "It's a nice excuse for a visit."

"I hated to trouble you," Ernie continued, practically dismissing Nicole's response as false niceties. "But I can't return."

That gave Billie pause. She frowned. "The administration won't let you back on campus?"

"*She* won't let me back," said Ernie.

"Dr Beaumont?" asked Nicole.

Ernie nodded. "Roger was supposed to drop my stuff off, but she canned him too."

"She fired Roger?" Nicole then mouthed "sous chef" to Billie.

"What happened, Ernie? You were months away from a retirement party. Do you know why you were dismissed?"

"*I* know why, but Beaumont will say something different."

"We want to hear the truth, from you," said Nicole.

"Well," said Ernie, "as the head chef, I'd been in charge of the faculty restaurant for twenty years. Dr Beaumont became president and organized a few private dinners. Not unusual, right? Dr Stein used to do the same thing. A visiting professor came, and we'd close the space for them. But Beaumont's private dinners were different." He stopped talking, spaced out for a second.

"Different how?" Billie asked, bringing him back.

"These weren't visiting professors or basketball coaches the school was trying to poach. These were young men."

"Students?" said Nicole.

Ernie shook his head. "Employees."

"Professors?"

"One. But mostly staff. Office workers."

"You said they were young," Billie began.

"Gotta understand everyone is young to me, but these men were far younger than Beaumont, you know?"

Billie sensed what Ernie was getting at, even if Nicole didn't. She tensed, waiting for Nicole to pick up on his cues. "These weren't professional dinners, were they?"

Ernie brought the teacup to his lips, but his hands trembled slightly. He set it back down without taking a sip. "She'd keep one girl as waitstaff. Then send me home before dessert."

"How often did that happen?" Billie said.

"A few times."

"And then what happened? What was the final straw?"

"You mean what did I see to get myself fired?" Ernie said.

Nicole and Billie nodded solemnly.

"I stayed late. She had told me to go home, but I hate leaving the kitchen without a final scrub down. So I stayed behind, and I saw what happened to the young man she was with." There was a sigh, a wobble to his voice. "He left with her, but he was sloshed out of his mind."

"Did he drink a lot at dinner?" Nicole asked.

"That's the thing," said Ernie. "He was served one beer."

"What did you do next?"

"I went out there. He was leaning on her, she was cooing in his ear. Saw he could barely stand, so I said I'll call a cab or contact the Safety Brigade."

"And did you?" Nicole asked, and Billie spied the desperation in her voice, the hopefulness that yes, Ernie did call someone.

He nodded, and Nicole visibly relaxed.

"That's the thing, though. I think I saved that one man, but not the others."

"Others?" Nicole whispered.

Billie cut in, "Can you describe any of these men?"

Ernie's gaze darted to Nicole. "One was Asian. A teaching assistant."

The nausea climbed Billie's throat.

"Another was your fella, Nicole. Calvin."

Nicole said, "He was being sexually harassed by Beaumont. Is that what you suspected?"

"I don't mean to sound harsh, especially since you kindly brought me my knives, but that's not what I would call simple harassment, and that was not what I suspected," he said. "I'm telling you that Calvin's a victim of whatever she put in his drink. When he left the restaurant he could barely stand. And he was only served one beer." He ran a hand over his chin. Billie understood now why he didn't want his wife home. He didn't want her to know that he hadn't done anything to stop Dr Beaumont. Billie didn't place any blame on Ernie. How could she? Ernie, however, blamed himself.

"I don't think Calvin was simply a victim of unwanted attention," Ernie said. "I think she raped him."

"Raped?" Nic said, clearly stunned.

"Yeah," said Ernie. "The college girls are always telling each other to protect their drinks. Well, in this instance, it got to the men too. He couldn't say no."

Nicole bolted from the chair. She fumbled for her purse and grabbed her shoes. She hadn't even properly slipped them on before she ran outside.

Billie made her apologies to Ernie and chased after her.

CHAPTER SEVENTY-THREE

Nicole rushed out of the apartment. Billie found her in the parking lot, circling the Hyundai like a Great White.

"Let's go," she said.

"Where?" said Billie.

"Kentwell. No, Calvin's place. No, Beaumont's. I want to murder her."

"And do what, Nic? You gonna confront her? Call Campus Police?"

"Maybe I will!"

"On the fucking college president?! Campus Police does her bidding. We need to stop and think." Billie was yelling now, attracting attention from an old woman who had just parked her Acura in a numbered spot.

Nicole threw up her hands. "Call Morales then, or Malley. God, you know enough cops."

"We'll get her. I promise."

Nicole kept pacing. "I knew she was a shady-ass woman. And here I was thinking she was just coming onto him. Flirting and making him uncomfortable. Bitch." She slammed her purse against the truck of the car. "Bitch!" Slam. "Bitch!" Slam.

Billie grabbed the strap, essentially stopping the onslaught.

Nicole stopped, leaned against the bumper, and collapsed. Billie joined her on the ground. Purses beside them. The car keys nestled against the tire.

A numbness settled over them.

Nicole leaned her head on Billie's shoulder.

"I accused him of cheating," said Nicole with a whimper. "It never occurred to me that he could've been...That the president of the goddamn college could..." her voice trailed. She couldn't say the word, the entire ordeal too horrible to consider.

As women, date rape was a shadow lurking over their shoulders on every outing. Entrusting their drinks to friends rather than strangers. Code words and signals. Horror stories as warnings. Bathroom stall scribblings reminding them to stay vigilant. Avoid creeps from these dorms/fraternities/classes. Doing everything right and it still not mattering. The shame that followed.

"I gotta talk to him," said Nicole.

"Maybe you should wait," said Billie.

"Don't say until I calm down."

"Okay, maybe you should wait until–"

But she didn't have time to finish. Ernie found them then, legs splayed, teary-eyed, and exhausted. He was carrying the box that Nicole had brought. He seemed trepidatious and slightly out of breath.

"Look what I found." He hefted up the box.

The girls slowly rose to their feet while Ernie plucked a beer bottle from inside.

"What's that?" Nicole asked, exhausted.

"Proof, maybe." He patted the cardboard top. "Roger packed up this box for me but he was fired before he could retrieve it and bring it over. He was escorted out by security, only allowed to take framed photos and the like. Anyway, this beer bottle is important."

Billie stepped closer, examining the brown glass in the emerging sunshine. There at the bottom was a bit of remaining liquid. The top had been taped closed, preventing the liquid from evaporating.

"Important how?" Billie asked.

"This brand of beer is special to Dr Beaumont. She brings it in. Some kind of IPA, brewed by a friend of hers, I think. We don't serve it on campus. She brings it in special."

Nicole looked at Billie who looked at Ernie. "This is the beer she puts drugs in."

Ernie nodded.

"You think that's enough?" Nicole asked.

"I'll call Morales," said Billie.

CHAPTER SEVENTY-FOUR

Later that evening, Billie stood outside Jeremy's door, her fist poised for a knock, but found herself incapable of announcing her presence.

She expected Jeremy to be angry with her; she worried more that he wouldn't be. That he wouldn't care about Billie's apology because he didn't care about her opinion.

She also worried she hadn't just enraged Jeremy, which had always been fairly easy to do. She was sick to her stomach that she had cut him so deep that he'd decided to exorcise her from his life. That feeling of guilt and shame lingering inside her body made her feel like she was about to jump off a cliff with no safety net. She felt like she was heading toward her doom.

And yet she knocked.

There were several moments of silence before she heard footsteps, then the peephole cover sliding over, before the agonizing minute of Jeremy fussing with the locks. When the door opened to reveal him standing there in unwashed sweats, his hair flat and unkempt, his eyes bloodshot and lifeless, Billie realized she would kill a man if it meant receiving Jeremy's beleaguered sigh of irritation at her showing up unannounced. For a split second she thought he was going to close the door in her face but, instead, he turned and walked away, leaving her to linger in the hallway like an unwanted kitchen odor.

She followed him inside, gently shut the door, and prepared to grovel. But the minute he turned around he looked so broken and small that all her words were forgotten. Instead, she took three large steps toward him, opened up her arms and enveloped him in a hug.

To Jeremy's credit, he did not reciprocate until she whimpered, "I fucked up, and I'm so sorry." She felt his body relax, his arms wrap around her back, and his chin rest comfortably on her shoulder.

Then he said, "You fucking should be."

A sound emanated from her, a mixture of a sob and laugh, that startled even him. "You eat something weird in your car again?"

When she pulled away, she realized she had been crying, and Jeremy seemed like he'd been on the verge of tears. She'd take that.

This was a moment. She was trying so hard to be firmly present, when all she wanted to do was snap a picture so she could relive it later.

The awkwardness eventually found them and they stepped farther apart. Jeremy opened the fridge and located two bottles of water. He tossed one to her over the half-wall that separated the kitchen from the living room. She caught it and said, "I spoke to Ernie, you know the chef at the faculty restaurant?"

Jeremy paused, the bottle halfway to his mouth. "He corroborated Calvin's story?"

"He did," said Billie. "He also mentioned seeing you in the faculty restaurant...with Dr Beaumont." She let that linger in the air. "Do you want to tell me what happened? You don't have to, obviously. Just know that I'm here for you."

Jeremy scoffed.

Moment ruined. She had ruined it.

"What?" she said.

"You're not here for me," he said. "You're here because you want a story. You want to know what I know."

"That's not true," she said, getting angry and defensive. "I care about you, asshole. I hate caring about you. You're mean and a dick, and yet I fucking care about you. So much.

It bothers me how much I care about you. And if a power-hungry college president..." she let that hang.

"Except she didn't," said Jeremy softly.

"What are you talking about? She sexually harassed Stew. She raped Calvin."

"And I slept with her, willingly."

"Under duress."

"No," he said firmly. Then, "Maybe. I don't know."

"She's a powerful woman. Webber didn't think he could say no to Katherine. Maybe you didn't feel like you could say no either. She controls the purse strings. Your ability to go to Spain and finish your doctorate. She controls your teaching assignments. She controls everything. No one would blame you."

"I blame me!" he snapped. "She didn't drug me. We had dinner at the faculty restaurant. She made me feel special, important. Told me she could ensure my Spain funding, get me out from under Dr Finkel. She even suggested I could get a full-time faculty position after I finished my doctorate." His voice grew soft. "I went home with her."

"She took advantage of you," said Billie. "You're the victim here."

"Don't you see? I don't feel like a victim. Calvin is a victim. Stew, a victim." He pointed to his chest. "Jeremy, not anything resembling a victim."

"That isn't true," said Billie.

"Let's agree to disagree," Jeremy said softly.

"Is that why you didn't want June's case?" said Billie. "Because you felt guilty?"

"I could barely look June in the eye. Couldn't imagine telling her that I would look into Alan's death knowing what I knew. And I was so sure Felicia was not responsible for his accident. She'd been at that school fundraiser. We all were there." He stared into the distance and Billie could see him pulling a memory into the foreground. "Alan and I had this big fight before he died. He wanted to write an exposé and use me as a source. I told him no. I told him what I just told you. You should've seen the look he gave me."

Billie moved so she was directly in front of Jeremy. She put her hands on his shoulders and forced him to look at her. "Listen, you're not responsible for what happened to Alan. Felicia Beaumont is, I'm almost certain. There was time unaccounted for. Time where Felicia and Katherine were nowhere to be found. So if we want to honor Alan's memory, we need to take her ass down. Morales is helping."

"Morales is no match for her lawyers."

"He's a detective. Lawyers aren't uncharted territory for him," she said.

Billie then flopped onto the couch and brought Jeremy down with her, his feet now resting on the coffee table. Their breathing grew quiet as their heartbeats connected in rhythm.

"And to think this all started because Celeste had an asthma attack," said Jeremy.

"And to think if Alan hadn't embarked on a personal vendetta there would be a lot more men abused in Beaumont's wake," said Billie.

Jeremy's voice shook as he said, "Yeah. You're right. Also I won't make a habit of saying that."

"God forbid you lay a compliment at my feet," said Billie with an awkward laugh. She felt simultaneously at ease and anxious with Jeremy. There was a fluttering in her stomach that unsettled her nerves. She did not like it. She did not *not* like it.

She shifted awkwardly and grimaced. Her back was sore from Brianne Druffner tackling her on the stairs.

"Hurt?" Jeremy asked.

"Bruised," said Billie.

"I'll get you an ice pack," said Jeremy, as he motioned to get up. But Billie tugged him back onto the couch. "There's no swelling. Just discomfort. Nothing that won't heal."

Jeremy nodded, then sighed. Billie could tell that he was repressing a confession of sorts. Some admission rested on the tip of his tongue that he was trying to swallow down.

"Just say it," said Billie. She expected him to tell her to leave. That he was OK now, and she was free to go.

He said, "Don't tell Nicole about what happened with me and Beaumont."

"All right," said Billie. Jeremy didn't look convinced and the doubt on his face ate away at her heart. "I won't," she said again, and she meant it. Nicole had said that she was going to meet Calvin at his apartment to talk things over. Billie couldn't bear to imagine the conversation they were having right now.

"I'm ashamed," Jeremy said, holding up a hand as if to silence Billie's protest. A protest she hadn't made.

"Feel your feelings," is all she replied. "But you have nothing to feel ashamed about." Billie squirmed on the couch. She might've bruised her ass too. "This is nice," she said. "Us being friends."

"Is that what we are now?" Jeremy asked, but his voice sounded soft and low.

Billie shivered. "Well, we're not enemies."

"Day isn't over," he said, facing her, his cheek resting on the couch cushion.

"That's true." She glanced back at him. "I'm sure I'll do something to piss you off."

"I typically count on it," he said, his voice still soft. The exasperation nowhere to be found.

Two inches. If she just moved two inches closer, she'd–

Billie's phone began to ring.

CHAPTER SEVENTY-FIVE

"I'm putting you on speaker," said Billie.

"Why?" said Celeste.

Jeremy shook his head, the universal signal for *don't tell her I'm listening*. Billie replied, "Uh, because I'm cooking."

"Oh, OK," said Celeste. "How are things going with my cousin's case?"

"Great," said Billie. "I'm sure you'll be happy to know I've nearly nailed Brianne's ass to the wall."

"That *is* great," said Celeste. "Actually I'm calling with good news. Maybe something that will help you. Help us, I mean."

Jeremy leaned forward, his brows raised in a hopeful manner.

"Let's hear it," said Billie. Then, realizing, she said, "*Me*. Let me hear it."

Jeremy gave her a look.

Celeste said, "A friend sent me this video that I think you'll be interested in. They follow an account for a guy, a kid really, who does weird cycling challenges and posts the videos to YouTube."

Billie's stomach wobbled a little. "Really?" she said.

"Yeah," said Celeste. "I'm going to text you the link. My friend thinks this was filmed at Dyckman Hill by the Englewood Boat Basin."

Billie bolted upright, knocking Jeremy off kilter. "OK." Her voice grew excited. Nerve endings tingled. *Don't get your hopes up.*

"The video was uploaded to YouTube on February 14th, and

there's slight editing so maybe it was really taken February 13th."

"And you think this will help us?" asked Billie.

"Yes," she said. "Because I'm pretty sure I spotted Alan in the background."

Billie stared wide-eyed at Jeremy.

"Celeste, I'm going to hang up and you're going to text me that link right away. Got it?"

"Hang tight." Celeste disconnected the call just as Billie's phone dinged with the incoming message.

Jeremy said, "Let's see what we have."

Billie clicked on the link and opened the video as large as her cell phone screen would allow.

The footage, clearly taken with a GoPro, opened on a teenage boy, sixteen maybe, dark-haired and wearing a blue bike helmet. He was cycling along River Road, the Hudson River to his right, the entrance to a closed Dyckman Hill ahead.

"Can't believe this is a February day," he said, slightly breathy. "Climate change is real."

The video continued for another ten seconds, and then Jeremy cried, "There!"

Billie tapped the screen, and slid the bar at the bottom back a few seconds. She resumed the video, and squinted. "Is that Alan?" The boy cycled past a man with dark hair. He could be Asian, but Billie couldn't discern.

"I recognize his Cannondale." Jeremy pointed to the phone. "See?"

Billie couldn't, so she said, "I'll take your word for it."

Jeremy tapped the screen and the video continued. They watched as the kid pedaled around cones and climbed Dyckman Hill, huffing as he moved up the steep incline.

Verboten. But the kid either didn't know or didn't care.

His head bobbed with the exertion, moving side to side. At one point Alan had his arm raised. "He was trying to signal the kid to stop," said Jeremy.

Alan the protector. He had gone after Brianne Druffner and the college president to protect Celeste. Now here he was, trying to help a dumbass teenager stay safe.

A truck drove past the bottom of the hill and honked the horn.

The video continued. The kid was cresting the hill, and Alan slowly disappeared from sight.

"Oh my God, I can't do this. The road is a mess," the kid whined, breathless. "This isn't safe. No wonder it's blocked off."

Finally common sense prevailed.

As the kid took a break on the road, he must've popped the camera off his helmet because he was then scanning the environment, including pointing the lens down toward the mouth of the hill, showcasing the rocks and broken asphalt. "When will they fix this?" he said. Popping his helmet back on, he said, "I'm turning back," and pedaled down toward the boat basin area.

Jeremy and Billie watched as the kid picked up speed, descended the hill, and merged back onto River Road. But while he was cycling his camera was recording a car driving past.

"Black Mercedes," Billie whispered.

"And?"

"Same color and make as the car that hit Gramps."

"Your grandfather got hit by a car?" Jeremy said.

"Oh, yeah," she said, pausing the video. "He's fine. Should be discharged later today. Assuming he doesn't stroke out."

"Billie!"

"I'm kidding. He has a mild concussion." This was all said while she stared at her phone screen. She rewound the video, then pressed *play*. Then, *pause*.

She bought the screen to within inches of her eyeballs.

Jeremy tugged the phone away. "Let me look."

"Hey!"

"You're hogging evidence," he said.

He too squinted at the car. "I see a window. It's open. I don't see a face, though."

Billie leaned over his shoulder. "There's an arm." Her breath hitched. "And look, a bracelet, gold with the crescent moon."

"That could be anyone from that boarding school of horrors," he said.

"No, Jeremy." Billie pointed to the screen. "Look at her hand." Jeremy leaned over and squinted.

"At the tattoo," said Billie.

CHAPTER SEVENTY-SIX

Gramps was lying in the hospital bed, fully dressed in a set of clean clothes that David had brought him, when his cell phone rang from the nightstand.

He fumbled for his glasses, then stared at the screen a beat too long before realizing he had to swipe up to receive the call. Which he knew, he was just flustered. He'd been waiting on the doctor to discharge him for the better part of an hour. *Where was this guy?*

"Abuelo," whispered the voice on the phone.

The Colombian kid. "Diego?"

The video screen lit up, and Gramps panicked. He didn't want the kid to see him in the hospital.

"Shh, I can't talk loudly," said Diego. He wasn't in the frame. He was pointing the phone at a large Victorian house with giant Greek letters above the door.

Gramps swung his feet over and planted them on the linoleum. He was no longer being monitored, therefore no longer tied to an IV (for dehydration, said the nurse. Yeah, dehydrate Medicare with the bill). "What are you calling for? You OK? What am I looking at?"

"Shhh," said Diego again.

"You called me," Gramps hissed. "You should've called Billie."

"I can't," Diego whispered. "She won't take the call. She keeps declining."

So I'm second fiddle?

He continued watching the screen. Two girls stood outside the house. Gramps easily recognized Brianne Druffner – the girl could play Nurse Ratched in a revival. But the other face was unfamiliar. She was young, like Billie, but with long, dark hair. Latina likely. Gramps wanted to ask Diego if this was a relation of his, then thought better of it. *See, I'm growing.*

"We should go inside," said the brunette.

"Why?" said Brianne, her arms crossed, a tough-girl stance meant to cover up that she was cold. "You don't want anyone to see you? God, you'll do anything to protect her, won't you? She's going to throw me under the bus, you know? I had nothing to do with Heath Vickery but she'll say I did. Felicia only cares about herself. Just like Katherine. They don't care about us."

The wind whipped the girl's hair, a mass of brown strands fighting against nature. "That's not true," she said. "I wouldn't have a job without Katherine. Without Felicia you'd be working fast food counters."

"You'd like that, wouldn't you?" Brianne sneered.

"No," said the girl. "I'm just saying we should be grateful. We need to protect them."

"Gratitude only goes so far when your ass is on the line. I have cops sniffing around me. I have to go in for questioning. That freaking Colombian kid did this to me. I should've known he'd been a plant." She stared at the brown-haired girl. "You're next, you know? Don't get cocky."

"Is that a threat?"

"Listen, every woman for herself. They'll want to trade information. I'll tell them who I gave the GHB to and, in return, they'll forget I had it in the first place." Brianne smirked.

Diego whispered, "Got her."

"So you're going to turn on Felicia?" the girl said. "That'll hurt Katherine too."

Brianne laughed. "I'm only going to do what she would – save my own ass. I'll tell the police that she manipulated me.

Just like she manipulated all those men. I'm a victim." Brianne turned as if she was going to head back inside. The girl grabbed her shoulder and twisted her around.

"Women stick together," she said. "Gunness girls look out for each other."

"You're not a Gunness girl," Brianne hissed. "You're pathetic. A wannabe. And sticking together only works when you have the same goal. My goal is to call the family lawyer and then that Morales detective." Brianne gave the girl a perfunctory nod as if that was the end of it.

Gramps's pulse quickened. If he still had been hooked up to a machine, alarms would be blaring from all ends of the unit.

"Diego," he warned. "I think it's time to go."

The brunette picked up a rock from the ground and weighed it in her hand.

"What are you doing?" said Brianne, gesturing to the stone.

"Just thinking," said the brunette.

"Well think quicker. I have shit to do."

The brunette nodded.

Brianne turned to go back inside the house. That's when the brunette tossed the rock at Brianne's head and the girl went down.

"Shit!" cried Diego. And, worse, the girl with dark hair had heard him. She turned and spotted him, her face now taking up the entirety of the phone screen. She held the rock up high, ready to smash it again against Brianne's skull. "Get in the house before I kill her."

"Don't go in that house," Gramps barked. "Diego!"

"I mean it," said the girl. "I'll bash in her brains and it will be all your fault. Get in the house."

Brianne was a monster, but she didn't deserve to die.

Diego whispered into the phone. "Don't worry, Abuelo. I can take her."

"Don't be a hero!" Gramps shouted, but the next thing he saw was his own phone screen turning black.

CHAPTER SEVENTY-SEVEN

Billie and Jeremy were racing to her Hyundai when the phone rang.

"Don't answer it," said Jeremy.

"It's Gramps," she said. "He's being discharged, and Detective Morales isn't going anywhere anyway." Billie picked up the phone and said, "Can David take you home? I have some business to–"

Gramps was nearly wheezing. She heard hospital noises grow, then fade in the distance. "I'm discharging myself." He sounded breathless, like he was power walking. Or, in his case, just walking.

"What's the emergency?" She shot Jeremy an exasperated look over the roof of her car. With Gramps, running out of beer was an emergency.

"Diego's in danger," said Gramps.

"What do you mean 'in danger?'" Billie said loudly.

"He went to that sorority house, followed the Druffner girl, but got more than he bargained for. A brunette was there and she attacked Brianne, then she forced Diego inside the house and he's trying to be a hero. You put these ideas into that boy's head."

"Did this brunette have a tattoo on her hand?" Billie asked quickly.

"I don't know. I didn't look."

"Shit. OK. It's got to be Rebecca." Billie motioned for Jeremy to get in the car. "We're on our way."

"Me too."

"You stay there," she said. "You don't have a car."

"I will not!" He shouted. "I called a taxi."

"A taxi?!" Billie fell into the driver's seat and barked at Jeremy to call the police. "Ring David. Wait for me." She disconnected the call and then sped out of the apartment parking lot – and into standstill traffic.

A marching band went past her, followed by a Girl Scout troop.

"St Patrick's Day Parade," she groaned. "How could we be so oblivious?!" She smacked the steering wheel.

"Get out," said Jeremy.

"What?"

"I'll drive. You make a run for it," he said. "Really? You'll let me run off into danger?" She realized how that sounded – as if she was offended when really she was touched.

"Of course! Now go!"

Billie scrambled out of the car, grabbed her bag and ran down the street, crossing over the main drag and into the residential part where she hoped she could easily snag a ride.

A black Acura sidled up by her and rolled down the window. "Need a lift?" said a man's voice.

"Not now, creep." She stopped and the car stopped also. She leaned slightly, peeked inside. "Matty? Matty!" She opened the passenger's side door, got in, and pointed into the distance. "Kentwell! And steer clear of Cedar Lane."

"Yeah, I know. There's the parade," he said. "I thought we were going to get your grandfather."

"We'll meet him there," she said.

"At the hospital?"

"Just drive and I'll explain." She wiped sweat from her forehead. An idea occurred to her. "Do you have your Glock in the trunk?"

CHAPTER SEVENTY-EIGHT

To her surprise, Billie showed up at the Zeta Omega house first. The front door wasn't open and at first glance there was no sign of Brianne, Rebecca, or Diego, which in itself seemed like an omen.

Matty leaned over the steering wheel, glancing suspiciously at the house. "What do you want me to do?"

"Keep trying Morales. Stay here and wait for backup. Don't let Gramps go inside."

"Then why ask about the gun?" he said, warily.

"Rebecca won't be armed. That's not her MO." She opened the car door and sprinted toward the house. Matty called after her, "This is insane!"

Billie leaped up the front stairs and twisted the doorknob. Locked.

She pointed to the backyard and signaled to Matty where she was headed.

Billie quietly lifted the gate latch and crept along the stone path. She listened, heard bird calls and local traffic but the house remained silent.

Bad sign.

She spotted an open window and lifted the sash. She dropped her bag inside then climbed in after, tumbling headfirst onto cold hardwood. Her hips and ass followed with a thud.

"Dammit."

She'd ended up in the first-floor powder room. A voice emanated from a grate near the pedestal sink. The vent, she assumed, led to the cellar, which meant the basement stairs were probably just outside the bathroom.

Billie dug around her messenger bag for the Taser and brandished it like a knife. She abandoned the rest of her gear – zip ties, duct tape, the supplies of a serial killer – and headed down the basement steps.

"Rebecca," she called out. "I know you're here."

Billie heard skittering noises as if someone was flitting around the cement floor.

She emerged into a dark space. Light filtered in from small windows coated in film.

"Diego," said Billie. "If you can hear me, say something."

She heard nothing. Whatever Rebecca had been doing had stopped.

Then a muffled sound came from a room in the far back. Billie eased herself along the concrete walls. Baby steps. No sudden movements.

She turned the corner and found Rebecca hovering above Brianne Druffner, who was bleeding from the head, mouth taped shut. She'd been hogtied with a thick cord. Her blond hair was matted with blood.

Billie had admittedly dreamed about shutting up Brianne, but not like this.

Diego, too, was there, sitting against the wall, his eyes wet with tears. He was bound and gagged. A wet stain darkened the bottom of his sweatshirt.

The air smelled like metal.

"Diego, you OK?" Billie asked, although suspecting he wasn't. The blood was dripping from his waist to the cellar floor. She needed some indication from him that he was still with her. Only his head lolled to the side.

Shit. *Shit*.

Billie asked Rebecca, "How much blood has he lost?"

"How should I know?" she replied. "He tried to jump me so I stabbed him in the side, I think."

"I need to staunch the bleeding," said Billie, glancing around frantically for a rag or towel. Finding nothing she pulled off her own hoodie and ran toward him. But Rebecca was faster. She flashed a butcher knife, causing Billie to skid to a halt, before pressing the blade to Diego's throat. "Drop the Taser."

Billie immediately lowered herself to a squatting position. "I'm putting the Taser down." She caught Rebecca's glance. Rebecca leaned forward and quickly snatched up the Taser. She didn't drop the knife but it was no longer piercing Diego's skin.

This would have to do.

"Bex," said Billie carefully. "He needs medical attention."

"Don't call me Bex," said Rebecca, her knuckles gripping the knife's handle. "I hate that name. Heath uses it to demean me. 'Bex, where's my smoothie? Bex, file these reports. Bex, reschedule my appointment with my trainer.' Oh my God, him dying was the relief I needed."

A voice called out from the top of the stairs. "Billie!" It was Matty. "Are you OK?"

Rebecca's eyes grew wide and she pressed the blade into Diego's neck. A trick of blood oozed from the wound and slipped down his throat.

"Don't come down!" Billie cried out.

"You want me to get my Glock?" Matty asked.

Rebecca pressed down harder this time.

"No!" Billie cried. "Please don't."

"OK," said Matty, clearly uncertain. "I'll stay here."

"Great," said Rebecca. "Now I'll have to kill him too."

"This seems like a lot of work," said Billie. "You'd have to also get rid of me, Diego, and Brianne. Seems implausible."

"I've been successful so far," said Rebecca.

"I think this goes above and beyond your current job responsibilities, you know?"

"I see you're joking, but I really am a good employee."

"I'm not joking," said Billie, her eyes flitting from Rebecca's manic face to Diego's terrified one, to the blood pooling below his torso. "You killed Webber before he could expose Katherine as a sexual harasser and abuser. You killed Heath before he could ruin VHG with his charity scam, not to mention get Katherine buried under sexual harassment lawsuits. You also killed Alan before he could write an article about Felicia Beaumont, college president and rapist. And if I hadn't come by you would've killed Brianne and Diego to cover it all up. Bex – I mean Rebecca – you're not just a great assistant, you're also a great serial killer."

"I wouldn't test me if I were you. I'm the one with power here." She brandished the knife, slicing it through the air. Billie retreated a step. Rebecca grinned.

Billie pressed on, treading carefully. "You don't have power," she said. "You're just doing other people's bidding. You're still an admin. A secretary."

"I have potential," said Rebecca.

"Did Katherine tell you that? Or Felicia? Felicia is a rapist. You want the admiration of a woman like her?"

"Katherine loves her so I love her. You wouldn't understand."

"You're right. I wouldn't because all I see are toxic women who care more about themselves than people. They don't love you. They're not your friends or family."

"My own family doesn't care about me, but Katherine does. She looks out for me. She gave me a gym membership and a clothing allowance. She put me in charge of company picnics and dinners. You know what she said when I hired the receptionist? 'Great job, Rebecca. You have an eye for talent.' Hear that? An eye for talent. Because of her I have an entire office that respects me. I have dinner with twenty people every week."

"Drinks out and the occasional band night at a Hoboken bar do not mean you have respect, Rebecca," said Billie. "Katherine and Felicia don't give a shit about you. To them you're an errand girl they can manipulate. They don't value you as a person, so why ruin your life for them? The minute you become an inconvenience they'll throw you under the bus."

"You sound like Brianne." Rebecca lifted her chin. "Felicia told me that she wished Brianne was more like me. Calm. Measured. Enthusiastic." Rebecca then yelled at Brianne, "You're such a fucking problem that Felicia wishes *you* were more like *me*! Ha. How does that feel? Who's pathetic now?" Rebecca pressed the knife to Diego's neck. Even gagged, Billie heard him scream.

"Rebecca, please. Be calm and measured now. Put the weapon down."

"No," she snapped. "If I'm caught, I'm fired. I can't lose my job."

"Your job? That's the least of your problems. You're not getting out of this. Cops can bridge a link. You prepared Heath's protein shakes. They can draw a line from the peanut butter powder you used in those shakes to Webber's poisoning."

"They won't," said Rebecca confidently.

Billie pushed. "Detective Amadi is smart. He'll figure out that you put erectile dysfunction drugs into Heath's smoothies. I assume Katherine asked you to do that, hoping he would cheat on her so she could file for divorce. So he wouldn't walk away with all those stock shares."

Rebecca said nothing, which meant Billie's assumption was correct.

"But why did you slip Heath GHB? And why was he at Kyle's place?"

"It's not Kyle's place," said Rebecca, shaking her head again. Her eyes were wide, her pupils blown. "Katherine owns that brownstone. She said that if the boner pills weren't working, we could try another plan – drug Heath, strip him naked, and set him up at the brownstone. We'd hire a girl and take a video. Blackmail him. It was genius, really. So I laced his last protein shake and led him away. I told him that Kyle was still living at the brownstone and that Katherine wanted him to be a man and kick Kyle out. But Heath got weird the minute we went inside. He headed upstairs and into the bathroom, then climbed into the bathtub. Said he wanted the elderly to swim the Mediterranean, and then he passed out. Just like Webber, he made it too easy. I turned on the faucet and let the water do its job."

"You let him drown."

"He can't take half the company if he's dead," said Rebecca. "And he certainly can't ruin Katherine's life."

"Yes," said Billie, the sarcasm bubbling to the surface. "Poor Katherine. She truly is the victim here."

"It's *her* company. As long as she's head of VHG I'm valued. These men will come and go. They mean nothing to her, but I'm her assistant. Her partner."

"It's a fucking office job, Rebecca. That's all. You have no real power."

"Really? I have more power than you realize." Rebecca raised the knife as if preparing to cleave Diego's head from his body.

Oh, shit!

"Wait!" said Billie. Then she had an idea. "I'm reaching into my pocket for something I think you'll want. Jewelry."

That roused Rebecca's interest.

Billie displayed a little, gold bracelet with a crescent moon charm.

"Where'd you find that?" Rebecca asked.

"In Webber's nightstand," said Billie. "The clasp is broken. It fell off your wrist when you were in Alan's apartment to steal his laptop – which is why you had to return before the cops found it. You then lost it again in Webber's nightstand when you stole his EpiPens, ensuring he wouldn't be able to save himself when he had the attack. I assume you swiped his house keys. The desk drawers at Tropic Reef don't lock."

Rebecca said, "I made a copy during lunch break. Put them back before he noticed." She then mocked Webber's voice.

"'This isn't Costco, Rebecca. We don't have lockers.' Ha! He probably died wishing it was."

"But you forgot where you lost the bracelet, right?" Billie asked.

"If I had known it had fallen into Webber's nightstand I would've gone back for it. It's so pretty, isn't it?" Her head tilted to the side, her eyes following the charm as it swung in Billie's grasp. "You're somebody when you wear it." Rebecca, sweaty and breathless, stepped toward Billie who instinctively retreated on her heels. "Give it back," said Rebecca.

Billie dangled the bracelet so it caught the light and pretended to examine the construction. "I just don't understand where you got this from." Billie then looked at Rebecca. "You didn't go to Gunness."

"No," she replied. "It was a gift."

"From Felicia?"

"If you must know, yes. That was hers. She said I could have it. She said I deserved it."

"When did Felicia give it to you?"

"At the fundraising gala."

"On February 13th, when you slipped out to find Alan."

Again Rebecca nodded. "She let me borrow her car. She told me the reporter was biking from campus and that I should follow him, see where he went and who he spoke to." Rebecca watched the bracelet, hypnotized, as it swung in Billie's trembling hand. "If I took care of him I could have the bracelet. 'Doors will open, Rebecca.'"

"Except Felicia has a bracelet. I saw her wearing it."

Rebecca's gaze snapped to Billie. "No. She gave me hers. Said I was an honorary Gunness girl now."

Billie shook her head, then pointed to Brianne. "She's wearing hers. Katherine obviously has hers. I saw Felicia a week ago and she was definitely wearing a bracelet that looked just like this one. So yours must be fake..." She let the thought hang. "Since the clasp never connects right. I mean, you lost it twice. Seems cheaply constructed. And the gold flecks a bit. Gold shouldn't do that."

Rebecca frowned.

Matty suddenly called out, "Police are here! I'm coming down!"

Billie tossed the bracelet in the air. Rebecca screamed and dropped the Taser as she attempted to catch the gold moon charm before it fell. That's when Billie swiped the Taser off the floor and hit the button.

CHAPTER SEVENTY-NINE

Evidence, Billie considered, was like ingredients. To make a proper dinner a cook needed quite a few odds and ends: noodles, cheese, sauce, and herbs. An apple by itself could take the edge off, but an apple was not a meal. To identify a suspect detectives enjoyed an eyewitness account, but that alone would not sate their hunger. A co-conspirator helped. A paper trail. Text messages or, better yet, a recorded voice admitting to the dastardly deeds. To truly be satisfied, justice required a feast.

As she and Jeremy sat in the small Kentwell theater watching student documentaries on everything from cheating scandals to stalker cases that went completely ignored, Billie was reminded of how lopsided the system was. To expose a woman like Felicia Beaumont, Billie needed to prepare a seven-course spectacle because apparently Rebecca was not talking to police. Not yet anyway. Morales said the girl had got a great defense attorney, paid for by Katherine Von Holm, and immediately clammed up. The one smart move she had made.

Diego had given a police statement of the entire harrowing ordeal from a hospital bed. After tasing Rebecca, Billie had managed to staunch the bleeding moments before the authorities, and Matty, arrived. Miraculously, all Diego had needed were stitches and rest. For now he was convalescing back at David's place. "I like it here," he had texted her that morning. "It's like having two older brothers. Also your abuelo keeps bringing me soup and magazines."

As for Brianne, she had also gotten patched up in the hospital and sent home, walking out with a concussion and minor head wound. Morales said they were building a case against Brianne for rape. Diego was a key witness but they would need others to come forward. Celeste had agreed to talk to the detectives about the harassment, but Bergen County required cooperation from the victims at Washington and Franklin. In the meantime, Brianne had secured a bulldog of a criminal defense lawyer and he had advised her to withdraw from Kentwell and stay away from the sorority house. Tasha was understandably thrilled, but something told Billie she was still keeping tabs on Brianne.

Nina Patchett-Borel quit her job as vice president of Tropic Reef, citing the toxic work environment as the reason for her departure. Billie had no doubt Nina would find herself in another corporate gig soon enough.

Kyle Olsen had turned himself in for evading police but posted bail. He had not been formally charged with Heath's murder, but Billie was sure Rebecca's criminal defense team would exploit him to drive doubt into the county's case.

Kyle was also fired from the company he had built.

And Katherine Von Holm...well, that remained to be seen.

Everyone had lawyered up. That's what money did for the wealthy. Protected them. Buffered them from the consequences of their actions. They'd rather pay attorneys than give in. That was where their power lay.

Maybe not everyone would be so fortunate.

Felicia Beaumont currently sat in the front row wearing a designer suit, her blonde hair a curtain between her and the gentleman seated to the left, a dean from the criminal justice department. Dr Whitlock sat in shadow behind her.

What do they say? If you aim for the queen, you best not miss. Well, Billie thought, if you poison her highness, she better swallow every bite.

Jeremy tensed beside Billie. Grabbing his hand, she flicked her chin toward the front where a Black girl stood before a large projection screen.

Tasha Nichols.

"There's no mic, so I'll talk loudly," said Tasha, "although I think the student films will speak for themselves. The first submission is for the collaborative category. The entire film was researched, edited, and produced by members of Sleuth Squad, the college's only civilian detective group. I present to you: *The Sisterhood.*"

There was a round of polite applause. Tasha caught Billie's eye before she sat down in the front row, next to several Sleuth Squad members that Billie had met last year.

Billie had suspected Tasha's film submission would be about the Jasmine Flores case, but the minute the film began to run, Billie wasn't so sure.

Faces flashed across the screen, mostly men, but not all.

"I worked in Human Resources," said a blonde man.

Another, a red-headed gentleman, said, "Campus Life."

"Maintenance," said another.

Then the faces flashed again. The voices rattled off colleges: "Kentwell. Ohio State. Minnesota. New Mexico. A shoe company."

"Oh, shit," Billie whispered, sensing that whatever the Sleuth Squad had planned, it wasn't going to be some artsy piece about an unsolved murder that they had hashed out on their subreddit.

Billie recognized the places as appearing on Felicia Beaumont's resume.

Jeremy said nothing, even as he reached for Billie's hand again.

She stared at their interlaced fingers, only daring to glance up when a voice on the screen said, "Thought I landed my dream job."

Another voice, "I was invited to fancy faculty cocktail hours."

"Five-course dinners. Fancy beer."

A man then seated himself on a stool, a colorless curtain behind him. The film was shot entirely in black and white, an interesting effect that unsettled Billie for a reason she couldn't pinpoint. This man was white, late twenties or early thirties.

Billie whispered to Jeremy, "Do you recognize him?"

He shook his head.

But Felicia Beaumont must've. She immediately rose from her chair, made some excuse, and started heading for the door, but was pushed back into the room by a disembodied hand. Felicia took out her cell phone, gestured to it wildly, and hissed, "I have to make a call."

The man on the screen said, "I was invited to a private dinner to talk about promotion opportunities. A new position was being created, and would I be interested in the job?"

The disembodied hand revealed itself as belonging to Esteban Morales.

The film continued but Felicia's interruption and the emergence of a BCDB police detective was causing a bit of a stir.

Tasha, however, seemed unsurprised. A smirk spread across her face.

"I went to the dinner," said the man, "at the dean's house...a few people were there...had dinner and then beer...everyone left...I blacked out...woke up in her bed, naked..." The man began to cry.

"Felicia Beaumont," Esteban Morales said, loud enough now to be heard above the film. A Sleuth Squad member pressed a key on the laptop, pausing the movie, the closed captioning frozen on her name.

"Dr Beaumont, you are under arrest for the sexual assault of–"

Jeremy bolted toward the back exit. Billie chased after him, not sure where the back door even went until she followed him into a courtyard.

Jeremy paced around a dry fountain, exhaling repeatedly as if he had just finished an ultra-marathon. "I was a coward," he said, hopping on his toes.

Billie wished for the millionth time that Vela was here to offer guidance. She'd say the right thing. All Billie could do was grab Jeremy's hand, steady him, and force him to face her.

"You're not a coward," she reminded him. Billie pointed to the door that led back into the theater. "Beaumont is the villain, not you."

Jeremy nodded, then dropped his chin onto Billie's shoulders. She felt him tremble, sensed the fight leave him – which was a relief, she imagined, for them both.

They'd slain the dragon. Now it was time for rest.

CHAPTER EIGHTY

Morales held the door open for Billie. "Five minutes," he told her, before adjusting his tie and shutting her inside.

She nodded, then tugged the metal chair away from the table and sat. Billie on one side, Katherine Von Holm on the other, in the BCDB's interrogation room.

"Cozy," said Billie.

"Don't tell me to get used to this," said Katherine with feigned indifference. "I'm not under arrest, nor will I be."

"Surprised your lawyer isn't here," said Billie, glancing around the empty space, her gaze flicking off cinderblock walls and the two-way mirror.

"I told him to leave. The detective asked if I could stick around to speak with you, and I said I'd be delighted." She smiled a wolfish grin. In the right light, even seemingly beautiful things appeared ugly. "But understand, dear girl, you won't get me to admit to anything."

"You've been advised well," said Billie.

"Good lawyers buy the best defense."

"They certainly cost more than I do. You could've just paid me the thirty grand, you know? Instead of stiffing me like some cheapskate."

"And why would I reward you," asked Katherine, "when you showed no loyalty?"

"That's what you value, huh?" Billie drummed her fingers along the table.

"You don't get to my level without demanding fealty."

"And here I thought you got to your level because your great grandfather built the company you are currently dismantling."

Katherine laughed. "What are you talking about?"

"How long have you been questioned today?"

Katherine crossed her legs. She was wearing a cream-colored suit; the pencil skirt had dark smudges from the grime that clung to the chair and table – dirt stemming from drug addicts, thieves, gang bangers. The filth of the common people. Katherine tried to hide the stain with her hands, but Billie noticed, and she made sure Katherine noticed her noticing.

"Hours?" Billie said.

"A few," Katherine replied suspiciously. "The detectives had questions about my relationships with Rebecca and Felicia. Naturally I came in to help."

Billie gave a perfunctory nod as she removed her cell phone from her pocket. "That would've kept you pretty busy."

Katherine frowned. "So?"

"So a lot can happen in a few hours. The crazy thing about modern living is the pace in which information goes viral. You remember Reilly McReady? Her mom was a Gunness girl too. And you love your Gunness girls. Luckily for Reilly, she went to a public high school. Her morals still seem intact. Anyway, she and Webber were friends. Did you know that? They were such good friends that he told her a secret."

Katherine said nothing in reply, but a flight response must've been triggered somewhere in her cerebral cortex. She rose from the table. Billie grabbed her wrist, the bracelet still there, and said, "Sit."

To Billie's internal astonishment, Katherine sat.

Billie continued, "You paid Webber nothing and expected him to be grateful for the suits you bought him so he'd be quiet that you were sexually harassing him. You had all the power. Webber threatened to leave and you told him that, if he did, no other company would take him. You'd make sure of that."

A bubble of sound came out of her mouth and it took Billie a beat to recognize it as a laugh. "You're making up a story. The sex was consensual. He enjoyed it."

"He didn't."

"You have no way of knowing what he thought."

"I figured you'd say that." Billie swiped through her messenger app until she found the audio recording. She pressed play. Katherine's voice rang out clearly.

"Webber, dear, I don't want to call every single CEO in Manhattan, but I will. They don't like disloyalty any more than I do. You try and leave for another job in this city or within the entire tri-state area, you'll see how far my reach is. The only job left for you will be in a Vermont Cracker Barrel."

Billie pressed stop.

"There's more, but I think you get the gist."

Katherine reached for the phone, but Billie stepped back, dropped it in her jacket pocket. "Katherine, you're not so old as to believe that destroying my phone will destroy that recording, are you? Like I said, Webber trusted Reilly with his secret. And this secret she spilled on her very popular YouTube channel. A new hashtag has emerged on social media. You're trending, but for the wrong reasons."

One. Two. Punch.

"Right now, VHG's board of directors are combing through employee records, preparing settlements for the men and women who have come forward to accuse you of sexual harassment. They're probably holding an emergency meeting right now," Billie said.

This time when Katherine jumped up Billie didn't try to stop her. "You might want to take your phone off silent. Shit's gonna blow up."

Katherine said nothing. She knocked on the door and waited until she was let out. Billie decided to stay behind. She kicked her feet up on the table and crossed her arms, reveling in the justice.

CHAPTER EIGHTY-ONE

Nicole invited Billie over for dinner. She said she had bought a new air fryer and was dying to try it out. "I got fresh salmon," she'd told Billie over text. "I went to a fishmonger and everything."

Billie gently knocked on Nic's door so as not to disturb the cranky neighbor across the hall who heard things as if Billie was wearing a microphone. She held a bottle of red wine close to her chest, a merlot the liquor store owner swore was the best $15.99 could buy.

Billie took him at his word.

Nicole flung open the door. She was dressed in sweatpants and a light beige sweater, like she had paused getting ready for a proper date and not just hanging out with Billie in her condo.

Billie stepped into the foyer as Nicole grabbed her phone off the kitchen counter and pressed a button. The music died down around them.

Billie thrust the bottle of wine out. "Brought you a prezzy."

Nicole accepted the bottled, peered at the label, and nodded approvingly.

"The guy promised this was a good one," Billie said while shucking off her coat.

Nicole shrugged. "Honestly, I'm not much of a connoisseur." Then, softly, "I'm glad you could come over."

Leaning against the counter, Billie nodded. "It's been a hell of a month. *Hell* being the operative word."

Nicole brought Billie in for a hug. "The messes we find ourselves in," Nicole said into Billie's hair.

They pulled away and Billie shot a glance at Nicole's paper calendar that was tacked up on the fridge with a clipper magnet. There had been several dates now crossed out – dinners with Calvin.

"Are you guys OK?"

Nicole teared up as she went straight for the bottle opener. "We've decided to take a breather."

"I'm sorry," said Billie, although she wondered if that was the right response. Nicole didn't say they had broken up and jumping to the assumption that a breather was a breakup might just be making the situation worse. But if Nicole thought that, she didn't show it.

Nicole ran a hand over her face. "I didn't handle this well. He had tried to tell me something horrible happened to him, and I immediately accused him of cheating on me. I apologized profusely, but I guess it wasn't enough."

She poured herself a glass of wine and took a sip. Then she took another sip, and another.

Billie had only ever used alcohol as anesthetic a handful of times, and it only ever ended in stomach upset and headaches, two things she could accomplish by eating fried food and smashing her face against the wall. Her anxiety meds seemed to do a pretty good job of dulling the edges though.

"He went through trauma," said Billie. "It's going to take time. You can see that, right?"

Nicole nodded. "I'm just so pissed for how I handled it. I'm finding it hard to forgive myself."

"You're not the villain," said Billie, remembering how she told Jeremy the same thing. "Felicia is."

"Toxic bitch." Nicole poured herself another glass.

Billie noted the cutting board on the counter and said, "What side dishes are we having? I can chop vegetables."

"You like asparagus?"

"I like how it makes my pee smell."

"Gross, but it's what I have. Oh, and mashed potatoes."

"Love them."

Nicole handed her a knife and Billie went to cutting off the tough ends. She then peeled potatoes and placed them in a pot of cold water.

While the food cooked, Billie sat at the table with a glass of seltzer. "Alan's sister is having a memorial for him this weekend if you want to come."

"Do you want me to come?"

"Jeremy could use the support."

"You guys are close now, I take it."

"Not super close."

"You've been through a lot together," said Nicole. "You're not at each other's throats like before."

Billie supposed that was accurate since they had made a truce. On his couch something had changed between them. "We're trying out friendship. Acquaintanceship, really. I guess I sorta value his opinion now."

"I think you always valued his opinion," said Nicole. "That was the issue, right? You worried he didn't value yours."

"I can handle a lot of things, but apathy isn't one of them. I'd rather someone hate me than not think about me at all. I care about Jeremy in some weird way."

"You like him," Nicole sang playfully. "He's attractive as hell."

He is, thought Billie, but the last thing she needed was to have some high school-style crush on a guy she competed with. "Maybe I should just hit up Morales for a booty call. Scratch that itch."

"You could," said Nicole, "But you won't."

"Why not?"

"Cause that will fuck up your weird thing with Jeremy. You guys might decide not to confront your romantic feelings for each other, but that doesn't mean they aren't still there."

"If Jeremy and I are going to continue partnering on cases, we can't kiss. We just can't."

"I'll take that action," said Nicole. "No way you two handle another case and don't end up in bed together."

"Let's switch topics. What is happening with your job?"

"I've been asked to stay at Kentwell," said Nicole. "I've been offered a sweet raise and my own office."

"Are you going to take it?"

"Yes," she said. "I saw how those other colleges cowered under pressure. Kentwell is going to need strong women at the helm."

"Women like you."

"Hell yeah, and my first order of business is to hire people, diversify the workforce."

Billie toasted Nicole's wine glass. "I'm here for it."

Nicole smiled just as the oven timer dinged. "Dinner!" She got up from the table and scuttled toward the kitchen.

CHAPTER EIGHTY-TWO

When Billie was a kid, and some relative died, her grandmother would bring sponge cake to the cemetery and pass it out among the mourners. So when they had gathered at the Englewood River Basin to memorialize Alan, Billie decided to take a page out of Grandma's playbook and bake a sponge cake. She held out the Tupperware container.

David peeked inside and cocked a brow. "Really?"

Billie shrugged. "June brought the wreath. I didn't want to come empty-handed."

"I'll have a piece," said Matty as he plucked a square of cake and popped it into his mouth. "Spongy," he said while chewing.

Billie frowned, then offered some to Celeste, who shrugged and took a piece. "I dig it," she said.

Billie pressed the Tupperware into Jeremy's chest, and he pushed it back. "Can't eat." He huffed out a shaky breath, so Billie grabbed his hand, but he flinched. "What are you doing?" he said.

"Comforting you."

"Please don't."

"It's OK if you want to cry," she said, half-kidding. She didn't want him to cry because then she would cry. Sure, her meds dulled her emotions or, as Vela put, made it easier for her to handle stressors. But if Jeremy broke so would she. How weird for her emotions to be linked to his? She hadn't felt this way since Aaron left.

"You worried about the lawsuit?" Billie asked him. The college trustees were going to get their asses handed to them in a class action lawsuit. They never properly vetted Felicia Beaumont and were potentially liable. Jeremy would get a lot of money out of Kentwell – deservedly so. The settlement was expected to be quickly resolved.

"No. Bob Whitlock has this," said Jeremy.

"It can't be Spain," she said. "You got the trip funded."

"I'm worried people are going to look at me differently once this all gets out."

Billie exhaled. "I'll treat you the same. With aggravation and mild disdain."

And that earned her a laugh. But not his hand. Jeremy wiggled out of her grasp.

June held out hers, though. "Take mine," she said to Billie. "I'm going to need your support."

Billie happily intertwined her fingers with June as she began the ceremony.

"First, thank you all for coming. Alan was my baby brother. I spent so many years looking out for him. He smoked like a chimney when he was on deadline. He ate way too much takeout. But he wore his bike helmet. He believed in justice, in righting wrongs, in helping his friends and family. He made his life's work uncovering toxicity and was done in by the system he attempted to dismantle. I'd like to think that he died valiantly, exposing corruption and toxic work culture, but really he was the best this world offered, and we're a little worse off for his absence. I lost a brother."

"And I lost a cousin," said Celeste, crying.

"I lost a best friend," said Jeremy.

"There is no replacing him," said June, letting go of Billie's hand to wipe her eyes.

Billie also began to tear up. On one side, David slung his arm over her shoulder. Matty encircled her waist. Jeremy had wandered off toward the water.

June nodded, her speech done. She picked up the wreath and handed it to Jeremy who was already at the water's edge. He tossed it like a frisbee across the river. June squeezed his shoulder, kissed his cheek, and rejoined the others. Billie spied a few reporters who had come to offer condolences. One asked, "How can we help?"

June replied, "Go after the bastards."

Matty said he was returning to the car. David had to get to work. Celeste had class.

Billie and Jeremy were left alone. This time when Billie grabbed his hand he didn't let go. She wouldn't have let him anyway.

Billie and Jeremy returned to the Levine house together. Not Billie's idea but Gramps's. Jeremy had wanted to head home. To process, he said. But Billie recognized that for what it was: avoidance.

"Gramps is requesting the honor of your presence," she said.

"He didn't text that."

She showed him the message chain.

"Huh," said Jeremy.

Their friendship had taken a weird turn in the past few weeks. They replaced the snipes and barbs with respect and admiration and, frankly, Billie missed the bickering. Perhaps they were settling into comfort. Treating each other as colleagues and less like nuisances. She wondered how long this would last.

They parked along the street and headed toward the house, but were stopped by Gramps's shuffling outside the garage. The door was open and Gramps was dancing back and forth with a broom, barking things at Diego, who was jotting them down on a clipboard. The scene made Billie slightly uneasy, reminding her of Katherine and Rebecca.

Some cases outstayed their welcome.

"What's going on?" Billie asked.

Gramps pivoted with a grin. He waved his arm in a wide arc. "Picture this as our new office."

Billie leaned slightly around her grandfather's frame and peered into the cluttered garage. "You serious?"

Gramps frowned, clearly disappointed by her lack of enthusiasm. "There's potential here, Billie."

She stepped around him and went inside while Gramps continued sweeping. Jeremy joined her, meandering from one dingy corner to another. He pointed, "One desk here." He turned, jerked his chin in another direction. "One desk there." He kicked an errant sheet of newspaper. "A waiting area. Shelving. Certainly doable."

"Permits?" Billie said.

"I know a guy," said Gramps with a shrug.

"There's so much to clean out," she added.

Gramps clamped a hand onto Diego's shoulders. "The kid can help."

"When he's healed," said Billie.

"For my hourly rate?" asked Diego.

"Of course," said Billie at the same time Gramps said, "We'll discuss that."

The whole time Jeremy was smiling.

"I'm sick of working out of the dining room," said Gramps. "I'm getting fat being too close to the kitchen like that."

Getting?

"And Nagel's won't be an option much longer," he added. "We're professionals." He jutted his thumb at Diego. "We have an employee now."

Sighing, Billie couldn't belabor the point. "It's just gonna cost money to transform this space properly. Insulation. Maybe plumbing. We don't have that kind of capital, especially after the roof repairs."

"We do the work ourselves," said Gramps.

"Since when do you know how to install a bathroom?" she said.

Gramps shrugged. "YouTube?"

"I can help," Jeremy cut in. "Financially. Not with the bathroom install."

Billie barked out a laugh, resulting in Gramps's confused expression. "Let's not look a gift horse in the mouth."

"It's just," she began, facing Jeremy. "You don't have to do that. There's nothing in it for you."

"Despite what you think, Levine, I'm not always looking for an angle."

"My apologies–"

"Actually–"

"There is it," she grumbled.

"I was wondering if you would both consider a partnership of sorts." Jeremy twisted slightly, as if merely presenting this idea gave him hives. "I don't want to lose my PI business but I'm also trying to finish my dissertation. I'm heading to Spain in the summer. It could help me out if we combined forces."

"I don't know–" Billie began but Gramps was running a hand over his scruff, obviously considering the idea.

"Whose name would go first?" he said.

Billie glanced at her grandfather. "That's your biggest concern?"

"Listen, we're building a reputation," said Gramps. "While you were out the other day, I fielded two calls for work. Within an hour. So, whose name would go first?"

"Well," said Jeremy, "I had thought Yang and Levine Investigations sounded smart–"

Gramps cleared his throat.

"But I'm open to suggestions."

"Would you still need me?" Diego asked.

Jeremy nodded. "There's only so much Billie and I can handle. I'll need you to cover the forty percent of her I can't."

354 MAKE A KILLING

Diego laughed, but stopped the minute Billie shot him a look. "This is not a roast," she said.

"So?" said Jeremy, glancing at her. "What do you think?" There was a smugness to his expression that made her uneasy. He already knew what she was going to say.

Damn him.

"Is this going to be OK?" Jeremy asked, hefting a box off the shelf.

Billie was sweeping a pile of dead spiders out the door. "Why wouldn't it be?"

"I don't know. I feel like, you and I...maybe we were better off trying to kill each other. Now it feels...weird."

"We're adults, Yang. We can figure out our shit. Besides, you can't change your mind now. Gramps is already mentally spending your money."

"Yang, huh? You only call me by that when you're trying to distance yourself."

"Last time I checked there's no doctor in front of your name."

"Ouch."

"You know what I mean."

Jeremy set the box down on the floor and opened the lid. Inside were backpacks, mostly from David and Billie's elementary school days.

Peering inside, Billie said, "We work well together. This could be good. And if it's not, Gramps is really clever at hiding bodies."

"I know you're joking, and yet..." Jeremy found an old black backpack with a tarnished VHG emblem on the front. He freed it from the box. "Good shape."

"It was my mom's. From the eighties," she said to him. "Take it to Spain."

"No way," he said. "My Nike backpack is just as good."

Billie went to Gramps's old workbench and found needle nose pliers which she used to pull out stitches, releasing the emblem into her hand. "They don't make them like they used to. And now, no free advertising."

"Their stock has plummeted."

"It's just a backpack now." —

"*You* take it to Spain," said Jeremy.

"Funny," said Billie. "Also a little dickish. I'm not going anywhere."

Jeremy blinked at her, his lashes thick and dark. "I'm not saying for you to accompany me for three months. God forbid. But you could come for a week or two. I got that generous stipend, remember. Two bedroom apartment."

"Are you serious?" she said.

"Like a heart attack," he said. "Which is probably what you'll give me. So two weeks, max."

"I don't know," she said softly. "I may not have the funds to get there. And then food."

"Jesus, Levine. We're talking a trip to Seville, not the moon."

She shook her head, as if waking up from a dream. "Fine. Fine. I'll go. I'll do it."

"Feel like we're both going to regret this," he said, but he was holding out his hand, a gesture of partnership. Not just in business, but whatever they were slowly becoming.

Billie reached across and clasped his hand. She felt she had greeted an electric wire. Her entire insides buzzed. Oh shit, Billie.

ACKNOWLEDGEMENTS

Billie Levine, as misguided as she is sometimes, would not exist without this incredible crew of people.

Thank you to my agent Liza Fleissig, and the entire Datura Books team: editors Desola Coker and April Northall; publisher Eleanor Teasdale; publicist and marketing team Caroline Lambe and Amy Portsmouth; and everyone else who works behind the scenes at Datura to bring Billie into the world.

I'm grateful to my writing friends – Melinda Michaels, Katrina Monroe, Elizabeth Buhmann, and Jill Ratzan – for their help with plotting, editing, and characterization. I love running a bad idea past them.

Thank you to my family and friends who have championed all the Billie books. I appreciate everyone who has bought copies as gifts, thus foisting my art upon unsuspecting readers.

Lastly, I want to thank the librarians who are fighting against censorship and providing access to books and art. We can't do this work without them.

ABOUT THE AUTHOR

Kimberly G. Giarratano is an author of mysteries for teens and adults. A former librarian, she is currently an instructor at SUNY Orange County Community College. She previously served as chapter liaison for Sisters in Crime. Born in New York and raised in New Jersey, Kim and her husband moved to the Poconos to raise their kids amid black bears and wild turkeys. While she doesn't miss the Jersey traffic, she does miss a good bagel and lox.

Visit her at www.kimberlyggiarratano.com